PALINDROME

"A palindrome is a literary device,
word, sentence or even poem that reads
the same forward and backward.
In Stuart Wood's new novel, palindrome is the
perfect metaphor for the book's identical twins,
Hamish and Keir Drummond, and their
relationship with Elizabeth Barwick."
—Bookpage

"A MASTER AT WORK." —Mystery News

"TAUT AND SUSPENSEFUL."
—Detroit Free Press

"MR. WOODS' BOOKS HAVE GOTTEN BETTER
AND BETTER, AND HE HAS WRITTEN HIS BEST."
—The Baltimore Sun

"IN THIS HIS SEVENTH NOVEL, STUART WOODS
HAS UPHELD—EVEN SHARPENED FURTHER—
HIS SKILL AS A WRITER. THE READER'S
ATTENTION IS RIVETED FROM THE FIRST PAGE
AND IS NEVER RELINQUISHED."
—Nashville Banner

"COMPELLINGLY TOLD...PALINDROME IS
A CHALLENGE, A PLEASURE, AND A THRILL
TO READ."
—London Free Press

PRAISE FOR PALINDROME

"Woods is in bestseller form with this fast-paced, multi-level tale of mystery and revenge."

—Publishers Weekly

"A tale of fast-paced suspense."

—Bookpage

"A smooth, fast-paced thriller . . . an atmosphere of total suspense."

—Oxford Review

"An exciting new novel of suspense."

—The Florida Times-Union

AND FOR *SANTA FE RULES*

"Whisks the reader from the page on a roller-coaster ride of breathtaking speed, sharp, totally unexpected turns and unflagging suspense. . . . A whirlwind story with a plot that twists more than Chubby Checker. Even the veteran mystery reader will be dazzled. . . . *Santa Fe Rules* is a delight."

—*L.A. Life*

"Long on heart-stopping suspense. . . . The plot has more twists than the Grand Canyon."

—*Palm Beach Post*

"Whether you are a mystery fan or not, this book will keep you reading until you've finished—no matter the hour. . . . It undoubtedly is headed for the top rung of the bestseller lists."

—*Richmond-Times Dispatch*

"Distinctly readable—told with speed and glamorous flourishes."

—*Chicago Tribune*

"Guaranteed to keep you guessing."

—*Detroit Free Press*

Also by Stuart Woods

Fiction:

Heat*
Dead Eyes*
Santa Fe Rules*
L.A. Times*
New York Dead*
Grass Roots
White Cargo
Under the Lake
Deep Lie
Run Before the Wind
Chiefs

Memoir:

Blue Water, Green Skipper

Travel:

A Romantic's Guide to the Country Inns of Britain & Ireland

*Available from HarperCollins*Publishers*

STUART WOODS

PALINDROME

HarperPaperbacks
A Division of HarperCollins*Publishers*

This book contains an excerpt from *New York Dead* by Stuart Woods. This excerpt has been set for this edition only and may not reflect the content of the final edition.

This is a work of fiction. The characters, incidents, and dialogues are products of the author's imagination and are not to be construed as real. Any resemblance to actual events or persons, living or dead, is entirely coincidental.

HarperPaperbacks   *A Division of* HarperCollins*Publishers*
10 East 53rd Street, New York, N.Y. 10022

A hardcover edition of this book was published in 1991 by HarperCollins*Publishers.*

Cover illustration by Robert Gantt Steele

First HarperPaperbacks printing: November 1991

Printed in the United States of America

HarperPaperbacks and colophon are trademarks of HarperCollins*Publishers*

10 9 8 7 6

This book is for Dick and Maud Hedger

Madam, I'm Adam.

anon.

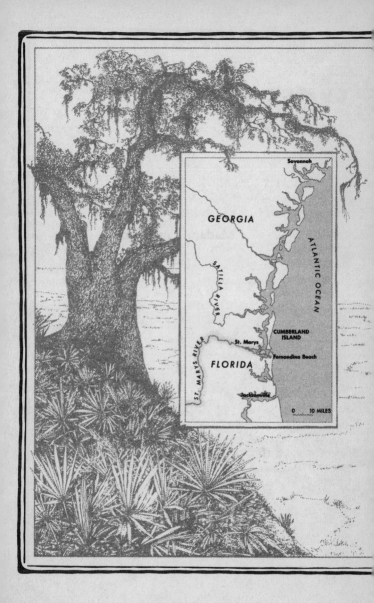

CUMBERLAND ISLAND

Highpoint

LAKE
WHITNEY

A T L A N T I C   O C E A N

Plum Orchard

Stafford

STAFFORD
ISLAND

STAFFORD
BEACH

LITTLE
GREYFIELD
BEACH

Greyfield

DRUM
POINT
ISLAND

Grand Avenue

DUNGENESS DOCK

Dungeness

DUNGENESS BEACH

N

JETTY

PROLOGUE

Miller was wakened from his doze by a puff of hot air, redolent of freshly cut grass and newly disturbed dogshit. Someone had let in the July night.

He tried to lift his head from the examination table, but his stethoscope caught and snapped his head back onto the cushion. He freed himself, swearing under his breath; some unthinking person had disturbed his quiet evening in the Trauma Center of Piedmont Hospital. Miller froze when he saw who had opened the door.

A young woman—he thought she was young, anyway—stood in the hallway, dressed only in khaki shorts and a badly torn T-shirt. Her left hand was partly raised, and she held her elbow tightly against her ribs, making her left breast seem larger than the right, which was exposed. Thick brunette hair spilled down to her shoulders. Her face was nearly unrecognizable as human. Both eyes were swollen nearly shut, her nose was flattened, and her cheeks were the color of rotting meat.

She shuffled forward a step, then stopped. She did not turn her head or speak.

Miller got off the table and moved quickly toward her, snagging a gurney as he approached her. "It's all right,"' he said, taking her right elbow and steering her onto the stretcher. He turned toward the admitting desk and said emphatically, but not loudly, "Nurse!"

A young woman holding a cup of coffee looked up from the desk, then quickly moved toward the gurney.

"In number two," Miller said, pushing the stretcher toward an examination room. Once there, he took a pulse while the nurse worked on a blood pressure. "Pulse is thready, hundred and ten," he said.

"Blood pressure is one twenty over seventy," the nurse recited.

"We need to get her clothes off. Can you move that much?" he asked his new patient.

"No," the woman said, without moving her swollen lips.

"Cut them off," he said to the nurse, who immediately went to work with the scissors.

Miller switched on a tape recorder. "She's got a fist-sized hematoma of the left breast; it's twice the size of the right; multiple bruising of the abdomen;

pain in the left chest." He listened with the stethoscope. "Both lungs good. Can you lift your left arm?"

"No," the woman said. "Hurts."

"Let's get stat chest, facial bone, and skull X rays;
I want a CBC, blood typed and crossed; I want four
units of whole blood ready. Start an IV with one
thousand cc's of normal saline."

While these things happened the woman lay perfectly still.

Another nurse came in with a clipboard. "I need
to get some information and a history," she said to the
woman. "Name?"

There was no reply.

"Ma'am, can you tell me your name?"

Still no reply.

"Is she conscious?" the nurse asked Miller.

Miller moved to his patient's head. Gently, he
opened her mouth, took hold of her upper teeth and
manipulated them. "The maxilla is movable," he said.
He bent close to her ear. "Can you hear me?"

"Yes," the woman replied.

"How did this happen? Did someone beat you
up?"

"Yes."

"Were you sexually assaulted?"

Silence.

"What were you beaten with?"

"Fists."

Miller took a deep breath. "Do you know the
man who did this?"

Silence.

Miller turned to the nurse. "Call the police."

"No!" the woman said with unexpected vehemence. "No."

"The police should be looking for whoever did this to you."

"No."

Miller shook his head at the nurse.

"Car," the woman said.

"Have a look outside," Miller said to a nurse. He conducted a pelvic examination and found vaginal bruising and tenderness. There was semen in her pubic hair, and he took a sample for a slide.

The nurse returned. "There's a Mercedes convertible out there. The motor was running. I parked it." She hung the keys on her clipboard and made a note of the license number.

Someone came in with the X rays.

Miller clipped them to a light box and peered at the chest. "Good lungs. Two broken ribs." He looked at the head shots. "Mmmm," he said. "I want a plastic surgeon to see her. Who's got the duty?"

"Griffin," a nurse said.

"No!" the woman on the table said.

"Griffin's good," Miller told her.

"Harry Estes," she said.

"He's good, too. You know him?"

"Yes."

"Can I tell him your name?"

The woman said nothing.

Miller went to the desk, looked up a number, and dialed.

"Hello?" a sleepy man's voice said.

"Dr. Estes? This is Martin Miller in the Piedmont ER. I've got a woman here I'd like you to see."

"Dammit, I haven't got the duty! Can't you read the list?"

"She asked for you. Says she knows you."

"What's her name?"

"She won't say."

"What's her condition?"

"She's been raped and badly beaten; the eyes are swollen shut; there are lacerations about the cheeks and eyes; the nose is flat. X rays show the maxillary sinuses are full of blood. The maxilla is movable; I think she's got a Le Fort three fracture."

"What did you say she was beaten with?"

"Fists."

"A Le Fort three is impossible."

"When you've seen her you can tell me that."

"I'll be there in fifteen minutes."

Harry Estes lived near the hospital; he made it in twelve minutes. On the way he tried to think what woman among his patients this could be. His main practice was in Northside Atlanta, the most affluent part of the city. The women he treated came to him for breast implants or reductions, nose jobs, face-lifts—the gamut of elective cosmetic procedures; occasionally, one was injured in a car accident. In his Northside practice he had never dealt with the results of a beating; no patient of his, to his knowledge, had ever been raped. He also consulted at Grady Hospital, the huge publicly operated facility on the south side of town. There, he could catch anything, and did. But

Piedmont Hospital was the richest, most fashionable in the city. Who could this woman be?

Estes parked his car and walked into the hospital. Miller met him in the lobby.

"Who is she?" Estes asked.

"She still won't say."

"Is she sedated?"

"No, I wanted you to talk with her, first."

Estes entered the examination room and stopped short. He did not recognize the woman; her mother would not have recognized her. He had never seen anything like this. He bent over the table and spoke softly to her. "It's Dr. Estes," he said, soothingly. "I'm going to take care of you, now; don't worry."

"Thanks, Harry," the woman said thickly.

Harry Estes was a rather formal man; only those patients who were his friends addressed him by his first name. He began to dread learning this woman's identity. On pretense of taking her pulse, he took her left hand from under the sheet.

The woman gasped.

"Sorry, I know those ribs are sore. We'll get them taped in a little bit." She was not wearing a wedding ring, but there was a faint mark. She may have been wearing one until recently.

Estes peeled back the swollen eyelids. Green. The pupils contracted. "Did you conduct a neurological examination?" he asked Miller.

"Yes. Normal. I didn't think it necessary to call in a neurologist. Do you want one?"

"Not if you're satisfied."

"Manipulate the maxilla."

·
6

Estes opened the woman's mouth, took hold of her upper teeth, and worked them back and forth. Her face moved with them. The woman's whole facial structure had been separated from her skull. He tried to keep his voice low and calm. "You're right, it's a Le Fort three fracture. I'll suture now." He injected Xylocaine into the woman's cheeks and left eyelid, then carefully closed four lacerations.

"There," he said. "You're going to be just fine."

The woman's face showed something like a smile. "Not bad work for somebody with no forehand," she said.

Estes's mouth dropped open. He knew in a rush who this was. He waved at a nurse. "Give her one milligram of morphine intravenously."

"Wait!" his patient said.

Estes bent over her. "What is it?"

"I want to see Al Schaefer. Nobody else. No name here."

"Did you say Al Schaefer? Are you sure you don't want Walt Hopkins?" Schaefer was a hotshot trial lawyer who specialized in big criminal cases. Hopkins, he knew, was her lawyer.

"Schaefer," she said. "Nobody else."

"All right," Estes said. "Are you sure you don't want . . . anyone else?"

"Nobody else."

Estes nodded at the nurse, who stood by with a syringe. She inserted it into the IV tube.

"You sleep, now, darlin'," Estes whispered to her. "I'll see you tomorrow."

His patient immediately relaxed.

Estes straightened. "Get some ice on her face and that breast, tape the ribs, then I want her in intensive care. Note on her chart that she's to have nothing by mouth. I want her to have a cranial CAT scan first thing in the morning; I'll schedule her for surgery when I've seen that."

"What's her name?" the nurse asked.

"Admit her as . . . P. J. Clarke," he said, reciting the first name that popped into his mind. He'd had dinner at the New York bar the weekend before. "Tell admissions not to badger her for insurance information or anything else. All her charges to my account, for the time being."

"Whatever you say, Doctor," the nurse said, scribbling on her clipboard. The other nurse applied ice packs, then the patient was wheeled out of the examination room toward the elevators.

"Let's look at her X rays again," Estes said to Miller.

Miller switched on the light box.

"She's got a very hard head," Estes said, peering at the film. "It's a miracle she hasn't got brain damage or, at the very least, a skull fracture, getting hit that hard."

"I wouldn't have thought a Le Fort three was possible from a blow with a fist," Miller said.

"Neither would I. Neither would anybody," Estes replied, staring at the X rays. "But it was no ordinary fist."

CHAPTER

1

Schaefer presented himself at the main reception desk of Piedmont Hospital and was directed to the room. He walked to the elevator bank, pressed the button, and waited, standing ramrod straight. He was only five feet seven inches tall in his shoes, and he made every inch count.

A large man in an ill-fitting suit stood outside Room 808, looking bored. Schaefer presented himself, and the man cracked the door and said something to someone inside. "The doctor wants you to wait a minute," the man said to Schaefer.

Schaefer, who was incapable of standing still, paced until a man came out of the room. Schaefer immediately placed him as one of several hundred Atlantans whom he thought of as the city's establishment, and with whom he had few dealings, unless their sons or daughters got into trouble.

"I'm Dr. Harry Estes," the man said. "May we sit for a moment?" He herded Schaefer toward a bench.

Schaefer arranged himself and made a point of not showing deference. "I have to be somewhere at six," he said.

"I understand," the doctor replied. "It was good of you to make a house call, as it were."

"Tell me, Doctor," Schaefer said, "is your patient's name really P. J. Clarke?"

The doctor smiled slightly. "I'm afraid that was a moment's whimsy on my part. She did not want to give the hospital staff her name."

"What is her name?" Schaefer asked. "That seems like a good place to start."

"Yes, of course," the doctor mumbled, rearranging his white hospital coat. "Her name is Elizabeth Barwick. In the wee hours of this morning she walked into the emergency room downstairs. She had been badly beaten and, apparently, raped. She declined to say who had beaten her, only that it had been done with fists. During the course of her emergency treatment she asked for me."

"Had she been a patient of yours?"

"No. I knew her socially. She and I were members of a group who used to play tennis at a mutual friend's house. I am a plastic and reconstructive surgeon. I think she knew she would need the services of someone like me at an early stage."

"What was the extent of her injuries?"

"She had received extraordinary trauma to the

face and head; she had two broken ribs; there was extensive bruising of the breasts and upper body; the vaginal area showed bruising and superficial bleeding. The emergency physician took what turned out to be a semen sample from her pubic hair."

"Excellent. What treatment has she been given?"

"Very little. She was X-rayed; her ribs were taped, and ice packs were applied to her face and left breast; I sutured four lacerations of the cheeks, eyelids, and forehead; she was sedated. She was X-rayed last night, and this morning she had a CAT scan."

"Was there any neurological damage?"

"Remarkably, none."

"What treatment do you plan?"

"I have her scheduled for reconstructive surgery the day after tomorrow. I want the swelling to recede a bit first."

"What is her state of mind?"

"She is lucid and calm. She has been since she was admitted. I want her to see a psychiatrist, but she insists on waiting until after the surgery. I rather doubt she's going to have much to say to him. She's very contained."

"Do you know why she asked for me?"

"No," the doctor replied, and something in his tone implied that he didn't understand it, either.

"Has she been photographed?"

"No."

"I'd like it done immediately. It will be embarrassing for her, but legally speaking, it's the single most important thing you can do for her right now. It should have been done before the ice was applied.

You might make a note, Doctor, to photograph any patient with trauma inflicted by another person. The pictures will always be important later."

The doctor stood. "I'll see to it. You're right, I should have done it earlier." He took off his glasses and massaged the bridge of his nose. "Ironically, she's a photographer, a rather good one."

Schaefer stood, too. "I'd appreciate it if you'd also give me a written description of her injuries and the treatment required—and don't leave out the psychiatrist."

"I'll go and dictate that right now and messenger it to you."

"Who, besides you and me, knows she's here?"

"Only a man named Raymond Ferguson. He published a book of sports photographs of her. She asked me to call him, but he hasn't seen her yet."

Schaefer was surprised. "No family?"

"Her parents are both dead. I'm not aware of any other relatives."

"Is she married, Doctor?"

Estes sighed. "Yes. To a man named Baker Ramsey."

Schaefer's eyebrows went up. "The running back for the Bobcats?"

"That's the one."

"Do you know him?"

"Yes."

"What do you think of him?"

"I once thought he was a fairly decent fellow. Recently, I've thought he was a jerk. Now, I think he's a monster."

The room was lit only by sunlight reflected onto the ceiling by drawn venetian blinds. It was more nicely furnished than most hospital rooms, but it was bare of anything connected with the occupant. There were no flowers, no clothes in the open closet, no books at bedside. There was only the long shape of a woman under the sheets. Most of her face was covered by dressings, and Schaefer was grateful for that. He pulled a chair over to the bed and sat down. Her eyes peeped out through slits.

"Ms. Barwick, I'm Albert Schaefer."

She spoke like a ventriloquist, her lips barely moving, but her voice was surprisingly strong. "Thanks for coming. Call me Liz."

"I'm Al. I was wondering why you asked for me."

"My own lawyer is Walter Hopkins. If I had asked Walt to handle this, he'd have written a strong letter, then he'd have written another strong letter, and in a couple of years we'd have a resolution. I want this matter resolved *now.*"

"I understand. Please tell me what happened to you last night."

"My husband came home and tried to beat me to death."

"I see. Did you—please understand I have to ask some very blunt questions—did you provoke him in any way?"

"Yes. I told him I wanted a divorce."

"That was all?"

"Yes. He didn't seem to like the idea."

"Of a divorce?"

"No, just of my telling him I wanted one. You understand, he wasn't like this when I married him."

Schaefer got comfortable in his chair. "Let me get some background, just to help me get a complete picture. Are you originally from Atlanta?"

"No, from a small town south of here called Delano."

"How small?"

"A little under five thousand."

"What did your father do there?"

"He worked for the railroad, until they moved most of the operations to another town, then he retired."

"How did you end up in Atlanta?"

"I got a scholarship to the University of Georgia. I was a fine arts major there—photography."

"Ramsey played for Georgia; is that where you met him?"

"Yes, but I didn't know him well there. It wasn't until I moved to Atlanta after graduation and got a job as a photographer on the *Constitution* that I got to know Baker. I was on sports, and I began to see a lot of him. He was charming and funny and smart—not really what I'd expected a pro ball player to be. After about a year of seeing him, we got married."

"Am I tiring you?"

"No. You have to understand that Baker was different then, a different person. But he wasn't doing well on the team, and they were talking about trading him. That's when things started to change."

"Tell me about it."

"We'd been married about a year and a half when

·
14

he started on an intensive weight program designed to put more muscle on him. He was tall, six-three, but light for pro ball—only about a hundred and eighty-five. The change in him was dramatic—physically and emotionally. He gained fifty pounds in an alarmingly short time. I read something in the paper about steroids, and I asked him about it."

"What was his reaction?"

"He hit me."

"Was this the first time?"

"Yes. Baker always had a cruel streak, I think, but he used it on the field and didn't bring it home often. But he was obviously on steroids by this time, and it changed him. He became incredibly aggressive on the football field—very hard to stop. The team stopped talking about trading him and gave him a new contract. But he changed off the field, too."

"He became more abusive?"

"More and more. I don't know why I took it for so long—some perverted sense of loyalty, I guess. I began living this peculiar, introverted life. I didn't see many friends, and all my energy seemed to go into just not making Baker angry. For the past two years I've been walking on tiptoe around him, and it was wearing me down. I had left the newspaper at Baker's insistence, and I was working on a book of photographs. I would hide out in the darkroom as much as possible. Foolishly, I kept hoping that he'd go off the drugs and be his old self again. Then, in addition to the steroids, Baker started using cocaine, and he became downright explosive. And that brings us up to this week."

"The other night, did he rape you, as well?"

"Yes, but I don't think it's necessary to go into that right now."

"I think it's better if you let me decide what's necessary right now."

"First, let me tell you what I want, and then you can ask me anything you think is pertinent, and I'll answer fully."

"All right, tell me what you want."

"I want an immediate divorce; I want a legally enforceable undertaking from my husband that he will never see or speak to me again; I want my personal belongings from the house; and I want a quarter of a million dollars in cash."

"Is that all? A quarter of a million dollars?"

"Oh, he's got a lot more than that, but I figure that's the maximum I can get from him without a fight, and I don't want a fight. I just want it over."

"What about your medical expenses? They're going to be considerable."

"I'm covered under his team medical insurance. Anything that doesn't pay, I'll handle out of my quarter of a million."

"I think your demands are modest. I don't see any problem in having them met right away."

"That's why I wanted you. I think the mere fact of your being my lawyer will intimidate Bake, make him move fast. You can add your fee onto the settlement."

"All right, I'll see what I can do. My fee is normally a third of the settlement, but I think we can achieve a net you'll be happy with. I've asked Harry

Estes to have your injuries photographed right away, before you improve any more. I'm going to need those photographs."

"All right," she said evenly.

"I need a photograph of you before . . . the incident, too."

"Call my publisher, Ray Ferguson, at Buckhead Press." She gave him the number. "He has a self-portrait I did for my new book."

"All right. I think I have all I need." He stood up. "Is there anything else I can do for you? Do you need anything?"

"Yes. When I get out of here, in a week or so, I'm going to need a furnished apartment for a few weeks. I'm going to need some clothes—jeans, size eight; a T-shirt; sneakers, size nine, just something to wear out of the hospital." She fumbled in a bedside drawer and held out some keys. "My car is in the parking lot downstairs; it's a silver Mercedes, the little convertible. I'd like you to sell it; it's less than a year old, get what you can. My safety-deposit-box key is on the key ring, too, number 1001 at the Trust Company Bank. Clean it out; the title to the car is in there; so is Bake's most recent financial statement. You should be able to use that to good advantage."

"Okay, I'll do all that." He scribbled his home number on his business card and left it on the bedside table. "Call me, day or night, if you need anything, anything at all. My secretary's name is Hilda; she's a wonder; use her as your own; I'll brief her."

"Thanks."

"You want me to call any friends?"

"No. No friends."

Schaefer walked to the door and paused. "You understand, of course, that this is not a conventional way to proceed, but your position is strong, and you have me on your side. I'm immodest enough to tell you that I don't think any other lawyer could pull this off without a lot of delays, but I think I can. If you don't care how I do it."

Something like a laugh came from Elizabeth Barwick, and she twitched from the pain in her ribs. "Believe me," she said, "I don't care how you do it."

Al Schaefer left the hospital parking lot and turned into Collier Road, listening to the hum of the twelve-cylinder BMW engine. He loved the sound, it helped him think. He thought now. At the Northside Drive traffic light, he tapped a number into the car phone and waited. The light changed and he drove on.

"Stillson, Immerling, Hoyt, and Thomas," a woman's voice said. Schaefer remembered the story, perhaps apocryphal, that the names Immerling and Hoyt had been transposed on the firm's original letterhead. That had been more than fifty years ago, and the legend still lived.

"Henry Hoyt, Junior, please," Schaefer said.

"Mr. Hoyt's office," a very serious secretary's voice said.

"This is Albert Schaefer. Let me speak to Henry."

"He may have already left for the day. May I ask what this is about?"

"Just tell him it's urgent."

"Who is it calling, again?"

"You heard me the first time. Put him on."

There was a pause while, Schaefer figured, Hoyt worried about the risk of snubbing him.

Finally, "This is Henry Hoyt."

Schaefer deliberately skipped any pleasantries. "Henry, you still represent the Atlanta Bobcats, don't you?"

"Yes, I do," Hoyt drawled.

"How long have you known me, Henry?"

Irritably, "I don't know, Al, fifteen years?"

"Do you know me to be a serious person, Henry?"

Near exasperation, "Yes, Al, you're a serious person."

Hoyt had good reason to know, Schaefer reflected; he had carved the man, his forty-eight partners, and his two hundred associates into a pretzel shape seven years before, in a huge personal-injury verdict against the firm's biggest client. The case had tripled his billings.

"Well, I'm serious now, Henry. Last night, one of your most expensive ball players tried to murder his wife, whom I now represent."

Weakly, *"What?"*

"I won't keep you in suspense, Henry. It was Bake Ramsey."

Involuntarily, *"Jesus Christ."*

"He very nearly succeeded in the attempt. I've just seen the woman; she will never be the same again, physically or mentally."

"Who knows about this, Al?" Hoyt was recovering.

"I know about it, Henry; *everybody wants* to know. I'm not sure how long I can keep a lid on it."

"It's a little early in the game for threats, isn't it, Al? You and I have to talk."

"You and I and Bake Ramsey, tomorrow afternoon at two o'clock in my office. Not a minute later. I don't want any team management there. I'll expect you to be authorized to act."

"I don't know about that."

"Oh, you've got plenty of time to explain it to them, Henry. If they balk, tell them that this attack probably took place because the team has been shooting old Bake up with steroids since well before last season."

"That's very dangerous talk, Al."

"It certainly is, Henry. Just two more things, then I'll say good night: I want you to tell Baker Ramsey who I am, just in case he doesn't know; then I want you to tell him that if he goes anywhere near his wife, I'll make sure he doesn't see the light of day for the next twenty years."

"Al . . ."

"Yes, Henry, I know; that's a threat. You just make sure Ramsey understands I can make good on it. I'll see you tomorrow at two."

Schaefer hung up and gripped the steering wheel. Sweat from his palms seeped into the soft leather. Once in maybe three or four years, he got to talk like that to a senior partner in an establishment law firm. It was better than sex.

Al Schaefer winged his way home.

CHAPTER

2

*R*aymond Ferguson sat next to the bed and looked at the sleeping Elizabeth Barwick. He was glad she was asleep; it gave him a moment to accustom himself to the transformation of the loveliest woman he knew into a swollen, discolored lump of flesh. He willed himself to stop feeling sorry for her—she would know it in a minute if he did, and she would hate him for it. He took a deep breath and touched her hand.

"Lizzie? It's Ray."

She opened her eyes as much as she could. "Hey, Ray," she said. She sounded as if she were smiling.

He fixed his eyes on hers as she pressed the button that raised the bed. "I hear you're going to live."

"You bet. Have you got something for me?"

Ferguson smiled and produced a package wrapped in expensive paper. "First copy," he said.

She took the package and ripped it open, ignoring the beautiful paper. "The Beauty of Sport," she read, "Photographs of Athletes by Elizabeth Barwick." She turned the pages rapidly, bringing the book close to her face. "The printing is gorgeous," she said excitedly. "You were right to take a chance on those people."

"I'll use them again and again," Ferguson said. "Are you happy with it?"

"Ray, it's just wonderful; you've made me look great."

"You've made yourself look great. By the way, good news: the Bobcats have bought ten thousand copies. They're offering them as a premium for season ticket buyers."

"That *is* good news," she said. "Maybe after today they won't want them."

"Don't worry about it," he said. "I've got them nailed for the order." He looked around the room. "They said you didn't want flowers; is there anything else I can get you?"

"Not at the moment. I'll let you know."

"Listen, Liz, have you given any thought to what you're going to do next?"

"Crawl into a hole for a while, I think."

"I've had an idea I was going to talk with you about, and maybe this is as good a time as any."

"Shoot."

"You know Cumberland Island?"

"Only the name. It's near Sapelo Island, isn't it?"

"No, farther south. It's the southernmost of the barrier islands off Georgia, just north of the Florida line. An amazing place."

"What makes it amazing?"

"Well, most of the barrier islands have been developed, often overdeveloped, like Hilton Head and St. Simons, but Cumberland has been in the hands of one family, the Drummonds, since the late eighteenth century. It's probably not a hell of a lot different than it was when the Spaniards discovered it. Old Aldred Drummond, the patriarch, built several big houses for his children, one of which is now an inn. Apart from those, there are only a dozen or so houses on the island. A limited number of people are allowed to visit the island every day, and the inn sleeps only eighteen. There's all sorts of wildlife and about eighteen miles of the most glorious beach you ever saw, with nobody on it."

"Sounds like heaven."

"If it ain't, it's close. I want a book of photographs of the place. I'd like to do the text myself. You want to take a crack at it?"

She was quiet for a moment. "I don't know. I used to have the urge to do nature stuff—I've always been a big fan of Ansel Adams and Eliot Porter. I envy Adams the chance to photograph the West before it got really tamed."

"Well, maybe this is like that. The island is in the hands of one old man, now, and he's over ninety. He lives in a sort of isolated grandeur in the main house, a giant of a place called Dungeness. When he goes, nobody knows what's going to happen. The developers are sniffing around, of course, and I hear the Parks Service has some ambitions. It's unlikely to be the same place in a very few years. I'd like it captured as it is before it goes to hell. I want a big book."

"That's interesting, Ray. God knows I'll need to get away when I get out of here."

"When will that be?"

"Surgery's tomorrow. I'll be out a few days after that, depending on how things go. I'll want some time entirely to myself after that, to get well."

"Think about the autumn, then. It's a beautiful time of the year at Cumberland. We have a cottage down there; it came from my wife's side of the family—she's a distant cousin to the Drummonds. It's not fancy, but it's comfortable, and you're welcome to it for as long as you like. There's even a storage room that might make a good darkroom."

"Mmmmm."

Ferguson shifted his weight. "I think, with the probable success of this book"—he tapped the book in her lap—"I could probably manage a bit more money for a Cumberland volume. It'll sell for years to come."

"You certainly know what tempts a girl. Let's call it a definite maybe. We'll talk about it in a couple of weeks, when I'm settled somewhere, all right?"

"All right." Ferguson seemed to be searching for words. "Listen, kid, I'm sorry this happened . . ."

"Don't, Ray," she said, squeezing his hand. "I'll start feeling sorry for myself. I just want to accept things as they are and make the best of them."

"Sure, I understand." He stood. "You think about Cumberland Island."

"I'll hardly be able to think of anything else," she said.

He gave a little wave, and closed the door behind him.

Elizabeth Barwick gazed adoringly at the book in her lap. She tried to hug it to her breast, but the pain stopped her.

CHAPTER

3

Schaefer walked into the smaller of his two conference rooms and looked it over. It was done in Art Deco style, the antithesis of what a conference room at SIHT would look like. Henry Hoyt would be immediately uncomfortable. Hoyt, Schaefer knew, was no fool, and he would have recovered himself after having been caught off guard by Schaefer's phone call the evening before. Never mind, Schaefer thought. I'll have him rattled again inside of five minutes.

He moved all but three chairs back to the wall and arranged the remaining three with two on one side of the table and one on the other. On the table in front of the single chair he placed a large brown envelope and a manila file folder, squaring them neatly. Unbuttoning the jacket of his silk Armani suit, he removed a Colt Cobra .357 magnum revolver from his waistband, popped the cylinder to be sure it was loaded, opened a slender drawer in front of the single chair, and placed the pistol there. He closed the drawer and stood back to survey the scene. Perfect.

Schaefer looked at his wristwatch; one minute past two. The phone on the conference table rang.

"Mr. Schaefer, Mr. Henry Hoyt and Mr. Baker Ramsey are here."

"Are Kimble and Brown ready?"

"Yes, sir."

"Tell Mr. Hoyt I'll be right with him," Schaefer replied. He hung up the phone, took it off the table, unplugged it from the wall, and placed it inside a credenza drawer. He left the conference room and walked down the hall toward the reception room, working to breathe slowly. Schaefer's offices were on the top floor of Atlanta's new IBM Tower, in a suite designed by Henry Jova, a top local architect. When he had signed the lease there had been betting in the Atlanta Lawyers Club that he wouldn't be able to pay the rent.

Two men—one white, one black—wearing polyester suits, were leaning against the wall near the reception room. "You know what to do," Schaefer said.

Both men nodded.

Schaefer led the two into the reception room. Henry Hoyt and Bake Ramsey stood up. Schaefer noted with distaste Hoyt's elderly Brooks Brothers suit. Only old money could get away with that sort of seediness, he thought. He noted Baker Ramsey with even more distaste. Six feet three, two hundred and forty pounds, fifty of it put on before the past season, when Ramsey's new weight and increased speed had made him the team's unchallenged star. His blond hair was cut in a trendy version of a Marine Corps white sidewall haircut; his neck was wider than his head; his biceps bulged against the sleeves of his custom-made suit.

Schaefer took Henry Hoyt's hand, simultaneously turning to his other two visitors. "Gentlemen, please take a seat. I'll be ready for you in just a few minutes." He turned to Hoyt. "Henry, how are you?"

Hoyt's attention was fixed on Schaefer, but Bake Ramsey was watching the other two men. A look of unease flashed across his face. Just to complete the picture, the white man, Kimble, unbuttoned his jacket, hooked his thumbs in his belt, and ran them around the waistband, hiking up his trousers and revealing a gold detective's badge clipped to his belt. He returned Ramsey's glance with a cold stare.

"I'm all right, Al," Hoyt replied. "This is Baker Ramsey."

Schaefer merely nodded at Ramsey, ignoring his outstretched hand. "Please come with me," he said to Hoyt. He led them to the conference room, indicated the two chairs, then sat opposite them.

"First of all, Al," Hoyt began, "I want you to understand that Mr. Ramsey and I are here merely as a courtesy and in a spirit of conciliation, not because of any implied threat you might have made in our conversation last night. Mr. Ramsey has explained to

me the events of a few days ago, and, while he may
have behaved somewhat rashly and is willing to de-
fray any expense of Mrs. Ramsey's resulting from the
incident, neither he nor I is of the opinion that any
substantial settlement is involved here. I just want
you to understand that clearly at the outset of this
meeting."

Schaefer smiled slightly, then began as if Hoyt
had not spoken. He opened the file folder in front of
him and retrieved two documents, passing copies of
both to Hoyt and a single copy to Ramsey. "Henry,"
he began, "before you are two agreements, one for the
signature of Ramsey, one for your signature on behalf
of the Atlanta Bobcats. If I may summarize briefly: in
his document, Ramsey agrees to an immediate, un-
contested divorce from his wife, Elizabeth Barwick;
he agrees not to see, write, telephone, or otherwise
contact her at any time in the future; he agrees to
make his residence available for Ms. Barwick to remove anything she wishes from the premises; and,
finally, he agrees to pay immediately to Ms. Barwick
the sum of five hundred thousand dollars in cash. In
return, Ms. Barwick agrees to waive any criminal
charges against Ramsey resulting from the events of
earlier this week, and to forgo any further financial
demands upon him."

Schaefer turned to Hoyt. "In your document,
Henry, the team agrees to pay Ms. Barwick five hundred thousand dollars, to guarantee that she will have
the full benefit of the team's group health insurance
policy, and that any of her medical or psychiatric bills
not covered by the policy will be paid by the team.

The team further agrees to reinstate the order for ten thousand of Ms. Barwick's new book of photographs, which was canceled by the team's public affairs office this morning. In return, Ms. Barwick absolves the team of any liability and agrees not to speak to the press about the events of earlier this week."

Hoyt looked up from the documents. "Al, I can tell you right now that neither Mr. Ramsey nor the team has any intention of agreeing to such an arrangement. Mrs. Ramsey can accept Mr. Ramsey's offer of expenses, or she can sue. That is our position."

Schaefer reached under the rim of the conference table and pressed a button, then picked up the brown envelope in front of him, opened it, and slid a photograph across the table. "Henry, have you ever met Ms. Barwick?"

"I haven't had the pleasure," Hoyt replied, picking up the photograph. "Ah, yes," he said, glancing at it, "she's quite pretty, isn't she?"

"She was quite beautiful at the beginning of the week," Schaefer said, sliding half a dozen other photographs across the table and spreading them before Hoyt. "This is how she looked yesterday. And, I should mention, these photographs were taken after Ms. Barwick had received emergency treatment and had partially recovered."

Hoyt picked up one of the photographs, which were in vivid color. The color drained from his face, and his mouth fell open.

The door to the conference room opened and a woman stepped in. "Excuse me, Mr. Schaefer, but Mr.

Hoyt's office is on the phone for him. They said it was urgent."

Hoyt dropped the photograph as if it were hot and turned to the woman, obviously grateful for the interruption. "Thank you, ma'am," he said. "I'll be right there." He rose from the table. "Excuse me, gentlemen. Bake, I don't want you to talk to him while I'm gone." He left the room.

Schaefer turned his attention to Bake Ramsey, who had been silent until now.

Ramsey's eyes, deep set in his muscled face, widened slightly as he stared with hatred at Schaefer. "You little Jew bastard," he said through thin lips. "You think I'm going to sign that thing?" He half-rose. "I'm going to wring your skinny little neck."

Schaefer quickly opened the drawer and placed the Colt Cobra on the table. The light gleamed dully on its blued surface. "Sit down, you muscle-bound piece of shit, or I'll make a big hole in your face," he said.

Ramsey froze, then sank back into the chair, staring hotly at Schaefer.

"You're going to sign that document before you leave this room, you overgrown turd," Schaefer said pleasantly. "You know who those guys out in my reception room are, don't you? They've got a warrant, and at a word from me, they're going to come in here and arrest you for attempted murder, rape, and aggravated sodomy. Then they're going to cuff your hands behind your back and take you downstairs, where there are a number of photographers and a television crew waiting, and stuff you into a squad car. They're going to take you down to Decatur Street and put you in a cell, and you're not going to get bailed out, I can promise you that. You're going to miss the exhibition game in New York this weekend, you're going to miss the season opener, and you're going to miss the goddamned Super Bowl, if the team gets that far, and the next twenty-five Super Bowls after that, do you hear me? You're going to sign that agreement, or I'm going to *burn you down, boy.*" Schaefer held the athlete's gaze.

Ramsey looked down at the table.

Schaefer put the pistol back in the drawer and closed it.

Hoyt reentered the room and sat down. "Some mix-up or other," he said. "I got cut off. Now listen, Al, we might be willing to come to some sort of reasonable arrangement, but of course, I'll have to consult with the team's owner and—"

He was interrupted by the opening of the door. "Excuse me, Mr. Schaefer," the woman said. "Mr. Furman Bisher, of the *Atlanta Journal* is on the phone, and he insists on speaking to you right away. There's also someone from the Associated Press on the phone, and he is very anxious to speak to you, as well."

"Thank you, Hilda," Schaefer said. "Would you ask Mr. Bisher and the other gentleman to hold on for a couple of minutes? And, Hilda, when you've done that, would you come back and bring your notary's seal?"

The woman left, and Schaefer turned back to Hoyt. "Now, Henry, I think you're beginning to get an idea of your position. If you leave this office without signing that document, I promise you that the world is going to fall on your clients and their football player." Schaefer took two pens from the drawer and placed them before the two men opposite him. Hilda entered with her notary's stamp and stood at the end of the table.

"Al, this is an outrage!" Hoyt began. "If you think you can bulldoze me into . . ." Hoyt stopped and watched Bake Ramsey as he leaned forward, picked up a pen, and signed the document.

Hilda moved to his side, stamped the document, and signed it.

Hoyt watched this ceremony apprehensively, then tried once more. "Al, I'm going to have to consult—"

"Henry," Schaefer interrupted, "you and I both know that you already have your client's authority to settle. Now let's get this over with."

Hoyt's shoulders slumped. He picked up the pen, signed the document, and the trusty Hilda notarized it.

Schaefer retrieved the documents and stood up. "Thank you, Henry. I'll expect the funds on my desk by noon tomorrow, as our agreement stipulates. A check on your firm's trust account will be fine. I'll return a copy of the agreement with Ms. Barwick's signature when she's out of surgery."

"All right," Hoyt said dispiritedly.

"Hilda, will you show these gentlemen to the freight elevator? I think they'll want to avoid some people at the main entrance to the building. And tell

Furman Bisher and the gentleman from the AP that I won't be available today."

Schaefer followed them as far as the reception room. When they had gone, he peeled off two hundred-dollar bills and gave them to the detectives. "Thanks, fellas," he said, shaking hands with both of them. "I'll see you next time."

As Schaefer returned, smiling, to his desk, he reflected that he had just paid his office rent for the next several years.

CHAPTER

4

Schaefer arrived at Piedmont Hospital carrying a small suitcase, his briefcase, a shopping bag from the fancy grocer across the street, and two dozen yellow roses. He found Elizabeth Barwick sitting up in bed, sipping orange juice through a glass straw. He took it away from her and set it on the bedside table.

"You shouldn't be drinking straight orange juice," he said, opening half a bottle of champagne and adding some to her glass. "It should be diluted." He handed her the glass.

She did not immediately drink. "Al, I've been thinking about my demands since we last talked. I think I overreached, and I don't want you to feel

badly if you get less. I've figured out how to do what
I want to do for about a hundred thousand."

Schaefer wagged a finger. "Business later, first
roses." He laid the flowers across her lap. "This room
needs a little more color."

"Thank you, Al, they're very nice."

"I want you to know that I would have been here
sooner, but Harry Estes wanted me to wait until you
were a day away from the surgery. How are you feeling?" He looked closely at her. All he could see was
her eyes and a strip of face where the mouth was. It
was obvious that her long hair had been cut. A tight
cap of gauze was wrapped around her head.

"I'm feeling well, if a little anxious. Harry says it
went extremely well. I'm leaving the hospital tomorrow."

"About that," Schaefer said, "I have some news."
He handed her a key. "That's to your new apartment.
It's a sublet—the owner is traveling for the next three
months. It's on a nice street in the Virginia-Highland
area. It's roomy, sunny, and it has a grand piano, if
that makes any difference."

She smiled. "Not much. I haven't played since
high school."

He knocked on the suitcase. "Hilda took charge
of the clothes; she said you'd look funny if I chose
them, so she got you a couple of changes—some un-
derthings, too."

"Thank Hilda for me."

"I sold your car to a friend of mine, got fifty-two
thousand for it. That was halfway between the

wholesale and retail price." He handed her a deposit slip. "I put it in your account."

"I'm very pleased with that."

"Now, about your settlement. First of all, we didn't talk about what you'd have to give in the arrangement. I had to promise them you'd never talk about what happened with the press, and that you wouldn't press any criminal charges against Ramsey."

"That's reasonable, I guess."

"How much did you say you could get by on?"

"A hundred thousand or so. Less, since you got such a good price for the car."

"Well, you're going to have to get by on"—he looked at the deposit slip in his hand—"six hundred sixty-six thousand, six hundred and sixty-six dollars and sixty-six cents." He handed her the slip.

"What?"

"I hit Ramsey and the team for half a million each. I figured that if the steroids have affected him the way you say, the team's as liable as he is. Your medical bills will come to me; I'll see that the team's insurance company settles them."

She stared at the deposit receipt. "You mean, I have over seven hundred thousand dollars in cash in my bank account right this minute?"

"That's right. My standard fee in these situations is a third of the settlement. The car money is in checking; the rest is in your savings account. Your banker likes you a lot." He handed her a card. "I think you should call Bill Schwartz at the Private Banking Division of the First National Bank just as soon as you're able. He'll help you maximize your earnings."

She took a long swallow of her orange juice and champagne. "Could I have some straight champagne, please?"

Schaefer produced two glasses and poured for them both. "What are your plans, Liz?"

"Healing and work. I'll tell you more about my plans later." She sipped her champagne. "Can I ask for one more favor?"

"Shoot."

"Will you buy a gun for me?"

"When I said 'shoot,' I didn't mean it literally."

"Will you?"

"No. And I don't want you to buy one for yourself. Don't worry, sweetheart, he isn't going to bother you; he's too afraid of me. I hosed him down pretty good. By the way, there's an exhibition game in New York this weekend; you can get into the house."

"Good. I'm anxious to wipe the slate clean."

"Baby, it's about as clean as it's ever going to get. Not many people get this kind of a fresh start. Make the most of it, but don't blow the money."

"Don't worry, my needs are going to be very simple for a while."

"Harry wants you to see a shrink. I think it's a good idea. You've got to be a very angry lady at the moment, whether you know it or not."

"I've got an appointment on Monday."

Schaefer set down his glass and stood up. "You finish the bubbly for me. I've got to be in court in an hour."

"Give 'em hell."

"You know it."

"Thank you, Al."

"Don't thank me; I did pretty good for myself."

"I'm glad."

"Something else; I had a good time doing it."

"That's always important."

"You remember that, kid. Whatever you're going to do, have a good time doing it." Schaefer left the room and whistled his way down the hall.

Doing well by doing good. He loved it.

The following day, Elizabeth Barwick checked out of Piedmont Hospital and vanished. The following weekend, her mother's furniture, her cameras and darkroom equipment, and everything else that belonged to her disappeared from the house she had shared with Baker Ramsey.

Over the next several weeks, one by one, her friends received a phone call. The conversations were much the same:

"Hi, it's Liz."

"Well, hi! Where you been keeping yourself?"

"I've been on the move. Bake and I called it a day."

"Sugar, it's about time. All your friends think so."

"It had to be done."

"Let's get together."

"I'd love to, but everything is so hectic. I'm going to be traveling for a while, and I've got so much to do."

"Around the world?"

"Maybe. I haven't decided."

"Send us a postcard."

"Sure thing. I'm sending you a copy of my book; it's out next month."

"Can't wait to see it. Can't wait to see you."

"When you least expect it."

"Take care."

"Bye."

CHAPTER

5

*L*iz Barwick leaned over
the rail and let the wind blow in her face. It was the
day after Labor Day, and it seemed a very long time
since she had performed such a pleasurable act. She
was aboard the *Aldred Drummond*, formerly a naval
landing craft, which had departed Fernandina Beach,
Florida, twenty minutes before. Cumberland Island
loomed ahead.

This was all very strange to her and, in a way,
frightening. At this moment in her life, she had no
connection with any human being, other than her
publisher and her lawyer. Since birth, there had always been someone to tell her what to do—her parents, teachers, professors, her boss at the paper; and,
in recent years, an increasingly volatile husband. Now

she was independent—well-off, too. She was also alone.

Her new car, a black Jeep Cherokee, shared the craft with a van from the island's Greyfield Inn. She leaned back inboard and caught her reflection in the Cherokee's window. She had been avoiding her reflection for the past two months, but now she studied the vaguely different face that stared back at her from under a floppy, broad-brimmed straw hat. It was remarkably free from apparent damage; indeed, a stranger might think the face quite normal. The nose was straight and long, almost as before; the teeth were fine, the jaw realigned; there was a splotchiness of the skin where scars had been cleverly removed. A lingering puffiness of the forehead and cheeks gave her a nearly Indian look, made her eyes seem unusually deep set. Under the straw hat were two inches of thick, dark hair—the same length all over, newly grown from a once-shaven scalp. The new hair already hid a thin, red scar which ran, from ear to ear, over the top of her head. Harry Estes had made the incision, then pulled her scalp forward, baring the skull, until he could see the orbs of her eyes from above, then he had reattached her facial structure to her skull, using four small titanium plates. The weight on her five-foot, eight-inch frame was down from one hundred and thirty to one hundred and three pounds.

Liz opened the car door and stood on the doorsill, the better to see the island. They were in Cumberland Sound, part of the Inland Waterway, and the island was showing its narrow southern tip, the bone end of the typical leg-of-lamb shape of an Atlantic Seaboard barrier island. The mouth of the St. Marys River opened to her left, and the sinister, black silhouette of a United States submarine could be glimpsed as it made its way upstream toward its new base at St. Marys. To her right, the Atlantic Ocean began to slip from view behind the low-lying island.

Beyond a small sea of waving marsh grass and a stand of trees, a gaggle of chimneys rose, hinting at something imposing under them. That would be Dungeness, the main house, Liz thought, remembering the map in her pocket, and, as they made their way up the sound, Dungeness Dock appeared in the distance.

Liz felt thirsty, and she moved toward the rear of the Cherokee, where a cooler rested. As she reached the back of the car and started around it, a shaft of timber appeared, rushing toward her face. She spun out of the way, suddenly terrified, holding her fragile new visage in her hands, trying not to tremble.

"Hey, I'm sorry, didn't see you," a pleasant-looking young man said, hefting the two-by-four onto his other shoulder.

"It's all right," she replied, leaning against the Jeep for support, trying to slow her heartbeat.

"You must be Liz Barwick," a woman's husky voice said.

Liz dropped her hands and looked at a fortyish, statuesque woman wearing a cotton shift, her salt-and-pepper hair falling loose about her shoulders.

"Yes," she said, feeling somehow cornered.

"I'm Germaine Drummond," the woman said, sticking out a hand. "I run Greyfield Inn."

"Hi," Liz replied, struggling to smile.

"Ray Ferguson told me you were coming, asked me to look out for you." Her brow furrowed. "You seem a little shaky."

"I'm okay; just a near collision with a piece of lumber." She nodded at the young man, who was making his way aft.

"Oh, that's Ron; he's a summer waiter at the inn. I'm sorry he scared you."

"It wasn't his fault." Liz moved to the rear of the Jeep again and opened the tailgate. "Would you like something to drink?"

"You could force a beer on me, I guess," the woman replied.

Liz opened two beers and handed Germaine one. "Ray told me about the inn. It sounds like a nice place."

Germaine nodded. "We try. Sometimes I wish it was in a populated place, so we wouldn't have to do things like run a daily ferry to Fernandina, and go over there once a week for groceries. By the way, give me a list the middle of every week, and I'll add it to your trip; charge you ten percent for the service."

"More than fair," Liz said. "How long have you owned the place?"

"I don't own it," Germaine said. "My grandfather does; charges me rent. I've been running the place since I kicked my husband off the island ten years ago."

"Your grandfather is quite old, isn't he?"

"Ninety-one. Still drives a jeep all over his island. We had to make him stop riding horses awhile back."

She nodded at the chimneys above the trees. "There's his house."

"It looks big."

"Forty rooms. I know, we counted them once, when I was a little girl. My two brothers and I spread out and each took a chunk, then compared notes. The place had a staff of three hundred in the old days, toward the end of the last century."

"Three hundred?"

"They grew their own vegetables, raised and slaughtered their own cattle and hogs and chickens, did their own building and blacksmithing, ran a school, had a doctor and a dentist in once a week— had an office and equipment for them. It was a working settlement. Grandpapa still grows most of his own food. Say, I know you won't feel like cooking after moving all your gear into the cottage. Why don't you join me for dinner at the inn tonight?"

Liz hesitated for a moment. During the past two months she had become accustomed to refusing contact with anybody, hiding away while she healed. "Thanks," she said finally. "I'd like that." It was time she came out of hiding.

"There's Greyfield Dock," Germaine said. "We'll be ashore in a few minutes. How long you down for?"

"I don't know," Liz said honestly. "Ray wants a collection of photographs for a book about the island. As long as it takes, I guess."

"It's about time he did that book; he's been talking about it long enough. I reckon I'll sell a ton of them at the inn."

A single-engine airplane appeared, low in the sky, and flew in two tight circles over the island.

"We've got a grass strip on the island," Germaine said. "The odd guest flies in, buzzes the inn, and we meet him."

The *Aldred Drummond* began a turn toward the slip.

"Better saddle up, I guess," Germaine said. "Come for a drink about six. Dinner's at seven-thirty."

"See you then," Liz replied, climbing into the Jeep.

The barge eased up to the bank and dropped her gate. Germaine drove the van ashore, and Liz followed in her vehicle. Greyfield Inn appeared on her left, a graceful mansion in the colonial style, with a broad, high front porch. Giant live oaks spread their long limbs over the lawn before it, dipping to the ground, their Spanish moss dripping from every branch. Germaine stopped the van and waved Liz alongside.

"You know the way?"

"Not exactly."

"Go out through the main gate and follow the road north. A couple of miles along, you'll come to a big, open field—that's the airstrip. A big house called Stafford is right next to it. Just past the strip, you turn right and, after about a quarter mile, bear right at the fork. Stafford Beach Cottage is at the end of the road."

"Thanks," Liz said, and drove toward the gates. She edged over to allow a beat-up old pickup truck to pass, headed toward the inn. The driver was a tiny, very black, old man with a fuzz of white hair. His chin was tilted up so that he could see over the wheel, and that and his intense concentration gave him an arrogant look.

She started north on a good dirt road, flat and straight. Palmettos occasionally brushed the Jeep's doors, and a forest of pines and live oaks occupied both sides of the road. She had gone less than a mile when, suddenly, a buck deer sprang out of a thick bunch of palmettos on her left, cleared the road with a single bound, and disappeared into equally thick palmettos on the other side. She had come within an ace of hitting it. She drove on, a hand clasped to her breast. The open field appeared as advertised, and she was in time to see a Cessna rolling down the runway, using less than half of it to get off the ground.

The airplane turned north over the beach, gaining altitude. Liz had always wanted to learn to do that. One of these days, she thought.

She passed Stafford House, found the road to her right, then bore right again at the fork. She came around a corner, and the house sat before her, under a huge live oak, nearly in the dunes. The single-story cottage was covered with weathered cedar shingles, and the trim was a freshly painted white. The beach must be only yards away, she thought; she could see birds wheeling low in the sky, just beyond the dunes. She turned the Jeep around and backed it up to the steps to the house.

Anxious to see her new home, she trotted up the front steps and emerged onto a wide deck. From here she could see across the dunes to the sea. The beach stretched away into the distance, north and south, not a soul on it. She tore herself from the view, fumbled for the key, and slipped it into the lock. To her surprise, the door swung open at her touch. Well, she supposed, maybe people leave their doors unlocked on Cumberland Island. She stepped in and stopped in her tracks. The faint aroma of fresh coffee was in the air.

"Hello?" she called. "Hello?" this time louder. Silence greeted her. She looked around her. She was in the living room. An assortment of old furniture was scattered around the sunny room; everything was neat and orderly. She moved straight ahead to the kitchen; it was just as neat. She walked to a countertop and placed her hand on the electric coffeepot. Still warm. A single cup sat, upside down in the draining rack. She opened the refrigerator. There was little there—three bottles of beer and an open can of condensed milk, still sweet smelling. She went and looked into both bedrooms. No one there, beds stripped, neat as a pin. Wondering, she returned to the Jeep and began to unload.

An hour later, she was unpacked, except for the darkroom equipment. That could wait until tomorrow. She put away her groceries and found some tonic water and a lime. Drink in hand, she wandered toward the deck. As she emerged into the late-afternoon sunshine, a sound met her ears—a series of high cracks. She saw a figure on the beach and went back for her binoculars.

She trained the ten-power glasses on the beach, and the figure became more visible, though still far away. A man—tall, slender, blond—stood in the light surf, a rifle at his shoulder, firing out over the water. His attitude was relaxed, yet concentrated. He wore only a sort of Tarzanian loincloth, and a knife hung in its sheath from his belt. He went on, monotonously firing at nothing Liz could see.

She hurried back into the house, found a camera case, and dug out a 35-mm body and a 300-mm lens. There was something odd, almost otherworldly about the man and what he was doing. She wanted a photograph. She walked outside, stepped up to the deck's railing, camera ready, and looked toward the beach. He was gone, vanished from the scene. How long had she been in the house? Half a minute? She estimated the distance from the surf to the dunes. It didn't seem possible that he could have vanished so quickly. She picked up the field glasses again and swept the area. Nothing.

Liz glanced at her watch. Five-thirty. She was due at the inn at six. She abandoned the deck and got into the shower, then slipped into a cotton dress, applied light makeup, and fixed a silk scarf over her short hair, pinning it behind her head. When she left the cottage, she carefully locked the front door.

CHAPTER

6

*L*iz climbed the broad steps of the inn and stopped on the front porch. A young couple was lounging in a swing at one end of the veranda, her head on his shoulder. Liz felt a moment of longing, even envy. She reflected that it was the first emotion besides rage that she could remember for the past couple of months. She entered the house and found it quiet. To her right, she discovered a small room with a bar, deserted. A sign said MIX YOUR OWN, so she did, pouring herself a small bourbon. She wandered out of the bar, exploring. A library next door held many volumes, most of them dusty and old. She walked back down the hallway and found a large sitting room, dominated by a full-length portrait of a beautiful young woman and filled with

53

odd objects and bric-a-brac. On the opposite wall, facing the picture of the young woman, was a portrait of a rakishly handsome man of about thirty, wearing riding clothes, a plaited crop in his hand. On a windowsill nearby was the skull of a loggerhead turtle, as big as a football. She tried to imagine the size of the whole turtle and failed. She browsed further around the room, and, with a shock, stopped in front of a framed photograph.

It was obviously old; the print was faded and yellowing. It was of a man, tall, blond, and slender; he stood in a light surf, firing a rifle toward the sea; he wore only a loincloth, and a knife hung from his belt. She had the irrational feeling that she had taken the photograph less than an hour before.

"That's my father," said a voice behind her, making her jump. She turned to find Germaine, a drink in her hand. She sipped the drink and smiled; revealing large, square, white teeth. "That was taken in the early fifties by my mother. They were both killed in nineteen sixty, taking off from the airstrip in an old Stearman biplane. A wire strut snapped and they lost a wing. We never knew which one of them was flying—they were both pilots."

Liz stared, speechless, at the photograph. "But—" she began to say.

"This is my grandmother, when she was nineteen," Germaine interrupted. "She died before I was born." She turned and nodded at the opposite wall. "That's Grandpapa, when he was in his late twenties. I'm sorry, were you about to say something?"

Liz shook her head. "No," she said, feeling foolish.

"This is my favorite room in the house," Germaine said. "It's full of family things—pictures, portraits, stuff my brothers and I collected when we were children. We found the turtle skull on the beach."

"It's huge," Liz said.

"After dinner, when it's dark, we'll take a drive and see if we can find a loggerhead or two laying their eggs."

Liz turned to ask about the turtles, then froze. Standing in the doorway was the man in the photograph, the man on the beach with the rifle.

Germaine, who was still talking, stopped and looked at her, then turned and followed her gaze. She smiled broadly. "Look who's here!" She crossed the room, and he met her halfway. They embraced. "Hello, baby brother!" Germaine said.

"Hey, big Germaine," the man replied, hugging her and laughing.

Well, thought Liz, at least she can see him, too; he must be real.

"Come here and meet somebody," Germaine called to Liz.

Liz walked over.

The man stuck out a hand. "I'm Hamish Drummond," he said, smiling, revealing what were obviously the family teeth, big and white against his tanned skin.

His blond hair was neatly combed—not like that afternoon—and he seemed so . . . *clean*, Liz thought. "I'm Liz Barwick," she said.

"Hi, Liz," he replied, still holding the handshake. "You down for the week?"

"She's down for longer than that," Germaine said. "Ray Ferguson sent her to do that book of photographs on the island he's been promising us."

"I'm glad to hear it," Hamish said, finally releasing her hand.

"I'm looking forward to getting started," Liz said, finding it impossible to take her eyes off him. He was not quite handsome; he was closer to beautiful. "It's a lovely island."

"It is that," he said.

"You haven't got a drink," Germaine said, tugging him toward the bar.

Liz followed them and found two couples there, drinking.

"This is my cousin, Jimmy Weathers, and his wife, Martha," Germaine said, introducing a short, balding man and a plump, pretty woman. "This is Liz Barwick, who's down here photographing things."

"We saw Grandpapa this afternoon," Jimmy said. "You seen him yet, Hamish?"

"No, I only got in this afternoon. I'll see him tomorrow."

Another couple entered the bar, then another, and the conversation turned to the island, its wildlife, and its beauty.

"I nearly hit a buck this afternoon," Liz said.

"You nearly hit Buck?" Jimmy asked.

"A buck, not Buck, Jimmy," Germaine pitched in.

"Pity you missed him, then," Jimmy said. "We could have had some of Germaine's venison for dinner."

Liz found a moment to turn to Hamish Drummond. "I saw you up at Stafford Beach this afternoon."

Hamish turned and looked at her, puzzled, then his eyes narrowed. "Did you? Did you really?" he said, more to himself than to her.

At dinner in the basement dining room, Liz found herself seated between Germaine and Hamish at a large table with half a dozen other people. As the remnants of a pâté were taken away and fat trout were served, the talk turned to work. "What do you do?" a man across the table asked Hamish.

"Financial consulting."

"Who consults you?"

"Right now, a merchant bank in London. Everybody's getting ready for the big move in the Common Market in 'ninety-two. What do you do?"

"I'm a psychiatrist," the man said. "So is Ann my wife. We practice in Savannah."

Hamish nodded, as if he had little interest in the subject.

"I develop resort property," Jimmy said, as if it were his turn.

"Well," the doctor said, "I hope you never get your hands on this place."

Hamish smiled slightly. "I wish I'd said that."

"Now, you'd be surprised what enlightened development could do for this island," Jimmy said.

"Make it available for a lot more people to enjoy. It would have to be done right, of course. Elegantly."

"Like Hilton Head?" the doctor said.

"Beautiful development, Hilton Head," Jimmy said, looking dreamy about it, missing the sarcasm.

"Wall-to-wall development," Germaine chipped in.

The table fell silent.

Liz turned to the psychiatrist. "What sort of practice do you and your wife have, Doctor?" She really didn't want to know; she had seen enough of psychiatrists over the past few weeks, but she felt the need for a change of subject.

"Well," the man said, "I was teaching at Duke University Medical School, and I retired last year. We moved to Savannah, and we both felt the need for some activity, so we started a part-time practice."

"We're working on a book, too," the man's wife said.

"A book on psychiatry?" Germaine asked.

"Not exactly," the man replied. "We're conducting a major study on identical twins, and the results will form a book on the subject."

"Hamish has a twin," Jimmy chimed in. "You ought to study those boys." There was something malicious in his tone.

Hamish suddenly stood up. "Excuse me, please." He left the table.

There was a silence in his wake, and, again, Liz tried to keep the conversation going. "Are twins particularly interesting to study?" she asked the doctor.

The doctor smiled. "Fascinating. Identical twins

have the closest of all human relationships—closer than mother and child. They enjoy a high degree of empathy, often are telepathic, know what each other is thinking. Sometimes, during our work, I've had the eerie feeling that a pair of twins were the same person—or, rather, different halves of the same person."

"Is that just because they grow up together, spend so much time together? Or do you read something more into it?" Liz asked, interested.

"Something more, though I'm not quite sure what. We've studied twins who were separated shortly after birth, who didn't even know they had a twin, and there were remarkable similarities in how they had lived their lives, the choices they had made—even though they were brought up in families that were very different. I've interviewed one such pair who seemed to choose the same brands of clothes and even had identical haircuts. They both had had a fantasy twin for as long as they could remember, played with him, talked with him. Neither was much surprised when he discovered that he had an actual twin."

"Boy, that's spooky," Jimmy's wife, Martha, said.

"That's not exactly a psychiatric term," the doctor said, "but it's properly descriptive."

"Do twins always get along with each other?" Martha asked.

"Always," the doctor said, "at least in our study. Their mothers seem to regard them as one person, so they don't have to compete for her affection. In fact, generally speaking, they don't compete with each other over anything; instead, they seem to form a unit and compete with others, as one person."

"I've always wondered why their mothers dress them alike," Martha said. "Couldn't that warp them in some way? Screw up their individuality?"

"Some twins we've talked to resisted dressing alike as children," Anna Hamilton said, "while others chose to do so. Some of them go on dressing alike for all their lives. Twins have a bond that lasts until they die—in fact, a significant percentage choose not to marry, so that they can remain with each other, although this phenomenon seems more pronounced among females."

"Can a mother always tell her twins apart?" Liz asked.

"Usually, at least after infancy, but not always. It's very common for parents to put ID bracelets on twins so they can tell them apart. Usually, as they get older, enough differences develop that it gets to be easier. One child may have some minor injury and have a scar; one may gain more weight—something like that."

Germaine leaned close to Liz. "Did you notice that, when Hamish arrived tonight, I didn't introduce him, that he introduced himself? That's a habit I got into when Hamish and Keir were growing up—I was wrong so often." She turned to the doctor. "Twins are palindromic," she said.

"That's very good," the doctor agreed. "A palindrome is the perfect metaphor for identical twins."

"What's that?" Jimmy asked. "That word?"

Germaine spoke up. "A palindrome is a literary

device—a word, or a sentence, or even a poem, that reads the same forward and backward. Exactly the same."

The group gathered around and watched. Some had flashlights, others used flash cameras, but the mother was not disturbed. The female loggerhead turtle lay over the hole she had dug with her flippers and dropped her eggs into it, dozens of them, each like a slippery Ping-Pong ball.

"We have an egg patrol," Germaine said to Liz. "We go down the beach, look for signs of a nest, then obliterate the signs. Otherwise the raccoons get at the eggs and eat them."

The loggerhead finished her work, pushed sand over the eggs, and, exhausted, began struggling back toward the sea. The moon lit the little band of watchers as they followed her painful progress across the beach. Then, finally, she reached the surf line and disappeared into the water. The group cheered.

Walking back to the Jeep, Liz fell into step with Germaine. Their bare feet left moonlit tracks on the damp sand. "Tell me, Germaine, why did Hamish excuse himself at dinner when Jimmy mentioned his twin?" Liz asked.

"Ah," said Germaine, "I'm afraid that Hamish and Keir might shake the good doctor's theories about the closeness of twins."

"Why?"

"Well, the boys were much the way he described when they were children, even as teenagers. Nobody could tell them apart—well, nobody but Grandpapa, anyway. They could fool me any time they wanted to. They were always together—always. If they were apart, they were nervous, unhappy. Once, I remember, Keir was ill with the flu when they were supposed to go to camp in the North Georgia Mountains, and Grandpapa forced Hamish to go without him. After he left, Keir couldn't sleep, wouldn't eat, wouldn't talk. A couple of days later, Grandpapa got a call from the director of the camp; Hamish had disappeared. He turned up that night. He had hitchhiked to St. Marys; he walked to the mouth of the river and *swam* across Cumberland Sound. At night. He was twelve."

"Jesus, he's lucky to be alive."

"I think if he had died in the attempt, Keir would have died, too."

"Did something happen to change the relationship?"

"Yes. The summer they were almost eighteen, when they were both about to go off to Princeton, something happened."

"What?"

"Nobody knows. But since that summer, it's more than twenty years ago, they haven't spoken to each other and haven't spoken about each other to anyone else."

They trudged along the beach in silence for a time.

"What about Keir?" Liz asked finally. "Where is he?"

"Nobody knows," Germaine said. "He turns up, unannounced, from time to time—never when Hamish is here—and then he disappears. A friend of mine ran into him in Paris, last year. I haven't seen him for more than three years. I don't even know if he's alive. Except, I always had the feeling that if Keir died, Hamish would die, too, and vice versa. Even now, when they must . . . *hate* each other, I still feel that. I don't know why."

Driving back to the inn in the Jeep, both women were quiet. Liz came into the bar for a nightcap, and, when she left to go back to the cottage, Hamish Drummond was sitting in one of the big swings on the veranda, an empty brandy snifter next to him, staring out into the darkness. Liz did not disturb his reverie.

When she got back to Stafford Beach Cottage, the front door stood wide open.

CHAPTER

7

Angus Drummond walked slowly down the front steps of Dungeness, the enormous house that had been his home since the day he had been born there, ninety-one years before. He walked slowly, as he did most things these days.

He lengthened his stride now, along the front of the old house, ignoring the peeling paint and dry-rotted windowsills. Dungeness, in Angus's mind, was as fresh and whole as the day his ancestor, old Aldred Drummond, had finished building it in 1820.

A brown-skinned boy in his midteens approached, leading a fine-looking horse. "You be riding today, Mr. Angus?" the boy asked.

Angus found an apple in his pocket and fed it to

the gelding, stroking his soft nose. "Not today, James," he replied. "I think I'll take the jeep."

It was a conversation they conducted each morning, never varying, each reciting his lines from a script they both knew would not change. Angus had last ridden some six years before. James would exercise the animal, keep him sweet for that day when Angus might reply, "Yes, James, saddle the gelding. I feel like a ride today." The boy led the horse away, and Angus strode toward his World War II–era jeep. He hoisted his backside into the metal seat, then, grasping his trousers legs, hauled his long legs under the steering wheel. The jeep started first try. Angus placed his panama hat on the floor, settled his steel-rimmed sunglasses on his prominent nose, and pointed the vehicle toward the sea. The jeep's transmission had only three gears, and he kept it in second as the road led into the dunes. He wound through the mountains of sand and grass, then emerged onto the open beach.

Cumberland Island has eighteen miles of broad beach, and there seemed to be no one on it that morning but Angus Drummond. He liked it that way. The wind was out of the southeast, as it often was, and, as he drove north, the jeep's speed made the day seem nearly windless. Angus saluted the two shrimp boats fishing barely a hundred yards off the beach and got a wave back from men on both.

A pair of brown pelicans kept pace with the jeep, skimming the water near its edge, hunting breakfast. Angus took some satisfaction in seeing them; a few years back they had been an endangered species. Now hundreds of them flocked on the island, where he protected them from their only enemy: Man.

From his perch in the jeep, Angus spotted the tracks of deer, wild horses, raccoons, and a dozen different birds in the damp sand at the edge of the dunes. There were few people on his island, but he was not short of company.

In the distance ahead he saw a black speck. He watched it as it grew larger, his prescription sunglasses bringing the image sharp. There were two people—no, one and some sort of apparatus. He slowed the jeep and pulled up next to a young woman standing beside a large camera on a tripod.

Liz smiled at the old man in the jeep, the wind mussing his thick, gray hair. "Mister Angus Drummond, I presume," she said.

He regarded her with suspicion. "You have me at a disadvantage, Miss, ah, Mrs.—"

"Ms.," she interrupted. "Elizabeth Barwick."

"Miz Barwick," he said. "Before I welcome you to my island I'll ask what you are doing on it."

"I am photographing it," Liz replied. "I hope in such a way that no one who sees the book I make from the photographs will ever forget how beautiful a place it is."

"Ah, um . . . ," Angus muttered, put off balance by the flattery.

"I'm a guest of the Fergusons," she said, nodding toward Stafford Beach Cottage. "Mr. Ferguson is my publisher."

"Ah, yes," Angus said. "He's not a bad sort. Doesn't come down here often."

Liz wondered whether Drummond's favorable assessment of Ray Ferguson was connected with the infrequency of his visits. "I arrived yesterday, so I haven't had a chance to see much of the island, but I couldn't resist the morning light. I had to get a shot of the beach."

"Well," he said, "I guess I'd better show you around a bit. Get in."

Liz folded the tripod and tucked it into the rear of the jeep, releasing the 4 × 5 field camera and nestling it in her lap. "I'm all yours, Mr. Drummond," she said.

Angus released the clutch pedal, and the jeep lurched forward. Liz sat back and enjoyed the morning. The jeep rolled north along the beach, and the sun beat down on them. "Where are you from?" Angus asked, and by the time they had come to the end of the beach, he knew everything about her that she was willing to tell him.

Angus slowed the jeep as they approached a band of water that lay ahead. Before them on the sand rested a flock of brown pelicans that Liz quickly estimated at five hundred.

"Do you mind if I take a photograph?" she asked.

"Don't be long," he said. "You've a lot of island to see."

She had the camera set up and her shot made in five minutes. "Thank you," she said, climbing back into the jeep.

Angus pointed at the land on the other side of the water. "That's Little Cumberland Island; I don't own that. An oversight of my ancestors. Don't ever try to swim across there. It's not far, but the current is strong." He put the jeep into gear and swung around. A moment later, he was following a faint track through the dunes, headed toward the interior of the island.

They drove along quietly, Angus occasionally pointing out some place of interest. They passed black workmen running an old road scraper and doing other maintenance jobs. Shortly, they pulled to a stop among a group of deserted-looking wooden houses.

"The old slave settlement," Angus said. "I built some more modern houses at Dungeness a long time ago for the workmen and their families, but I never pulled down the old slave settlement." He nodded at an elderly black man who was coming out of a tiny church. "And here comes its only resident." He raised his voice. "Good morning, Buck," he called. "Come over here and meet somebody."

The old man shuffled across the few yards that separated them. "Hey, Mist' Angus," he said. "How you doin'?"

"Pretty good. Buck, this is Miz Barwick. She's staying down to Stafford Beach. Miz Barwick, this is Buck Moses, who worked for my daddy and me for most of the past century. Buck is our only officially retired citizen. I still work."

Liz remembered having seen him in his truck. "Hello, Mr. Moses," she said.

"Now, you call me Buck, just like everybody else," the old man said, with a toothless grin.

"Buck is the only man alive who knows more about this island than I do," Angus said. "He taught me what I know, but he kept a few secrets to himself, didn't you, Buck?"

"Now, Mist' Angus, you know I can't hide nothing from you. You see right through me."

"That's a laugh." Angus snorted. "Well, Buck, we've got some territory to cover. We'll be on our way." With a wave, he drove on.

"How old is he?" Liz asked.

"Nobody knows; not even Buck," Angus replied. "I'm ninety-one my last birthday, and the first time I remember Buck he must have been twelve or thirteen. That'd make him at least a hundred and five, but he might be older. He was my best friend when I was a boy; taught me everything. My son, too, and my grandsons. My daddy spent most of his time in New York, so I didn't see much of him. Buck took up the slack. Then, when my boy was killed in that plane crash in 'sixty, old Buck was right there with the twins, too. I expect Buck believes *he* owns Cumberland Island, and in a way I suppose he's right. He's going to outlive me, I know it."

Angus drove on in silence for a while, then pulled off the road and drove along a track for a way, ducking tree branches. Finally, he stopped and waved an arm. "Lake Whitney," he said.

Liz saw a lake nearly covered with water lilies. As she watched, a doe waded into the water on the other side, a hundred and fifty yards away.

"We're downwind," Angus said. "Go ahead and take your picture."

Liz quietly got set up and had the deer framed when a commotion broke out in the water on the other side of the lake. She snatched her head from under the black cloth, away from the upside-down image, and looked. The deer was screaming, thrashing about in the water. Then it went down and disappeared, while the water continued to churn.

"Well, I'll be a son of a bitch," Angus said, wonderingly, almost to himself.

"What happened?" Liz asked weakly, too stunned to move.

"It's Goliath," Angus said. "Miz Barwick, you're a lucky girl. You could live on this island for nearly a hundred years, like I have, and not see a thing like that."

"Who's Goliath?" Liz asked.

"He's the biggest alligator I ever saw, and the last time I saw him was a good fifteen years ago. He was a twelve-footer then; God knows how big he is now."

Liz stood, looking at the spot where the doe had disappeared. The water was glassy smooth again. She suddenly realized that she had not pressed the shutter release.

"Let's get going," Angus said.

"The poor deer," Liz said, climbing into the jeep.

"Gators got to eat, too," Angus said with a shrug. He got the jeep going again and pointed it away from the lake. "See you don't take any swims in Lake Whitney, nor any place around it. Gators can walk, too."

They were on what passed for a main road now. Angus swung around a sharp bend and drove down a straight stretch. They passed through a gate and came to a flat lawn. Ahead of them sat a gracefully designed Palladian mansion, gleaming white in the sun, framed by giant live oaks. Angus stopped the jeep. "That's Plum Orchard," he said. "I built it for my boy, Evan, after the last war."

"It's beautiful," Liz said. "Who lives there now?"

"Nobody," Angus said, swinging the jeep around. "I keep a roof on it, keep it painted. I wouldn't want to see it fall down. Maybe one of my grandsons will come back and live in it one day. I'll be gone by then." For a moment the old man looked stricken; then he looked up and paid attention to his driving. For the remainder of their drive they talked about the island and its history and how Angus Drummond had shaped it.

It seemed to Liz that, in a couple of hours, they had covered more ground than most new acquaintances did in weeks. They warmed to each other.

When the jeep pulled up at Stafford Beach Cottage, Liz climbed out and retrieved her tripod. "That was a wonderful tour," she said. "I hope I'll get to see Dungeness one of these days, too."

"I'd be honored to show it to you," he said. "You're a young woman of some substance, Miz Barwick." He grinned. "If I were fifty years younger, I'd do something about it."

"Thank you for that," she said. "Call me Liz."

"I'll call you Elizabeth," he said. Then he put the jeep in gear and drove away.

Liz watched him go, then trudged into the house with her gear. It occurred to her that Angus Drummond, at ninety-one, was the most attractive man she had met in years. She wondered if that was a comment on him or on her.

Germaine Drummond was at her desk off the kitchen at Greyfield Inn when she heard her grandfather's jeep. She got up, opened the screen door, and stuck her head out. "Hey, Grandpapa!" she called. "You want a cup of tea?"

Angus sat in the idling jeep and looked at her for a moment. "Germaine," he said, "you call my lawyer and tell him to come over here and see me. Next week will be soon enough." Then he drove on.

Germaine stepped out into the drive and ate a little of his dust. He was finally going to make a will. She felt weak with relief.

CHAPTER

8

*L*iz stood naked before the mirror and, for the first time since she had struggled into the Piedmont Trauma Center, looked deliberately at her reflection. At first it was something of a shock. Her hair was still short enough to be spiky, and she was still thinner than at any time since pre-pubescence, but the Cumberland sun had given her color, and the last of her bruises had faded, taking their yellow tinge with them. The person who stared back at her seemed a reasonably healthy woman. Her thoughts returned to the couple she had seen on her first visit to the inn. How long since she had leaned against a man in that way? How long since she had made love? She laughed at herself. A reasonably healthy woman, indeed!

She slipped into a favorite cotton nightshirt and padded, barefoot, into the kitchen to fix herself dinner. She put a steak under the grill and, while it cooked, opened a bottle of California Merlot and poured herself a glass. She took her meal out onto the deck and ate it greedily while the light died and the blue sea beyond the dunes faded into a slate gray. She had an appetite at last, and the wine was good, too. She poured herself another glass and sat on a chaise, hugging her knees, sipping the wine while half a moon rose from the Atlantic Ocean. She was dug in, now, and that day she had taken a good photograph, the one of the pelicans on the beach. Except for her loneliness, this felt very much like contentment.

A fresh breeze swept in, bringing with it the promise of autumn, though that season comes late on Cumberland. She shivered a bit, then walked through the darkening cottage to the kitchen, where she washed her dishes. When the kitchen was neat, she returned to the living room and stretched out on the sofa. She sipped the last of her glass of wine and watched the moon swing across the sky, turning the room white and leaving her in shadow. She did not remember falling asleep; she only knew how good it felt.

When the noise woke her she knew exactly where she was, in spite of the wine, and she knew where the noise came from: the kitchen. There was the closing of the refrigerator and the scrape of a chair on the linoleum floor. She lay still, trying to keep her breathing steady, wondering what to do. Then she became angry. This was her house, and intruders were not welcome. Quietly, she felt for her large camera case, found what she wanted, and moved toward the kitchen, weight on the balls of her feet, afraid to breathe. She stopped at the kitchen door and tamped down her fear for a moment. Then she eased her head around the doorjamb. A man was sitting at the kitchen table, drinking something. The moonlight through the window was weaker at the back of the house, but even in the dimness she could see that he was naked.

For some reason, this made her even angrier. She brought her hand up, shut her eyes tightly, and fired the strobe light.

"Jesus Christ!" the man yelled. There was the sound of furniture overturning.

When she opened her eyes he was backed against the kitchen wall, shielding his eyes, trying vainly to see. The strobe had a five-second recycle time, and she counted aloud—"Thousand one, thousand two, thousand three"—as she moved toward the kitchen counter. She could tell he was starting to see again by the time she reached the knife rack. "Thousand five," she said, and fired the strobe again.

"Will you stop that! Are you trying to blind me?" he shouted.

Liz had the chef's knife, now, the one with the twelve-inch blade. She stepped in front of him, knife at the ready, and fired the strobe again, while shutting her eyes tightly. "Maybe I'm trying to blind you," she said, her voice shaking with anger, "and maybe I'll do worse with this knife. What are you doing in my house?"

"Christ, all I wanted was a beer," he said, rubbing at his eyes. "It's even my beer. I put it in the icebox before you came."

"All right, so it's your beer; it's *my house,* and I didn't invite you."

"Just take it easy," he said, shielding his eyes from another possible burst of light. "I didn't mean to disturb you; I thought you were out."

"I'm not out, I'm here!" she said, nearly shouting, "but even if I were out, it's *my house!*"

"I'm sorry I invaded your privacy. Let me tell you who I am."

"I know who you are," she said. "You're Keir Drummond." Her own eyes had adjusted better to the dim light, and she could see now that he was not naked, merely wearing the loincloth she had seen him in before. She walked to the door and switched on the light. "Have a seat," she said, indicating the far end of the table with her knife.

"Thanks," he replied. He sat down again and picked up his beer, but he kept his eye on the knife. "So you're Liz Barwick," he said.

She went to the fridge and got a beer of her own. She didn't want it, but somehow she felt at a disadvantage because she didn't have one. "That's right," she said, drawing up a chair to the opposite end of the table. "Why have you been coming into my house?"

"It's just that my present quarters are without an icebox and a coffeepot," he said.

"And where are your present quarters?"

"So you're a photographer," he said, ignoring her question.

"That's right. And I expect you know why I'm here."

"I know what you've told the others."

For a moment she had the feeling that he could see into her, that he knew not just why she was here, but everything else about her since the day she was born. She shook it off. "Then you know why I'm here," she said tartly. She had known they were identical, of course, but still, she was amazed at how perfectly like Hamish he was—in appearance, anyway. There was something beneath the surface that was different. "That brings us to the question of why *you're* here," she said, anxious to get the ball back into his court.

"I told you. I wanted a beer."

"Here on the island."

"This is my home. Why shouldn't I be here?"

"Why don't your sister and your brother know you're here?"

"I don't have a brother," he said mildly. "I'll see Germaine soon enough."

"What about your grandfather?"

"He's the reason I'm here. He's going to die soon."

She felt somehow that this was more than a general prediction of the health of a man in his nineties. "I met him today," she said. "I liked him."

"And he liked you."

"So you've seen him?"

"No."

"Then why do you think he likes me?"

"Grandpapa would like a girl who would come after an intruder with a flashgun and a kitchen knife."

"What was I supposed to do, call the cops? And I'm not a girl, I'm a woman."

He laughed. "I'll take your word for it."

She was taken by the warmth that radiated from him when he laughed. He seemed suddenly at ease, carefree, and boyish.

"So where do you live, what do you do?"

"I live wherever I like; I do whatever I please," he said teasingly.

"That's no answer."

"It's a truer answer than you know. As you get to know me better, you'll find that I'm a teller of the truth, though it's not always to my advantage."

"Oh? Am I to get to know you better? Will you be creeping into my kitchen every night, frightening me to death?"

"If you like."

"I don't like. If you want to come around here, do it at a decent hour and knock on the door like a human being. And you're too old to be a Peeping Tom." It was only a guess, but it turned him red.

"I think I'd better be going," he said, half-rising. He nodded toward the knife. "If it's all right."

"It's all right," she said.

"I do apologize for intruding upon you," he said, suddenly serious and courtly. He reminded her of his grandfather for a moment. "I'll be off, but I hope I'll see you again." He walked to the back door, which stood open.

Liz rose and crossed to the sink counter, replacing

the knife in its rack. "Then I don't suppose I'll be needing this," she said, turning.

He was gone. It was if he had simply dematerialized. She walked out the back door and peered into the trees, their leaves bright with moonlight. A moment later, a puff of wind chilled her, and she thought she heard something large moving through the brush. She was left with the disconcerting feeling that she had dreamed the whole encounter.

Liz walked back inside, turned off the light, and went to her room. As she settled into the bed, it occurred to her that there was one very big difference between the twins. Keir Drummond had reacted to her as a woman. She was still angry with him, but she felt the attraction, too. In spite of her recent longings, the thought unsettled her, made her wide awake.

She was lying on her side, and she suddenly realized that her hand was between her legs. She spread herself and felt with her finger. A rush of feeling—old memories and sensations—swept through her body and mind, and, in a moment, rose to a climax.

Soon, she was sleeping soundly.

CHAPTER

9

James Moses stood and, once again, presented the gelding to Angus Drummond, who declined, as always these days. James, now fifteen, had been taking care of the horse since he was seven, when he had had to stand on a stool to curry the animal. His grandfather, Buck Moses, had delivered him to Drummond the summer he had finished the first grade.

"You got sump'n this boy can do, Mist' Angus?" Buck had asked.

Angus had cast an appraising eye over the small boy for longer than a moment. "I reckon he'll keep busy in the stables," he had said, at last.

James had been terrified of the amazingly tall white man the first summer. After that, he had gotten used to his imperious ways, had even learned to tell when the old man was pleased. He had been nine when he had learned for sure that Angus Drummond was his father.

His mother had died that year, old at fifty, and another, older boy had taken the occasion of her funeral to explain to him why his skin was so much lighter than hers. The relationship had seemed impossible to him at the time, but he had come to accept it, even if old Angus had never given the slightest hint that he did.

This morning, at first so like hundreds of others, suddenly became different. Angus Drummond stopped as he was about to turn toward the jeep and regarded James gravely.

"You'll be going back to school at Fernandina pretty soon, won't you, boy?"

"Yessir," James replied. "Next week."

"You like going to school with those white children over there?"

"I always been to school with white kids," James replied. "They're okay."

"They don't give you a hard time?" Angus asked.

"How you mean, sir?" James asked back.

"About being colored."

"A couple of boys called me a high yeller one time," James said, shrugging. "I saw 'em about it. They didn't do it again."

"You're getting big," Angus said. "Tall. You going out for football?"

"Yessir, I played end on the freshman team last

year. I reckon I'll make the varsity this year. I like basketball best, though."

"Yes," Angus mused, "you'll have the height for that."

"Coach says I might get a scholarship somewhere if I practice a lot."

"Good, good," Angus said. He gazed off toward the sea for a moment. "What do you do with yourself on the island when you're not working around here?"

"I do some hunting and fishing," James said. "Granddaddy shows me the good places."

"What do you hunt?"

"I get a deer or two every year for meat, but I like bird shooting the best. I got me a good dog."

"What do you shoot birds with?" Angus asked.

"I use Granddaddy's old single-shot twelve-gauge. Can't never get but one at a time, though."

Angus looked at him in a way James had never seen before. "You come on with me," Angus said. He turned and started up the steps to the house.

Surprised, James just stood for a moment; then he tied the gelding to the banister rail and hurried to catch up. Angus was already into the house, turning left off the entrance hall into his study. James followed him, taking in the old oak paneling, the leather-bound books, the marble fireplace, the mess of dusty papers on the huge desk, the crystal decanters on the butler's tray filled with red and amber liquids. He had been in this room once, as a small boy, had sneaked in here, gazing awestruck at the grandeur of the place, until his mother, who cooked for Mr. Angus, had found him and tanned his backside. The room was as big as he remembered it. Must be forty feet long, he thought.

Angus Drummond went to a glassed-in gun cabinet, dug in his pocket for a key, opened it, and took out a double-barreled shotgun. He broke it, checked to be sure it wasn't loaded, then picked up an oily cloth and wiped it as affectionately as a mother might clean a child's face. He leaned back against the desk, hefting the gun, sighting along the barrels. "I had this pair of guns made in London, before the last war," he said. "They were made by an outfit called Purdey, in South Audley Street—famous people; you'll hear about them one of these days. I guess it took a man a year to make these guns, not counting the engraving, which I've always thought exquisite. The stocks are of burled walnut; the weight is perfect. You'll be as tall as me, so they'll fit you one of these days before long." He held out the gun. "Take it," he said. "I'll leave you the other one in my will."

James stepped forward and reached slowly for the beautiful thing, half-expecting it to be snatched away at the last moment. He stood, holding it awkwardly in front of him. "Thank you, sir," he said.

"That gun doesn't need babying," Angus said gravely, "but don't abuse it. Use it well. Don't hurt yourself or anybody else."

"Yes, sir," James said, looking wonderingly at the weapon.

"It's worth a lot of money these days, but don't ever sell it. If you take care of it, your son will get good use of it, and his son, too." Angus opened a cupboard and took out a sheepskin sleeve and a mahogany box. He took the gun from the boy, dropped it into the sleeve, and handed it back with the box. "Some cleaning things. Purdey made those, too." Angus looked at the boy, and his eyes seemed to water. "You take this gift with my affection, James," he said.

"Thank you, Mister Angus," James said. "I'll always take the best care of it."

"I know you will," Angus replied. "Now, go on out of here and shoot some birds with it."

James turned and walked slowly from the room with his treasure. At the bottom of the front steps of the house, he almost started to run, but willed himself to walk slowly. Then he remembered the gelding. He tucked the shotgun under an arm, held the cleaning kit in one hand, and, with the other, took the reins and led the horse toward the stables. He had not yet reached the corner of the house before he began to cry.

Angus Drummond watched the boy from the window until he was out of sight; then he sat down at his desk, blew his nose noisily, unscrewed the cap from his Parker pen, and, in long, looping strokes that belied his age, started to write his will.

CHAPTER

10

*L*iz left the cottage to wander; she didn't much care where. Since her travels with Angus Drummond had been to the north, she drove through the dunes, onto the beach, and turned south. She went slowly, savoring the morning sun. When she had driven a couple of miles, she saw a Drummond emerging from the sea. There was something cool in the smile that greeted her that made him Hamish. She stopped the Jeep, and, as he jogged toward her, she thought how impersonal the smile was. No, *impersonal* was not the word; *unsexy* was. She might have been a man, so little warmth did he emit in her direction. This pleased her, because she was not yet ready for a man; it annoyed her, too, because it pricked her pride. She was accustomed to being a beautiful woman, and even though she was still regaining her looks, she was vain enough to want a reaction from him.

"Good morning," he said, stopping alongside the Jeep. Water streamed from him, ran in rivulets through the curly blond hair on his chest, over the brown skin. She had only seen him carefully groomed before; in his present state he might have been his brother, except that she thought him a bit heavier.

"What are you up to?"

"Taking in the sights," she said. "How's the water?"

"Great. Shall I show you around a little?"

"Sure, hop in."

He walked around the Jeep, grabbed a towel and some shoes from the sand, laid the towel on the seat, and climbed in. "Onward," he said, pointing down the beach.

Liz drove on. "How long are you here for?" she asked.

"Couple of weeks, maybe a month. I like it this time of the year."

"Where do you live?"

"New York. I spend a fair amount of time in London, and I have a summer place on Martha's Vineyard. How about you?"

"Atlanta, until recently."

"And where do you live now?"

"Here."

He smiled. "That's good. You'll like it."

"I already do."

"I can tell." They were nearing the southern end

of the island. Hamish pointed at a track through the dunes. "Take that," he said. "We'll have a look at Dungeness."

She slowed and swung the Jeep into the sandy ruts. "I hope your grandfather won't mind."

"Not at all. He likes you."

"How do you know?" She was reminded of her conversation the night before with Keir.

"He told me so. I had dinner with him last night, and he talked of little else."

"I'm flattered."

"You should be. From what I've been told, he always had superb taste in women."

She felt a need to change the subject. "You get along well with your grandfather?"

"I always have. When my folks were killed, I guess I became grandson and son combined. He doted on me." He pointed again. "Bear right at the fork. The left turn goes down to the mud flats at the southern tip of the island. Good clamming there, if you like that sort of thing."

"I'll keep it in mind."

They were passing under trees now, and there were buildings ahead. They pulled into a courtyard and stopped. She could see various pieces of equipment in what must have been the maintenance barn, and facing that was a long stable. A teenaged boy with café-au-lait skin was brushing a gray horse under a huge live oak tree.

"Morning, James," Hamish called.

"Hey, Hamish," James replied, waving his brush.

"This is Elizabeth Barwick."

"Hey," he said, grinning.

"Hey, James," she said.

"Come on," Hamish said, "I'll show you a small sight." He led her from the courtyard down a path through some trees. After a minute's walk, they emerged into a clearing at the edge of a salt marsh, and a low wall was before them. As they neared, tombstones became visible. "The family plot," Hamish said, pushing open a wrought-iron gate.

A large stone dominated the graveyard. Liz read the inscription. "Aldred Drummond, Master of Cumberland Island, 1740–1829."

"And master he was," Hamish said. "He ruled this island like a king. They say he hanged a few men who deserved it."

"How did he happen to come here?" Liz asked.

"He got the island in a king's grant in 1765. Eleven years later he was at war with his king. He was meant to be a delegate from Georgia at the signing of the Declaration of Independence, but he was delayed en route, and Button Gwinnett replaced him."

"Almost a father of his country," Liz said.

"Almost." He moved along a row and stopped at another stone. "My parents are here, in the same grave," he said.

"Germaine told me about their deaths."

He waved a hand. "A scattering of other Drummonds, and then this." He showed her to a very old stone,

Sacred to the memory of
General Henry Lee of Virginia,

Obiit 25 March 1818, aged 63.

which lay horizontally over a border of bricks.

"He was Light-Horse Harry Lee, Robert E. Lee's father," Liz said. "How did he come to die here?"

"He fell ill on a ship that was passing Cumberland and was put ashore here to die."

Hamish pointed at another stone, this one lying horizontal, covering the grave. Liz read the inscription.

The remains of General Henry Lee were removed under an act of the General Assembly of Virginia to Lexington Virginia May 28, 1913.

Hamish continued, "Old Aldred buried him in the family plot, and when the remains were moved to Virginia, the family kept the grave as it was."

"I don't recall ever seeing an empty grave in a cemetery."

"Nor do I." Hamish chuckled. He looked around the little graveyard. "I always thought I'd be buried here someday, but I guess not."

"Why not?"

Hamish pointed to the edge of the marsh, only a few feet away. "The sea has come too close over the years. As it is now, if we got a big spring tide and a southeasterly gale at the same time, the place would be flooded. Grandpapa's having all the graves moved inland a bit, to higher ground. He's got a professor and some students from the Anthropology Department of the University of Georgia coming down to do the job soon. The graves are too old just to be dug up and the coffins transplanted. This place needs a finer touch, and Grandpapa is anxious that as little as possible be disturbed. He'd planned on being buried here, too, and he's disappointed about that, but he's not anxious to have the sea coming into his grave."

"It's a nice place. I wouldn't mind lying here until Judgment Day."

Hamish smiled his cool smile. "All you have to do is marry a Drummond."

"A high price to pay," she said jokingly. "Are you married?"

"I was; it didn't work out. We were married in New York on rather short notice—a mistake for both of us, really, except for my son, Aldred."

"Do you see much of him?"

"Not as much as I'd like, but I get him for a while in the summer. He's five, now; when he's a little older I'd like him to spend his summers here."

Liz got the Jeep started and, following Hamish's directions, drove toward the main house. They passed a row of old automobiles, rusting to bits. There was an early-fifties Studebaker convertible among them. "My father used to have a Studebaker," she said, pointing at the car.

"I'm afraid that when things stop getting used around here they just get left where they stand," Hamish said. He pointed out a large collapsed building as they passed. "That was the gymnasium. It housed a pool and a squash court. It just fell in on itself one day."

"Such a waste," she said.

"There were other things on the island that needed the money more, I guess. Grandpapa keeps up the roads and everything else himself."

The huge main house lay before them. It was the first time Liz had seen it. "Grandpapa's jeep is gone," Hamish said. "He's out there prowling around his island. One of these days we're going to find him dead in that jeep."

"There are worse ways to go," she said.

They passed through the arched gateway and onto the main north-south road.

"Can you drop me at the inn?" he asked.

"Sure."

They drove on in silence until the turn for the inn appeared. She dropped him at the back door. As he got out of the Jeep, Germaine appeared.

"Some mail for you, Liz," she said, handing over a thick envelope.

"Thanks," she replied, glancing at the envelope. It was from Al Schaefer. "Thanks for the tour," she said to Hamish. "Come up to Stafford Beach Cottage for a drink sometime."

"Sure," he replied, waving as he passed through the screen door into the kitchen.

He won't come, she thought as she drove away. She wasn't sure why, but she knew he wouldn't.

Back at the cottage, she opened the letter from her lawyer.

"Dear Liz," Al had scrawled on a notepad, "I thought you might like to have this. Hope all is going well. Let me hear from you if there's anything you need."

She unfolded the attached document. It was her final divorce decree. For the first time in weeks she laughed aloud.

CHAPTER

11

Angus Drummond sat in his jeep and munched a sandwich, now and then washing it down with a sip of mineral water. He used to like a beer with his lunch, he reflected, but lately it made him sleepy. He was parked at the old wharf at Plum Orchard, the house he had built for his late son, Evan. He gazed west over the marshes toward the mainland and tried to remember the last time he had been off the island. Four or five years, anyway. He finished his sandwich and got out to stretch his legs, strolling slowly down to the dock. A fish jumped well clear of the water, delighting him and scaring up a bird from the long marsh grass. When he turned back toward the jeep, his grandson was standing there, bare chested, wearing an old pair of jeans, leaning against the hood, grinning at him.

"Good morning, Ha—" He stopped and looked closely at the man. "Good God, Keir!" They met half-way and embraced. He held the younger man back from him and looked at him closely.

"Hello, Grandpapa," Keir said. "Did you think I was dead?"

"No, no, they couldn't kill you, but I swear I thought I wouldn't see you again before I die."

Keir laughed. "You, die? You'll outlive us all."

"Not much chance of that, boy," Angus said with some feeling. "Come on, take a drive with me." He pulled his grandson toward the jeep, and in a moment they were driving north through the woods. "Well, tell me what you've been doing with yourself. It's been how long?"

"Too long. I'm sorry I was away for such a time."

"Where have you been?"

"I've been in Europe, mostly. I spent quite a lot of time in Rome. Wrote a few stories, sold one to *Harper's.* I'll send you a copy when it comes out."

"You do that. I want to read it."

"I thought I'd write something about the island, but I hear somebody's beat me to it."

"You mean the Barwick girl?" Angus grated the gears as he shifted down for a deep rut in the road. "I'd better send the scraper up here for that one," he muttered, half to himself. "Yes, she's taking pictures for a book; don't know if she's writing anything. Have you seen your sister?"

"Not yet. I'll get down to the inn soon, don't worry."

"When did you get in? Your brother's here, you know."

Keir pointed into the woods. "You know, I think the armadillo population has increased since I was last home." The little armored creature scurried under some dead palmetto leaves.

Angus sighed. Somehow, he'd hoped that something might have changed between his twin grandsons. "How long will you be with us?"

"Oh, a few days, at least. We'll see. I need to stop in New York and cement a few magazine contacts before I cross the water again."

"You know," Angus said, "I would have thought Cumberland would be a good place to write your stories. I'm not going to be around much longer; I'd like to see more of you."

"I want to see more of you, too, Grandpapa, but, well, there are too many distractions here."

"More distractions than Rome?"

"Ah, but there are no armadillos in Rome; no deer, no gators. Those are the distractions."

"I always thought pheasant was the ultimate distraction, myself." Angus chuckled. "I always had a hard time concentrating during the pheasant season."

"You still hunting with your Purdeys?"

"No, I haven't fired a gun for a couple of years, I guess."

Keir laughed. "Maybe you *are* dying, at that!"

"I'll tell you how close to death I am," Angus

said. "This morning I gave one of those shotguns to James."

"James Moses?"

Angus looked at him for a moment before answering. "That's right. James Moses. That boy has been at my beck and call for years, and I never so much as tipped him a dime. He's a good boy, smart; he'll do well, if somebody pays some attention to him. You might do that sometimes, Keir; pay some attention to James. You'd like the sort of boy he's grown into."

"I'm afraid I won't be around long enough to be of much use to James, Grandpapa. I just came to see you, really. I'll have to be off again soon."

"Don't come back to bury me, you hear?" Angus was adamant. "Don't you go buying any airplane tickets with your money just to see me put in the ground. I always hated funerals, myself. I won't go to mine, if I can help it."

Keir looked at his grandfather and smiled. "Grandpapa, if I come back to see you buried, it'll be for my own peace of mind, not out of any sense of duty. I know how you feel about funerals. I won't embarrass you after you're dead."

Angus looked around him. "I don't know what's going to happen to this island when I'm gone," he said sadly.

"It will always belong to you," Keir said, "and I'll see that nobody ever builds anything on it that you wouldn't like, not while I'm alive, anyway."

"That's the way I like to hear you talk!" Angus

grinned. "Your cousin Jimmy would like to pave over the whole place, I expect."

"Don't worry, Grandpapa. I'll keep your island wild."

"Excuse me a minute, Keir," Angus said. He pulled over and, leaving the engine running, got out, walked a few yards into the woods, unzipped his fly, and took a long, satisfying leak. He zipped himself up and returned to the jeep. His grandson was gone. On the front seat was a tiny conch shell. Angus picked it up. It had been polished to a high gloss. The boys had done that when they were little; they'd scrape the shell and rub it against their noses, letting their body grease slowly raise a gloss.

Angus shook his head. They were strange, his grandsons, especially Keir. He put the shell in his shirt pocket and drove away.

12

Al Schaefer was still floating on the best week of his career, when he had earned more than three hundred thousand dollars from Elizabeth Barwick's settlement. There had been weeks when he had won a judgment for more money; weeks when a larger check had arrived; but there had never been a time when he had initiated a case, settled it, and received such a huge payment in a single week. And, since he had no partners and felt no need to reward either of his two associates with a bonus, it was all his.

First, he had set aside thirty-three percent of his fee, the maximum combination of U.S. and Georgia income tax he might have to pay; that came to a hundred and ten thousand dollars. Then he had put a hundred thousand into long-term CDs at a good rate. Finally, he had sent a check for thirty-five thousand dollars to the American Civil Liberties Union. His country, his security, and his conscience thus accommodated, and all his ordinary office and personal expenses taken care of by his other income, he was left with eighty-eight thousand dollars and change with which to amuse himself without guilt. He thanked his stars that his divorce had been final five months before, so he would not have to share the loot with what's-her-name.

Al started with Las Vegas. He called a friend who had a very nice little business jet, who let him have it for running costs and crew expenses; then he called a girl he knew—a perfect Vegas girl—and they departed on a Friday morning. They checked into a high-roller's suite at Caesars Palace, and for two days Al did little but eat, drink, screw, and play high-stakes poker. He slept all day Sunday, played poker again that night, and, at checkout time on Monday morning, he calculated that, after all his expenses, he was thirteen thousand dollars ahead. Now he had over a hundred grand to play with.

Al turned to the girl, with whom he was having breakfast in bed. "Do you really have to be back tomorrow?

She shrugged. "Not if I quit my job," she said.

"Why don't we look in on LA for a few days?" He grinned.

She grinned back. "Jobs are easy to find."

By three o'clock they were lounging poolside at the Beverly Hills Hotel, not too close, because Al was terrified of water. He called for a phone, rearranged his appointments, talked to his broker, and did some business. That night they dined at Michael's in Santa Monica, and the next day Al rented a Porsche 911 Cabriolet and they drove up to Santa Barbara for lunch. The week blew by: a chopper to Catalina, dinners at Spago and Rex, the studio tour at Universal, shopping on Rodeo Drive. Last Saturday night, driving back from dinner in Malibu, the music gave way to sports news.

"Hey," she said, "the Bobcats are playing the Rams tomorrow. Let's take it in."

"Nah," Al said. "I'm off the Bobcats for life."

Back at the Beverly Hills, she was tired; Al wanted a nightcap. She went upstairs; he headed for the Polo Lounge, got a table by himself near the garden door. They'd go back tomorrow; he was gaining weight, and he wasn't really accustomed to this much time away from work. He rested his head against the banquette cushion and swirled his Armagnac. Life was sweet. Or it was until he opened his eyes. Baker Ramsey was seated at a table near the door with a blonde. Al had walked right past him.

Al's first impulse was just to get out; Ramsey looked drunk, and he didn't want a scene; but Ramsey was between him and the door. Al glanced over his shoulder toward the empty dining room and the garden beyond. He put a fifty-dollar bill on the table, slid out of the booth, and headed toward the garden. Outside, he seemed trapped, at first; then he saw a sheltered passage that led away from the tables; he emerged in more gardens, near the bungalows.

Al took a deep draft of the California night air, laced with the scent of bougainvillea. There was a moon, and the gardens were lovely. He decided to explore for a few minutes; he didn't want to run into Ramsey in the lobby. He wandered slowly through the gardens, following no special path. A few minutes later, he emerged at the pool. The area was empty, lit only by the underwater lights.

Al eased his small frame onto a comfortable chaise, not too near the water. When he was a boy some overenthusiastic bullies had nearly drowned him, had put him in the hospital. The smell of chlorine and the thought of inhaling water still brought him irrationally near panic. He liked looking at water, he just didn't like being too near it. He'd wait here a few minutes, then go back to the room. After all, Ramsey had a game to play tomorrow; he'd leave soon.

Al reflected that things had never before been so good. He'd made a lot of money for a long time, and now he was comfortably rich. He was out of a bad marriage; he was getting more big cases than ever; he was only forty-two; he had his health. He dozed.

He was dreaming something bad. He wanted to scream, but he couldn't; he wanted to breathe, but he couldn't. He woke up.

A huge hand covered his mouth and nose. He felt himself lifted from the chaise until his feet no longer touched the ground. An arm clamped around his neck, and he beat at it, tore at it. The lights in the pool seemed to be dimming when, suddenly, he could

breathe again. He sucked in air, and, when he was
about to yell, the arm tightened around his neck.

"Not a sound," a voice said, close to his ear. "You
make a noise, and I'll break your neck."

Al scrambled for a toehold, but there was nothing
under him but air. He wedged his hands between the
arm and his neck and tried to pull it away, but he
couldn't budge it.

"Where is she?" the voice said.

"What?" Al managed to reply.

The arm tightened again, and the hand went
over his mouth and nose. Half a minute passed as
he struggled, then he was allowed to breathe again.
"I'm going to ask you just once more, and unless I
like the answer . . ."

"What do you want to know?" Al managed. He
was becoming very frightened; he tried to think of a
way to stall. Jesus, he was in a busy hotel; somebody
had to come.

"Where is the bitch? Tell me where she is, and I'll
let you go. Otherwise . . ." He put the hand over Al's
mouth and nose again.

Al, in spite of his terror, was beginning to think;
he had enough air to hold his breath for a few seconds. This guy had a hundred pounds on him, but
there was one place he might be vulnerable. Al
couldn't get to his crotch the way he was being held,
but there was one place. He felt backward with his
feet, ran his heels up the other man's legs. Then he
brought his right knee up nearly to his chest and
drove his heel down hard into Ramsey's knee.

This time, it was Ramsey who made the noise, an angry grunt, followed by a low, continuous growl.

Al became a little tiger, squirming, reaching back for his captor's eyes, driving elbows backward, anything he could do to hurt the man. The hand left his face, and he was able to get a breath. Then, suddenly, the arm went from around his neck, and Al tried desperately to run, but a hand grabbed his suit collar and spun him around. He was facing Ramsey now, and he went for the eyes again. Then Ramsey hit him. Al took the punch in the upper abdomen, just below the solar plexus. He folded in half and fell to the tile poolside, clutching his belly, gasping for air. He might have been paralyzed, so difficult was it for him to move.

Ramsey stood, looking down at him. "Now, you're going to tell me where she is," he said, and he was smiling.

Al had just managed to get a tiny breath, when he found himself hoisted by his feet, facing Ramsey. He tried to shout, tried to move, but the pain in his middle was too much. Now he was being carried toward the pool. Knowing what was coming, he struggled wildly; then he was in the pool to his waist, upside down. He had precious little air in his lungs, and, with his failing strength, he tried to stop himself from inhaling water. He was ten years old again, drowning at the neighborhood pool, held under by two bigger boys. It was his worst nightmare.

Then he was out of the pool, hanging upside down, just over the water.

"One last time," Ramsey said. "Tell me."

Al was terrified, but his response to fear was to fight. "Fuck you," he sputtered. Ramsey wouldn't kill him here, not in this place. "Fuck you," he repeated. "You don't have the guts to kill me, you muscle-freak faggot!"

Then Baker Ramsey put Al Schaefer back into the pool.

13

CHAPTER

13

*L*iz was driving through the woods south of Lake Whitney when the road crossed an earthen dike, and something caught her eye. She stopped the Jeep and walked quietly, slowly, back onto the dike. The creatures had not moved.

On a mud bank below the dike were arrayed at least a dozen baby alligators, none longer than about fifteen inches, she reckoned. She returned to the Jeep and started unloading equipment. She chose the 4 × 5 Deardorff field camera and a heavy, wooden tripod, then grabbed her big bag, full of lenses and sheet film. She practically tiptoed back onto the dike and started looking for the best vantage point, which involved edging slowly down the bank of the dike toward the water. She stopped. A large log floated in the water a

111

few feet from where she stood. Where there are little alligators, she told herself, there are big alligators, and alligators look like logs in the water.

She examined it closely. It was a log.

Heaving a sigh of relief, she began to set up her equipment. Soon, she had set up the tripod with one leg in the water and was fixing a 305-mm lens to the boxy camera. She wanted a tight shot. She heard an odd, high-pitched, guttural sound coming from the direction of the young reptiles; she peeked at them from under the cloth. The little alligators sat motionless, seeming to ignore her. The log was drifting slowly away, moved by the ripples when she disturbed the water.

Her position was awkward. She was at the bottom of the bank, having a hard time setting up her shot. She shook off a moccasin and gingerly put a foot into the water, looking carefully about for snakes. The water was cool to the touch; she felt for the bottom and, wrinkling her nose, pushed down through the ooze until she met firm resistance. Now she was in a sitting position behind the camera; she got her head under the black cloth and began framing and focusing.

It was a good shot. She squeezed the cable release, hoping the click would not frighten the little creatures. They kept perfectly still, and she loaded another sheet of film, rechecking her exposure meter; she went under the cloth for a second shot. Then the log came to life.

Under the cloth, she was aware of a heavy splashing, combined with a hiss that quickly became a roar. From her awkward position, she wrenched her foot from the sticky bottom and started crawling, backward, up the dike, giving a fine view of what was coming after her.

Time slowed to nothing; everything seemed to move in the slowest of motion. The enormous alligator seemed to walk on the water as it came toward her, jaws agape, making its awful noise. Instinctively, she tried to put the camera between her and the gator as she moved backward on her hands, pushing with her feet. There was screaming coming from somewhere, and she realized it was from her. On the gator came, starting up the bank after her. The camera fell toward it, and a leg of the seasoned hardwood tripod went into the beast's mouth, immediately becoming splinters.

On she traveled, backward in this slow-motion nightmare that would never end. She reached the roadbed at the top of the dike, the gator in pursuit, and began trying to get her feet under her, stumbling, scraping her knuckles until she was running, running, afraid to look back.

Then, when she thought she could spare a look back, she ran into something that held on to her.

"Easy, easy," he was saying, "just come over here to the Jeep. It's all right, now, he's gone."

Liz was gulping great lungsful of air, sobbing, whimpering.

"Just calm down, now, you're all right," Keir Drummond was saying, repeating himself in a soothing, rhythmic voice. He took her under the arms and sat her on the passenger seat of the Jeep.

"Where . . . did you . . . come from?" she gasped.

"I wasn't spying on you, if that's what you mean. I was just . . . here."

"Spying is okay," she said, wiping the tears from her face with the back of her hand. "Just as long as you're here."

"I didn't save your life or anything, you know. You did that. I was just here to keep you from running all the way to Greyfield."

"I would have, too," she said, nearly laughing, shaking as she said it.

Keir reached out and pulled her into his arms. He said nothing, just held her head in one hand while he rubbed her back with the other.

Liz could feel her heart pounding against her rib cage, against him. She held on to him tightly and cried. He was warm and safe and she just wanted to hold on to him for five or six weeks.

He kissed her ear and made shushing noises.

Gradually, she got control of herself and gently pushed herself away from him. "My camera," she said, finally. "Did the sonofabitch get my camera?"

"You stay here, and I'll have a look," he said.

She watched him as he walked onto the dike and edged cautiously down to the water, looking around him. She was astonished at how close to her the spot was; she felt as if she'd run at least half a mile.

He came back with the camera, the splintered tripod still attached, and, in the other hand, her shoe. "The camera looks okay," he said. "I don't think it got into the water." He returned to the spot and brought back her bag. "You're still in business, but with a bipod."

"I've got a lighter one," she said, sadly unscrewing the camera from the wrecked tripod, "but it's not heavy enough for the view camera."

"I'll fix it for you," he said.

"It'll never be the same. I'll just have to order another one from Zone VI." She looked at her watch. "It's cocktail time," she said. "I'll buy you a drink, and, if you're brave, I'll cook you some dinner."

"I'm brave enough for that," he said.

They sat on the deck over the wreckage of their dinner, bathed in the light of a hurricane lamp, and finished off a second bottle of wine. Liz was feeling very warm and cozy and not a little drunk. She watched him as they talked and marveled at the difference between Keir and his brother. This twin emanated warmth—the corners of his eyes and mouth worked differently; a sense of humor was there behind the eyes. She wanted him, and she pushed back the irrationality of her feelings. She had not slept with many men, and she had always been cautious about it.

"How big do you reckon Goliath was?" Keir asked. "Nobody's seen him for years."

"Oh, about seventy-five feet," she said.

"I didn't ask you how big he *seemed.*" Keir laughed. "Really. I'd like to know."

"I swear, I don't have a clue," Liz said. "He was one hell of a lot bigger than anything I ever saw at a Florida reptile farm, and I think I saw one about twelve feet there when I was little, when Daddy and Mother took me to the beach one time."

"You were very lucky," Keir said. "I wish I had been there a little earlier so that I could have fought him off with my bare hands. Then you'd be pitifully grateful."

She smiled at him. "I'm pitifully grateful that you were there at all." She swirled the wine in her glass. "So where have you been since I last saw you? Following me around?"

He raised a hand. "I promise you, I haven't. I really was just passing."

"On the way to where?"

"No place in particular. I just roam, sometimes. I've been away a long time, and I miss Cumberland. I guess I've been pretending I was a little boy again, hunting with Buck Moses."

"Have you seen Buck?"

"Yes, the first day. He'd know I was here, even if I didn't look him up. He's like that."

"Have you seen your grandfather?"

"Yes, a couple of times. I had lunch at Dungeness yesterday. It was quite like the old days."

"You should see him more often."

"The old man isn't as lonely as you think. He's very self-contained; he doesn't like much company. He just likes his island around him."

"Have you seen Germaine?"

"We had a drink last night and caught up. I told her I'd met you."

"Seen anybody else?" She watched him closely.

"No one else to see." He picked up her hand and

inspected the palm, turning it toward the lamp. "Long life line. A break in it, near the end of the first third of your life. Means a major change." He picked at more lines with his fingers. "Change for the better," he said. "True?"

"It would almost have to be," she said.

"You want to tell me about it?"

"No. Not now, anyway. I'd rather hear about you. What do you do? How do you support yourself?"

"I write. Not a hell of a lot, but I write. I'm good at it. It doesn't support me, but there's a little money from my parents that keeps me from having to write when I don't want to."

"Where have you been living most recently?" she asked, framing the question carefully. She didn't want generalities.

"Rome."

"Where in Rome?"

"I have a little flat in the Piazza Navona. It gets the sun in the mornings and the shade in the afternoons."

She reached for his hand. "Let me have a look at your palm, now."

He closed it. "You don't want to know too much."

She wrinkled her brow.

He reached out and massaged her forehead with his fingertips. "No furrows there, please. No worries, especially about me." Then, as if he had done it before, he moved his hand to her cheek and kissed her lips.

As if she had done it before, she kissed him back.

He pulled her to her feet and put his arms around her, kissing her again.

She responded more easily than she would have believed possible. For the moment, she had no past, and his didn't matter. Soon, without seeming to walk, they were in her bed and naked. She received him easily, lustily, and they made each other happy.

This is just physical, she told herself, just something I need at this moment.

Sometime in the night, she felt him leave the bed, and she fell asleep, expecting him to return. He did not.

The next morning, she woke feeling all rosy; then she remembered the night and suddenly felt guilty. Why? She was a grown-up; she could sleep with whom she liked. She thought about it until she had rationalized away the guilt and was left with only a warm, sweet memory.

CHAPTER

14

*L*iz stuck her head into the little office at the inn. Germaine was talking on the cellular telephone that was the inn's only electronic contact with the mainland. "Buy a girl a cup of coffee?" Liz asked.

Germaine covered the phone with her hand. "I'll be with you in a minute; help yourself."

Liz walked into the kitchen, searching for coffee. Hamish Drummond was sitting at the otherwise empty staff table, sipping from a cup and reading a newspaper. She poured herself a cup of coffee from the pot on the stove and joined him.

"Morning," he said, smiling. The usual detached charm.

"What's in the papers?" she asked. "I haven't seen one for a while."

"The news is bad," Hamish said, "for the Atlanta Bobcats anyway. Bake Ramsey hurt his knee, and it looks like he's out for most of the season."

"I don't follow football," she said. Not anymore. Baker had never been seriously injured before, she remembered—not in college, not in the pros. She wondered how he was taking it. Then she dismissed her ex-husband from her mind. He was no longer her concern. "Anything else of importance?"

He held the paper back and cast an eye over the front page. "Mmm, let's see—unilateral disarmament; first man on Mars; Second Coming." He shook his head. "Nothing as important as Ramsey's knee."

"Now we know what your priorities are."

"Damn right. I had money on that game. The 'cats should have creamed 'em." Hamish stood and drained his cup.

Germaine entered from her office. "You off, then?"

"Yep. A boat's coming for me from Fernandina."

"You're leaving us?" Liz asked.

"Yeah, for a week or so, anyway. Got to go to New York, make a few bucks."

"Okay. Have a good trip."

"Thanks." He snaked an arm around his sister's neck and kissed her on the lips. "Take care."

"You, too. You will come back?"

"Once I do this deal I can afford some time off. I'll come back and wait tables or something."

"That'll be the day," Germaine said dryly.

Hamish grabbed his bag, left by the back door, and headed for the inn's dock.

Germaine poured herself some coffee and sank down beside Liz. "Whew, busy morning until this minute. Nice to have a break." She peered at Liz. "Something's different; you look awfully pleased with yourself."

Liz blushed. Was she so easily read?

Germaine's eyebrows went up. "Ahhhhh," she crowed quietly.

"Ah, what?" Liz asked, avoiding her gaze.

"He told me you'd met. You've gotten even better acquainted."

Liz was shocked. "He told you that?"

"Nope." Germaine laughed. "You did. It's written all over you."

"I don't believe you," Liz said, feeling redder.

"Listen, you were wound pretty tight when you got here. Now, suddenly, you're all aglow." She looked ashamed of herself. "I'm sorry, I didn't mean to pry."

"It's okay." Liz sighed. "I should probably get your advice anyway."

"Enjoy! That's what I do."

"You do? Who with?"

Germaine nodded in the direction of the dining room. Liz turned to see a nineteen-year-old male backside in tight jeans pointed at her as Ron, the waiter, swung a mop back and forth across the floor.

"You're kidding," Liz said.

"Nope. The first year or two I ran the inn, I nearly went nuts I was so horny—we almost never get a single man as a guest here. Then I discovered the pleasures of young flesh. They come here to work for the summer. It's perfect."

"Well, I'll be damned," Liz said.

"Me too, probably, but it's worth it. The funny thing is, they *love* it, being with an older woman. At that age they've maybe screwed a cheerleader or two, but that isn't much experience. I send 'em away ready for anything." She leaned close. "Ol' Ron, there, will be the hottest thing on campus when he gets back to school. And the nice thing is, I'm having to *make* him go back. He wants to stay on for the winter!"

"You salty old thing, you!"

"Damn right. I'll be forty next month, and I'm still nuts about young flesh!"

The two women dissolved into laughter, so much so that Ron turned and looked questioningly at them.

"Girl talk, sweetheart," Germaine called to him. "Don't mind us."

Ron gave her a broad wink and went back to his mopping.

"To tell you the truth," Germaine said, "I was thinking of offering him to you, you seemed so lonely, but I guess that's all taken care of, and I can't say I blame you. I've always thought my baby brothers were the dishiest things around."

"Well, I don't know where this is going. He seems pretty slippery, your brother."

"That's true enough. He might just get up and go; you should take that into account."

"I'm not looking for anything permanent," Liz

said truthfully, then she grinned. "But I do hope he sticks around for a *little* longer."

They burst out laughing again. When they had recovered themselves, Germaine looked at her more seriously. "It's been awhile, has it?"

"Awhile."

"How long you been divorced?"

"It was final after I arrived here."

"It ended badly?"

"He put me in the hospital."

"Shit," Germaine said. "My ex slapped me once, and I broke his nose with my fist."

Liz laughed in spite of herself. "I was outclassed in the muscle department, believe me."

"I hope you stuck him for a lot."

"I did, but if he ever gets his hands on me . . ."

"Jesus, no wonder you wanted to come someplace like this."

"Well, when Ray made the offer, it did seem the answer to a prayer."

Germaine grinned. "And Keir was the answer to another prayer?"

"Well, let's just say he's awfully nice to have around."

"I'm glad to hear it. I've been worried about both of you. Just don't get too involved; he really is capable of vanishing into thin air. Does it all the time."

"I'd thought as much."

Germaine slapped her palms on the table and rose. "Well, I've got a grocery order to make up and phone in. You finish your coffee, and we'll talk some more another time."

"Thanks, I'd like that."

Germaine headed for her desk, and Liz idly turned her attention to the newspaper that Hamish had left behind. A banner above the masthead read,

BOBCATS' HOPES DASHED
AS RAMSEY BASHES KNEE
IN L.A. OPENER

Once again, she pushed Baker Ramsey out of her mind.

She scanned the front page and stopped at the bottom.

ATLANTA LAWYER FOUND DEAD
IN BEVERLY HILLS POOL

She read on:

Albert Schaefer, a prominent Atlanta trial attorney, was found dead on Sunday morning in the swimming pool of the Beverly Hills Hotel by a lifeguard who arrived for work. His body was fully clothed when found.

A Beverly Hills Police Department spokesman confirmed that death was by drowning and stated further that the alcohol content of Schaefer's bloodstream was elevated.

The investigating detectives surmised that Schaefer had fallen into the pool while drunk, during the early hours of Sunday morning, and had been unable to save himself. The lawyer's ex-wife confirmed that Schaefer was a nonswimmer with a fear of water, and the spokesman said that foul play was not suspected.

Liz had known Al Schaefer only briefly, but she was shocked and immensely sad at the news of his death. Then she looked again at the headline.

L.A., she thought. No, it was a coincidence. But if it was a coincidence, why was she suddenly so frightened?

15

CHAPTER

15

*B*aker Ramsey looked through half-closed eyes at the nurse on top of him. Her name was Mary Alice, and she rose and fell upon his body, making little whimpering noises, her starched skirts pushed up around her waist, the front of her uniform unbuttoned to allow her large breasts to spill out into Ramsey's kneading hands.

"Oh, you, you, you . . . ," she whispered as an orgasmic shudder ripped through her.

Ramsey came, too, but more quietly. This one was good. He'd see some more of her. He held her off him as she tried to collapse onto his chest. "No, baby, you can't go to sleep," he cooed at her. "You've got to get back down the hall. If you get caught, we can't fuck again, right?"

She ran her fingers down his huge arms. "God, what muscles!" she said. "You jocks are really something!"

Ramsey placed his hands under her buttocks and, as easily as a normal man would hoist a doll, lifted her off him and onto her feet beside the hospital bed, careful not to bump her against his knee.

She giggled as she looked for her panty hose under the bed. "You're the only man I ever knew who could pick me up like that."

"We'll do it again," he said.

"How long do you need?" she asked, kissing him lightly. "Shall I come back in an hour?"

"Not tonight, baby," he replied. "I've got surgery at seven; I need some sleep. You wore me out, anyway."

"Sure, I'll bet," she said lasciviously, rubbing her hand over his penis. "I'll check on you during the night, anyway."

"Don't do that," he said. "I'm a light sleeper; you'll wake me up. Just put down on your clipboard that you looked in. Don't worry, I won't die in the night."

"Whatever you say, Bake," she cooed. She gave his limp penis a final kiss and swung out of the room, smoothing her skirt as she went.

Ramsey waited until her footsteps had receded before he gingerly removed the ice pack from his knee and swung his legs over the side of the bed. The clock on the night table read just after 2:00 A.M. As he stood he caught sight of himself in the full-length mirror on the wall. Automatically, he flexed his biceps, then struck a bodybuilder's pose. Right, he said to himself. That's what turned the girl on—all that muscle. He'd seen the look in her eyes when he'd checked in to the hospital that afternoon, and he hadn't been the least surprised when she came to his room after midnight. He took one more look at himself in the mirror. Women loved him like this. Except Liz, the bitch. She'd started to go off him when he began to put on the heavy muscle.

Ramsey moved across the room, limping; he had used crutches, for effect, when he had checked in to the hospital, but he could walk without them, especially with another kind of help. He took a small bag from the closet; from that he removed a small leather case, unzipped it, and chose from the row of bottles. He held it up in the moonlight and read its label: XYLOCAINE. He took a disposable syringe from the little case, tore off the wrapping, and plunged it into the rubber neck of the bottle, sucking some of the contents into the plastic implement. He returned the bottle to the case, limped back to the bed, and sat down, crossing his legs, the injured knee on top. Carefully, he began injecting the painkiller, choosing the soft tissue, varying the depth of his stabs. He massaged the knee gently. Damn that little prick, Schaefer. The bastard had done this to him with one kick. Who'd have thought he could have ruined the knee so easily? He'd used his little medical kit to hold off the pain until he could get into the game with the Rams. Then, one tackle, and he had had an excuse for his injury. Now the pain began to ebb away, and Ramsey could walk back to the closet without limping. What the hell did it matter if he made it a little worse? They would fix it in the morning, anyway.

He got into some jeans, moccasins, and a shirt; then he took the spare pillows from the closet and arranged them under the sheets. He cracked the door and looked down the hall; the nurse was at her station, her back to him. He tiptoed across the hall and headed down the fire stairs; they ended in the main lobby, which was deserted at this time of night. In a moment, he was out of the hospital and into the empty street, avoiding the emergency exit. Looking carefully both ways, he limped across the street and disappeared into the Brookwood Hills neighborhood, a quiet, old subdivision of medium-sized houses that had, in recent years, become expensive. Soon, when the Xylocaine had taken full effect, he no longer had to limp.

It took him twenty minutes, moving in the shadows, to find the place. He passed through the backyard of the house next door and spent a moment taking a length of rope from a child's swing.

Ray Ferguson opened his eyes, alert, unsure about the sound he had heard. He looked at his sleeping wife, then got out of bed, listening. The back door opening, that was what the sound had been; he often forgot to lock it. He sat very still, straining to hear. Another sound, this one from his study. The publisher got slowly up from the bed, so as not to disturb his wife, and went to the closet for his shotgun.

He had bought the weapon years before from a small-town hardware store, a short-barreled pump twelve-gauge that had belonged to the local police force, the man had said. There had been some burglaries in the neighborhood that year, and he had been worried. He had loaded the weapon with number-nine bird shot, the smallest available. He didn't want to kill anybody; he'd have bought buckshot for that. He just wanted something to frighten somebody away, if it came to that. Now, he thought, it has come to that.

He walked quietly to the stairs in his bare feet and started slowly down them, listening. He stopped at the bottom and turned toward the study. That was where the sound had come from. At the door he stopped, afraid. "All right, you in there," he said, surprised at how strong his voice sounded, "I've got a shotgun. There's an outside door in there, and you'd better be out of it in five seconds. Now, get going!" He listened hard again.

"Ray?" It was his wife's voice, sleepy, upstairs. He ignored her.

There was absolute silence from the study. His eyes had become accustomed to the darkness now, and the moon was sending slatted rays through the venetian blinds in the room. It was a big room, with a vaulted ceiling and exposed beams. He released the safety on the shotgun and pumped it noisily. "You'd better get moving, buddy," he said loudly, "unless you want a snoot full of double-aught buckshot!" Still, only silence.

"Ray?" his wife called again. "What's happening?"

"Stay there," Ferguson said to her. He stepped

cautiously into the study, the shotgun at port arms. A board squeaked under his bare foot. Something soft brushed against his face, and, suddenly, he couldn't breathe. He was swept up, off his feet, then lowered to his tiptoes. In panic, he dropped the shotgun and clawed at the rope around his neck.

"Where is she?" a voice said, close to his ear, hot breath on his neck.

The rope slacked minutely. He pushed with his toes, trying to lessen the tension. "What?" he managed to croak. The rope went tight again, before Ferguson could get his fingers under it.

"Just once more, and if you don't tell me the truth, I'll tear your head off. Where is Elizabeth?"

The rope stayed tight until Ferguson was at the brink of unconsciousness, then it slackened. He bit at the air, sucking it in.

"Last chance, Ferguson; the very last chance."

Ferguson began to weep.

"Ray?" The voice was startlingly loud. She was standing in the door to the study. "Oh, my God!" she screamed.

Ferguson went limp. He knew he would tell Ramsey anything, now. "Please don't hurt my wife, Baker," he said.

CHAPTER

16

Liz dreamt the dream about Baker Ramsey. He was stalking her through a house, their old house. She slipped from room to room, hiding under beds, behind draperies, but he always found her. She would run, but he always caught up, following her in a leisurely fashion, playing with her, tomcat and mouse. Finally she was cornered; it was a room with no furniture, no place to hide. She cowered, crying, "Don't hit me, Bake, please." Smiling, he put a huge hand to her cheek. As his flesh touched hers she screamed.

"Christ, it's only me, take it easy! No one's going to hurt you." Keir held her shoulders, then put a hand to her cheek again. "Easy, now, you must have been dreaming. I'm sorry I frightened you."

She stared at him, having trouble shaking the dream. "Try knocking next time," she said coldly.

"I really am sorry," he said meekly. "I thought you'd be awake at this hour."

"What time is it?"

"Nearly six."

"Swell," she said, swinging her feet off the bed. God, I sound like an awful bitch, she thought. "I didn't mean to be cranky. Want some coffee?"

"I'll make you some while you dress."

"Okay, give me ten minutes for a quick shower."

He disappeared toward the kitchen; he was wearing the loincloth again, with the knife at the belt. She went into the bathroom and splashed cold water on her face and brushed her teeth; five minutes in a warm shower relaxed her, made the dream recede. You can't start treating him as if he were Baker, she reminded herself as she toweled her hair dry. It was getting longer; soon it would benefit from the attentions of a good hairdresser. She got into some khaki shorts, a polo shirt, and her usual boat moccasins, then headed for the kitchen, where the smell of coffee greeted her.

"No kidding, I thought everybody got up this early," Keir said as he poured her coffee.

"Only to take pictures." She sipped the strong, black liquid gratefully.

"Okay, I'll get you some pictures today." He grinned.

"Where?"

"Trust me."

Ten minutes later they were in her Jeep, headed

up the beach. A huge red sun hung just above the horizon.

"So, are you ready to tell me where you're living?" she asked.

"In a secret place," he said, smiling slightly.

"And how do you get around the island?"

"In secret ways."

There was something mischievous in his speech; there was, too, something different about him, something looser, freer. She wondered if he knew Hamish had left the island.

"How come you're wearing the loincloth today?" she asked. "It's the first I've seen you wear it since the first time I saw you."

He grinned. "This is how we dressed as kids on the island. Dad handed that down."

"We?" she asked. It was the first reference ever to his twin.

"We?" he asked back, puzzled.

"You said, 'the way *we* dressed as kids.' "

"I said the way *I* dressed. You're deaf."

He seemed perfectly serious. But that slip meant something, she thought; she just wasn't sure what.

"Turn here," he said, pointing at a narrow track through the dunes. "You'd better put it in four-wheel drive, too."

She did as he said, and soon they were through the dunes and into thick woods, following what seemed to be a disused road. A moment later the water of Lake Whitney flashed through the trees.

"I'm not going anywhere near that lake," she said

firmly, shuddering at the memory of her encounter with Goliath.

"Don't worry, we won't get that close. Stop anywhere here, and bring the Hasselblad. The view camera might be a little tough to handle in here."

She followed him straight into the trees, along an overgrown path that she wouldn't have noticed without him. They came to the edge of a clearing on the shore of the lake, and he stopped.

"We'll take up a position in a moment," he said, "and then there'll be no talking or moving. That means *no* moving, not even to scratch an itch or swat a mosquito, so get comfortable. We may be here for a while."

She followed him along the edge of the clearing, still in the trees, until he motioned for her to set up her tripod. He sat down and watched her, then nodded at the spot next to him. She focused the wide-angle lens on the clearing and sat down cross-legged, holding the cable release. He held up a hand as if to say, Don't talk, don't move.

They sat for more than an hour. She knew, because she could see her wristwatch. She could see him, too, since she was sitting slightly behind him. He sat, completely motionless, as if he were in a trance; an occasional blink of the eyes was his only movement. She tried to follow suit, and, as the time passed, she became more and more uncomfortable. Still, she did not move, not wishing to earn his disapproval. After more time had passed a sort of numbness set in, and her mind drifted. Then she snapped back.

A large blue heron appeared and sat in a tree

forty feet away. It was in her camera frame, but too far away for a good shot with the wide-angle. Still, she thought, if this is what he brought me to see, I'd better shoot something. She raised her hand slightly to press the shutter, but he looked at her sideways and shook his head almost imperceptibly. This annoyed her; she was not cut out for sitting still this long. She wasn't a goddamned Indian, after all. Then there was a movement on the opposite side of the clearing.

She concentrated her attention there, and her aches seemed to dissolve. As she watched, a small deer, a doe, moved cautiously into the clearing, ears twitching, then stopped, as if assessing the situation. Then, just as Liz was about to fire the shutter, the doe was followed by a pair of tiny fawns, identical, and so young they were still awkward in their movements. The doe walked to the center of the clearing and began to lick something in the grass. The fawns followed her and imitated her action.

Keir nodded slightly, and Liz fired the shutter. The doe jerked her head up at the tiny, muffled click of the shutter, froze in that position for a minute or so, then returned to her licking. Liz was torn between advancing the film and taking a chance on spooking the doe, or just sitting and enjoying the sight. Slowly, she moved her hands toward the camera. It took her half a minute, but she managed to wind the film without betraying her presence. Then, just as she was ready to shoot again, the doe left her spot, walked to the lakeside, followed by the fawns, and drank.

Liz fired one more shot, then the three animals walked slowly across the clearing and departed the way they had come. Keir held up a hand to indicate that she should still not move. They sat still for another two minutes, then he motioned for her to follow and walked back toward the car. Liz followed, silently stretching her limbs, trying not to whimper with relief.

When they reached the track, Keir spoke. "Well, how did you like that?"

"It was wonderful," she said, grateful to be able to speak again. "I would never have gotten that shot if you hadn't taken me there and made me shut up. I wouldn't ordinarily have had the patience."

"Patience is everything," he said, a trace of sadness in his voice. Then he brightened. "How about a swim?"

"In Lake Whitney? Not on your life!"

"How about the Atlantic Ocean? That safe enough for you?"

"Does it have giant alligators?"

"Not usually."

"You're on."

They drove back to the beach, and Keir shed the loincloth and ran into the water. After a look up and down the beach, she stripped and followed him. They had to go out some distance before the water became deep. They swam idly for a few minutes and engaged in some banter and play that reminded her of college, then they ran out of the water toward the Jeep. They ducked into the shade of the car, for the sun was becoming hot, and he kissed her and pulled her to him.

"You ever made love on a beach?" he asked.

"Sure," she said, "and once was enough; too much sand." She looked up at him. Was she going to tumble into the sack with him, just like that?

He looked at her carefully. "Am I pushing you?"

She thought about that for a moment, just for a moment. What did she really want? She took a deep breath. "A bed is better than a beach. How about your place?"

"It better be yours," he said.

They had made love for an hour that morning before Liz went into the kitchen and found the note from Germaine.

CHAPTER

17

When she turned around he was gone. She had crossed the room to pick up a book; he had been staring out the window. She was becoming accustomed to this trait of his, and she thought she even liked it. If he could come and go as he pleased, so could she. She thought of him running, half-naked, through the woods, to some warren, some hideaway where he curled up and slept until he was hungry. He was a wild animal, and she liked him that way; he seemed disinclined to make any civilized demands upon her—fidelity, fixed abode, fashion. Baker, on the other hand, had demanded all those things, even when their marriage was at its worst. Keir seemed to have no expectations of her at all, except to make love when he wanted her, and, so far, she was willing to meet that one.

She remembered Germaine's note: "I need to talk to you." By "need" did she mean "want"? Did "talk to you" mean she wanted to pour out her heart about some problem? No, Liz thought, finally, it was a southern sentence; it meant: I have important information to impart.

God, she was getting analytical, and just when she felt most free from the need to analyze. She had money, time, and work to do. She was safe, there was breakfast in her belly, and she had been fucked to a pleasant soreness, to put it crudely, and she felt crude, elemental. Everything in her life had been reduced to the essential; there was no worry, no plan outside purposeful work and the satisfaction of appetites. She glowed with the simplicity of it all. In this context, Germaine's information could not be important.

Still, her curiosity got the better of her. She dressed and drove to the inn. She passed through the front gate, and as she approached the house there was a clatter from above, and a helicopter sat down on the wide front lawn. As the rotors slowed, Germaine and Ron appeared on the front porch and watched.

Three men spilled from the machine, which was marked as belonging to the National Park Service. One of the men was dressed in the summer uniform of a ranger; the others wore suits; one carried a brief-case.

Liz parked the Jeep and met Germaine at the bottom of the inn's front steps as the chopper's turbine wound down.

"It's Grandpapa's lawyer," she said, anticipating Liz's question. "Ward Cheatham. Cheatham's his name, cheat 'em's his game," she muttered. "The other guy's our congressman; I can't remember his name. I don't know who the Smoky is." She grabbed Liz's arm. "You stay right here; I've got to talk to you."

Germaine walked out to meet the men, shook their hands, exchanged a few words, then said something to Ron. The boy led the others to the inn's van, and they drove away. Germaine returned and led Liz up the steps to the broad front porch and one of the large swings.

"What was that all about?" Liz asked, as they sat down.

"Who knows? Grandpapa asked me to call Cheatham for him; my guess is, he wants to make a will. I don't know why the hell he brought the feds along. Ron's driving them to Dungeness." Germaine settled herself and looked Liz in the eye. "Bad news, buddy," she said. She reached over to the table alongside the swing and picked up a newspaper. "I'll tell you flat out, then you can read the details, and you'll know as much as I do." She cleared her throat, as if looking for an excuse not to talk. "Ray and Eleanor Ferguson are both dead—night before last, I think."

Liz felt as if she had been struck hard in the chest. Without speaking she reached for the newspaper.

ATLANTA PUBLISHER AND WIFE IN APPARENT MURDER/SUICIDE

The bodies of Raymond E. Ferguson, head of his own publishing house, Buckhead Press, and his wife, Eleanor, were found in their home by a cleaning lady early yesterday. Mrs. Ferguson had been shot, and her husband hanged.

A federal form found in Mr. Ferguson's desk indicated that he had purchased a shotgun in 1982, and the weapon was found near Mrs. Ferguson's body. A source in the Atlanta Police Department theorized that the Fergusons had quarreled, and that, in a rage, Mr. Ferguson had turned the shotgun on his wife. He then, apparently, went next door and took a rope from a child's swing and hanged himself from a beam in his study.

Neighbors said the couple had lived quietly in the Brookwood Hills house for more than twenty years and were well-liked. "No one can believe that this has happened," said their next-door neighbor, Mrs. James Thready. "They were tremendously kind people, and it is impossible for me to believe that they weren't kind to each other as well."

Homicide Detective Sergeant Lee Williams, in charge of the case, said that there would be no official

statement until a thorough investigation had been conducted.

Liz began to cry. Germaine gathered her to her
breast and stroked her head. "You go right ahead,
sugar; you're entitled."

Liz wept for Ray and for the circumstances. She
wept out of anger, and, as she did, a cold fear came
to her, and she suddenly stopped crying.

"What?" Germaine asked.

"I have to use your telephone," Liz said, sniffling.

"Of course, Liz, go right ahead."

Liz took the newspaper and walked downstairs to
Germaine's office. When Al Schaefer had died she had
put it down to an accident, but now the only other
person she had been close to since she had been released from the hospital was dead, too. It could be a
coincidence, of course, but she had to know. She dialed Atlanta information and got the number of the
Homicide Bureau of the Atlanta Police Department. It
took only a moment to be connected to Detective
Sergeant Lee Williams.

"Sergeant Williams," he said, and the voice was
rich and deep, with African-American intonation.

"Sergeant, my name is Elizabeth Barwick; I'm
calling about the murder of Raymond Ferguson and
his wife."

"Murder? Do you know something I don't, Ms.
Barwick?"

"I think they were murdered."

"First things first," Williams said. "May I have
your address and phone number, please?"

"I'm outside Atlanta, and I don't have a phone. Please just listen to me."

"Just a minute, please," he said. He covered the phone with his hand and spoke to somebody else. "All right, go ahead, tell me everything."

There was an electronic beep on the line.

"I believe the deaths of Mr. and Mrs. Ferguson may be connected to the death of Al Schaefer, a couple of weeks ago."

"Schaefer, the lawyer? Was he acquainted with the Fergusons?"

"He met Ray through me. They didn't know each other well."

"So why do you think their deaths were connected?"

Liz's resolve began to weaken. She was at the point of committing herself to accusation, now, and she knew that if she did, there would be no turning back. The beep sounded again; Williams was obviously recording her. She took a deep breath. "They were both connected with me. I think my ex-husband may have killed them both."

"What is your ex-husband's name?"

"Baker Ramsey." There, it was out.

There was a brief silence. "The running back for the Bobcats?"

"That's right."

The detective took a deep breath. "Could you spell your name for me, please?"

She did so.

"And you were married to Bake Ramsey?"

"Yes. Our divorce became final less than a month

ago. Al Schaefer was my lawyer; Ray Ferguson was my publisher. He published a book of my photographs, and I've been working on another one for him."

"And why do you think Ramsey would want to kill both these men—and Ferguson's wife, too?"

"Sergeant, can I just begin at the beginning?"

"Go ahead, I've got plenty of time."

Liz began with the night Baker Ramsey nearly killed her, and brought the policeman up to date.

"I see," Williams said finally. "You've been the victim of domestic violence at the hands of Ramsey, but why would he want to kill Schaefer and the Fergusons?"

"I know it isn't rational," she said, exasperated, "but Baker is completely crazy. He's stoked up on all sorts of steroids; he's capable of anything. Look, he was in Los Angeles the night Al Schaefer drowned; the Bobcats were playing the Rams the following day. Why don't you just check on his whereabouts on the night the Fergusons died. I'll give you odds he was in Atlanta."

"So were half a million other people, Ms. Barwick, but I'll look into this, I promise. Now how can I get in touch with you?"

"You can't."

"Be reasonable, Ms. Barwick. If you really believe Ramsey did this, and you really want to help me, then I've got to be able to get in touch with you."

"You know everything I know; there's nothing else I can tell you. I can call you back later, if you like. I have to borrow a phone."

Williams sighed. "All right, call me back this time tomorrow, and we'll see where we are then."

"All right. And, Sergeant?"

"Yes?"

"It is very important that Baker Ramsey not know that I've spoken to you, I hope you can understand that. He's already come close to killing me once, and I don't want him any madder at me than he already is."

"I understand, Ms. Barwick. I won't tell him I've spoken to you."

"Thank you. I'll call you tomorrow."

Williams gave her another phone number. "That's my cellular phone; if I'm out of the office, you can reach me at that number."

Liz wrote down the number, then hung up and put her head down on Germaine's desk. She hoped she hadn't sounded hysterical; she knew the whole business must sound improbable to the detective, but she knew in her bones that Baker had done this, even if she couldn't explain to herself exactly why.

CHAPTER

18

Detective Sergeant Lee Williams knew where Baker Ramsey lived; somebody had pointed out the house to him once. He was nearly to the house when he heard a report on a radio sports show.

"Bake Ramsey, the Bobcats' star running back, came through his knee surgery in fine form and will be watching team practice from the stands at Bobcat Farm this afternoon."

Williams swung the car around and headed north. Bobcat Farm was the team's headquarters, a large spread near the little town of Roswell, north of the city. Williams was a Bobcats fan, and he was excited about a visit to a place that rigorously excluded the public.

Twenty minutes later, he pulled up to the gate of Bobcat Farm and showed his badge to the guard. "Atlanta PD. I want to see Bake Ramsey."

The guard asked him to wait while he made a telephone call, then came back to the car. "Drive straight up the road to the main building. Mr. Smith, the public relations director, will meet you there."

Williams drove slowly up the drive, taking in the grounds. In the distance, he could see a scrimmage taking place on the practice field. The main building was a faux southern mansion, and a middle-aged man wearing a Bobcats polo shirt was waiting for him on the front steps.

"Hi, I'm Bob Smith," the man said as Williams got out of his car.

"Detective Sergeant Lee Williams, Atlanta PD," he replied, careful to avoid mention of the Homicide Bureau.

"I understand you want to see Bake Ramsey. Can you tell me what it's about?"

"Just some routine questions," Williams replied. "I hope he may be able to help me with some information."

"Is this to do with an active investigation?" Smith asked, standing his ground. "Bake can't be disturbed right now. He's learning some new plays."

"It's official police business," Williams said, "and I can wait until he's finished. I've got all day."

Smith still did not move. "I'm afraid that won't be possible," he said.

"Mr. Smith," Williams said in a flat voice. "I'm going to talk with Mr. Ramsey today. Now, I can do it here and now, or I can radio for a warrant, arrest Ramsey, and talk to him downtown. What's it going to be?"

"It's as serious as that?" Smith asked, looking worried.

"It may not be serious at all, I don't know, and I won't know until I've talked to Ramsey himself. Now, I know it's your job to protect the players, but the best thing you can do to protect Ramsey is to get me to him right now."

Smith hesitated only a moment. "Come with me, please." He led the way through the front doors of the mansion, past a reception desk, into a room that might have been the library of an antebellum house. "Please wait here, and I'll ask Bake to join us. Can I get you a drink?"

"No, thanks."

Smith left the room, and Williams had a look around. All the books on the shelves were about football, and one wall was filled with leather-bound Bobcats playbooks. Williams was a little nervous about speaking to the Bobcats' star. Ten minutes passed, then Smith returned. Bake Ramsey was right behind him, on crutches. He was wearing shorts and his player's jersey, and his left knee was wrapped in a huge bandage. Smith made the introductions and sat down.

"I'd like to see Mr. Ramsey alone," Williams said to him.

"Against team policy, I'm afraid," Smith replied firmly. "No interviews of players at Bobcat Farm without a PR man on hand."

"I'm happy to have Bob hear what we say to each other," Ramsey said, speaking for the first time. He seemed cool, relaxed, unworried.

"As you wish," Williams said, sitting down. "Mr. Ramsey—"

"Call me Bake; everybody does." Ramsey smiled at him.

"Thanks, I'm Lee," Williams replied, smiling himself. He was happy to keep it informal; he didn't take out his notebook. "Bake, you were in Los Angeles for the opener with the Rams, weren't you?"

"Right. That's where I hurt my knee."

"The game was on Sunday?"

"Right again."

"When did you arrive in Los Angeles?"

"On Friday afternoon."

"Do you remember what you did on Saturday night?"

"Sure, I had dinner in my room and went to bed early."

"Were you alone?"

Ramsey grinned. "No, there was a young lady with me. She stayed the night."

"May I ask her name?"

"Brenda. I never got her last name. We met in a bar on Friday evening and, well, we got along."

"You have her number?"

"Afraid not. She was a throwaway, you know what I mean?"

"Where were you staying?"

"At Le Parc"—he spelled it—"it's a suite hotel in West Hollywood. The team always stays there."

"Can anyone else confirm you were there that evening?"

"The room-service waiter, I guess." Ramsey seemed to be trying hard to help. "He's the only other person I saw that night."

"Okay. Now, where were you on Tuesday, in the evening?"

"That's easy; Piedmont Hospital. I checked in around five that afternoon and had my surgery at seven the next morning."

"Did you leave the hospital any time that evening or night?"

"Nope. They put you right to bed when you go into the hospital."

"Did you have any visitors that evening?"

"Just the doctor, right after I arrived, and the nurse on duty. A new nurse came on at eight; she checked on me from time to time."

"Remember her name?"

"Yeah, it was Mary Alice Taylor. She was very nice."

"Bake, did you know a lawyer named Al Schaefer?"

"I only met him once. He represented my wife when we got divorced."

"Did you ever see him again?"

"Never, just that once."

"Did you know Raymond and Eleanor Ferguson?"

"Sure. Ray was my ex-wife's publisher."

"Did you know him well?"

"Not real well. Liz—that's my ex-wife—and I

had dinner with them a couple of times. She knew him a lot better than I. He was a nice guy, though; I liked him. I was sorry when I read about his death." He grinned slightly. "I wasn't quite so sorry about Schaefer. He cost me a lot of money."

Williams smiled. "Lawyers are like that. So you disliked Schaefer, then?"

"Not really, he was just doing his job. I only met him the once, for ten or fifteen minutes, maybe. The team lawyer and I went to his office to work out the settlement."

"And was the settlement easily reached?"

"Like I said, it only took ten or fifteen minutes. I didn't want to be rough on Liz; I gave her what she asked for."

"Where is the ex–Mrs. Ramsey now?"

"I don't have a clue. I heard she left town after the divorce. She told a mutual friend of ours that she was going around the world. That's okay with me."

Williams stood up. "Well, that's all I need, I think. Thanks for your time. Thank you, Mr. Smith." He turned and walked toward the door.

"I'll walk you out," Ramsey said. "I know old Bob wants to get back to work."

Smith's eyebrows went up, and Ramsey shook his head. Williams walked slowly, so that Ramsey could keep up.

"Is that knee going to put you on the reserve list?" Williams asked.

"Just between you and me?"

"Sure."

"I'll be back by midseason. The team wants it thought that I'm out until next year."

"Don't worry, I never meet any sports writers."

"You got any kids?" Ramsey asked.

"A boy, thirteen. He's playing junior-high ball; he might make a running back one of these days."

"Hang on a minute." They were in the entrance hall, and Ramsey turned to the receptionist. "Let me have one, Sheila." The woman went to a closet behind her desk and tossed Ramsey a football. "And a couple of my house seats for Sunday." He turned back to Williams. "What's your boy's name?"

"Martin."

Ramsey took a pen from the reception desk and signed the ball, "To Martin, from another running back, Bake Ramsey." He handed the ball to Williams.

Williams looked at the ball and hesitated.

"Come on, it's for the kid, it's not a bribe."

Williams took the ball. "Thanks, it'll make his whole year."

Ramsey smiled and handed him two tickets. "*This* is a bribe. It's two for the home game on Sunday."

Williams smiled back. He couldn't pass this up, the boy would never forgive him. "Consider me bribed." He laughed.

Outside on the steps they shook hands.

"You've talked to Liz, haven't you?" Ramsey said.

"Liz?"

"My ex-wife. There can't be any other reason you'd come to see me. Liz is a sick girl, real paranoid.

She's told people I beat her up; that's not true, I never laid a hand on her. Now she's got it in her head that I killed Schaefer and the Fergusons, I guess." He looked sad. "Well, I'm happy to help you in any way I can. I've certainly got nothing to hide."

"Oh, I wouldn't worry about it," Williams told him. "This is just all routine."

"Well, if you talk to Liz, tell her I'd like to see her again; talk over old times."

"Take care," Williams said, and walked down the steps to his car. Outside the front gate, he stopped and checked his address book for the telephone number of a detective he knew on the Los Angeles force. The man owed him a favor. When he was on the line, Williams asked him to pay a visit to Le Parc in West Hollywood, then he turned his car toward Piedmont Hospital.

Williams showed his badge to the nurse at the hall station. She was young and pretty, and she had a mischievous air about her. "Could I speak to Mary Alice Taylor?"

"She's the night nurse; doesn't come on until eight. What's this about?"

"Just some routine questions."

The nurse grinned. "Sure, that's what the cops always say when they're hunting down somebody for a foul deed."

Williams grinned back. "I don't suspect her of some foul deed, I promise." He didn't want to come back at eight and miss his dinner at home, and he didn't want to go looking for this girl right now; he had other work to do. "Maybe you can help me at that. Can you tell me what procedure is for the night nurse, regarding checking on patients?''

"Same as during the day, except during the day I have doctors to fool with. She's got the better deal, believe me.''

"How often would she check on her patients at night?''

"She'd make rounds every hour, more often if a patient has to have periodic medication.'' She indicated the bank of monitors behind her. "It used to be constant, but these keep an eye on the patients in serious condition, and half the patients on this ward are just waiting for elective surgery the next morning. They get a sedative at bedtime, and, after that, they're just lumps.''

"Do you know Mary Alice Taylor?''

"Sure, we were in nursing school together.''

"Is she a conscientious sort of person? I mean, would she make her rounds as prescribed, or would she more likely take a nap?''

"Oh, Mary Alice would definitely make her rounds.'' She grinned again. "With some patients, the cute ones, she might even make them more often than necessary.''

"Do you think she might find a pro football player cute?''

"You bet she would; Mary Alice has a thing for jocks. We had Bake Ramsey on the ward for knee surgery the other day, and she was still turned on when I relieved her the next morning.''

"So she would have paid special attention to somebody like Ramsey?''

"Listen, if I know Mary Alice, she probably gave him a sleeping pill, then came back during the night and checked under the sheet, just to have a look."

Williams laughed. "I get the picture, and that's all I need to know." He thanked her and left.

Late that afternoon, his Los Angeles contact reported back.

"Ramsey's story checks," the man said. "He and a girl had dinner in his room. He wasn't seen again until the next morning."

"Tell me something," Williams said. "How far is Le Parc from the Beverly Hills Hotel?"

"Five minutes in a car. Nobody walks anywhere in LA."

Williams thanked the man, then hung up. He went over his notes again of the conversations with Ramsey and with the nurse at Piedmont. Ramsey seemed fully alibied, and he had impressed Williams as being at ease and open.

The detective closed his notebook and sighed. This seemed to be a dead end. He felt perfectly satisfied with Ramsey's account of himself, except for one point. By Ramsey's own admission, he had been within minutes of all three victims at the times of their deaths. It was a big country, but Ramsey had been close to three possible murders, two thousand miles apart.

Williams didn't like coincidences, but he didn't know what the hell he could do about it.

That night, his son slept with the football.

CHAPTER

19

After she had phoned Detective Sergeant Williams a second time, Liz returned to the cottage in a horrible mood, made of half rage, half depression. Keir Drummond was sitting on the deck with a beer in his hand, watching the light fade on the dunes.

She flopped down in the chair next to him.

"Could I be kissed?" he asked.

"Not at the moment," she replied.

"What's wrong?"

"Have you ever heard of Bake Ramsey?" she asked.

"No. Who's that?"

"You're not a football fan, then?"

"I enjoy it; I don't keep up."

Liz told him everything; she told him about Bake and her marriage, about Al Schaefer, about the Fergusons and her conversations with the policeman.

He put a hand on her cheek. "I'm sorry you had to go through all that," he said. "Does the cop believe you?"

"I don't think so. Now he's talked to Baker, and he buys his story." She explained about Ramsey's alibis for the two nights.

"Well, look, a cop can only do so much. Even if these deaths are murders as you say, if Ramsey's got good alibis, what more can the guy do?"

"It stinks," she said. "He's getting away with it." She began to cry.

Keir gathered her up, took her into the house, and cuddled her on the living-room sofa.

"Not only have I lost good friends," she said when she had recovered, "I've lost a publisher. The work I've done here means nothing, now. There's no one to publish it."

"Listen to me," he said firmly. "If what you're doing is any good, you can find another publisher."

"But Ray was going to write the text. I'm no writer; I can't even write a decent letter, let alone a book. It needs somebody who loves the island the way Ray did."

"It seems to me that you love the island the way Ray did. Why don't you have a shot at the text yourself?"

"I suppose I should, but I don't know if my heart is going to be in it after this."

"It's a big heart; it can handle a lot. You'll get past

this, don't worry. This island will take hold of you again and make you want to do the book."

She grabbed a tissue from the coffee table and blew her nose loudly, then put her head on his shoulder. "I'm glad you're around," she said, then she reached up and kissed him. "There, I owed you that. I'm sorry I was nasty to you before."

"You were upset; it's okay."

"I'm still upset," she said. "Baker killed all three of them, I know it, and he's going to get away with it."

"Look, I know how strongly you feel about this, but you've got to leave room for some doubt. It is just possible, after all, that the deaths are a coincidence."

"I suppose it is possible, but if you knew Baker the way I know him—the way he's been the past couple of years, you'd know that he's perfectly capable of this, and, moreover, he's devious enough to cover himself. It's his craftiness that makes him so dangerous. And if he gets away with these murders, he'll think he can get away with *anything.*"

Keir stroked her hair. "Do you think he might try to hurt you again?"

"If he did kill Al Schaefer and the Fergusons, he did it because of his hatred of me. I can't imagine he's gotten it out of his system."

"You're safe here. I'll take care of you."

"I'll have to leave here eventually; I can't spend my life hiding."

"I won't let anything happen to you."

"I believe you," she said, kissing him again. "I'll feel safe as long as I'm here with you."

"Good."

She raised her head. "But I'll tell you this: if any other friend of mine suddenly dies violently, it won't matter how good Baker's alibi is, I'll get a gun and kill him myself."

"Easy, now," he said, cuddling her, "don't let him make you mad. If he makes you angry and afraid, then he's won."

"You're right," she said, making a conscious effort to melt the hard, icy ball in her chest. "I won't let him win." She stood up. "I'm going to start living like a normal human being again, and right now. Let me get you another beer."

There was a knock at the front door. She looked around and saw James Moses standing somberly at the door, holding an envelope.

"Evening, Miz Elizabeth," he said quietly. "I got an invitation for you from Mr. Angus. He said wait for your answer."

"Thank you, James." She took the envelope and opened it.

"Evening, Mr. Hamish," James said.

Liz winced.

"My name's Keir, James," Keir said pleasantly. "Good evening."

The boy seemed embarrassed, and Liz stepped into the breach. "Please tell Mr. Angus that I'd be pleased to accept," she said to him.

"Yes, ma'am," James said, smiling. He turned and left without another word. A moment later Liz heard a horse trot away.

"What did Grandpapa want?" Keir asked.

She passed him the heavy piece of stationery with its old-fashioned handwriting. "He's invited me to dinner," she said. "Told me to dress."

"You know, I think he's got a little thing for you," Keir said, smiling.

"You know," she replied, smiling back at him, "I think *I've* got a little thing for *him.*"

CHAPTER

20

*L*iz drove through the gates of Dungeness, wearing her only silk dress, a relic of her social life in Atlanta. She didn't remember why she'd brought it to the island, but she was glad she had. She wondered who else was coming to dinner.

James Moses stood on the front porch of the huge old house, wearing a white cotton jacket, the sleeves of which were a bit too short for him, and a black bow tie. "Good evening, Miz Elizabeth," he said, bowing stiffly. "Welcome to Dungeness."

"Thank you, James," she replied, as she reached the top of the steps. "Has anyone else arrived yet?" She wondered where the regular servants were, if there were any.

"There's not anybody else," James said, looking surprised. "Just you and Mr. Angus."

While James held the door, she entered the large entrance hall in time to see Angus descending the grand staircase. He was wearing a freshly pressed dinner suit she thought must be very old, although it did not seem much out of style, except, perhaps, the waistcoat, which was double-breasted, with lapels. A heavy gold watch chain stretched across it, and diamond studs gleamed on the stiff shirtfront, in the light from the chandelier.

"Good evening, Elizabeth," Angus said. "Welcome to my home."

"Good evening, Mr. Drummond."

He met her at the bottom of the stairs and offered her his arm. "I would be pleased if you would call me Angus," he said.

"Of course, Angus," she replied.

He led her to his study, and she began to feel that she was in another century. The room, which she calculated must be forty feet long and half as wide, was entirely lit by tall candles, placed in silver candelabra. At the opposite end of the room from Angus's desk, a table was set for two. "I thought we'd dine in here," he said. "The dining room is more suitable for forty than for two."

James spoke up. "May I get you some refreshment, Miz Elizabeth?" he asked, moving toward a butler's tray filled with decanters and an ice bucket. She asked for bourbon, and Angus requested a martini, watching closely as James made the drink and nodding approval when he had finished.

Liz took her drink from a silver tray and sipped it. "What a handsome room," she said, looking about at the high shelves of leather-bound volumes and the polished mahogany paneling.

"I'm glad you chose that word. I've always thought that old Aldred Drummond made this room to be handsome, not beautiful. It's a man's room, and it's always been my favorite. I have probably spent more time here than in any other place on earth."

She looked at the gun case and the rack for fishing rods, then at the old-fashioned file cabinets and map drawers. "I think it must reflect you as much as old Aldred," she said, and he beamed with pleasure.

"It certainly holds a lot more books than he originally allowed for. It is the library of six generations. We always had a bookbinder on the place until a few years ago, when the last one died."

"What sort of staff do you still have here?"

"Just a maid and a cook to take care of me. Of course, there's a gardener and a maintenance crew of a couple of dozen to keep the roads, the docks, and the airstrip."

She stopped before the fireplace in the center of the room and gazed at the painting over the mantel. It was a naval battle scene, and the fires on the burning ships cast an amazing light. "Is it a Turner?" she asked, not willing to believe her instinct.

"It is, and one of his best, I'm told. My grandfather bought it in London in 1889. I've got the bill somewhere. It was a hundred pounds, I think."

"He was always one of my favorites," she said.

"You probably appreciate it more than I. It was

always there for me to see when I was growing up, and I suppose I've gotten used to it. When I was a boy, though, it was the source of many dreams about fighting at sea. I think it was the reason I joined the navy in 1917, right out of Princeton."

Liz did a quick calculation. "You finished Princeton at what, nineteen?"

"I'd been well tutored most of my life, and I was somewhat ahead of my classmates."

"Were you in the first war?"

"I served in a frigate in the North Sea. It was my greatest regret that I did not arrive there in time for the Battle of Jutland, the previous year. I was never even shot at."

Liz's grandparents were both dead, and she was enchanted with the notion of knowing someone directly connected with a past she viewed as distant history. "What did you do after the war?" she asked.

"Like a lot of well-off young men of my day, I traveled. I spent three years in Europe—Paris, Rome, Florence, Budapest, Prague, Warsaw, Vienna, Dresden, Berlin." He showed her to one of a pair of wing chairs and sat opposite her.

"When you finished your traveling, then what?"

"I went to law school at Duke University, but I never practiced, never even took the bar. My father thought the law would be useful in managing the estate, and he was right to an extent. My father died the summer I graduated, and from then on, I was here—with a lot of time spent in New York, London, and the Continent, of course. I stopped traveling abroad when the last war broke out, and I never wanted to again after that." He crossed his long legs and sighed. "It's a vanished world, now, but in my memory, Europe still exists as it was." He sipped his martini and gazed into the fire. "When I heard that Dresden had been destroyed, I wept."

"I plan to travel, when I've finished my book," she said. "The whole of my European experience was a guided trip to Paris when I was in college."

"See the world, all of it," he said, with vehemence. He looked at her. "You're still doing the book? After what's happened to Ray Ferguson?"

"Yes," she said.

"I was sorry to hear about Ray and Eleanor. They were decent people; they shouldn't have died like that."

"You're right," she said, and tried not to think about Baker Ramsey. "Keir convinced me I should finish the book, although I didn't need much convincing. If you don't mind my staying on."

"Of course not. You've been seeing Keir?" he asked.

"Quite a lot," she said, and felt herself blushing.

"He's a good boy," Angus said, "they both are, but they're different."

"You're the first person who's said that. Everybody else talks about how much alike they are."

"They were always different, to me. They could fool me for a time, if they tried, but I could usually tell them apart. I sometimes wish Keir had led a more conventional life, but he seems happy, happier than Hamish in some ways, although Hamish has been more the success. I think Keir feels more than Hamish."

"I've felt that, too," Liz said. "Hamish seems, well, colder. Do you know why they . . . stay away from each other?"

"I don't," Angus said, "but I stopped letting it drive me crazy a long time ago. If they want to go on pretending that the other doesn't exist, well, I reckon they must have their reasons, and I respect their wishes. If I didn't, I'd never see either of them, they'd never come around. As it is, I see Hamish fairly often, but I hadn't seen Keir for three years, until recently." He leaned forward and rested his elbows on his knees. "You know, when I was younger I thought that my progeny would succeed me as I succeeded my father, that Cumberland would always be kept as it was by future generations. Then, my son, Evan, died in that airplane crash, and I thought his sons would be here. Now I know that neither of them, no matter how much they love this place, is the man to continue for me."

"What about Germaine?" Liz asked.

"Germaine has her hands full with her inn, and I believe she's content with that."

James reentered the room. "Excuse me, Mr. Angus; dinner is served."

Angus escorted Liz to the table, seated her, and turned to a bottle of champagne in a bucket of ice beside the table. "Krug 'fifty-three," he said, showing her the bottle. He peeled away the foil and freed the cork from its wire cage. "I love old champagne. Not quite as fizzy as it was, I'm sure, but the color, the flavor!" He removed the cork and poured her a glass. "It's been in my cellar for thirty-five years—hasn't moved an inch in all that time."

Liz drank from her glass, and turned to report to him.

"Let me tell you," he said. "Big, yeasty, not too many bubbles. Perfect."

"You're right, of course." She laughed.

He seated himself and looked up as James entered with two covered dishes. He placed them before the diners and lifted the covers; there were a dozen fresh shellfish on each plate. "My clams, from down on the flats behind the house. Best in the world."

Liz savored the sweet flavor. "I can't disagree."

Angus watched James as he left the room. "I've been training him all afternoon to serve dinner. The maid's too clumsy, and the cook's in the kitchen. He's doing well, isn't he?"

"Yes, he is. He seems a very nice boy; did he grow up on the island?"

"Yes, he did," Angus replied, forking a clam into his mouth. "He's my son."

Liz stopped, her fork in midair. Then, for something to do instead of speaking, she ate the clam.

"His mother worked on the place. She was Buck Moses's daughter, by his fourth wife. I liked her, and I'd been a widower many years. We . . . comforted each other. She died some years ago and Buck has raised the boy since then—Buck and now, me. Buck's getting too old." He sipped his champagne. "I've never told another soul that," he said. "Indeed, I admitted it to myself only a short while ago." He peered at her across his glass. "I wonder why I told you."

"I'm glad you did," she said. "It's flattering when someone you like tells you his closest secrets."

They finished the clams, and James came and took away the dishes. Angus got up, went to a sideboard, and retrieved an empty wine bottle and a full decanter. "Do you like claret? Red Bordeaux, I mean. The British call it claret, and I think it's a nice word."

"I do. I haven't drunk all that much of it, though."

"I want you to know about this bottle, because as long as you live, you may never have another wine as good. This is Chateau Lafite-Rothschild 1929, the finest red Bordeaux of this century, maybe ever." He poured a small amount in his glass, twirled it, plunged his nose deep into the glass, and inhaled. "Perfect. It's my last bottle; I wanted to drink it before I die, drink it in good company." He poured them both a glass and sat down.

Liz imitated his action with the glass, then sipped the wine. "I've never tasted anything so wonderful," she said, and she meant it.

James returned with a platter and presented two pheasant, sizzling. "I shot these myself last week with my new shotgun," he said, smiling.

Angus smiled back at him. "I've always managed to keep a good cook," Angus said when the birds had been served. "I think that's why I've lived so long."

They ate in silence for a while. Finally, Liz asked, "What's going to happen to James when you die?"

"I've thought about that," Angus said. "I'd leave

him to run wild on this island, if I thought he'd stay. But he won't. He wants to go to college, to see some of his country and the world. I'll see that he can do that, then I can only hope that Cumberland will draw him back the way it always draws back the people who love the place. I'll try and make it easy for him to come back."

"Do your grandchildren know they have an uncle?" Liz asked.

"I think Keir knows, but I'm not sure about Hamish and Germaine; they may have had their suspicions. I don't much give a good goddamn what anybody else thinks. Like that little weasel, Jimmy. He thinks he's going to *develop* Cumberland Island. He has some surprises coming!"

Liz was tempted to ask about the surprises, but she didn't want to pry.

They finished their dinner with a blueberry pie and a honeylike dessert wine from Angus Drummond's cellar, then they repaired to a leather sofa before the fire.

"I don't think I've ever had a better dinner in my whole life." Liz sighed, accepting a brandy snifter from Angus. "And certainly not one where everything came from the backyard, so to speak."

"It's been awhile since I've entertained a beautiful woman," Angus said, sipping his brandy. "I'd forgotten how satisfying it can be."

"Thank you." It was at this moment, she thought, when a younger man would move on her. She wondered if he were about to, and, if he did, what she would do.

"Will you accept a gift from me?" he asked suddenly.

"I beg your pardon?" she asked, surprised.

"I'd like to give you something. Will you accept it?"

She hesitated only a moment. "Yes."

Angus rose and walked to his enormous desk. He brought back an envelope and a sheaf of papers. "I assure you it's not an inappropriate gift for an old man to give a young woman." He handed her the envelope. "Wait until I die to open it. I don't much like being thanked, and, I assure you, you won't have long to wait."

She looked at him, alarmed. "Do you know something I don't?"

He laughed. "No, but at my age, I could go at any moment. Lately, I've been feeling that it might be soon."

"All right," she said, laying the envelope in her lap, "I'll respect your wishes about waiting, but I'll thank you anyway. Even though I don't know what it is, I'm very grateful that you would want to give it to me."

Angus looked nonplussed for a moment, then he began shuffling the papers in his hands. "I'd also like to ask a small favor of you—nothing to do with my gift."

"Of course."

"I'd like you to witness my will."

"All right. I was at the inn when your lawyer arrived the other day. Germaine thought you might be making one."

"He didn't prepare this, I did. I told you I was trained as a lawyer, and when Cheatham paid me his visit earlier this week, I decided I didn't need a lawyer any longer." He turned red, apparently at the thought of Cheatham. "Do you know what that sonofabitch tried to do?"

"Easy now," she said, placing a hand on his arm. He took a deep breath. "He brought my congressman and a man from the government here to . . . the congressman wants to introduce a bill in the Congress that would turn Cumberland Island into a national park. Wants to pay me thirty million dollars for it."

Liz said nothing.

"Said it would be a monument to me. The idiot."

"I can imagine what you must have told them," Liz said.

"I fired my lawyer, and I told the government man to go to hell. Then I told the congressman this: I said, I'm making a will, and I'm going to put a clause in it leaving fifty thousand dollars to the campaign fund of the principal opponent of any congressman or senator who introduces such a bill in Congress."

Liz burst out laughing. "Oh, that's wonderful! What did he say?"

"He said, 'Well, of course we want to respect your wishes in this matter, Mr. Drummond.' "

She started laughing again.

"I did it, too, I put the clause in my will."

"Good for you," she managed to say.

"Now, I don't want you to think that I drew this up hastily, because I didn't. I've been working on this document for a month, and it's just the way I want it.

I've made it very difficult, I hope impossible, for anybody to ever make any radical change in this island. When Aldred Drummond got the grant of this place, he made it into a seat for himself and his family, and we Drummonds have been prolific enough to see that there'll be family around for a long time to come."

"It's your property, Mr. Drummond," Liz said, "and I think you should do whatever the hell you want to do with it."

"Good girl," he said, smiling broadly. "Now, listen to me. This document is my last will and testament; I am of sound mind, if not body; I'm not crazy, and I wasn't drunk when I wrote it, even if I am a little bit right now; it contains what I intend for this island and my family, is that clear to you?"

"Yes, it is."

He produced an old Parker pen and signed it. Then he pointed at the place for her to sign. "Sign and date it right there."

Liz did so. "Why did you want me, in particular, to witness your will?"

"Because you're damn near the only person on the island at the moment who's not either a beneficiary or cut out of it. You've no ax to grind."

"That's certainly true, but don't you need two witnesses for it to be legal?"

"You're perfectly right, in the state of Georgia you need two witnesses. Don't worry, I'll find another one before it's too late." He walked to his desk and deposited the will there. "Enough of business," he said, "let's get back to the brandy. Did I tell you about the brandy?"

Sometime after midnight, Angus Drummond walked her down the front steps of Dungeness, put her into her Jeep, and kissed her on the cheek. "Don't worry," he said, "there are no policemen to check your breath on the way home."

Liz reached up and kissed him firmly on the lips. "Thank you, Angus, for a fine dinner and a wonderful evening and for whatever is in this envelope."

She drove back to Stafford Beach Cottage, happily drunk, her skirt blowing in the breeze. When she got home, she felt thirsty and went to the refrigerator for a cold bottle of mineral water. Her thirst slaked, she turned toward the bedroom, thinking of other appetites. Sadly, he wasn't there, but then, she thought, I'm too far gone anyway.

CHAPTER

21

In the late afternoon Liz left the cottage with the Jeep full of gear and headed for the west side of the island. As she drove past the landing strip, a single-engine airplane set down and taxied up to the road. She slowed as Hamish Drummond got out and helped down a woman and a small boy. She pulled to a stop. "Hello, there," she called. "You're back early."

He smiled at her. "Yes, I finished sooner than I had expected. Liz, meet Hannah Drummond, and this is our son, Aldred."

Liz sized up both of them quickly. Hannah was in her midthirties, with blond hair swept straight back and tied. Everything in her appearance and bearing said, "ex-deb; old money; thoroughly conventional."

The boy was a smaller image of his father, tousle-headed and crafty looking. He watched her appraisingly. "I like your Jeep," he said. "Can I drive it?"

"You're still a bit young for that," his father said, mussing his hair further.

"You did it when you were little," the boy said reprovingly. "You told me."

"Sure you can drive it sometime, Aldred," Liz said. "I'll come and find you at the inn." She turned back to Hamish. "Can I give you a lift?"

"Thanks, but we buzzed the inn. They'll send out the van." As he spoke, the van emerged from the trees on the other side of the strip, with Ron at the wheel.

"I'll see you later," Liz said. "I'm off to photograph the sunset. Any suggestions for the best spot?"

"Plum Orchard," Hamish replied. "You'll have an unobstructed view across the marshes from the dock." He waved and turned to their luggage.

Liz turned north for Plum Orchard. She turned left at the fork, and soon the mansion appeared, bathed in the golden afternoon light. Not wanting to drive across the lawn, even if it was neglected, she followed the road around the back of the house, then toward the dock. She slowed to let half a dozen of the island's wild horses move grudgingly off the road. One of them, she noticed, was hobbled. She had never seen anyone but James Moses riding a horse on the island, let alone a wild one.

She pulled the Jeep onto the grass near the dock and got out. The sun was well above the horizon, and she turned to setting up her 4 × 5 view camera. When she was ready, the sun was still too high, so she

walked over to inspect the old boathouse. She peeked
through a broken pane at the inside. The doors, surprisingly, were open, and there was a length of new
rope coiled on the rotting catwalk inside. She went
back to her camera, unfolded her camp stool, and
waited.

The sun crept slowly westward, growing larger
and redder as it sank, lighting the salt marshes from
a low angle, casting long shadows. She framed a shot
and took it, then reloaded. She got four well-spaced
shots before the last bit of the sun's rim sank below
the horizon, then she got two more in the afterglow
of day. Well satisfied with her work, she slowly
packed her gear, enjoying the creeping dusk. It was
nearly dark, but the sky was still vividly blue when
she climbed back into the Jeep and moved up the road
toward the house. It was then that she saw the light.

It blinked at her as she drove, a pinpoint of lumi-
nescence from behind a lowered blind in a dormer at
the top of the house. She was first surprised that the
house still had electricity, then she wondered who
could be there. She pulled up behind the house and
beeped at the horses, who did not want to leave their
spot; then, on an impulse, she pulled off the road.

She climbed out of the Jeep and stood, listening.
There was no sound but the snorting of the horses and
grass snapping as they grazed, and the crickets coming
alive in the dusk. She retrieved a small flashlight from
the Jeep and walked up the back steps of the house.
The door was securely padlocked, and there was
nothing on the other side of the panes but an empty
kitchen, its old appliances covered with dust. She

walked slowly around the house, examining each window and looking for another door. There was a porch at the side of the house facing the water, but the door there was also locked. She continued to the front door, locked also. But when she came to the end of the house facing away from the marshes, there was another door, and even though it was padlocked, the screws fastening the hasp to the door came loose when she tried the lock. She turned the knob and pushed the door open.

It squeaked, and she was startled to hear the noise echo loudly. She stepped through the door and pointed her little light ahead of her. She was standing at the edge of an indoor swimming pool, empty of water, its diving board poised over what seemed an incredibly distant bottom. The thing must be twelve feet deep, she thought, and there was no shallow end. Had she not had the flashlight, she might have tumbled into it. The huge room was tiled, accounting for the echo.

She walked alongside the pool toward another door, each scrape of her soles ringing harshly in the darkness beyond her light's beam. The next door was open, too, and she entered a hallway inside the mansion proper. There was a smell of dust and dead air. Shortly, she emerged into a sitting room which contained only a few pieces of furniture, all of them covered with muslin. Then she came to the main entrance hall and stopped to admire the grand staircase. Momentarily forgetting her purpose, she was overcome with curiosity about the house that Angus Drummond had built for his son. She prowled on,

entering the drawing room, then a library, its shelves
bereft of books. Even in the thin beam of her flashlight, she was impressed with the proportions of the
place. It was big, but the scale was human. She went
back to the entrance hall and found the dining room,
then she was brought up short by the sudden presence
of another person with a flashlight.

It took her a moment to realize that she was facing a large mirror, and that she was the other person.
Heaving a sigh of relief, she turned toward the main
staircase. The steps creaked lightly as she climbed,
then she was on the second floor. The rooms were
empty, though she found a bedroom with wallpaper
that suggested Germaine as a little girl. Farther along,
there was a room that must have belonged to the
twins. An elderly rocking horse occupied its center,
waiting patiently for riders. She touched it, and it
quivered on its springs.

At the end of the hall she found a room still
furnished, and she knew that it had belonged to Evan
Drummond and his wife. There was a four-poster bed
with a sagging canopy, a dressing table, and a chaise
longue. Two dressing rooms opened, one on each side
of the bedroom, empty but for a pair of gentleman's
white kid gloves, lying forlornly on a shelf. She
picked them up, and, although they were dusty, they
seemed never to have been worn. She replaced the
gloves and left the room to its ghosts.

The light had come from a dormer, and that
meant another floor above. Liz found the stairs again,
and started up the narrower steps to what must be the
attic. As she turned at the landing, she was aware of

another source of light, and she switched off hers. She stood for a moment, letting her eyes adjust. The light came from a door that stood ajar at the top of the stairs. She listened hard for evidence of someone there but heard nothing.

She began climbing the last steps, instinctively walking on the outside of the treads to prevent squeaking. She reached the door and edged around it, holding her breath. She was greeted with the sight of an attic wonderland. Dozens of boxes were piled up in an orderly manner; odd pieces of furniture were scattered about the large room; a tall floor lamp with a fringed shade leaned against a wall; empty picture frames were scattered about.

As she moved farther into the attic, a long rack of clothes appeared—ball gowns and other dresses, a suit of tails and a linen suit that had once been white. She turned the corner and found the source of light. At the far end of the room a lamp stood on a small table, burning brightly, casting its light over a room within a room. A sofa formed one border and an old oak double-decker bunk made the other. A large coffee table sat between them, and the lamp and its table were at the end.

The top bed of the bunk was neatly made up with sheets, a pillow, and an old army blanket. A hat rack stood in a corner of the area, holding a pair of jeans and a couple of polo shirts.

Then there was a creaking noise from behind her, and the door slammed.

Liz whirled around, emitting a sound—half scream, half shout—in spite of herself. She was still alone in the room. A rattling noise caused her to spin again, but it was only the edge of the shade slapping against the window as the wind caught it. The door had been blown shut.

She let out a moan of relief and sank onto the sofa, raising a small cloud of dust. She held a hand to her breast, willing her heart to stop trying to escape her rib cage. As her breathing returned to normal, she noticed a large, old-fashioned scrapbook on the coffee table before her; she opened it to be confronted with a rather formal family portrait taken on the front porch of Plum Orchard. Evan Drummond gazed, clear eyed, into the camera, his hand resting lightly on his wife's. A girl of eight or nine or so stood behind and between them, a hand on each of their shoulders, and at their feet, sitting cross-legged on the porch and looking only momentarily still, the twins, aged about five or six, she reckoned, dared the camera to take their picture. They were all informally dressed, as if they had been happened upon by an itinerant photographer on a quiet Sunday afternoon.

Liz turned the page and found more photographs, some formally posed, some clearly family snapshots, yellowing at the edges. The parents soon disappeared from the album, but Germaine and the twins grew older as Liz turned the pages, stopping when the boys were eighteen or so. She flipped slowly back through the book, watching the twins grow. At times, she thought she could just distinguish, by some hint of gaze or bearing, which was Hamish and which Keir, but they were startlingly identical. She wondered what it must be like to be the mother of boys of whose names one could not always be certain, or, closer to home, what it must be like to be in love with one of them, knowing there was a duplicate.

It occurred to her at that moment, for the first time a serious thought, that she might be in love with Keir Drummond.

Suddenly, she felt the intruder, that she must not be found in this place, nor ever admit that she had been here. She felt that she was at the center of Keir's world, at a place where he could still admit the existence of his brother. She got herself up and out of there, fearing his sudden return. She ran down the stairs, her flashlight bobbing before her, knowing that if he caught her there, he would never speak to her again.

Late that night, when she was asleep, he came into her bed. She turned to him sleepily, and he held her close, rubbing the back of her neck.

"Where have you been?" she murmured.

"Around," he replied, kissing her.

"I missed you," she said, throwing a leg over his.

"Not as much as I missed you," he whispered, moving on top of her.

CHAPTER

22

They spoke in a patois no white person could understand, even though they were alone together at the old slave quarters. There were elements of both Gullah and Geechee, spoken by inhabitants of islands farther north in Georgia and South Carolina, but much of the dialect was peculiar to the slaves on Cumberland and their descendants, and now only Buck Moses and his grandson James spoke it.

"Big changes coming," Buck said.

"What kind of changes, Granddaddy?"

"A big wind going to blow through Cumberland. Everything change. I'm glad I ain't going to be alive to see it."

"You're not going to die, Granddaddy. You outlived four wives and everybody else on this island. I don't think you're ever going to die."

Buck Moses grinned toothlessly. "Tell you the truth, I just about believe that myself till right recent." His face grew sober again. "But I'm going to die, just like everybody else. I'll outlive your daddy, though."

It took James a moment to sort out who his grandfather meant, and then he was shocked. Buck had never spoken of this before.

"You knowed, didn't you?" Buck asked.

"Maybe," James replied, still cautious of speaking about it.

"He won't never say it to you," Buck said, sipping the hot tea he had made from herbs. "Not to your face. But he'll let you know. I knowed him since he was a baby; he won't let it pass. Could mean trouble for you."

"What kind of trouble?"

"Angus a rich man. He got a lot of kinfolk. Folks don't let go of money easy, and ain't going to be nobody to help you on this island."

"They going to think I want his money?"

"You crazy if you don't." Buck snorted. "You just like everybody else, you got to eat, got to have a roof. You going to need it."

"I can make my way," James said, offended. "You taught me all my life how to live off this island. If I can't make it on the mainland, I'll hunt my living here."

"Maybe, maybe not," Buck said. "They maybe

don't want you here when they know you his son. They maybe run you off."

"They got to find me first," James said.

Buck laughed out loud. "That's right, they got to find you. You give 'em a hunt, eh?"

"Yessir." James was quiet for a moment. "Granddaddy, anybody else know about this?"

"Folks got eyes. Germaine might be guessing, Hamish and Keir, too."

"They like me, don't they?"

"Sure, boy, but you don't know folks when they fighting over money. Keir won't do nothing to hurt you. I don't know about Hamish and Germaine. Hamish funny sometime."

"What's the matter with those fellows?" James asked. "How come they don't like each other?"

"Those boys love each other; that's why they like they are."

"But you can't talk about one of them to the other one, or he'll walk off. That don't be the way folks act when they love one another."

"There's a reason," Buck said.

"What reason? What could be so bad they won't even know one another?"

"I know. I'm the only one who know. Sometime I think them boys don't know theirselves. But I know."

"Tell me, then."

"I ain't going to tell nobody," Buck said vehemently. "I'm taking it to my grave. But they going to come face to face before long, and I just hope . . ." His voice trailed off.

"Hope what, Grandaddy?"

"I ain't talking about it no more," Buck said. He finished off his tea. "I'll tell you something. When Angus die, you go see Miz Elizabeth."

"How come?"

"Angus in love with her. He do her right, she do you right."

"But Granddaddy, he's what—sixty or seventy years older than Miz Elizabeth."

"Don't make no difference. I know Angus; I knowed him since he was born. He like a pretty woman. Ain't been one around here for a long time, and he lonesome."

"Don't make no sense to me." James sighed.

"You listen to me, boy. When Angus die, you go see Miz Elizabeth. She help you."

"If you say so, Grandaddy."

Buck Moses got up and walked to the window. "Big wind coming to Cumberland," he said.

CHAPTER

23

*L*iz stopped by the inn to leave her grocery order. It was late morning, the guests had been dispatched on foot, by bicycle, and by van to various parts of the island, bearing packed lunches, and there was no one about but the kitchen staff and Ron, who was mopping the stone floor in the staff dining room. Liz left her list on Germaine's desk and went looking for her. She had fallen into the habit of stopping by for tea or coffee.

She trudged up the stairs, had a look around the deserted library and living room, and emerged onto the front veranda.

"Good morning," a voice said.

Liz turned and saw Hannah Drummond, Hamish's ex-wife, sitting on a big swing, a book in her lap.

"Join me for some coffee?" the woman asked. There were a pot and two cups on the table before her. "I got some for Hamish, but he and Aldred are out in the jungle somewhere."

"Sure," Liz called and joined her on the swing. Up close, Hannah Drummond looked even better. She was carefully but not heavily made up, perfectly neatly dressed in khaki trousers and a madras shirt, and her hair was still pulled back so tightly that Liz wondered how she could blink.

"Hamish becomes a little boy again when he and Aldred are together," Hannah said as she poured the coffee. "I think he relives his childhood that way. They're probably out there right now getting snake-bit."

"No snake would dare bite a Drummond on this island," Liz said.

"You're probably right." Hannah laughed. She handed Liz her coffee. "I hear you've been spending time with a Drummond."

"Angus?"

"No, Keir."

"That's right."

"What's he like?"

"You've never met Keir?"

"No. Not quite, anyway. I saw him once."

"On the island?"

"No, in New York. I was doing some shopping on Fifth Avenue, and I stopped at the skating rink at Rockefeller Center for lunch. This was some years ago, when Hamish and I were still married, and I was pregnant with Aldred at the time. Anyway, I had just paid my bill when I looked up and saw Hamish on the ice, skating with a girl. I was absolutely floored—Hamish had never played around with other women—not that I knew about, anyway. They were skating around, quite gracefully together, and I just sat there and stared at them while I got madder and madder.

"Finally, I got up from the table and walked to the railing around the rink and just stood there. I wanted to see his face when he saw me. They came around again, and he looked right at me, and, to my astonishment, skated right past me. I stood there for two or three more circuits, and he went right past me just as coolly as you please.

"Then, they stopped skating, and he left the girl for a moment, went to the men's room, I guess. I walked over to her and asked the name of the man she was with. 'His name is Keir Drummond,' she told me."

"Did you speak to him at all?" Liz asked.

"No, I just left and went home. I was absolutely stunned. I couldn't figure out if it were some sort of weird practical joke, or if I had really caught my husband with another woman. That night, I told Hamish about my experience, and he dismissed it out of hand, said I must be hallucinating."

"Why didn't you know he had a brother?"

"He never told me. It wasn't until a month or so after that that Germaine visited us in New York and put me in the picture. I was mad as hell, and Hamish and I had a big fight about it."

"He wouldn't admit that he had a brother?"

"Not for a minute. I was beginning to think *he* was crazy."

"But you learned to live with it."

"Exactly. I mean, he was perfectly normal in every other respect. It seemed the only way to handle it."

"That's been my experience with Keir, too. He either just ignores any question about a brother or denies everything. Do you have any idea why they're this way?"

"Not a clue, and neither did Germaine. It apparently started the summer they were eighteen, right before Hamish left for Princeton."

Both women were silent for a moment, as if they had run out of things to talk about.

"Would you like to meet Keir?" Liz asked finally.

Hannah started to speak, then stopped. "No, I don't think so," she said at last. "I'm pretty much over Hamish, now, and I don't want to get more involved with his family. It's really none of my business anymore."

"I understand," Liz said.

They were quiet again, then Hannah spoke. "What's Keir like?" she asked, almost sheepishly.

"Like Hamish, but different. I mean, you know how alike they are. Hamish has always seemed sort of, well, detached, removed. I don't think I could get close to him."

"I know what you mean," Hannah said, nodding furiously. "I found that terribly attractive. It was a challenge, to get past that and find out what he was really like."

"Did you?"

"Sometimes, at little moments. In bed, mostly, I think. It's funny about some men—you can only really know them in bed."

That certainly seems to be the case with Keir, Liz thought, but she felt too shy to mention it. Hannah Drummond was talking as if they were old girl friends, when they'd only just met. There was an embarrassed silence. "How long are you staying?" Liz asked, to get the conversation moving again.

"I'll go back in just a few days, and Aldred will follow a little later."

"He won't get to see much of Hamish, then."

"Oh, he spent some time with him on Martha's Vineyard early in the summer."

Germaine came through the screen door, mopping her brow. "Whew, actual labor this morning," she said, plopping down next to them on the swing. "I've got a chambermaid with the curse this morning, so I'm doing double duty. Funny, when I've got the curse I work!"

"You seem really busy this season," Hannah said.

"It's true. I've only got eighteen beds, and I could fill three times that many if I had them."

"Why don't you expand?" Hannah asked.

"It's crossed my mind, but it won't happen while Grandpapa is alive. He wants it the way it's always been."

"Not many people are in a position to keep things the way they've always been," Hannah said, rather wistfully. "It must be nice."

"To tell you the truth, I've never much liked

things the way they've always been," Germaine said. "I don't like living in the past."

"Will you expand when your grandfather dies?" Liz asked.

"You bet I will. He knows it, too; he just wants me to wait until he's gone."

"How will you do it?"

"I'll build an annex out back, but don't worry, it'll be in the style of the house. I don't want you to get the idea I'm going to screw up the place."

"I know you wouldn't do that, Germaine," Liz said. "There isn't an ounce of developer in you."

Germaine pointed toward the gate. "Speak of the devil," she said.

The inn's van pulled up and Germaine's cousin Jimmy Weathers got out, followed by another man. Jimmy was carrying a large leatherette case.

"And it looks like he's brought some plans," Germaine said.

"You mean, he's planning some sort of development on the island already?" Liz asked.

"That's right."

"But how can he do that? He doesn't own any of it, does he?"

"Not yet, but Grandpapa has fired Cheatham, and if he didn't make a will, then his estate will be divided among his heirs; that's me, Hamish, Keir, little Aldred, and guess who."

"But you could outvote him."

"No, my lawyer tells me he could force a division of the property, and that means the island."

Liz watched Jimmy's back as he strode confidently into the inn. She felt good knowing that Cumberland Island was now safe from Jimmy and his kind. She thought of telling Germaine about her grandfather's new will, but she felt, somehow, that Angus Drummond would want to tell his grandchildren about that himself.

CHAPTER

24

Sergeant Lee Williams had his hands full keeping his son, Martin, from simply floating away. In spite of the weight of a Bobcats ball cap, a Bobcats pennant, and the football Bake Ramsey had given him, the thirteen-year-old's body kept threatening to leave the ground and not come back; he was that excited.

"Are they gonna be good seats, Daddy?" he asked, for the fourth or fifth time.

"I expect so," Williams said again. "I don't think Bake Ramsey would give us bad seats, do you?"

"Just as long as they're between the forties, it's okay," Martin said. "Even between the thirties." He sighed. "Hell, if they're between the end zones it's all right with me."

"You watch your language, boy," his father said sternly.

They followed the crowd along the stadium passage until they came to a sign pointing to their row number, then they began climbing. They emerged from the tunnel into brilliant sunshine, and the fifty-yard line was before them.

"Hot damn!" the boy yelled. "Look at that! And we're right on the aisle!"

"Martin, I'm not going to tell you again about your language; you're getting a real problem about that, son. Now, if I hear one more blue word out of you, we're going home right that minute, you got me?"

"Yes, Daddy," the boy said sheepishly, as they sat down.

The day could not have been more perfect, Williams thought. It was in the seventies, there was not a cloud in the sky, and the boy had every reason to be excited; they were, indeed, in the best seats in the stadium. Williams had not been entirely certain whether he liked Bake Ramsey, but at this moment, he could have kissed him.

They were surrounded by well-dressed Atlantans in their autumn finery. As Williams watched the prosperous-looking crowd, all friends and relatives of the players, he reckoned, a very pretty girl moved past them and took the seat next to Martin. Williams was glad he had made the boy wear his good clothes. A band struck up somewhere, and a roar rose from the crowd as the Bobcats ran onto the field.

"Look, Daddy, there he is—on the crutches, see!"

Bake Ramsey swung onto the field behind the team, dwarfing the assistant coach who walked beside him. He was dressed like the coaches, in blue trousers and a white, short-sleeved team shirt. Even from that distance, Williams could see the rippling muscles in his forearms.

"That guy is really pumped up, ain't he, Dad?"

"*Isn't* he," Williams remonstrated. "Yes, he's got the muscles, all right. You ought to see him up close."

"You reckon I could meet him after the game?"

"Well, I don't know about that; we weren't invited. He was nice enough to give us these seats, so let's don't get pushy, okay?"

The girl next to Martin turned to him. "You're a Bake Ramsey fan, are you?"

"Yes, ma'am," Martin said, "I sure am." He held up his most prized possession. "He gave me this football. Really, he gave it to my dad, but it was for me. He autographed it for me, see right here?" He held up the pigskin for her to see.

Williams was relieved that the boy was speaking politely.

The girl smiled and stuck out her hand. "I'm Mary Alice," she said.

Martin shook her hand respectfully. "I'm Martin. This is my dad."

"Hi, I'm Lee," he said, offering his hand.

She shook it and turned back to Martin. "You want to meet Bake after the game?"

"Oh, boy, I sure would like that, Mary Alice!"

"Well, he's a friend of mine; I'll see what I can do."

Martin turned back to his father. "Dad, can I? Is it okay?"

"Well, let's just see if it's convenient for Mary Alice after the game."

She winked at Martin.

Williams looked at her closely. High on her left cheek, nearly covered by makeup, was what seemed to be a large, ugly birthmark. He compared the cheek with the other one and made out the swelling. No, he concluded, it was not a birthmark; it was a bruise.

After the game Williams and his son followed Mary Alice into the bowels of the stadium. They were stopped twice, but her name was on a list, and soon they entered a waiting room. In a further room, a press conference was being held by the coach and some of the players.

"Wait here, and I'll find him," Mary Alice said. She left them in the waiting room and edged her way around the press conference. Martin went and stood, goggle eyed, at the door, taking in the proceedings.

Williams took a chair next to an office door, which was ajar, and a moment later he heard voices.

"Now you listen to me, you little sonofabitch," a familiar voice said. "You jack up the price on me again, and I'll break your arms for you."

"Listen, Bake," another voice said, "it's what it cost me; I'm not making out on this. You don't want the stuff, say so, and we'll forget it."

Williams turned to his right in time to see, through the open door, Bake Ramsey holding the shirtfront of a smaller man dressed as an assistant coach. Ramsey let go of the shirt and took a small package from the man.

"All right, as long as you're not sticking it to me." He took a wad of money from a pocket and peeled off some bills. "I'll want the same next week."

"Okay, but don't give me a hard time if the price goes up."

Williams got up and moved away from the door, toward the next room and the press conference. He knew a drug buy when he saw one, but he wasn't busting anybody today, especially Bake Ramsey, in the team's dressing rooms, with the press standing by and his son dying to meet the guy. A moment later, he saw Ramsey ease himself into the press room on his crutches and start answering questions. When it was over, Mary Alice led him into the waiting room.

"Bake, I want you to meet Martin," she said. "He's your biggest fan, I think."

Ramsey's personality had undergone a major change. "Hi, Martin," he said, bathing the boy in a big smile. "Did you like the game today?"

"I'd have liked it better if you'd been playing, Bake," the boy replied.

Ramsey looked up and saw Williams. "Oh, hi, there. This is *your* boy, huh?"

"It sure is," Williams said, trying to smile.

"Well, Martin, you come on with me a minute," Ramsey said. He took the boy and left the room.

Mary Alice turned to Williams, all smiles. "He just loves kids," she said. "I knew he'd want to meet Martin."

"I sure appreciate the thought," Williams replied.

"He'll remember this day forever." He nodded. "You hurt your face?"

She became unsettled. "Oh, uh, yes, I had a fall. Stupid thing; fell over my own feet."

"Sure," Williams said. "I do it myself all the time." Sure.

Ramsey returned, leading Martin, who was clutching a Bobcats jersey to his breast, grinning madly. "Well, Martin, if you and your dad will excuse us, Mary Alice and I have to be somewhere." He stuck out his hand, enveloping the boy's.

"Sure, sure, thanks, Bake, I really appreciate it."

Mary Alice gave them directions to the parking lot, and they left.

"Dad, look at this," Martin said, holding up the jersey. "It's his own jersey, the one he was wearing when he got hurt playing against the Rams; see the grass stains?"

"That's really something, boy. You got lucky today, huh?"

All the way home, the boy jumped up and down on the car seat, hugging the jersey.

Williams was thrilled with his son's joy over his day, but there was a sick feeling in his own belly. The day had lent weight to at least some of Elizabeth Barwick's allegations: Bake Ramsey was probably violent with women, and he was very likely using drugs. If those things were possible, then what else might be?

He was beginning to feel snookered, and he didn't like it.

CHAPTER

25

James Moses gripped the wheel of the jeep tightly and concentrated on carefully following Angus Drummond's instructions.

"Now, see the *H* on the gear knob? That shows you where the gears are. You push in the clutch and put it in first gear."

James did as he was told.

"Now, give it some gas and let out on the clutch gradually."

James tried, and the jeep gave a jerk and stopped running.

Angus sighed deeply. "Try it once again; you'll get the hang of it."

James tried again and got the jeep going. Clutching the wheel, he aimed down the beach. The tide was out, and his road was wide. He got through the gears and began to enjoy himself. "This is fun!" he shouted over the wind.

Angus laughed aloud. "I'd forgotten how much fun it was when I learned to drive," he said. "That was in a car not all that different from this one, about eighty years ago. It was an old Model T Ford pickup truck that was missing just about everything but four wheels and a steering wheel and some seats. All right, stop the car, and we'll try shifting again."

When an hour had passed, James was driving smoothly and was a little more relaxed. "Is it any harder on a road, Mr. Angus?"

"Not much, and there isn't much in the way of traffic to worry about on the island."

"Granddaddy wouldn't ever let me drive his truck," James said.

"I don't know why not," Angus replied. "That old heap was just about done for when I gave it to him, and that was a long time ago." He pointed at a track through the dunes. "All right, let's try it in four-wheel drive."

James worked the levers as instructed and powered up the track and over the crest of the dunes.

"Now, when we get a good-sized storm, or maybe a hurricane, somebody has to come out here with the tractor and open up these tracks again, or they'll just disappear," Angus said. "You remember that. When I'm gone, there's nobody on this island who'll think about things like that. Germaine and the twins think this island just maintains itself, that it's a wild place. Well, it's wild all right, but somebody has to make sure the maintenance crew keeps the roads repaired, and the grass on the landing strip cut, and a roof on all the buildings, or it'll just go to hell."

"Yessir," James said. He wondered why he was being told all this.

Then they began a tour of the island, and Angus showed him more of what had to be done—the bridges over the creeks, the traps for the wild hogs that rooted up things, the transformers that managed the electricity brought from the mainland, the piers and pilings on the landward side of the island, the wells that supplied fresh water. They finished up at Dungeness.

In the study, Angus brought down a cardboard box and took out of it a cloth-bound book measuring about nine by twelve inches and an inch thick. Angus opened it and began turning pages.

"I've been working on this for two years," he said, "and I just got the bound copies from New York last week. This book tells the history of this island from the time the Indians were the only settlers; it covers the Drummond family history, and there are maps from a survey that I did about twenty years ago. I drew them myself. There are descriptions and plans of every structure on the island that I built, and drawings of the others. Everything I could think of about this island is in this book, and I've had one bound for every living member of my family. Everyone except Jimmy Weathers, that is. In his hands, this might be dangerous information." He closed the book and handed it to James. "This copy is for you, son," he said.

James took the book and noticed that at the bottom, stamped in gold, was JAMES MOSES DRUMMOND. He ran his finger over the stamping. "If it's for me, why does it have this name on it?" he asked.

"Because that's your rightful name, James," Angus said.

James didn't know what to say. This was the only time Angus had ever mentioned this, and he was speechless.

"You take that book and you read it," Angus said softly, "and then you read it again. You need to know the things in that book, and I've been too long telling them to you."

"Yessir," James said.

"Go on about your business, now, and come see me tomorrow. We'll look around the island some more."

James did not go to sleep that night until he had finished the book. He would read it again the following day, he knew, and the day after that.

CHAPTER

26

"**T**he swelling is completely gone," the doctor said. "I'd say you were making a remarkable recovery." He looked Ramsey in the eye. "A very remarkable recovery."

Ramsey avoided his gaze. "Yeah? That's great."

The doctor looked at the assistant coach, Manny Davis. "Manny, will you excuse us for a minute?"

"Sure, Doc," Manny said. He walked to the other side of the exercise room and pretended to fiddle with a piece of equipment.

"Bake," the doctor said, "I've never seen that rapid a reduction of swelling after this sort of surgery without the use of massive doses of antiinflammatory drugs." He paused but got no response. "That means steroids, Bake."

"I've always been a fast healer," Ramsey said.

"You're looking very pumped up, too. What's your weight gain since last season?"

"My speed's up, too, Doc. I've been working at it."

The doctor looked undecided. "Bake, you know what team policy is."

Ramsey turned and looked him in the eye for the first time. "Team policy is to win football games," he said. "That's what I do."

"But . . ."

"And I take a drug test every week, just like everybody else on the team, right?"

The doctor just looked at him.

"Now, I'm planning to play in another three weeks," Ramsey said, "and I don't think the team's management would like it much if something got in the way of that. You catch my drift?"

The doctor sighed and stood up. "Yeah, Bake. Just go easy on the knee; light running is okay, if the swelling doesn't come back." He picked up his bag and turned for the door. "And I don't think it will. I'll tell Coach I expect you to be ready for the Dolphins game, barring complications."

"Well, don't tell anybody else," Ramsey said. "He wants to spring me on the Dolphins."

"Sure," the doctor said at the door. He went out and closed it behind him.

Davis came back to where Ramsey was sitting. "What did he say?"

Ramsey walked to a bench and began loading

weights onto the machine. "Ready for the Dolphins," he said, "barring complications. You make sure there are no complications. Just keep getting me what I need." He stretched out and began to do bench presses. From outside came the unintelligible blare of the coach's bullhorn.

"I'm having a little problem with supply," Davis said tentatively. "The feds busted a plant in Mexico last week, and there's talk of a drought."

"Manny," Ramsey said, puffing against the weight, "you're a pretty good backfield coach. You'll never make head coach on an NFL team, you don't pull that kind of weight. But you might—just might— handle offensive coordinator."

"That's all I want, Bake. You know Harley's retiring at the end of the season."

"Yeah, and you might be up for it. But, Manny, unless I have an uninterrupted supply of what I need for the rest of the season, you're not even going to keep the job you've got. I'll see to that."

"Bake, you don't have to talk to me that way. You know damn well I'll do my best."

"I just hope your best is good enough, Manny," Ramsey said, racking the weights and sitting up. "If the Bobcats drop you, you wouldn't even get a decent job in college ball. I'd hate to see you coaching at some jerkwater high school next season."

Davis looked at him, puzzled. "Bake, I probably know as much about sports medicine as most doctors, and I would have said that knee would be ready in two weeks, not three."

Ramsey looked at him and smiled. "I've got something else to do in two weeks," he said. "In the meantime, you just keep peeing into those little jars for me."

CHAPTER

27

*L*iz came back to the cottage in the late afternoon from a good day's work to find Keir sitting on the deck with a drink. He had slept with her most nights lately, but not the night before. She had missed him more than she had meant to, and not just the sex. There was an attachment growing here, and she both wanted and resisted it.

"Home is the hunter, home from the hill . . . ," he said.

"And the photographer, home from the shoot," she replied, grabbing his drink and taking a sip. "Where were you last night?"

He smiled slightly. "Riding on the wind, soaring like the hawk."

"You're so fucking poetic when you don't want

213

to give a straight answer to a question," she said, turning his face up and kissing him.

"Straight answers are boring, don't you think?"

"Not always," she said, flopping down on the lounge with him, pulling his arm around her shoulders. She stole another swig from his drink.

"Hey, do you think I'm made of bourbon?"

"I think you're made of snakes and snails and puppy dogs' tails, at very best."

"That's the nicest thing anybody's said to me all day," he said, kissing the top of her head.

"Nobody ever says anything to you but me, because you don't see anybody else but me," she said. "Not that I mind, much."

"Wrong. I see Buck Moses; I see Grandpapa; I see Germaine."

"Not much, you don't. I don't know about Buck, but you don't see much of your grandfather or your sister."

"More than you know."

"Why don't we see some people tonight?" she asked. "I'm going to dinner at the inn; want to join me?"

"Thanks, but no," he said, with a touch of regret in his voice.

"Why not?" she asked. Now and then she felt like goading him about Hamish. He must know his brother was at the inn; he seemed to know everything that happened on the island.

"What you call the inn I still think of as Greyfield House. Grandpapa's old-maid sister, Jenny, lived there when I was a kid; my great-grandfather built it for her. I loved her, and I loved the house; I don't like it with strangers sleeping and eating there."

Well, she thought, that's the most direct answer I've ever had from him. She got up. "I'm into a shower and out of here," she said.

"I like you a little sweaty," he said, catching her hand. "Can I interest you in a roll in the hay?"

"What a charmer!" she shouted. "A real smoothy! A roll in the hay, yet!" She headed for the shower, stripping off clothes as she went.

When she came out, he was standing at the bathroom sink, rubbing the fog off the mirror with his hand. He was wearing only some old khaki shorts, and she admired his lean, brown body for a moment as she toweled dry.

"Your hair's getting longer," he said, turning to look at her. "It doesn't stick up on top anymore."

"And about time, too," she said, snapping at his bare legs with her wet towel.

"Ow!" he yelled. "You're vicious with that thing!"

"A woman scorned," she called over her shoulder as she went into the bedroom.

"I didn't scorn you; I invited you to bed."

"You scorned my dinner invitation," she said, picking a cotton sheath from her closet and pulling it over her head. She deliberately did not put on underwear; she knew he liked that. She grabbed a brush and ran it through her hair. A quick look in the mirror told her that her sunburn would do for makeup. She slipped into some low shoes and turned her back to him. "Zip me up?" She knew that the open dress came exactly down to the crack of her ass.

"I'm better at unzipping these things," he said.

"Well," she said, grabbing her car keys, "stick around and you might get to unzip it when I get back."

"Maybe," he said.

"See you later, then," she called, heading for the back door. Her voice was gayer than she felt. Somehow, she had thought she might goad him into coming to the inn with her, but she should have known better. She had been anxious to get out of the house before he pulled her into bed; she would have given in, she knew, and she wanted to exert a little control. At least she would have time for a drink in the bar before dinner.

She parked in front of the inn and saw young Aldred Drummond sitting in a crook of the giant live oak on the broad lawn. The tree must be two hundred years old, she thought. Its limbs touched the ground in places—perfect for a small boy to climb. "Good evening," she called out.

"Hello, Miss, uh . . ."

"I'm Liz," she said, walking over. "You having a good time on the island with your father?"

"Yep," he said. Apparently a man of few words.

"You been to the beach yet?"

"Nope."

"Well, I live up at Stafford Beach Cottage. When you go to the beach, why don't you get your dad to bring you to see me?"

"My dad's going to Jacksonville tomorrow, and I can't go with him," he said.

"Maybe your mother can bring you to Stafford."

"Mom's leaving tomorrow. That's why Dad's going to Jacksonville. He's taking her to the airport. I'm staying with Germaine."

"Well, if I can arrange it, would you like to come up to Stafford for lunch tomorrow? You can go in the water, and you can play in the dunes, too."

He looked doubtful.

"Maybe I'll even let you drive my Jeep," she said.

"Oh, boy, yes!" he practically shouted. "Will you ask my mom?"

"Sure, I will."

He scrambled down from the tree. "I'd better go now. I've got to have my supper with Ron in the staff room."

"Okay, I'll see you later."

He ran up the steps and into the house; she followed more slowly. The front porch was deserted, and when she entered the house, so was the main floor. She had a look in the living room and library, then turned into the little self-service bar. She was pouring herself a Wild Turkey when a familiar man entered.

"Evening," he said, "drinking alone?"

"Not anymore," she replied. "What's your pleasure?"

"Can you make a decent martini?"

"Just watch me." She grabbed the gin and vermouth and went to work. It took her a minute to place the man. "How's your book coming, the one on twins?"

•

"Pretty good," he replied. "We're looking forward to a publication next fall. I'm sorry, I didn't get your name last time we were at the inn. You're here for some photographs, I believe?"

"That's right. I'm Liz Barwick."

"Douglas Hamilton. Call me Ham. This is our third time down here this year; we love it."

"So do I." She handed him his drink. "How's that?"

He sipped it and stared at the ceiling. "Classic. How's your work coming?"

"I'm getting a lot of beautiful stuff. It's easy on Cumberland; all you have to do is point the camera."

"Good." He sipped his drink, and they both seemed at a loss for words.

"Doctor . . . ah, Ham?"

"Mmmm?"

"Can I engage you in a little shoptalk for a moment?"

"Sure," he said, flopping down on a sofa. "Let me guess. You have this friend and she has this problem."

"Nothing like that. Just a hypothetical question about twins."

"Shoot."

"These twins—"

"Male or female?"

"Male."

"Identical?"

"Perfectly. They're fortyish. They had the sort of ultraclose relationship as boys that you described as typical of identical twins the last time we met."

"I remember. The closest of all human relation-ships."

"Until they were eighteen."

"What happened when they were eighteen?"

"Nobody knows. Or nobody who'll say, at any rate."

"They grew apart?"

"No, one day they just stopped speaking to each other."

"For how long?"

"Until the present moment."

The doctor's face registered surprise. "Extremely unusual. I remember one case of women twins who fought over a man. They were both in love with him, and when one of them announced their engagement, her twin wouldn't speak to her again."

"For how long?"

"For a couple of years, until the couple were di-vorced. When the twin with the man had to choose between her husband and her sister, she eventually chose her sister." He sipped his martini. "These hypo-thetical twins of yours, what do they have to say about each other? Haven't they ever given anyone who knows them a clue to what breached their rela-tionship?"

"No. What's more, neither will so much as ac-knowledge the other's existence."

The doctor's face collapsed in astonishment. "That's very disturbing," he managed to say.

Liz was worried by his reaction. "Why disturb-ing?"

He didn't answer at first. "Well," he said finally.

"For identical twins who have grown up ultraclose, as you put it, not speaking to each other for twenty years would put an unbearable emotional strain on both of them. I've known of cases where identical twins were forcibly separated from each other, and the effects on both were, in each case, terrible—worse, perhaps than losing a twin to death, because each knew that the other was alive somewhere, and they couldn't reach each other. There was a case in World War II where one twin ended up in a concentration camp, and the other escaped. The twin in prison died of the effects of the camp, and the other—well, pined to death. Wouldn't eat, because he knew his brother was in that camp."

Liz didn't speak.

"With your hypothetical twins—it's difficult even to imagine a trauma that would cause them not to speak for so long a time. But that's not the really disturbing part. The fact that neither will even acknowledge the existence of the other is terrifying, psychiatrically. What you're talking about is a kind of voluntary schizophrenia."

"I see," Liz said, for lack of anything else to say.

"Liz, if your twins were real, and not hypothetical, then I have to tell you that I believe they would both be very seriously disturbed human beings."

There was the sound of footsteps on the stairs outside the door, and, a moment later, Hannah Drummond walked in. "Good evening, Liz," she said brightly. "Are you tending bar?"

"Sure," Liz managed to say.

"Then I'll have a Scotch on the rocks, please."

Two couples entered the room, talking cheerfully. Dr. Hamilton got up and came to the bar.

"I'll have another martini, as long as you're at it," he said. He produced a card from his pocket. "We're leaving in the morning," he said quietly, "but if you ever want to talk further about this, please call me."

Liz poured the Scotch and mixed the martini, but, under the countertop, her hands were trembling.

"There she is," a voice said.

Liz looked up to see Germaine leading an elderly man into the bar.

"Liz, I want you to meet Dr. Blaylock. Doctor, this is Liz Barwick, the lady I was telling you about."

"I'm very pleased to meet you," the man said in a courtly manner.

"Liz, Dr. Blaylock is the head of the Anthropology Department at the University of Georgia. He's brought a group of students down to move the family graveyard."

"Yes, Hamish told me about it. Angus wants to get it onto higher ground, doesn't he?"

"Afraid of the crabs getting his bones, I think," Germaine replied. "I wonder if you'd do us all a favor and photograph the place before they move the graves? No matter how perfect a job they do, it's never going to look quite the same again, and I'd like to remember it the way it is now."

"Sure, I'll be glad to," Liz said.

"I'm afraid we'll have to get you up early," Dr. Blaylock said. "We plan to get an early start tomorrow morning."

"Suits me," Liz said. "I'm an early riser. You've got one empty grave down there, you know."

"Empty?"

"Better tell him about Light-Horse Harry Lee," Liz said to Germaine. She looked up to see Hamish enter. He came around the bar next to Liz and made himself a drink while Germaine introduced him to Dr. Blaylock and explained to the anthropologist about the Lee grave.

"That looks like a lot of work for one man," Hamish said to the man.

"Oh, I've got half a dozen students who'll do the dogwork," Blaylock said. "My job is just to direct them and to restrain their enthusiasm for their work. They have to be taught to go slowly, given the age of some of the graves, or they'll just make a mess of it."

"Are your crew staying in the inn?" Liz asked. She hadn't seen any students.

"No, they're camped out with our equipment, down near the cemetery." He sipped his drink and laughed. "Heaven only knows what they're up to."

Hamish laughed. "The same thing we were all up to at that age, I expect."

"Oh, God," the professor said.

At dinner, Liz watched Hamish as he entertained Dr. Blaylock with stories of the island. She couldn't find anything disturbed about him, nor about Keir, come to that, though he was less conventional than most people. She glanced across the room at Dr. Hamilton. He had just been issuing opinions off the top of his head; he didn't know the Drummond twins, and he was in no position to pass judgment on them. She began to relax and enjoy the evening.

She turned and spoke to Hannah Drummond, who was sitting next to her. "I invited Aldred to come up to Stafford Beach Cottage tomorrow," she said. "Would you mind if he came?"

"Not at all," Hannah said. "I'm leaving tomorrow, and Hamish is taking me to the airport. I'm sure Germaine would be happy to have him off her hands."

"I've got to take some photographs down at the cemetery tomorrow morning. How about if I pick him up on the way back? Say, about nine?"

"Perfect. We'll be leaving for the airport about then."

"Tell him to bring his swimsuit."

When Liz got home, pleasantly tired and wanting Keir, the house was empty. Maybe he had felt snubbed when she had declined to make love to him, but she didn't care much. If he wanted to be antisocial, that was his problem. She had no trouble falling asleep. But when she woke in the night, and he wasn't there, it hurt.

CHAPTER

28

*L*iz loaded the Hassel-
blad equipment into the Jeep and drove south toward
Dungeness. It was seven o'clock, and she hoped that
was early enough to get her photographs of the cemetery done before the professor and his crew of students went to work.

She parked near the equipment sheds, and as she
began to unload her gear, Angus Drummond drove up
in his jeep, with Dr. Blaylock, the anthropologist, in
the passenger seat.

"Good morning," she said to both men.

"Morning," Angus replied, but he seemed preoc-
cupied. Dr. Blaylock didn't speak at all.

She fell in beside Angus as they walked down the

path toward the cemetery. "I'm going to photograph everything before they begin work," she said.

"A good idea," Angus replied. "I'd like to have some pictures of the place, if you'll make some copies for me."

"Of course." They walked along quietly for a moment. "Is something wrong?" she asked finally, unable to contain her curiosity.

"Problems," Angus replied. He seemed disinclined to say more.

They arrived at the little cemetery to find a group of half a dozen young people gathered in a knot, talking worriedly.

"Good morning," Angus said to no one in particular. "Now, I'd be grateful if you'd tell me exactly what happened here last night."

No one spoke for a moment, then a tall boy said, "It started in the middle of the night—three, four o'clock, I'm not sure just when."

"What started?" Angus asked. "Speak up, young fellow, and let's get to the bottom of this."

"We're camped over there," he said, pointing. The bright orange of a tent could be seen through the trees twenty yards away. "This noise started."

"What sort of noise?" Angus asked. He was becoming impatient.

"All sorts," a girl said. "There was some rustling in the woods, then some animal noises. At least I think they were animal noises."

"They sounded human to me," another girl said.

"They sounded *inhuman* to me," a boy piped up.

•
226

"Was that it?" Angus demanded. "Just noises?"

"They seemed to be all around us," the tall boy said. "I had the feeling that, any second, something was going to come at us. By this time, we were all awake. The noises were pretty loud."

"Then what happened?" Angus asked.

"Then we got out of here," the boy replied. "We ran like hell, and somehow, we ended up on the beach. We walked to the inn from there."

"They woke me up about six," Dr. Blaylock said. "I couldn't make any sense of it. The boy at the inn drove us down here, then I came to get you."

"Was anything disturbed?" Angus asked.

"Nothing," the tall boy replied, "except Dr. Blaylock's stuff was gone."

"Something was stolen?" Angus asked the professor.

"Two toolboxes," he replied. "I've been years collecting that equipment."

"What was in the toolboxes?"

"The things I excavate with—trowels, brushes of all sorts, a lot of jars and containers."

"Anything that would be of value to a thief?"

"Not unless he was an archaeologist or an anthropologist. What do you make of all this, Mr. Drummond?"

"I don't know what to make of it; nothing like this has ever happened before. Oh, we've occasionally had some hooligans from the mainland, who'd come over here in a boat and steal something, break a window or two, that sort of thing. Just teenage vandals.

I expect that's who it was. You young people spread out in the woods, here, and let's have a good look around. I expect we'll find your toolboxes."

Somewhat reluctantly, the students did as they were told. Half an hour later, they all gathered at the graveyard again. Nobody had found anything.

"I'll tell you what I think," one of the boys said. "I think something doesn't want us to mess with these graves."

Angus laughed. "You mean you think we've got ghosts around here, son?"

"Well, I don't know, sir, but there was something here last night."

"There was a hooligan or two here last night," Angus said. "Ghosts don't have any use for toolboxes. Besides, no ghost would dare show his face on this island. I'll do the haunting around here, myself, when I'm gone."

"I don't know what to do," the professor said. "Nothing like this has ever happened on a dig before."

"I'll tell you what you do," Angus said. "You go over to Jacksonville today—I'll send you on the inn's boat—and you buy whatever you need to work, and I'll pay for it. Then, tomorrow, you get started."

"I'm not sleeping another night in these woods," one of the girls said, and the others murmured their support.

"All right," Angus said. "If you're scared, then you can all stay at the inn as my guests. Germaine's got a little bunkhouse that construction crews some-times use, and I'll see that it's cleaned up for you."

They looked happier at that news.

"Tonight, you pack up your belongings and the rest of your tools, and I'll send the van for you. Until then, you'll be working in daylight, and the ghosts won't come around. Neither will hooligans, I expect."

"Go on, now," the professor chimed in, "get your gear together."

The students did as they were told, Angus and Dr. Blaylock left, and Liz began setting up. The sun was still low in the sky, and the light was good for bringing the inscriptions on the tombstones into sharp relief. She took shots of each grave, then got wide-angle shots from the four corners of the plot. Satisfied that she had preserved the place for posterity, she packed her gear and loaded it into the Jeep.

It was nearly nine, now, and Liz drove to the inn to pick up Aldred Drummond for his day at the beach. The boy was finishing his breakfast in the kitchen, and there was a pile of luggage at the back door.

"Mom and Dad are going to Jacksonville," Aldred said, pointing at the luggage, "but I'm going with you today."

"That's right," Liz said. "It's just you and me all day."

He leaned close to her. "And I get to drive your Jeep, right?"

"Right," she said. "We won't tell anybody about that."

Hannah Drummond appeared and said her good-byes to her son. "You be good, now, and I'll see you next week."

Hamish Drummond wandered into the kitchen.

"We're off as soon as the van's back," he said, and, as he spoke, the van pulled up to the back door and discharged the students. "You two have a good time today," he said to Liz. "And Aldred, you do as Liz tells you, all right? Don't give her a hard time."

"Yessir," the boy said.

"Let's get going, Aldred," Liz said. "The Jeep awaits us."

Hannah handed her a canvas bag. "Here's his swimsuit and towel and whatever else he wanted to take with him."

Liz said her good-byes. "I'll have him back at the inn for supper," she said.

She hustled the boy out of the inn and into the Jeep. When they had cleared the dunes, she stopped and pulled him into her lap. "Okay, Aldred, now you're the driver. Here's the gear stick."

"I know, I know, you put it in drive," the boy said, and she did it for him.

"Now, I'll work the pedals, and you steer."

They meandered down the beach, the boy squealing with delight.

"Faster, faster!" he said.

Liz pressed the accelerator, and the Jeep moved down the wide beach at forty miles an hour, a delirious child at the wheel, and Liz ready to grab it if he strayed too far from the center.

Late in the afternoon, sunburned and sand encrusted, the two made their way on foot from the beach through the dunes toward Stafford Beach Cottage, Aldred running madly ahead. Where, Liz wondered, does he get the energy? She was exhausted, and he hardly seemed tired at all.

"Can I have a Coke?" Aldred called back to her.

"Sure, run on ahead. The house is unlocked, and the Cokes are in the fridge."

He sprinted down the last dune and up the steps to the deck. She paused at the top of the dune to catch her breath and watched as he ran through the living room toward the kitchen. Then he stopped. She wondered what could keep him from a cold soft drink. He stood in the door for a long moment, then he turned and walked slowly back through the living room and waited for her on the deck.

"What's wrong?" she called to him as she trudged up the steps. "Aren't you thirsty?"

He looked confused. "Liz," he said, "there's somebody in the kitchen."

Now she understood his confusion. She took a deep breath. "Well, let's go and see who it is," she said, wondering how she was going to explain this to him.

Hand in hand, they walked through the living room and stood in the kitchen door. There was a half-empty bottle of beer on the kitchen table, but no one was there. Liz sighed.

"Liz," the boy said, "I . . . I thought that was my dad, but it wasn't, was it?"

"No," she said, "it wasn't." She led him back into the living room. "Sit down for a minute," she said, "and I'll try and explain this to you. But we're going to have to keep it strictly between you and me, all right?"

"All right," he said, climbing onto the sofa beside her.

And so she tried to explain to Aldred Drummond about his father and his uncle. The boy took it amazingly well, she thought.

As the light was failing Liz heard a car stop outside the cottage. Gently, she moved the sleeping Aldred's head from her lap, tucked a cushion under it, and started for the door. She met Hamish Drummond there before he could knock.

"Hi," he said. "I thought I'd come and take him back to the inn; save you the trip."

"Come on in," she whispered, pointing at Aldred. "He's all tuckered out."

"You haven't spent much time around kids, have you?" He laughed. "We'd have to try hard to wake him, now."

"In that case, can I offer you a drink?"

"Sure, thanks; got any bourbon?"

She fixed them both one and they went out onto the deck. "I didn't hear your plane come in," she said. "I usually hear what comes and goes from the airstrip."

"I had some shopping to do on the mainland, so I took the *Aldred Drummond* back this afternoon." He sipped his drink. "You've settled in here very well," he said. "Looks like you've always lived here."

"I'm a nest builder," she said. "I could make a jail cell seem like home in fifteen minutes."

"That's a God-given talent; I could live in a suite at the Connaught Hotel for a year, and it would look like a jail cell."

Liz remembered how Keir had made a home in the attic of Plum Orchard. Maybe there were some differences between the Drummond twins after all.

"What's your situation here?" he asked.

"My situation?"

"Well, Eleanor Ferguson had a lifetime lease on this cottage, and, after what happened to Ray and Eleanor, I guess the lease has expired."

"Oh." That had never occurred to her. "And I may be an unwelcome guest, you mean?"

He smiled. "I doubt it. Grandpapa seems to like you; if he'd wanted you out he'd have been around here huffing and puffing before Ray and Eleanor were in the ground."

"You think I should speak to him about it?"

"No, let it ride. He likes what you're doing here—the book." He grinned. "And apart from the book, well, he's behaving like a teenager about you."

"I'm flattered," she said, though she couldn't quite imagine Angus behaving like a teenager.

Hamish frowned. "If he should die suddenly, though—and God knows he could at any moment, at his age . . ."

"Who would I talk to then?"

"It could get sticky, if Grandpapa dies without a will."

"Sticky? Would you and Germaine want me out?"

"No, certainly not, please don't misunderstand. It's Jimmy Weathers."

"I'm sorry, I don't understand."

"If Grandpapa dies intestate, Jimmy will be an heir; he's a grandchild, just like Germaine and me."

"I've never understood about that; just whose son is Jimmy?"

"My father had a younger sister, who died some years ago. Jimmy is her son. The way old Aldred Drummond set up the estate originally, if the inheritor—that's Grandpapa, at the moment—dies intestate, his children inherit. If the children are dead, as in this case, then the estate is divided among the grandchildren. There are no guidelines as to how the estate would be divided, so Jimmy could make a great deal of trouble. He wants to develop the island, so naturally, he'd want the beachfront property. Germaine wants the inn, and I want Plum Orchard, so I'm not sure we could keep the best of the beach out of Jimmy's hands. That would mean this cottage, of course; everything would have to be negotiated."

"Perhaps your grandfather will make a will and save you all a lot of grief."

Hamish shook his head. "I'd like to think that, but every time Germaine or I mention it, he gets angry. We've brought it up so often, that it would be just like him to neglect to do it, just to spite us."

Liz was tempted to mention Angus's new will, but again, she felt he would tell Hamish and Germaine when he wanted them to know. "He doesn't strike me as a spiteful man," she said.

"Willful, let's say. He never liked anyone to try to persuade him to do something."

"He loves you both. I think he'll do the right thing," she said.

"I think he will, too," Hamish said, "but I worry about it."

Liz said nothing more. The family's problems fascinated her, but she felt she should keep quiet.

"Well," he said, downing the remains of his drink, "I'd better get that boy home and get some supper into him."

They went back into the living room, and Hamish picked up Aldred gently and laid his head on a shoulder.

Liz got Aldred's bag and walked them out to the car. "I've loved having him," she said.

"He's loved it, too." Hamish smiled. "I can tell by how unconscious he is."

"Can he come back again?"

"Well, he'll be off home soon; I'd like to spend what time he has left with him."

"Sure, I understand. When he wakes up, tell him I enjoyed myself as much as he did."

"I will. Thanks for the drink." Hamish laid the boy on the front seat, got into the car, and started it. "Don't worry about the cottage," he said. "If it comes up, I'll see what I can do."

"Thank you," she said.

With a wave, he turned and drove toward Grey-field.

Liz was back in the house before she remembered

what Hamish had said: that if Angus Drummond's children were all dead, then the grandchildren would inherit. But Angus Drummond's children were not all dead. James Moses was alive.

CHAPTER

29

Sergeant Lee Williams stood in the staff cafeteria at Piedmont Hospital and looked for Mary Alice Taylor. He found her alone at a table, eating what looked like a diet meal.

"Hi, Mary Alice," he said, "Remember me? Lee Williams?"

"Oh, sure. Hi, Lee," she said, brightening. "Have a seat. What brings you to Piedmont? Visiting a friend?"

"No," he said, settling in with his cup of coffee. "Actually, I came to see you."

"Well, that's nice," she said, looking slightly confused. "How's Martin?"

"He's just great. It's hard to get him to take off Bake's jersey, even if it does come to his shinbones."

"I'm glad he came down and met Bake. Bake loves kids."

"Well, he was certainly nice to Martin."

"What brings you to see me?" Mary Alice asked. "And how on earth did you find me?"

"Well, to tell you the truth, Mary Alice, I came to see you before we met, but you weren't here that day. It was just a coincidence that we met at the game."

She cocked her head. "What sort of work do you do, Lee?"

"I'm a police officer," he replied quietly.

She took in a little breath and paused before she spoke. "I see, and why did you come looking for me?"

"I wanted to talk with you about Bake Ramsey. This was before I knew that you and he had been . . . seeing each other. As far as I knew, he was just a patient here at the time."

"You came to see me when Bake was having his knee surgery?"

"After that. But I wanted to talk with you about the night before he had the surgery. Do you remember that night?"

She flushed just slightly.

"Was that when you met Bake?"

"Yes. What is this about, really?"

"Mary Alice, can we talk in confidence? It's important that you don't tell anyone else about our conversation."

She hesitated. She knew that he meant Ramsey, but she was curious. "I guess so," she said finally.

"You were on duty all that night, weren't you?"

"Eight till eight. I worked an extra half-shift for a friend."

"How many times did you see Bake during that night?"

"At least once an hour," she said. "It's procedure to check frequently on patients."

"Did anything happen that night that could have caused you to miss a round, miss checking on Bake, I mean?"

She was cautious, now. "No, I don't think so."

"You made a regular check on him at least every hour all night?"

"That's the procedure."

I'm not getting anywhere, he thought. She knew something that he wanted to know, and she wasn't going to tell him. He decided to try shaking her up a little. "Mary Alice, did you have sexual intercourse with Bake Ramsey that night?"

She was rattled, but she held on. "I don't see what a question like that could possibly have to do with the police," she said. She hadn't denied it, and that was enough for him.

"After you and Bake made love, did you come back into his room again?"

She dug in. "I think I've already answered that question, and I think it's time you told me what this is all about," she said. She was recovering her composure. She wouldn't budge now, he knew.

He tried another tack. "Mary Alice, would you say that Bake Ramsey has a violent nature?"

She laughed. "He's a pro football player, isn't he?"

"Has he ever been violent with you?"

"Why do you ask?"

"Because I think if he hasn't already, he will."

She sat, frozen, staring at him, unsure whether he was friend or foe.

"I think he's already hit you on at least one occasion," Williams said. "In fact, the bruise hasn't entirely gone yet."

Her hand went involuntarily to her face, but she said nothing.

He pulled back. He was getting nowhere, now, and he didn't want to alienate her. "Listen, I apologize for what must seem to be some very rude questions. It's no fun for me to ask these things, but I'm worried about Bake."

"Just what is it you think he's done?"

"I'm not positive he's done anything, but I have some reason to believe that he has been violent with women in the past."

She didn't speak but looked away.

He pushed back from the table. "May I give you some advice? This is personal, not business."

"If you like."

"I know that if I tell you that you shouldn't see Bake anymore, you're not likely to listen to me. I'm a stranger, after all. But I think you want to be very careful not to make Bake mad. I don't have to tell you what a powerful man he is, and he—well, he may not have been himself recently." He took a card from his pocket and put it on the table. "Here are my numbers—home, office, and car. If you remember anything else about the night before Bake's surgery, or, if you just feel you need some help or advice, then please don't hesitate to call me. I mean that."

She picked up the card and tucked it into a pocket of her uniform. "Thank you," she said.

He gave her a little wave and left the cafeteria. She might call, he thought; she just might. Especially if Ramsey roughs her up again. Especially if he makes *her* mad.

Williams rapped on the glass door of his captain's office. Captain Ed Haynes waved him in.

"How's it going, Lee?" Haynes asked, pointing to a chair.

"I've had it worse, Ed," Williams said, sitting down. Ed Haynes had been his partner twelve years before, for the first four months after he'd made detective, so they were on informal terms. "I got something sticky I wanted to talk to you about."

"Sticky?"

"Well, iffy."

"You mean you've got a hunch and no evidence."

Williams laughed. "You're right, Cap."

"You guys always forget that I used to do your job. Tell me about it. Is it the Ferguson case?"

"Partly; it's more complicated than that. A little while back I got a call from a woman who says she thinks her ex-husband killed both the Fergusons and Al Schaefer."

"Schaefer was an accidental drowning in LA," Hayes said.

"Right; in the swimming pool at the Beverly Hills Hotel. But it may not have been accidental." Williams crossed his legs. "I thought what she had to say sounded pretty wild, but I looked into it. Turns out her ex was in LA the night Schaefer was murdered; he was staying at another hotel five minutes away. What's more, he was checked into Piedmont Hospital the night of the Ferguson killings, and that's only a few minutes from their house, even on foot."

"Does he have alibis for those two occasions?"

"He's accounted for his whereabouts both nights, but I think there might be holes in his stories, if I can find them."

"Motive?"

"He knew the Fergusons through his ex-wife, says he got along fine with them. I haven't been able to turn up anything to the contrary, except from the ex-wife, who says he hates her so much he might have killed them just because they're her friends."

"Doesn't sound good. What about a motive for Schaefer?"

"That's a little better. Schaefer represented his ex-wife in the divorce. Every divorced man hates his ex-wife's lawyer."

Haynes grinned. "I can vouch for that. Schaefer could be easy to hate, too, if he was the opposition."

"Also, if the ex-wife's story is true, the guy has a history of violence. She says he put her in the hospital, nearly killed her."

"That would look good in court, but you gotta make a case, first." Haynes put his feet up on the desk. "Who's the guy?"

"You don't want to know."

Haynes's eyebrows went up. "Oh, yes I do."

"Bake Ramsey."

"Oh, shit. I didn't want to know that."

"Don't say I didn't tell you."

"You talked to anybody else about this? I mean *anybody?*"

"No."

"Then for Christ's sake, don't! Now, tell me what you want; I know you want something I'm not going to want to give you."

"I want to go to LA. I've had some help from a buddy out there, but I can't ask him for much more. I need to punch through Ramsey's alibi."

"What about the alibi for the Ferguson killings? Why don't you punch through that instead?"

"I've already tried. My witness is stonewalling, but I hope she might come around later. In the meantime, Ramsey's a time bomb."

"A time bomb? You think he's going to kill somebody else?"

"The ex-wife says he's zonked out on steroids. I've done a little reading on the effects, and one of them is markedly increased aggression. To tell you the truth—and this is another hunch, of course—I think he might be capable of killing anybody who annoys him." He tossed a newspaper clipping onto the desk.

Haynes read it all the way through, nodding. "The ex-wife could be right, I guess. Is she in any danger?"

"I don't think so; he doesn't know where she is."

"Where is she?"

Williams shook his head ruefully. "I don't know, either. She wouldn't tell me, and our new telephone equipment wouldn't give us her number when she was on the line. The tech people think she was talking from a car phone, and I can't find a current address for her in Atlanta."

"Okay," Haynes said, taking his feet down and putting his elbows on his desk, "let's sum up. You think you've got two murders, two thousand miles apart, one of which belongs to another police department; your initial break is from a very possibly disgruntled ex-wife; you've got a practically nonexistent motive in the Ferguson case, and a so-so motive in the Schaefer case; you've got geographic opportunity in both cases, but your suspect has alibis for both; you've got no witnesses or physical evidence in either case; and your suspect is one of the most famous men in Atlanta, and the media would go bonkers if even a whiff of this reaches them. Does that about cover it?"

"Pretty much."

Haynes began to look uncomfortable. "Lee, I didn't want to bring this up, but I think it bears on what we're talking about."

"Yeah?"

"On the child murders case awhile back, you made some bad guesses, didn't you?"

Williams's ears burned. It was patently true that he had guessed wrong; a man had been convicted. But it was the first time his captain had brought it up. "I guess you could say that," he replied finally.

"You pushed too hard on your hunches when everybody else knew we had our man. I'll tell you the truth, Lee, that's why you don't have a partner at the

moment. The attitude around here—I think it's unjus-
tified—but the attitude is that nobody wants to be
made to look bad by a guy who depends too much on
hunches. You understand that, don't you?"

"Yeah, Cap, I understand it." It killed him to
admit it, though.

"And now you want to go to LA to poke around.
I expect you know that would involve a fax from me
to the LA chief of detectives, letting him know I've
got a man on his turf, and, of course, a copy of that
would have to go to our own beloved chief, one of
whose personal bugaboos is unnecessary travel during
investigations."

"I hadn't thought that far ahead."

"Well, I have to." Haynes stared at the ceiling.
"Looking at it as a detective, which I no longer am, of
course, I'd say you've got a pretty good hunch."

Williams leaned forward. "Thank you, Ed."

"Then again, looking at it as the commander of
the homicide squad, which I currently am, and which
I would like to stay, I'd say I want something more
from you."

"Such as?"

"A single piece of evidence; a collapsed alibi; another murder of somebody else Ramsey knows, who
was breathing the same air at the time of expiration."

"And what if he does kill somebody else, Cap?
How're you going to feel then, after what I've told
you?"

Haynes stood up, walked to the door, and opened
it. "You haven't told me a thing, Lee. This was just an

informal chat about a hypothetical case. Have a nice day."

Williams got up and walked out of the office.

"Lee?"

Williams stopped and turned.

"If there's room on some of your plastic for an airline ticket, and you want to take a couple of vacation days on the West Coast, well, who's to stop you? And then, if you can get a clean collar out of your little vacation, I might see my way clear to reimburse you out of discretionary funds."

Williams grinned from ear to ear. Now he had a chance—a slim one, maybe, but a chance—to pull himself out of this hole with his colleagues. He needed one heavy bust, and this could be it.

CHAPTER

30

*L*iz walked down the path toward the graveyard, and, as she approached, the murmur of voices reached her through the trees. There was the scrape of a tool on earth. The disinterment had begun.

She had expected to see somebody knee deep in a grave, shoveling for all he was worth—a daylight version of a scene from some old horror movie. Instead, she found Dr. Blaylock and his students on their knees, scraping at the earth with small tools and their hands. Blaylock looked up, saw her approaching, and rose to meet her.

"I didn't mean to disturb you, Doctor," she said. "I just wanted to watch for a bit."

"You're not disturbing me, Miss Barwick," he said. "In fact, I wanted to speak with you."

"Oh?"

"Yes, I understand that there's a black man on the island who's more than a hundred years old."

"That's right; his name is Buck Moses."

"It occurs to me that it might be useful to speak with him. An old retainer like that who's probably attended a lot of family burials—maybe even dug a few graves—might tell us something about the materials the coffins were made of."

"Perhaps he might," she agreed.

"We don't have a vehicle here, and I wonder if I might intrude on your good nature to the extent of asking you to see Mr. Moses and, perhaps, bring him here to talk to me."

"I'll be happy to, Dr. Blaylock," she said. "I'll drive up to the old slave settlement, but I should tell you that Buck could be just about anywhere on the island. He has an old pickup truck, and he gets around."

"Well, perhaps you could leave him a note."

"I'm not even sure he reads. Let's leave it this way: I'll go up there now, and if I'm not back in an hour, just assume I didn't find him. He'll turn up eventually, though."

"That's very kind of you."

Liz indicated the digging. "You're making delicate work of this, I see."

"Oh, we're approaching this as an archaeological dig—partly because of the site's age, and partly so my students can have the experience. Mr. Drummond was interested in having it done that way, too. If he had simply wanted the graves moved, a few careful men with shovels could have done the job. This graveyard goes back to the eighteenth century, at least; Mr. Drummond tells me the site was an old Indian burying ground before that, so there's no telling what we'll turn up." He frowned. "We'd be moving a bit faster if my toolboxes hadn't disappeared the other night."

"Dr. Blaylock," a girl called out.

Liz and the doctor turned to see one of the students holding up a broken clay pipe.

"You see what I mean?" The doctor smiled. "That will make their day." He returned to the digging.

Liz got back into her Jeep and drove up the north-south road that bisected the island. She took the fork for the slave settlement, and, shortly, pulled up before the church and stopped. "Buck?" she called out. "Buck Moses?"

She was greeted with silence. She walked among the old frame cottages, peering into a window here and there. All were empty but Buck's, which he shared with his grandson. She opened the front door of the church and stepped in. It was a tiny building, with a few benches and a rudely constructed pulpit. It could never have held more than twenty people, even if most of them stood.

Did Buck Moses read? There was no way of knowing, but she decided to leave a note anyway. She found a pad and pencil in the Jeep, wrote down her message, and walked to Buck's little house. She was looking for a way to wedge the note in the door, when she leaned on it and it swung open. She put her head inside. "Buck?" The cabin was neatly kept, with a wood stove and an old settee. In back there was a bedroom.

As Liz was about to close the door, her eye fell on two objects resting near the stove. On the floor, partly behind a stack of wood, were two large, gray, metal toolboxes.

She stepped back and closed the door, and, as she did, James Moses rode slowly into the clearing on a large horse. He threw a leg over the saddle and slid down.

"Hey, Miz Elizabeth," he said, smiling handsomely. "You come to see us?"

"I came to see your grandfather," Liz said, holding up the paper. "Will you give him a note for me?"

"Sure, I will."

"Dr. Blaylock wants to talk to him down at the Drummond family cemetery at Dungeness, wants to ask him about some of the burials."

James's smile disappeared. "Granddaddy ain't going down there," he said. "He don't hold with messing up that graveyard; he told me so."

"Oh. Well, I said I'd pass on the message, and I have." She turned toward the Jeep, then stopped. "James, did you have anything to do with scaring those college kids down at their campsite the other night?"

James poked at something on the ground with a toe. "Granddaddy says those folks got no right poking 'round that graveyard, says there's spirits going to be mad about it. Maybe it was the spirits."

"Well, Dr. Blaylock has been missing two tool-boxes since that night. There was nothing much of value in them, just things he needs to do his work."

"Yes, ma'am," James said. "I heard about that."

"Do you know anything about it?" she asked gently.

"You'd have to talk to my granddaddy about that," James said, and he didn't seem inclined to say more.

"I see," Liz said.

"Miz Elizabeth," James said slowly, "Grand-daddy says things going to change around here soon; says a big wind coming, going to change everything." He looked back at the ground. "I think he don't want it to change while he's still alive. I think he wants to keep it like it is right now."

"Well, that's understandable," Liz said. "Still, everything changes sooner or later."

"He's worried about it," James said. "I haven't seen him worried about much before, but he's worried about this, keeps talking about it."

"Old people are like that, James," she said. "They don't want things to change. They want them to be the way they've always been. Young people like you welcome change, but as you get older, it doesn't seem so welcome. I think I've come to understand how your grandfather and your . . . Mr. Angus feel about the island, how they want to protect it. But there's not really much they can do about it. They're both very old men, and their time will come soon. You and

Germaine and the twins will have to protect the island, then."

"I guess that's the natural way," James said. Then he looked up at her, worried. "But I don't think natural changes is what Granddaddy's talking about. He thinks something's going to happen here soon, and he don't like it. I'm scared."

Liz was nonplussed. "Well, James, if something happens, we'll just have to do the best we can, and I think that might be pretty good, don't you?"

The boy smiled again, a little. "Yes, ma'am, I think it might."

Liz said good-bye, climbed into the Jeep, and started back toward Stafford Beach Cottage. She cut across the island toward the beach, which took her past Lake Whitney. Slowing to drive across the earthen track that separated the lake from a smaller pond, she looked ahead of her and stopped. A man's hand protruded from the high grass on the lake's shore. She wouldn't have seen it, except for the sunlight reflecting from a gold Rolex watch on the wrist.

She watched the hand to see if it moved. It did not. She got out of the Jeep, and, to keep her courage up, walked quickly toward where the man lay. She could see none of him because of the grass. She stopped, and, taking a deep breath, dug in her heels, took hold of the wrist, and pulled hard, to get him into the road.

To first her surprise, and then her horror, she sat down hard in the roadway. In her lap was a man's arm, brutally severed, well above the elbow.

CHAPTER

31

*L*ee Williams got off the
airplane at LAX in a state of some excitement. He had
not traveled a great deal—New York once, Florida a
few times—and here he was in what he, like many
first-time visitors, thought of as Hollywood.

He quickly discovered that there was nothing
very glamorous about Los Angeles International Airport. It was like airports anywhere, albeit with palm
trees, and it seemed not as big as Atlanta's Hartsfield
International.

While he waited for his bag he checked in with
Avis for the car he had reserved.

"Wait outside on the curb for the bus," the
woman explained; then he asked for and got directions to West Hollywood. Getting a rental car in Hol-

lywood turned out to be a pain in the ass. He waited a considerable time for the bus, then rode some distance to a huge parking lot. Eventually, the bus stopped behind his Chevette. He tossed his bag in the backseat, showed his rental contract to a guard at the gate, and began to find out how big Los Angeles is.

Checking the line drawn on his map, he made his way, gawking, to West Hollywood. He was surprised at how few tall buildings there were and how flat it was until he began to climb into the hills. The suite hotel, Le Parc, was tucked away on a side street, and in a few minutes he was checked into a living room with a kitchenette in one corner, a bedroom, and a bath. This is pretty nice, he thought; roomy and nicely decorated. He called downstairs and found that the night concierge came on at eight.

With the three-hour time change, it was only midafternoon locally, and he became a tourist. On foot, following directions from the deskman at the hotel, he found the Chinese Theatre, which represented to him everything he had loved about the movies all his life. He fitted his feet into the prints of Gary Cooper and James Stewart; he wandered past those of Judy Garland and Clark Gable and Marlene Dietrich; he wallowed in what could never be again. Then, content, he wandered back to the hotel and took a nap.

His wake-up call came at seven-thirty; he showered, shaved, and changed into a blazer and open shirt—he had been told that things are pretty informal in Hollywood—then he went downstairs in search of the night concierge.

The man was tall and vaguely handsome, and Williams wondered if he had once been an actor. He identified himself. "Remember when the Atlanta Bobcats were here to play the Rams a few weeks ago?"

"Sure, a lot of the teams stay here."

"Remember Bake Ramsey?"

"Sure, Bake got hurt that game."

"Bake tells me that he had dinner in his room the night before the game with a girl named Brenda. Remember anything about that?"

"I remember him coming in with her early that evening," the man said, "but I don't remember her leaving." He grinned. "Probably she didn't leave until the next morning, when I had gone off duty."

"And they had dinner in the room?"

"You'll have to check with the room-service captain on that."

"One more thing: when I checked in they parked my car downstairs in the garage and gave me a plastic card to get in and out with. Does every guest with a car have that same arrangement?"

"Yes, everybody."

"So, in order to get his car out of the garage, Ramsey could have just gone downstairs and driven away, then come back later without having to see a parking attendant or anybody else?"

"That's right."

"Tell me, did you arrange for Bake to meet Brenda?"

The man shook his head.

"Look, I'm from out of town; I'm not looking to

make trouble for you; I just have to know how it was."

"I didn't set him up. My best guess is a bar on Melrose called the Goal Post. It's a sports bar, and a lot of girls hang out there."

"Thanks," Williams said, slipping the man ten bucks.

He found the room-service captain and the waiter who had served Ramsey and the girl. On Ramsey's instructions, the waiter had not been back for the tray until the following morning; he checked the fire stairs and found that Ramsey could have walked down to the garage without being seen by anybody, and that his room key would have let him back into the fire stairs.

Ramsey could have left Le Parc, gone to the Beverly Hills Hotel, and returned, unnoticed. So far, so good.

At nine o'clock the Goal Post was not crowded. Williams took a seat at the end of the bar, near the waiters' station, and ordered a beer. A soccer match was on the TV above the bar.

"That's a lousy game," he said to the bartender.

The bartender shrugged. "It's all that's on. The owner wants sports on the TV and that's all the sports there is tonight."

"Not very crowded, huh?"

"It'll pick up. Nobody much comes in before ten. I don't know where the hell they go this time of night." He moved away to serve another customer. A moment later he was back. "You from out of town?" he asked.

"Atlanta. My first trip here."

"Business?"

"What else?"

"Well, we run a pretty good joint here. Drop in whenever you're in town."

"Thanks, I'll do that."

"You want something to eat?"

"Can I eat at the bar?"

"Sure, anything you want." He handed Williams a menu. "The beef is good."

"I'll have the New York strip, medium, loaded baked potato, any salad dressing you got."

The place was starting to fill up, now, and most of the customers seemed to know the place well.

"You get mostly regulars, do you?"

"Yeah, we're a little off the tourist track. How'd you find us?"

"The concierge at Le Parc."

"Harry? Yeah, I know him. Used to be an actor, once. So did I for that matter."

"Tough line, huh?"

"I make more here in a night than I ever made in a week as an actor."

Williams's steak came, and he ate hungrily. He kept an eye on the bar, and soon there were three single girls bellied up. "Pretty good talent," he said to the bartender.

"Yeah, we get a lot of jocks; they get a lot of girls."

·

"Say, were you working the night before the Rams' game with the Bobcats a few weeks back?"

"Sure, I always work on Saturdays."

"You know Bake Ramsey when you see him?"

"Yeah, Bake's always pussy hunting in here when he's in town."

"You remember who he ended up with that night?"

"Oh, yeah, he picked up Brenda."

"Is Brenda in here a lot?"

"You're a cop, aren't you?"

"You made me, pal."

"I can always tell. Took me a little longer with you, though; guess it's because you're an out-of-towner."

"I guess so. Tell me about Brenda."

"Why don't you get Brenda to do that?"

"Huh?"

The bartender nodded at a blonde half a dozen stools away. "That's Brenda," he said.

She had been there for three-quarters of an hour, Williams realized. "Send Brenda a drink on me," he said. Here came the tricky part. How did Brenda feel about black guys?

Not bad, apparently. She toasted him with her new drink and gave him a little smile. She's nice looking, even if she is hanging out in bars, Williams thought. She wasn't a flashy dresser, didn't look like a bimbo.

The bartender came back. "Funny about you being a cop," he said.

"How's that?"

·

"So's Brenda."

Williams burst out laughing. That was going to save a lot of time and a lot of charm he wasn't sure he had anymore. He got up and walked down the bar to where she sat. "Hi," he said, smiling. "I'm Lee Williams. The bartender tells me you're a cop."

"He tells me you're one, too," she said, pleasantly. "Listen, no offense, and thanks for the drink, but I just spent ten hours in a black-and-white with a cop; I used to be married to a cop; I spend my whole fucking life with cops. That's why I come in here; to meet somebody who's not a cop."

"Oh," Williams said. "Well, this isn't entirely social. I'm on the job."

"You work West Hollywood?" she asked, looking bored. "What division?"

"I work homicide out of Atlanta, Georgia."

"Well, you're a long way from home, Lee. All right, sit down and tell me about it. You on an extradition out here or something?"

"No, Brenda, believe it or not, I came all the way from Atlanta just to find you." He smiled. "And here you are."

"Lee," she said, "you are full of enough shit to be an LA cop, you know that?"

"Brenda, I wouldn't shit a fellow cop. I came out here to find you and talk to you about Bake Ramsey."

She stared at him disbelievingly. "No shit?"

"No shit. Can I sit down?"

"You sure can, Lee. This is the greatest line I ever heard in my life."

He sat down. "It's no line," he said. "Let me

prove it to you. The night before the Rams game with the Bobcats, you came in here and met Bake Ramsey."

"Sammy could have told you that," she said, nodding toward the bartender.

"Then you had dinner with him in his suite at Le Parc the following night."

She looked at him narrowly. "You're a better cop than I thought."

"And later that night—very late, in fact—you and Bake had a drink at the Beverly Hills Hotel."

"You were tailing us, weren't you?" she asked.

"Brenda," he said, "can I buy you another drink at the Polo Lounge?"

"Let's take my car," she said.

She drove a Japanese sports car and drove it well. Shifting down for a corner, she said, "I'm six years on the job. I just passed the exam for detective, and I want homicide so bad I can taste it."

"Well, Brenda, this is your lucky day. Tonight, you're on a homicide case."

She grinned broadly. "No shit?"

They were given a table in the Polo Lounge.

"This is a movie business hot spot," Brenda said. "Look over there."

Williams looked. There were two couples in a booth. One of the men was Charlton Heston.

"Jesus Christ," he said. "And the other guy looks familiar, too."

"I don't know him," she said. "Maybe he's from Atlanta."

"You come here a lot?"

"Whenever I can get somebody to bring me. The headwaiter knows I'm a cop, and he gives me a good table."

"So I'm not only in Hollywood, I'm at a good table in the Polo Lounge."

"You're in Beverly Hills."

"It's all Hollywood to me, kid."

"So, how'd you know I brought Bake Ramsey here?"

"Elementary, my dear Brenda. He had to be here, because he's my suspect. I'll bet he didn't know you were a cop."

"Nope. I always tell them I'm an assistant casting director at Paramount. All jocks want to be in the movies."

Williams laughed. "You're a trip, Brenda. Jocks are your thing, huh?"

"I won't be coy with you, Lee. I like sex. I like jocks. I like sex with jocks. They're always in good shape, and they're a lot safer than your average guy in a bar; they've got reputations to lose. Did you say Bake is your *suspect*?"

"Ramsey left the table for a while when you were here, didn't he?"

"Yeah. I went to the ladies'—that's right out in the hall there. I took my time, and when I came back, he wasn't at the table. I figured he had to go, too; he came back after a few minutes."

"How long for your trip to the john, plus the time he took to return to the table?"

She stared into the middle distance for a moment.

"No less than fifteen, no more than twenty minutes."

"That's time enough."

"Time enough for what?"

Williams took two photographs from his coat pocket. One was of Ramsey; he showed her the other. "Think back to that night. Did you see this man in the Polo Lounge? Or anywhere in the hotel?"

She stared at Al Schaefer. "Yes," she said, "he was sitting right over there, by himself." She pointed to a table near the outside terrace. "And he got up and went out those doors, right before I went to the ladies'."

"Brenda, you've got a cop's memory," Williams said, "and I love you for it. Is there anything special you remember about Bake's behavior that night?"

"You mean here, or later?"

"Either."

She stared away for a moment. "Bake spilled a drink, a glass of water. It was all over his shirtfront when he came back from the men's room, and he was dabbing at it with a handkerchief. That's the only unusual thing I can remember."

"That's just wonderful, Brenda."

"Now tell me what the fuck is going on," she said.

"Well, it's like this, it's the wildest sort of coincidence, but they happen sometimes. You came in here with Bake Ramsey. The guy in the photograph was Albert Schaefer, an Atlanta lawyer who represented Bake's ex-wife in a divorce action. Bake must have hated him, because Schaefer got up and went out—

side—who knows why? And as soon as you left the table, Ramsey followed him, and he drowned Al Schaefer in the hotel swimming pool."

"Christ, I read about that drowning; it was made as accidental. I didn't realize it was the same night."

"Well, Brenda, I've got some really good news for you. I'm going to nail Ramsey for two other murders in Atlanta, and when I'm through with him, he'll be available for extradition to California, and I'm going to see that you get a piece of him. That ought to help you get into homicide."

She beamed at him. "Listen, Lee, you're staying at Le Parc?"

"Yes."

"Why don't we go back to your place?"

Williams smiled at her gratefully. "Sugar, I'd just love it, I really would, but I've got this wife that scares the living shit out of me. She has me believing that if I got in bed with another woman in any hotel in the world, she would be there to kick the door down and kill us both in our sleep. I'd never be able to do it, believe me."

"I don't," she said, patting his cheek, "but I like you for thinking about your wife."

32

The helicopter's blades slowed, and the engine wound down. Before the rotors had stopped, a man of about forty dressed in khaki shirt and trousers and a Stetson hat stepped to the ground.

"Good afternoon, Bob," Germaine said as he approached the front porch of the inn, where she and Liz were waiting. "Why don't you come around back?"

"All right," he said, eyeing the guests who littered the front porch. He waited until they were out of sight of the guests before asking any questions.

"Now, why don't you tell me exactly what happened, Germaine?"

"Bob, this is Liz Barwick; she's living up at Stafford Beach Cottage. Liz, this is Bob Walden, our sheriff."

"Hey," the sheriff said.

"Nice to meet you," Liz replied.

They reached Liz's Jeep.

"Liz had better tell you about it," Germaine said. "She's the one who found it."

Liz explained how she caught sight of her find at Lake Whitney. She went to the rear of the Jeep, popped the tailgate, and pointed at a sheet of green plastic. "That's it."

As the sheriff approached the Jeep, Liz and Germaine involuntarily moved back a step.

"I don't want to see this, do I?" Germaine said.

"Probably not," Liz replied.

Sheriff Walden gingerly unrolled the plastic and looked at the arm. "Jesus Christ," he said softly. "I never saw anything like that before."

"And I never want to see anything like that again," Liz said, turning away.

"Miz Barwick, why did you bring it with you? Why didn't you leave it where you found it and get some help?"

"I thought there was a man attached to it, and I tried to pull him out of the grass," Liz said. "When I realized what had happened, I thought I'd better bring it with me, or it might not be there when I got back with help."

"You sound like you know what happened," the sheriff said. "I'd like to know, too; tell me about it."

"It had to be Goliath," Liz said.

"Goliath?"

Germaine spoke up. "We've got a big gator in a lake on the north part of the island."

The sheriff looked at the arm again. "The way it's mangled above the elbow, it looks like it was torn off. Those are teeth marks, I reckon."

Liz did not look.

"You have any idea who it belonged to?" the sheriff asked.

"I think it's my cousin, Jimmy Weathers," Germaine said. "That's his watch, anyway, or one like his."

"Are you sure it's his arm?"

"Well, I never expected to have to identify him by his arm," Germaine admitted, "But the hair on it is light brown, like Jimmy's. I last saw him this morning; he was going around the island with an architect."

"And where's the architect?" the sheriff asked.

"I hadn't thought about that," Germaine said.

Hamish Drummond came out the back door. "Hi, Bob, what's going on?" he asked.

The sheriff nodded toward the back of the Jeep.

Hamish looked at the arm, grimaced, and turned away.

"That's Jimmy's wristwatch, isn't it?" Germaine asked him.

"Could be. Who found it?"

"I did," Liz said.

"I hope the hell it was at Lake Whitney," Hamish said.

"It was. On the dike thing where the road goes."

"Good. I'd hate to think that old gator was roaming around down here somewhere."

Angus Drummond pulled up in his jeep, followed closely by Buck Moses in his battered pickup. "I saw the helicopter," he said. "What's going on?"

Everybody filled Angus in.

"Did you see any of the rest of him?" Angus asked Liz, not unkindly.

"No. I just wanted to get out of there before I saw that alligator again."

"Again?" Hamish asked. "You saw him before?"

Liz nodded. "I was taking pictures down there one day, and he came after me. I was lucky to get away; as it was, he ate half my tripod."

"How big was he?" Angus asked.

"He looked gigantic," Liz said, "but mostly, I just saw jaws."

"He twenty foot," Buck said.

"How long since you saw him, Buck?" Angus asked.

" 'Bout a year. He twenty foot if he a inch."

"I believe it," Angus said.

"I believe it, too," the sheriff replied, "after looking at that arm."

Angus and Buck had a look at the arm, and the sheriff gingerly removed the wristwatch from the wrist. "Nothing engraved on it," he said, "but there'll be a serial number, and if he registered the warranty when he bought it, they'll have a record. I can check it with a phone call." He dropped it into a plastic bag and zipped it shut, then he wrapped up the arm again.

"I want to refrigerate this while we take a look at your lake," he said to Germaine.

Germaine shuddered. "All right, come on with me, and I'll get you a cooler and some ice." She stopped. "Somebody's got to call Jimmy's wife, too, I guess. Any volunteers?"

Nobody said anything.

"I didn't think so." Germaine sighed, then started for the house again.

"Could that arm belong to anybody but Jimmy?" Angus asked when they had gone.

"Germaine says everybody else is accounted for except the architect who was with Jimmy."

It occurred to Liz that one other person was not accounted for: Keir Drummond. She thought about the arm. It could be Keir's, she realized with a thump of her heart; still, she had never seen him wear a gold Rolex wristwatch, and she didn't think he was the sort who would choose something that gaudy.

"Well, it's the first man we've lost to Goliath," Angus said. "God only knows how many of my deer he's taken."

Germaine returned with a cooler of ice, the sheriff, and another man. "This is Henry Rhinehart, Jimmy's architect," she said. "He just got back to the inn. I've told him what happened."

Rhinehart looked stunned.

"Where did you last see Jimmy Weathers?" the sheriff asked.

"We were walking the beach," he said, "and then Jimmy wanted to look at something else; he didn't say what. He headed off through the dunes, toward the interior of the island."

"How long ago was that?"

Rhinehart looked at his watch. "About three hours. It took me that long to walk back to the inn."

"How much light we got left?" the sheriff asked nobody in particular.

Buck Moses looked at the sun. " 'Bout five hours," he said.

"Well, I guess we'd better go up there and see if we can find the rest of him. Maybe we'll get a shot at that gator, too."

"You ain't gon' find that boy," Buck Moses said.

The sheriff seemed to understand that he was in the presence of a backwoods expert. "Why not?"

"That gator, he gon' take his kill and stick it up under somethin'—a log, a rock—somethin' under the water. You put folks to lookin' in the water, and the gator gon' get somebody else."

"Well, I'm not anxious to get in the water with a twenty-footer, myself," the sheriff said.

"You're not going to kill that animal, either," Angus said firmly.

"That's a man-eater, Mr. Drummond," the sheriff replied. "I've got to do something about him if I can."

"That's my gator, and he's on my island. He was doing what comes naturally, and nobody's going to shoot him for it."

"Ain't no gator gon' come out of the water to get at a man," Buck said. "He got Jimmy, Jimmy was in the water."

"Why would he go in the water?" the architect asked.

"Dunno," Buck replied. "But the gator ain't gon' come out of the water at him."

"He had a go at me," Liz piped up.

"Was you in the water?" Buck asked.

"Yes," she admitted. "About knee deep."

"You lucky you got a knee," Buck said.

"Don't I know it."

"All right, all right," the sheriff said. "What I need is as many armed men as I can get—rifles and shotguns with double-aught buckshot."

"I don't want anybody shooting at that gator," Angus said.

"Well, we've got to have a look for the rest of this body, and I'm not going to ask any man to do that unarmed," the sheriff said.

"Just as long as you understand that nobody shoots at him unless he's in danger," Angus said, "then I'll scare up some weapons."

An hour later, the group arrived at the end of the dike.

"All right, Miz Barwick," the sheriff said, "where did you find the arm?"

Liz pointed. "There; about fifty feet along the dike, sticking out of the grass. I only saw the hand and the wrist."

"I want two men right behind me," he said and pumped the lever-action thirty-thirty in his hands.

The sheriff walked slowly out on the dike, keeping his attention on the high grass along the lakeshore, followed by Buck Moses and the architect, both clutching shotguns.

"He ain't gon' get you, sheriff!" Buck cackled. He seemed vastly amused by these white men.

"About there," Liz called, and the group stopped.

The sheriff moved the grass aside with his rifle barrel. "There's some blood, a lot of blood." All three men began poking in the grass with their rifles.

"Looka here!" Buck called out. "Gator done dragged him in right here!"

"Miz Barwick," the sheriff called, "could you come out here with your camera?"

Liz took a deep breath and walked along the dike to where they stood.

"Please photograph the bloody place, here, where you found the arm, and that spot in the mud, there, where it looks like something was dragged into the water."

Liz did as she was told, but she was trembling.

A few minutes later they regrouped at the cars.

"I don't know what the hell else to do," the sheriff said, mopping his brow. "I never had one of these on my hands before."

"Ain't nothing else you can do," Buck said. "Gator done gone with Jimmy. We ain't gon' see Jimmy no more."

"You don't think that gator would come out of the water to get a man, then, Buck?" the sheriff asked.

"Naw, sir," Buck said. "Jimmy done gone in the water." He paused. "Or somebody done put him in there."

Everybody turned and looked at Buck.

"Who would hate Jimmy enough to do that?" the architect asked.

Buck grinned toothlessly. "Jes' about ever'body, I reckon."

33

CHAPTER

33

*L*ee Williams was in his captain's office at nine sharp on Monday morning. He watched as his boss hung up his coat, moved around his desk, and flopped into his chair.

"So, how was your weekend?" Haynes asked.

"Could hardly have been better." Williams grinned.

"Tell me."

"I've got a witness who will place Bake Ramsey at the Beverly Hills Hotel, in the Polo Lounge at the same moment Schaefer was there, and who will testify that Ramsey had time to drown Schaefer in the pool, and that he returned to his table in the lounge wet."

"How good is your witness?"

"She's an LAPD cop who was Ramsey's date that night."

Haynes smiled broadly. "That's pretty good."

"It's gold plated. Not only that, but the head-waiter will testify that Ramsey left the lounge by the same route that Schaefer did."

"Even better. Did he sneak out of his hotel, past the staff?"

"He did. Guests can easily come and go through the garage without being seen."

"Good work. It's not good enough for an indict-ment, though, unless LA Homicide can tie in a witness at the pool or some physical evidence, and they're not going to get extradition without an indictment."

"That's okay with me; I want to bust him here, first."

"How you going to do that?"

"I think I can break his alibi for the Ferguson killings; it's just going to take me a little more time."

"What do you need?"

"I want the crime lab to go over the Ferguson residence one more time. I'm going to need a print, or some fibers, or something."

Haynes nodded. "I'll take care of that. Anything else?"

"Just the time to work on his girlfriend. She's his alibi. I want to find the ex-wife, too, the Barwick woman. I'm going to need her."

"You working on much else?"

"Nothing pressing."

"Okay, take all the time you need, just give me a good bust."

"Yes, sir!"

When Williams left the office, his lungs seemed too full of air. This was a glory bust; he'd nail Ramsey for the Fergusons and hand him to LAPD on a platter, and everybody in the city would know his name. It was a career-making case, and he wasn't going to blow it.

He picked up the phone and called Mary Alice Taylor's home number.

"This is Mary Alice," a honeyed voice said. "I'm not home, but you know I want to hear from you, so leave a message at the tone."

"Mary Alice, this is Lee Williams. It's important that you and I talk right away, so call me, please." He left all three numbers. "And, Mary Alice, it's important that you don't see Bake or talk to him before we get together. This is for your own good, believe me."

When by the end of the day she hadn't called, he waited until half past eight o'clock and went to Piedmont Hospital. When he got off the elevator on her floor, there was another nurse at Mary Alice's station.

"Excuse me," he said, "but is Mary Alice Taylor working another station tonight?"

"You'll have to see the supervisor," the woman said. "I'll call her for you."

Williams showed his badge to the supervisor.

"She didn't turn up for work tonight," the nurse said, "and she wasn't at home when I called."

"Is that unusual for Mary Alice?" Williams asked.

"Yes, it is, but my assumption is that she probably went out of town for the weekend and didn't get back. I expect I'll hear from her in due course, and she'll certainly hear from me."

"I'd like to have her home address, please," he said. "It'll save tracking it down through the phone company."

The nurse went to a card file and wrote down the address for him.

"Do you know what kind of car she drives?"

"No."

"It's a Volkswagen," the substitute nurse said.

"A Rabbit?"

"No, a bigger one."

"Jetta?"

"That's right. A white one. She bought it new this summer."

Williams thanked her and left.

Mary Alice Taylor lived in a large, attractive apartment development in the northwest quadrant of the city. Williams flashed his badge to the security guard at the gate and asked directions to her apartment. It was a ground-floor one-bedroomer on a nice street, and the living-room lights were on. He rang the bell, and, when there was no answer, he walked through a flower bed and looked through the window into the lighted room. Nothing seemed out of order.

He returned to the guardhouse and asked for the head of security; shortly, a black woman in uniform turned up. He showed his badge. "I'm looking for Mary Alice Taylor in 198. She hasn't turned up at work, and there's reason to be worried about her."

"You'll need a warrant, if you want to go into her place," the woman said.

"Listen, lady, this is a serious matter, and I don't need a warrant if you'll let me in. I'm not going to disturb the place, I just need to look inside."

"Oh, all right, but I'll have to go with you."

"I wouldn't have it any other way."

The door yielded to a pass key, and Williams was inside. The apartment was well furnished—it looked as though she'd lived there for a long time, had bought things for the place. In the kitchen there was an open jar of spaghetti sauce on the counter with a film of mold over it, and a pan waiting on the stove. He explored further, not knowing what he might find. The bedroom door was closed.

Williams turned the knob by grasping it close to the door. It was dark inside; he felt for a switch, and an overhead light came on. The bedspread and top sheet were on the floor, and there was a spot of dried blood in the middle of the bed. Not enough for a shooting or stabbing, he reckoned. He looked more closely and saw something else. The blood was from sex, he was sure, and the other thing looked like semen. He could see three pubic hairs on the sheet.

He had a quick look around the room, then checked the bathroom. There was a used hand towel on the sink, and it was bloody.

He went back into the living room, took out his notebook, and rewound her answering machine.

"Hey, sugar," Bake Ramsey's voice said. "It's Friday about noon. We're off to Miami this afternoon, so

I don't guess I'll see you until the first of the week. I'm sorry about last night; I'll make it up to you."

"Miss Taylor, this is Tiffany's; your wristwatch is ready, if you'd like to call for it."

"Hi, it's Bake. It's Saturday morning, and I thought I'd catch you at home. I hope you're not still mad. I'm in Miami; please call me." He left a number.

The next message was William's own. Then:

"Miss Taylor, it's the duty supervisor at Piedmont Hospital. It's eight-twenty Monday night, and you were due here at eight. Please call in as soon as possible."

Williams turned off the machine, sat down, picked up the phone gingerly, with two fingers, and dialed. "Who's this? Okay, this is Lee Williams; I have a possible crime scene, and I want a team out here right away—everything—the works, except no meat wagon; there's no corpse." He gave the address. "Also, I want a plate number for a new Volkswagen Jetta, white, registered to Mary Alice Taylor at this address, and I want an APB out on it right away. Check with the captain if you have to, but I'll take the responsibility. If the car is found parked, I don't want it touched until I get there. I want to know if the Bobcats played Miami this past weekend, and if they did, how and when they traveled, coming and going. I want to know if Bake Ramsey was with them, coming and going. I'll be at this number if you need to reach me." He gave the number, then hung up and dialed again.

"Hello?"

"Captain, it's Lee. I'm afraid I've lost my witness."

The doorbell to Mary Alice Taylor's apartment rang.

"Hang on, Captain." Williams got up and opened the door.

Bake Ramsey was standing on the doorstep; he looked puzzled. "What the hell are you doing here?" he asked.

CHAPTER

34

"**H**i, Bake," Williams said, managing a surprised smile, "what are *you* doing here? I didn't expect to see you, either." Ramsey was staring at him very hard. "Mary Alice didn't show up for work tonight, and the hospital called the cops. I took the call."

"Why didn't she show up?"

Williams took Ramsey's huge arm and led him up the steps to the parking lot, talking all the time. "That's what I'm trying to figure out, myself. You have any idea where she could be?" He stopped and leaned against his car.

"No, I haven't seen her since last week."

"When last week?"

"Thursday night. We had a date."

"Did you talk to her after that?"

"Nope. I called her a couple of times from Miami. I was down there with the team."

"When did you leave?"

"Friday afternoon."

"And when did you get back?"

"This morning. It was a night game, and we stayed over."

"I see." This was squaring with what he knew so far, but Ramsey's stories always squared.

"Look, has something happened to Mary Alice?" Ramsey showed just the right degree of puzzlement and concern.

"Not that I know of. We have to check these things out when we get a call, though. Listen, you go on home, and I'll call you when I get some more news."

"Okay," Ramsey said reluctantly. He gave Williams his number. "Maybe I should take a look inside and see if anything looks wrong."

"Don't worry about it. Security is in there, now, and there's nothing too unusual. We'll lock up and get out in a minute. I'll call you. Good night, Bake."

"Good night, Lee." Ramsey ambled over to a Mercedes, got in, and drove away.

Williams breathed a sigh of relief; he wanted Ramsey out of there before any more cops arrived. He had the gist of Ramsey's alibi, now, though it wouldn't be admissible, because he hadn't read the man his rights. He could always do that later, when he knew a crime had been committed.

A moment later, a police van arrived, and people

spilled out. Williams reentered the apartment with the group and got them to work. Two hours later, they left with their evidence, and the security lady locked the apartment behind them.

"Anything else I can do for you?"

Williams handed her his card. "Please let me know if Mary Alice Taylor returns to her apartment—make sure that all your people know to look out for her—and I'd like to know if Bake Ramsey enters the grounds at all."

"The football player?"

"That's the one."

"You got it."

She handed him a key and a plastic card. "Here's a spare key for the apartment, should you want to get in again when I'm not here. The card will let you into the back gate of the complex, which doesn't have a guardhouse."

He thanked her for her help and got into his car. There was fear in his heart as he drove away. He was afraid that, without Mary Alice Taylor's help, he wouldn't be able to break Ramsey's alibi for the Ferguson killings. But mostly, he was afraid for Mary Alice Taylor.

35

CHAPTER

35

*L*iz sat in the cottage's living room and drank bourbon. It had gotten dark, and she hadn't bothered to turn on a light. The silence was broken by the scuff of a bare foot on the kitchen linoleum, and she knew Keir was back. She no longer jumped when she heard such a noise; he came and went that way so often that she had begun to think of it as normal.

"Hi," she said, when he had time to reach the living room.

"It's not like you to sit alone in the dark," he said, sliding onto the sofa next to her.

"It's not like me to sit alone in the dark, drunk, you mean."

"How come you're drunk?"

"Because I found Jimmy Weathers's arm this afternoon—that alligator did something with the rest of him—and I can't forget it. I thought bourbon might help." She rested a hand on his bare thigh. "Why do you wear that loincloth?" she asked. "I always meant to ask you."

He laughed softly. "When I was a kid, I went naked a lot. Somewhere around puberty, I became a little self-conscious about it—I think I thought something was going to grab my crotch, and it had recently become terribly important. The loincloth was as close as I could get to naked and still protect my little cock."

"Not so little."

"It was, then."

"You're not surprised about Jimmy?"

"Buck Moses told me."

"I didn't think an alligator would do that. I mean, even when he came after me, I didn't really think he was a man-eater."

"Goliath is something special, you know. He's had precious little experience with man, and I think he must regard us as just larger-than-usual animals to hunt."

"Buck said he wouldn't come out of the water to attack a man; is that true?"

"I don't think anybody knows, anybody who's alive to tell us, anyway."

"Do you think he's really twenty feet long?"

"Yes, I do. I read somewhere once that the largest gator ever found in the United States was in Louisiana, in the last century. He was nineteen feet, two inches long, and the reason they found him was he

was so old, he had crawled out of the water to die. I
don't think they get that big anymore, because men
kill them before they're old enough. But Goliath has
been sitting out there in that lake for God knows how
long—a hundred years?—with nobody to hunt him
and plenty to eat. I wouldn't be surprised if he were
the largest alligator alive."

"How do you know he's a 'he'? Have you
checked?"

"Females don't get that big."

"Why do you think he went after Jimmy?"

"Maybe Jimmy got near his young."

"That's what I did. I was trying to photograph
the little ones when he came at me."

"Just before he attacked, do you remember a
noise like this?" Keir made high-pitched grunting
noise in his throat.

"Yes! Exactly like that! How did you know?"

"That's the distress signal of the little ones. They
make that noise, and mama and papa come running.
I'll bet that was the last sound ol' Jimmy heard, except
for his own screams. I just hope poor old Goliath
doesn't come down sick from eating such a poisonous
meal." Keir chuckled to himself.

"How can you talk like that about him?" she
demanded drunkenly. "He was a human being, and
he's dead! He was your cousin, for God's sake!"

"So what?" Keir said with some feeling. "If he'd
had his way—and he very likely would have—he'd
have raped this island from one end to the other; he'd
have built on most of it and paved over the rest,
believe me. It would look like Hilton Head and all the

other barrier islands that the developers got their hands on."

"But he couldn't have done it," she protested.

"Sure, he could. Grandpapa won't make a will, and he was playing right into Jimmy's hands."

"But he *has* made a will!"

"You don't know what you're talking about. He has a thing about it; every time somebody brings it up, he throws a tantrum, threatens to disinherit us all."

"He's made a will. I know because I witnessed it."

There was a stunned silence.

"Keir, I saw the document; he told me what it was; I signed my name as a witness. And he told me he'd done it in such a way as to keep any part of the island out of Jimmy's hands."

Keir leaned forward and put his face in his hands. "Christ, I don't believe it," he said, and then he began to laugh. "So, poor old Jimmy died for nothing; just a good dinner for a passing alligator and his brood. Christ, what a joke on him! What a joke on me!"

"On you? What do you mean?"

Keir went on laughing. It was a haunted, despairing sound, and Liz hated it. "Stop it!" she shouted, slapping him across the back of the head. "Shut up!" She hit him again.

He sat up and took a deep breath. "Oh, Jesus," he said pitifully. He turned and slipped his arms around her, put his head in her lap, and hugged her body. "The man who loves you is a pathetic creature." He sighed. "He can't love anything without destroying something else. Love and destruction, that's all he's capable of."

She leaned over and rested her cheek on his shoulder. "Shhh," she said. "You don't know what you're saying."

She didn't want him to say any more; there were some things she just didn't want to know. She stretched out on the sofa and pulled his head to her breast. "Shhhh," she breathed softly. "You don't have to tell me. I love you, whatever you are, whatever you've done."

She stroked his hair until the bourbon and her day overcame her, and she fell asleep in his arms.

CHAPTER

36

*L*ee Williams arrived at Dekalb-Peachtree Airport, a general-aviation field on the north side of Atlanta, twenty minutes after he got the call. He turned in through the main gate, and he could see, a block away, what he was looking for; two police cars, an ambulance, and the crime lab van were gathered in a parking lot, separated from a line of single-engine airplanes by a row of pine trees. He swung into the lot and stopped next to the ambulance; he could now see that the vehicles surrounded a white Volkswagen Jetta. The group of men were standing sullenly about; he had kept them waiting.

"Can we crack this car, now, Lee?" Mike Hopkins, the lab man, asked.

"Just a minute." He walked slowly around the car;

here and there it was grimy with black fingerprinting powder. He looked inside. There was a nurse's uniform in a dry cleaner's plastic bag lying on the backseat. There was a black leather handbag on the front passenger seat. He didn't like that. No woman would deliberately leave her handbag in a car in plain sight. There was nothing else to see inside the car.

"Okay," he said, "pop the trunk." He walked around to the back of the car and stood while an officer tried keys on the trunk lock. Williams tried to breathe normally.

"Here we go," the man said, as a key turned.

The lid came up to complete silence from the gathered group. They all winced at the smell.

Hopkins stepped forward, looked into the trunk, and spoke into a hand-held dictating machine. "The victim was discovered in the trunk of a 1989 Volkswagen Jetta, registered in her name. The body is lying in an unnatural position, which presumes death before entering the trunk; the odor of decay is moderately present. The body is entirely nude and is cold to the touch." He manipulated an arm, then a leg. "Rigor mortis is not present." He stepped away from the car and let the photographer get on with his work.

Williams stepped away with him. "How long?"

"I can tell you better later."

"Best guess."

"Over the weekend. Saturday, probably."

"Was she raped?"

"Too soon to say. They usually are when they're found nude."

"One thing you should know: she had sex with

her boyfriend, by his account, on Thursday night. It may have been pretty rough. You might see if you can differentiate between any bruising from that session and whatever happened at the time of her death."

"Thanks, that's good information."

"When can I have some results?"

"Preliminary"—he glanced at his watch—"ten o'clock tonight. Conclusive, tomorrow, the day after."

"Give me as much as you can tonight," Williams pleaded.

"I'll try. It may be an easy one, who knows? If it'll help, I think cause of death will be a broken neck; I don't think she was strangled."

"A powerful man, then?"

"That's a reasonable assumption."

"Anything else you can tell me now?"

Hopkins looked at his feet. "She's badly beaten up, you can see that. Looks like the guy wanted to hurt her a lot before he killed her."

"Uh, huh. Do you think he just meant to beat her up, that maybe she got the broken neck from a blow to the head?"

Hopkins shook his head slowly. "I think he meant to destroy her."

Williams nodded. "Okay, that fits my scenario."

Williams drove slowly away from the airport. The ambulance overtook him, no lights blazing. There was no hurry for Mary Alice Taylor.

It occurred to him that, in all his years as a policeman, he had never, until that day, seen the dead body of a victim he knew personally. It made a difference.

37

Williams arranged the chairs carefully. He had borrowed his captain's office for the morning, and he didn't want to use an interrogation room just yet; he wanted to get Ramsey on the record, first. Nervously, he picked up the phone and dialed a number.

"Medical examiner's office."

"Hopkins, please."

"He's on his way, Sergeant," the woman said. She knew the detective's voice by now.

"Did he finish?"

"He's got everything with him."

"Good. Thanks." He hung up and waited impatiently. It took Hopkins another twenty minutes to get there, and, looking at his watch, Williams

saw that he had only five minutes before his scheduled meeting.

"Sorry to be so late," Hopkins said, puffing as he
sat down.

"It's okay; I appreciate your getting this done so
quickly. What have we got?"

"Pretty much what I thought last night. She was
beaten badly with fists, and her neck was broken."

"Rape?"

"Not exactly. She had some bruises which would
correspond with Thursday night's intercourse with
the boyfriend, but she had more recent, more serious
damage to the vagina and anus, which occurred closer
to the time of her death."

"Which was?"

"Some time between midnight Friday and noon
Saturday."

"What was the nature of the more recent damage?"

"Not sex, not in the usual sense, anyway." Hopkins opened his old-fashioned briefcase and took out
a large Ziploc bag. He placed it on the captain's desk.

Williams had trouble keeping his face expres-
sionless. The bag contained a pointed wooden stake.
"It looks like the sort of thing you'd buy at a garden-
ing store," he said.

"It is. I don't know if you remember, but at the
airport, the bit of land between the parking lot and
the airplane tie-down area had recently been seeded.
The area had been cordoned off with string, and a
'keep off' sign put up. I think this is one of the stakes
the string was tied to."

"I don't remember it in or around the car. Where did you find it?"

"In her colon," Hopkins said. His eyes focused on the floor. "All of it. That's why we didn't see it sooner."

"Jesus God," Williams moaned. "It's twelve inches long!"

"It's fourteen inches long."

"Was she alive when it happened?"

"Yes, and she's had it in her vagina, as well."

Williams looked at the stake again. It was of rough lumber, not planed or sanded.

Hopkins read his mind. "There were a number of splinters present in both areas."

Williams looked up and saw Bake Ramsey and another man approaching the glassed-in office. "Anything else? I'm out of time."

"Nothing that would be of any immediate help. The car had some prints that weren't the woman's. I've given them to your people for running, but they're consistent with what might be picked up in a gas station or car wash. The driver's door handle and the trunk latch area showed signs of having been handled by someone with a cloth or gloves. That's your man, I'd bet."

"Thanks, Mike," Williams said. "Now you'll have to excuse me. I've got this meeting."

Hopkins handed him the written report and left. Williams quickly put the report and the bagged stake in a desk drawer, then he rose to greet Baker Ramsey.

"Morning, Lee," Ramsey said, sounding somewhat subdued. "This is Henry Hoyt, the team's lawyer. You said to bring one."

"Morning, Bake," Williams said, trying to settle himself down and sound normal. "Morning, Mr. Hoyt, I'm glad to meet you. Bake, I want to express my sympathy for the loss of your girl. I know it must have come as an awful shock." He managed to say this with a straight face.

"Thank you, Lee," Ramsey replied softly. "Yes, it was a shock. I can't imagine who'd want to hurt Mary Alice." His voice rose. "I'd sure like to get my hands on the guy for five minutes."

If you would just do that, Williams thought, you'd save us all a lot of trouble.

"Is Mr. Ramsey under suspicion?" the lawyer asked.

"We don't have a suspect, yet, Mr. Hoyt," Williams lied. "It's just that Bake seems to have been one of the last people to see Miss Taylor alive, and I need his statement on the record." He went to the door and beckoned to a woman. She came in with a stenographic machine, plugged it in, and sat down next to a desk. "Miss Jordan, here, will take down everything we say, then she'll type it up. Later, I'll ask Bake to read it and sign it, if it's accurate."

"I see," Hoyt said. "This is standard procedure, Bake."

"Now, Bake, the department insists that I tell you that you have the right to remain silent, and you have the right to have an attorney, which right you have availed yourself of. If you choose to answer my questions, and you're later charged with a crime, your

•

answers could be used against you in a court of law. Do you understand these rights?"

"That's standard, too," Hoyt said.

"Sure, I understand my rights," Ramsey said.

"Let the record show that Mr. Henry Hoyt, Esquire, is present, representing Baker Ramsey; also present are Sergeant Lee Williams of the Atlanta Police Department and Miss Evelyn Jordan, a stenographer and court reporter. Are you willing to answer my questions, Bake?"

"Of course," Ramsey said. "I'll do anything I can to help. I'm very upset about Mary Alice's death."

"I'm sure you must be. Let's begin at the beginning. When did you meet Miss Taylor for the first time?"

"When I checked in to the hospital for my knee surgery a few weeks ago."

"By the way, how's the knee coming?" Williams asked. "You can keep this out of the record," he said to the stenographer.

"We thought I'd be ready next weekend, but the doctor and the coach want to wait another week."

"Okay, back on the record. Did you see Mary Alice Taylor often?"

"Yeah, we were going out steadily."

"Did you have an intimate relationship with her?"

"Yes."

"By that, I mean were you having regular sexual intercourse with her?"

"Yes, very regularly."

"When did you last see Mary Alice?"

"Last Thursday night. We had dinner at her house."

"Did you have sexual intercourse with her that evening?"

"Yes, a couple or three times."

"Did she exhibit any signs of distress during your sexual relations?"

"Well, there was some blood."

"And yet you continued to have sex with her?"

"It was only the last time that she bled some, and it wasn't all that unusual. She didn't want to stop; she never did."

"Did you leave a deposit of semen on her bed that night?"

"I guess so."

"Was the sexual intercourse entirely voluntary on her part?"

"Entirely. She loved sex."

"Did you have to persuade or force her?"

"No, not at all. It was pretty much the way we usually made love. Listen, is this really necessary? It's pretty personal."

"I'm afraid so, Bake." It's a little late to object, isn't it? Williams thought to himself. "Let me change the subject, if talk of sex makes you uncomfortable."

"It's not that I'm uncomfortable; it's just private."

"Let's talk about dinner. You say you ate at her apartment?"

"Yeah, she cooked." Ramsey suddenly looked uncomfortable. "Well, uh, she was cooking, but we didn't exactly eat it. We, uh, started fooling around in the kitchen and she spilled something, and then we went into the bedroom and made love."

"And this lovemaking was entirely voluntary," Williams said.

"Yes, I said so before."

"Bake, you later left a message on Mary Alice's answering machine which was apologetic, as if you'd done something to offend her and were sorry. What was that about?"

Ramsey suddenly looked furtive. "It was, uh, just something personal."

"This is a very personal interview, Bake. What was your apology for?"

"I'm not going to talk about it," he said vehemently.

Williams paused and pretended to jot a note on a pad. Ramsey would talk about it as soon as he had time to make up a good story. "What time did you leave her apartment that night?" Williams said finally.

"I went home some time after midnight, maybe twelve-thirty."

"And you did not see Mary Alice Taylor again?"

"No, I didn't. The team left for Miami on Friday afternoon, and we didn't get back until Monday."

"And you went with the team?"

"Yes."

"How did you travel?"

"By air. We always do."

"Who did you sit next to on the airplane going down?"

"An assistant coach, Manny Davis."

"And coming back?"

"Manny again. We're good friends; we sometimes room together on the road."

"Did you room together that weekend?"

"No, I had a room to myself."

"What did you do on Friday evening?"

"I had dinner with Manny in the hotel restaurant, and then I went to bed early, about ten."

"What time did you get up?"

"I usually wake up about eight."

"Where did you have breakfast?"

"In the dining room with Manny and a couple of other players, Ralph James and Bobby Martino."

"What time?"

"About nine. There was a light workout that day, and I went out to the practice field on the team bus."

"How long did you stay there?"

"Until about four in the afternoon. When the bus got back, I had a nap."

"And what did you do between that time and the game the next day?"

"I watched some TV, and I had dinner with Manny again. We went out to a seafood place and had a couple of drinks at a sports bar called the End Zone."

"Anybody see you there?"

"Everybody. I got into a little altercation with a guy there."

"Were blows exchanged?"

"Nah, just some name-calling. The bartender broke it up."

"What time did you get back to the hotel?"

"Around midnight. I wasn't playing the next day."

"And what time did you get up?"

"Around eight. I had breakfast downstairs with the same guys."

The rest of Ramsey's story was much the same. His time, except when he was alone in his room, was accounted for, and that time overlapped the period when Hopkins had said the girl had died.

"On Friday night, did you leave your room again after you went to bed at ten o'clock?"

"Not until breakfast the next morning."

"Is there anyone who can corroborate that?"

"No, I slept alone."

"Do you know how to fly an airplane?"

"Nope. Never had a lesson."

"Do you know anyone in the Miami area who has a private airplane?"

Ramsey looked puzzled. "No."

"Do you know anybody in Atlanta who has one, or who sometimes rents one?"

"No. Well, yes, a couple of guys on the team fly those little single-engine jobs."

"Have you ever chartered an airplane, Bake?"

"Not for several years."

"When was the last time?"

"About four years ago, when my mother got sick."

"How did you go about chartering the airplane?"

"The team fixed it up. They're real good about stuff like that."

Williams stretched. "Well, I guess that's about it."

Ramsey made to get up.

"Oh, just a couple more questions, Bake."

Ramsey sat down again. His lawyer was looking bored.

"Bake, did you ever hit Mary Alice Taylor?"

"No, of course not."

The lawyer was suddenly alert. "I don't think that's an appropriate question, Sergeant."

"I think it is. Never, Bake? You never slapped her, even?"

"No, I don't do that sort of thing."

"Bake, in July of this year, did you beat up your wife and put her in the hospital?"

"Now just a minute," Hoyt said, half-rising.

"Answer the question, Bake. Did you beat your wife nearly to death?"

"I don't have to take this kind of stuff," Ramsey said, rising.

"Let the record show that Ramsey suddenly refuses to answer questions," Williams said to the stenographer.

"What would you say, Bake, if I told you that I can produce your ex-wife as a witness, and that she will testify that you beat her so badly that she had to have major reconstructive cranial surgery? And that her doctor will testify that she could have died from her injuries? What would you say to that?"

"This interview is concluded," Henry Hoyt said.

"Oh, just before you go, Mr. Hoyt, let me show you and Bake something." He reached into the desk drawer and took out the bagged stake. "The medical examiner removed this from Mary Alice Taylor's rectum during the autopsy last night. The man who killed her did that to her." He was trying not to shout.

Hoyt blanched at the sight of the stake. "Stop this, Sergeant, or I'll report your conduct to your captain!" The lawyer had gone pale, and sweat was starting to run from his face.

"It's not my conduct that's in question, Counselor, it's your client's conduct!"

"We're getting out of here right this minute, Baker," Hoyt said, grabbing his client's elbow and steering him from the office. "Good day, Sergeant; your superiors will be hearing from me."

"Go on, get him out of here," Williams said, then sank back into the chair.

"I got all that, Lee, anything else?" the stenographer asked.

"Cut it at Ramsey's refusal to answer, and get it typed up as soon as you can," Williams said, trying to calm himself.

Captain Haynes appeared. "I was next door," he said. "You kind of lost it there at the end, didn't you?"

"Sorry about that, Cap. At least I waited until the end."

"You going to get this guy?"

"You better believe it!"

"Whatever you need, Lee. I want him, too."

"I want an officer to confirm Ramsey's story with the assistant coach and two players."

"Okay. Ramsey was in Miami, though. I saw him on TV Sunday, on the sidelines at the game."

"And I want to go to Miami. I caught him lying in LA; maybe I can catch him out in Miami, too."

"Go. What's your theory?"

"The girl was found at a general-aviation airport. I think Ramsey got somebody to fly him to Atlanta on Friday night; he killed the woman, then flew back to Miami; it's the only thing that makes sense. I want somebody checking that out from this end; I'll do it in Miami."

"Don't spend your own money this time. I'll sign the chit."

"You think we're going to start getting heat from the Bobcats' owners about this?"

"Not yet; they won't want it in the papers. When it comes out, then they'll yell bloody murder."

Williams managed a smile. "That's appropriate." He didn't feel like smiling, though; this was becoming personal. The sight of that stake had made it impossible to keep any detachment. He *wanted* Bake Ramsey.

CHAPTER

38

*L*iz found Germaine in her office at the inn, adding up receipts.

"Come on in, kiddo, and sit yourself down," Germaine said. "You look beat; didn't you sleep last night?"

"Off and on," Liz said, sinking into a chair.

"You still thinking about your discovery at Lake Whitney?"

Liz nodded. "Can't get it off my mind."

"I can't get it off my *guests'* minds," Germaine said, giving up the calculator and turning in her chair to face Liz. "If I'd let them, they'd all be trooping up there to take pictures of the gator. I've had to tell my girls who conduct the nature tours not to let anybody out of the van when they're near the lake. All I need is to have a guest eaten."

Liz managed a smile. "From their reaction to Jimmy's demise, it sounds like having a guest eaten would be good for business."

Germaine laughed. "Maybe you're right." She jotted a note on a pad. "Choose guest to send to Lake Whitney on foot. I've got just the one, too; he sent the wine back last night; I had to drink it myself, and now I'm hung over."

"Poor Germaine."

"And that's not the worst of it. Ron went back to school yesterday, and I'm already horny. What am I going to do?"

"Poor, poor Germaine! Hung over *and* horny."

"I can see I'm not going to get any sympathy from somebody who's so well supplied with a man. How is my little brother, anyway? I haven't seen him for days."

"I'm not sure," Liz replied.

"You haven't seen him either?"

"I saw him last night, but I'm not sure how he is. It was the first time I've seen him depressed."

"Well, you're one up on me; I've never seen *either* of them depressed. They've always been the happiest people I know."

"Germaine, Keir's got me worried about something, and I don't know who else to ask about it but you."

"Shoot. I'll help if I can."

"It's something he said to me last night. He said

he couldn't love somebody without destroying something else."

Germaine looked astonished. "Keir said that?"

"He did."

"I've never heard either Keir or Hamish say anything of the sort, and if I heard it from anybody else but you, I wouldn't believe it. Certainly it has no foundation in any fact I'm aware of."

"There's something else. He said it in connection with Jimmy; it was almost as if he were saying he had something to do with Jimmy's death."

Germaine said nothing, just looked at her.

"Do you think Keir is capable of . . . I mean, he was very upset about your grandfather's refusal to make a will—he said that if Angus died intestate, Jimmy would automatically inherit a chunk of the island."

Germaine looked as if she was trying to decide how to respond. "No," she said finally, "I don't think Keir could do that, no matter how much he hated Jimmy. He's right about the line of inheritance, though."

"Then what was he talking about?"

"I think you'd better screw up your courage and ask him."

"I don't think I have that much courage."

"Then you'd better learn to live with it."

Liz sighed. "There's something else. I think I may have contributed to . . . whatever is bothering Keir. There was something I knew that I didn't tell him until last night. I haven't told you or Hamish, either, even though Angus didn't really ask me not to."

"What do you mean?"

"I mean that Angus invited me to dinner awhile back—right after his lawyer was here with the congressman and the Forestry Service people. After dinner, he produced a will and asked me to witness it."

Germaine's eyes grew wide. "He's made a will, then? You're sure?"

"I'm sure. He told me that he had made it himself, without his lawyer's help, and that he was of sound mind and all that, and that he wanted me to witness it."

Germaine leaned forward in her chair. "What did it say?"

"I don't know. I only saw the signature page. He did say, though, that he had arranged things so that Jimmy wouldn't be able to get his hands on any of the island."

"Well, that's a moot point, now. The important thing is that he's made the will, although with Jimmy out of the picture, it probably won't make much difference. Why didn't you tell me about this before?"

"I was worried that I might seem to be meddling in your family business."

"You aren't meddling; you just did what he asked you to. It was a perfectly straightforward thing to do."

"There's something else, something that may make me seem the meddler again."

"Oh, no, Liz," Germaine said. "I know he likes you a lot, but I hope you don't mean he's made you a beneficiary."

"Please don't be alarmed about that, Germaine. I know I'm not a beneficiary, because he said the reason he was asking me to witness the will was that I was the only person around who didn't have an interest in it."

Germaine leaned over and placed a hand on Liz's arm. "Please forgive me; I know I must have sounded like the disinherited relative talking to my grandfather's doxy."

"It's all right; I understand."

"A will has to have two witnesses, though, doesn't it?"

"Yes. He said he would find another one."

"I wonder who? He was right; you're about the only person he knows who isn't mentioned in the will; certainly he would remember the servants."

"There's something else," Liz said slowly.

"What?"

"I think I am truly meddling in family business, now, but it might be worse if I didn't. I couldn't tell Keir this last night; I thought he might be too depressed to react properly."

"What are you talking about, sugar?"

"It's James Moses."

"You mean he's mentioned in the will? I should hope so, after all the help he's been to Grandpapa."

"James may be a more . . . significant part of the will than that."

"How do you mean, more significant?"

"Angus told me that James is his son."

Germaine's face collapsed. "He *what*?"

"Surely that doesn't come as a complete surprise? There is a resemblance, after all."

Germaine put a hand to her breast. "Surprise?

Honey, that's the single greatest shock I've had in my life!"

"I thought everybody in the family must at least suspect it was true." She could see Germaine's mind begin to work, now.

"Well, I wasn't around when James was born. My ex had taken me away at that point. I guess James must have been five or six when I came back to the island."

Liz waited while Germaine's mind got around to the point.

"Jesus H. Christ!" Germaine said suddenly. "I hope to God he *has* made a will, because if he hasn't . . ."

"Keir told me about Aldred Drummond's will, about how the estate would be divided if the owner died intestate."

"The children inherit first, then the grandchildren," Germaine breathed.

"So that must not be how Angus wants it to happen; otherwise, he wouldn't have made the will."

Germaine laughed. "It's just coming to me; James Moses is my . . . Well, I'll be . . . shit, I almost said, I'll be a monkey's uncle. That's wrong; I'm a monkey's niece!"

"Germaine!"

"I'm sorry, I know it's not nice to call them monkeys. I'm just a little addled, I guess, having found a brand-new uncle."

"Are you upset?"

"Just stunned."

"I'm sorry I shocked you so. I figured you must

have an idea about it. Do you think Hamish and Keir know?"

"Probably. They're smarter than I am."

"Well, why don't you see if Hamish knows, and I'll tell Keir."

Germaine shrugged. "Okay."

Liz got up to go. "Germaine, your grandfather loves you and the twins; he wouldn't do something crazy at your expense, even if he loves James, too."

Germaine put her head in her hands. "Jesus, I hope not."

That night, Keir took the news about his new uncle differently. "I've always liked James." He shrugged. "I guess I can't like him any less because he's my grandfather's son." He smiled wryly. "It's a good thing Jimmy isn't around to hear the news. Jimmy would have murdered the boy."

CHAPTER

39

Miami was hot and humid, and Lee Williams didn't like it much. He liked it even less when he found that Bake Ramsey's alibi for the weekend was practically impenetrable. He confirmed the football player's every move during that weekend, and he couldn't prove that Ramsey was not in his hotel room between 10:00 P.M. Friday and 8:00 A.M. Saturday. Not yet, anyway. There was still the airport check to do.

First, he checked with Miami Flight Service and discovered that no aircraft had filed a flight plan from the Miami area to Atlanta Dekalb-Peachtree Airport during the hours in question. When he sounded disappointed, the man explained that airplanes aren't required to file flight plans. "Any light aircraft could

just fly to Atlanta under visual flight rules, if the
weather was okay, and as long as the pilot checked
with air traffic control before entering a terminal control area on his route of flight," he said.

"Are you saying that such a flight would be untraceable?"

The man nodded. "It might be untraceable, even
if the pilot didn't care if it was traced. If he didn't
want to be traced, he could use a false tail number to
identify himself, or he could just do what the drug
dealers do: turn off his transponder and stay off the
radio."

"I see."

"Would your man have made a round trip?"

"Yes."

"In that case, he'd probably need fuel. Miami–
Atlanta–Miami has got to be farther than the range of
just about any light aircraft I know about. Of course,
he could buy fuel at any number of airports along his
route that would be open all night."

Williams thanked the man and left. Now his only
hope lay in legwork, checking all the airports. He
climbed into his rented car, turned the air condition-
ing up full blast, and started driving.

He started southwest of the city at Tamiami Airport, checking with each charter service and flight
school, and he came up empty-handed. He then
worked his way north to Miami International, with
no better luck, then to Opa-Locka and the smaller
Opa Lock West. In each place he could find no trace
of an airplane flying to Atlanta and back on the Friday
night. He stood next to a small Beechcraft trainer at

Opa Lock West and mopped his brow. "I've checked all the Miami airports I could find," he said to the flight instructor he had been questioning, listing the fields he had visited. "Have I maybe missed one?"

"Well," the young man said, "there's Dade-Collier."

"Where the hell is that?" Williams asked, searching his road map again.

"It's this really weird place out in the Everglades. It was built purely for airline training purposes; there's a ten-thousand-foot runway and an instrument landing system, and that's about it."

"A ten-thousand-foot runway in the Everglades?"

"Yep, you can go out there and practice instrument approaches in a 747, if you've a mind to."

Williams mopped his brow again and asked directions.

An hour and a half later, after getting lost twice, he drew up to a gate in the middle of nowhere. A sign said, DADE-COLLIER TRAINING AND TRANSITION AIRFIELD. He drove slowly until an enormous runway appeared, heat shimmering from its concrete surface. There was a tower, which looked deserted, a low building, and only one airplane, a small, twin-engine job, parked on the apron, some distance from the tower. No other aircraft of any kind was in sight, in the air or on the ground.

"What a fucking waste of time," he shouted, banging on the steering wheel. Then he took a deep breath and drove toward the building. As he pulled up, a man came out to meet him.

"What can I do for you?" the man asked. "This field isn't open to the public."

Williams flashed his badge. "I'm trying to trace the flight of a light aircraft from the Miami area to Atlanta last Friday night, and I wonder if you could help me."

"Mister, that sort of stuff don't fly in and out of here," the man said, shaking his head. "This is purely a training field; general-aviation aircraft can't take off or land here without a permit from Dade County, and nobody's even applied for a permit in weeks."

Williams slumped. This had been his last hope. He was hot, tired, annoyed, and thoroughly defeated. "Well, thanks, anyway," he said to the man.

"Don't mention it," he replied, and started back into the building.

"Excuse me," Williams said.

The man turned around. "Yeah?"

"If general-aviation aircraft have to have a permit to use this place, and nobody's applied for a permit recently, then what's that over there?" He pointed to the twin-engine airplane parked some distance away.

"Well, you got me there, mister," the man replied. "It turned up last weekend, and nobody has a clue what it's doing here."

"Why don't you and I go over there and have a look at it?" Williams proposed.

The man shrugged. "Sure."

They got into the car and drove toward the airplane.

"It's a Cessna 310," the man said. "A nice one, too."

Williams stopped the car and made a note of the airplane's registration number, which was painted in twelve-inch letters on the fuselage. Both men got out and approached the aircraft.

"How do you get into it?" Williams asked.

"There's only one door; it's on the other side."

They walked around the aircraft, and the man stepped up onto the port wing and peered inside. "Uh, oh," he said. He hopped back down to the pavement. "I'm not opening that door. You do it."

Williams stepped up onto the wing, as the man had done, and looked inside. Someone was slumped over the pilot's control yoke. Flies buzzed about him, and the odor of corruption leaked through the door seals.

Williams hopped down from the wing. "I think we'll let your local sheriff's department open that door," he said.

An hour later, Williams phoned his captain from the airport office.

"I think I found the guy who flew Bake Ramsey to Atlanta and back," he said.

"What did he have to say?" Haynes asked.

"He didn't say anything; he died of a broken neck a few days ago. We found him in his airplane at an almost-deserted airfield about forty miles north of Miami."

"Oops," the captain said. "Listen, one of our guys checked at Dekalb-Peachtree and found out that an airplane refueled there about three A.M. on Saturday morning. I've got the tail number." He read it out.

It matched the number on the piece of paper in Williams's hand. "Bingo," he said.

"Can we tie Ramsey to the airplane?"

"The Dade County Sheriff's Office is dusting the plane right now." He paused. "But, Captain, I've got a fairly certain feeling that they won't find a trace of Ramsey on that airplane. I think the sonofabitch has snookered us again."

"Come on home, Lee," Haynes said. "You've had enough Florida sunshine."

"You're damn right, I have," Williams replied, trying hard to suppress his fury and failing.

CHAPTER

40

*L*iz found Angus Drummond at the family cemetery, where there seemed to be excitement among the group of students and their leader, Dr. Blaylock. She stayed on the other side of the low wall that enclosed the graveyard and watched them. They crowded around a large hole and watched as small amounts of earth were expelled by someone down so far that Liz could not see his head.

"It's intact!" a voice said from the grave, and there was a little round of applause. "I can get my hand under the coffin; the supports have held, too."

"Is this the first coffin you've found?" Liz asked a girl at the edge of the group. "Yes," the girl said excitedly.

"What does he mean by supports?"

"Well," the girl said authoritatively, "when you bury somebody, you put a couple of lengths of wood crosswise in the grave for the coffin to rest on. This keeps it out of any immediate water that might have collected in the grave, and when the coffin is lowered, the supports allow the ropes to be withdrawn again. This grave is from 1881, and rope was a valuable commodity then, especially on an island, where it would have had to be brought in from the mainland."

"Toss me the rope," the voice from the grave said, and two coils were passed down to him. The students began erecting a tripod over the grave; when they were done, they hung a block and tackle from it, passed a rope through the sheave, and lowered the end into the grave.

A male student appeared from the grave, drawing up a wooden ladder after him. "Okay, you can hoist away," he said.

The group massed on the end of the rope and began to hoist. Shortly, a wooden coffin, very dirty, emerged from the grave, and the students manhandled it onto the ground.

Angus Drummond, who had been watching from the graveside, stepped over and wiped the top of the coffin with his hand, then took a handkerchief and rubbed until a brass plate appeared through the grime. "Dorothy Callaway Drummond," he read aloud. "Eighteen thirty-seven to eighteen eighty-one."

"That corresponds with the tombstone," Dr. Blaylock said. "All right, some of you get to work cleaning up that casket."

Students fell to work with soap, water, and brushes.

"The coffin is in remarkable condition to have been in the raw earth for nearly a hundred and ten years," Blaylock said.

"That's because it's made of live oak," Angus said. "Before Aldred Drummond died, he specified a coffin for himself of live oak from the island's trees, lined in lead. Every Drummond coffin since that time has been made the same way. I'd be willing to make a considerable wager that when you get old Aldred's box up, it, too, will be intact."

The coffin stood clean, now, if stained, its rich wood gleaming dully.

"No varnish left," Blaylock said, running his hand along the wood.

"It wasn't varnished," Angus said. "The coffin was rubbed with teak oil."

"May we open the coffin, Mr. Drummond?" Blaylock asked.

"No, you may not," Angus said. "That was not part of our arrangement, and I won't have the remains of members of my family unduly disturbed. Dorothy Drummond was my grandmother."

"Of course; I understand," Blaylock said.

"I'd like you to get her into her new resting place without delay," Angus said. "The ground has already been consecrated. We'll have a proper service when all the remains have been moved."

"Right away," Blaylock replied. "All right, young people, let's load the casket on the truck. Carefully, now."

Angus turned and saw Liz. "Good morning, my dear," he said brightly. "How nice to see you."

"It's good to see you, Angus," she said.

"You've arrived just in time to meet my grandmother," he said, waving at the coffin, which now rested in the truck bed.

"So I heard. That's fascinating about the coffins."

"You think so? Come along, then, and I'll fascinate you some more."

He led her away from the graveyard, back toward the main house. Soon, they came to the cluster of maintenance buildings that sat behind the mansion. Angus opened a large door and motioned for Liz to go ahead of him.

The room was well lighted by a skylight set in the roof, and, immediately, the clean, pungent scent of wood shavings reached her nostrils. They were in a carpentry shop, well equipped with power tools, and others, some of them obviously quite old, were stored neatly on pegs along the rear wall. The side walls were covered with large racks which held lengths of lumber.

"We don't often cut down a live oak," Angus said. "Takes them too long to grow to have them fall to some obnoxious human's ax, but now and then a hurricane will blow one down or wound it so badly that it makes sense to harvest it. The lumber is sawn at our own sawmill, down in the woods, and left here to dry."

In the center of the room, on sawhorses, rested three coffins, one of them already lined in sheet lead, the other two still only bare wood inside. In a corner of the room, a smaller coffin sat on the floor.

"We keep a supply in stock," Angus said. "We hadn't made one for a while, but it seemed a good idea to do so now. Jimmy Weathers won't be needing one, but I will, soon, and so will Buck Moses. He'll be buried in the family plot with us."

"What about the child's coffin, in the corner, there?"

"That was never needed, thank goodness. It was built when the twins' mother was pregnant with them. We were ready for anything."

"And the third large one?" she asked.

"Always good to have a spare," Angus said. "You never know."

Liz ran her hand along the side of one of the coffins. "It's so smooth," she said.

"It's very dense wood, almost like iron. When you sand it down, it stays smooth for a long time." He paused. "That one is mine."

"It does seem a little longer than the other two," she said.

"I've spent my whole life looking for clothes, beds, and other things that were big enough for my frame," Angus said. "I don't intend to be cramped in my grave."

"Angus," she said tentatively, "there's something I want to tell you."

"Go right ahead," he said.

"When you had me to dinner and asked me to witness your will, you told me about James Moses."

"Yes."

"Although you didn't say so, I had the feeling you were telling me about both the will and James in some confidence."

Angus said nothing.

"If that was so, then I'm sorry to say that I've broken your confidence."

"How so?"

"Germaine and Keir, and probably Hamish, as well, have been upset, I think, about your not having made a will."

"They've brought it up often enough," Angus said irritably.

"I think it was a reasonable concern, and things reached a point where I felt I had to tell them about it."

"That's all right; I would have gotten around to it myself."

"I'm glad, but I'm afraid I also told Germaine and Keir about James being your son."

Angus chuckled. "I'm not sure I'd have got around to that, but I'm glad you did. Otherwise, they'd have learned about it at the reading of the will, and it would have been something of a shock, I suppose."

"It's a shock now," Liz said, "but less of one, I think, than if they'd learned about it after you were gone."

"What was their reaction?"

"Nothing that you or James would have to worry about, I think. They both took it pretty well, although Germaine was truly shocked at first."

"Well, they'll have time to get used to the idea."

"I think it helps a lot that they all love James anyway, relative or not."

"I know they do. It's only lately that I've let myself feel strongly about the boy. For a long time, I didn't want to think about it."

"From what they've told me, Jimmy's death somewhat simplified things."

"That's God's truth. I'm sure the little brat would have stirred up all sorts of trouble when he read the will. There would have been lawsuits for decades. Now old Goliath has done us all a service."

"All but Jimmy."

"God forgive me for speaking ill of the dead, but I have to say I never liked the boy, from the time he was a gnat. He was nothing but an irritant to the family his whole life long. His mother, my daughter, was a rebellious thing, married badly, had only the one child, thank Christ. She died, drunk at the wheel of a car, in Jacksonville. Her husband drank himself to death some years previous."

"Jimmy had a wife."

"I must have been prescient; I left her a bit in the will, providing he had no control over it. She isn't a bad little thing; I always felt sorry for her."

A truck rumbled past.

"Well," he said, looking at his pocket watch, "I think I'll go and see Grandmother Dorothy put to rest. She died before I was born, so I missed her first burial. Will you come with me?"

"Of course. I'm glad I made a clean breast of things and that you're not angry with me."

"Nonsense. You did what any reasonable, concerned person would have done under the circumstances. And," he said sheepishly, "you did something for me that I didn't have enough courage to do for myself. Now, come on, let's get our respective cars, so you won't have to bring me back."

The two walked from the carpentry shop arm in arm, and Liz felt comfortable with herself for the first time in days.

CHAPTER

41

Williams sat down across the desk from Haynes. His captain gazed impassively at him. There was no hint of either anger or sympathy in his eyes.

"All right, let's go over it again," he said. "From square one. Start with Schaefer."

"I can prove by two witnesses, one of them a Los Angeles policewoman, that Ramsey was in the Beverly Hills Hotel when Albert Schaefer was drowned in their swimming pool."

"That's opportunity," the captain said. "Motive?"

"He killed Schaefer because he hated his guts. Schaefer represented Ramsey's ex-wife in the divorce proceedings, and Schaefer always got big settlements for his clients. I asked around."

"Motive," the captain said. "Now the Fergusons."

"Ramsey was checked in to Piedmont Hospital for knee surgery at the time the Fergusons died. He screwed the night nurse, and I think she covered for him, or at least failed to check on him, so that he was able to leave the hospital in the middle of the night, walk or drive to the Fergusons', which was nearby, and do the deed."

"Opportunity, maybe. Motive?"

"I'm damned if I know. The ex-wife didn't shed any light on that when she phoned, and I haven't been able to find her. It's hard to believe, but all of her friends say they don't know where she is, and I believe them."

"So we're shaky on the Fergusons, even in theory."

"I'm afraid so."

"The motive for Mary Alice Taylor?"

"I talked to her about the night she met Ramsey, and she struck me as evasive. I warned her not to tell Ramsey we'd talked, but I think she did. He killed her because he knew she could blow his alibi for the Fergusons."

"Why did he torture her?"

"To find out what she'd told me. She would have denied telling me anything, of course, since she didn't, but he obviously didn't believe her."

"And Ramsey flew up here from Miami and back in the middle of the night to kill her?"

"Right. He must have known the guy whose body we found. We haven't been able to make a connection, yet, but they could have met at some bar or something. Ramsey must know thousands of people. This airport in Florida is perfect; it's not attended twenty-four hours a day, so the guy could pick up Ramsey there and deliver him back, all in the wee hours. We know the airplane came to Dekalb-Peachtree because it took on fuel there—the refueler saw only the pilot; we just can't place Ramsey on the plane; it was clean."

The captain leaned back in his chair and put his feet on his desk. "It's all perfectly plausible," he said. "But we can't prove any of it. We'll just have to wait until he kills somebody else and hope he makes a mistake."

"I don't think he's going to kill anybody else," Williams said.

"Why not? He seems to enjoy it."

"Because there isn't anybody else to kill. He's had reasons for killing five people, but now he's home free. Why should he kill anybody else?"

"Unless . . ." The captain took his feet down and leaned forward, elbows on his desk. "Oh, boy, I think I just had a flash."

"Tell me."

"The wife."

"You think he wants to kill the wife?"

"Why else is she taking so much trouble to cover her tracks? She hasn't told a single friend where she's gone—you said that. Why? She's afraid Ramsey will find her, that's why."

"That makes sense," Williams admitted.

"Not only does it make sense, it gives us a motive for the Fergusons and a better motive for Schaefer."

"I don't get it, Cap."

"They knew where Elizabeth Barwick is! Christ, she had to tell somebody. Who better than her lawyer and her publisher?"

"But why all three of them?"

"Maybe Schaefer wouldn't tell him. He was a gutsy little guy, Al was."

"So he tried to find out from the Fergusons?"

"From Raymond, at least. Maybe he killed the wife just because she was there."

"He threatened the wife to get the husband to tell him," Williams said, excited now. "That had to be the way it was. So now Ramsey knows where his ex-wife is?"

"Maybe. Or, on the other hand, maybe the Fergusons didn't tell him, either."

"No, I don't believe that. Ferguson would have talked to protect his wife."

"I think you're right. I also think you'd better find Elizabeth Barwick in a hurry, or she's going to be real dead real soon."

"If she's not already," Williams said.

"We'd have heard about it, wherever she is."

"But she could be anywhere. She could be in Paris or Tokyo or fucking Moscow, if Schaefer got her a big settlement."

"Try her bank," the captain said. "Everybody's got to have access to his money. Try credit cards."

Williams was raring to go now. "Okay, I'll try all of them."

"Start with the biggest banks and work your way down. Let's assume that she's got some real money, from her settlement from Ramsey. She'd want some help with it, either a stockbroker or a bank. Hang on, I've got it! Try the private banking departments of the big banks—Trust Company, C & S, First Atlanta, Bank South."

Williams was already moving.

He started with the Trust Company Bank, and he immediately made a mistake. "Do you have a customer named Elizabeth Barwick?" he asked the director of private banking.

"I'm sorry," the man said, "we do not divulge the names of our clients." And he held to that position. He wasn't telling anything, even whether or not she banked there, without a court order.

On his next stop, Williams got foxier. He got off the elevator on the fourteenth floor of the First National Bank Tower and presented his badge to the receptionist. "I want to inquire about one of your customers," he said.

"Just a moment, please." The woman dialed a number and spoke with someone.

A moment later, a man walked into the reception room. "May I help you?" he asked.

"I want to inquire about one of your customers, Elizabeth Barwick," Williams said, and held his breath.

"Oh, yes," the man said. "She's one of Bill Schwartz's customers. Follow me."

Williams exhaled as slowly as he could and followed the man down a hallway to an office where he was introduced to a red-haired man with glasses who appeared to be in his early forties.

"Mr. Schwartz, I'm making inquiries about Elizabeth Barwick in connection with a police investigation."

Schwartz looked alarmed. "Surely Liz Barwick hasn't done anything wrong."

"Certainly not," Williams replied. "I didn't mean to imply that. We think she might have some valuable information for us, and we can't find her. Could you give me her address, please?"

"I'm afraid I can't do that," Schwartz said.

"Mr. Schwartz, let me be as plain as I can. I have reason to believe that Elizabeth Barwick is in great danger. I must tell you that if you decline to help me, you may be contributing to her violent death."

"I'm extremely upset to hear that," Schwartz said, and he looked upset. "But I'm afraid that I still cannot help you find Ms. Barwick."

Williams was starting to get angry now. "Mr. Schwartz, I'll go to the president of your bank if necessary, and—"

"Detective Williams," Schwartz interrupted, "you misunderstand me; I'm not refusing to tell you where Ms. Barwick is; I *don't know* where she is."

"Oh, no," Williams said, running a hand across his face.

Schwartz got up and went to a filing cabinet. "In

the circumstances I don't think I would be violating confidence if I told you that Ms. Barwick opened an account with us in July of this year. Her lawyer arranged it; I never even met her. She deposited . . . certain funds with us and asked us to manage them. She also asked us to pay certain bills for her." He removed a file from the cabinet and consulted it. "In August she made a lot of purchases, the last among them, a car, on August thirtieth. I had a moderately large sum in cash delivered to her on the following day, at her written request, and that was the last contact I had with her."

"Do you know if she has any credit cards?"

"She does; the usual ones. The bills are sent to me."

"If I could have a look at the receipts, maybe I could track her that way."

"There haven't been any receipts; there haven't been any bills."

"Has she cashed any checks?"

Schwartz consulted the file, then tapped some instructions into the computer terminal on his desk. "No," he said. "Nor has she used her Private Banking Card, which lets her withdraw up to five hundred dollars a day from our teller machines and several thousand others around the country. I suppose the cash I sent her has been meeting her needs."

"What kind of car did she buy?"

Schwartz picked up a piece of paper. "Here's the title. It was a Jeep Cherokee, black." He read off the license number.

Williams jotted it in his notebook. "I can at least

put out a bulletin on the car. Is there anything else you can tell me that might help find her?"

"I wish there were. I can only tell you that she hasn't touched any of her investments; I handle those."

Williams dug out a card. "If you hear from her, I would be very grateful if you would insist that she get in touch with me immediately, at any hour of the day or night. Just say that her life may depend on it."

"I will most certainly do that," Schwartz replied.

Williams sat in his car and telephoned his office. He was connected to Captain Haynes.

"Captain, I need an APB on Elizabeth Barwick's Jeep Cherokee, black." He read off the license number.

"Sure thing. I'll do it right away. How far do you want to go on this?"

"I think she's in Georgia. She told me when she called that she read about Schaefer's death. It would only have made the Atlanta and LA papers, I think."

"We'll add the bordering states," the captain said, "just in case."

"Another thing. I think we have to assume that Ramsey knows where she is. I want to put a round-the-clock tail on him."

There was a long silence at the other end of the line.

"Captain?"

"Lee," Haynes said finally, "I'm not going to be able to do that."

"But, Captain, it's the only real chance of finding the woman before Ramsey kills her."

"I understand your feelings," Haynes said carefully, "but I can't do it."

The man said "can't," not "won't," Williams thought. "Captain, have you been getting some pressure?"

"Let's just say that one Henry Hoyt, Jr., of a prominent Atlanta law firm, called the chief, and the chief called me."

"I see," Williams said.

"I hope you do, Lee," the captain replied. "I'll do what I can for you on this one, but I can't go much farther without some really substantial evidence to confirm your theories. Those are my instructions."

"I understand, Captain," Williams said, then he hung up, stunned at this turn of events.

He started the car and began driving, with no particular destination in mind. He was numb with depression. Ramsey was going to walk on five murders, and probably commit a sixth, and there wasn't a damn thing he could do about it. There was something, an old police method, one he had never used. He asked himself if he was really that angry, that frustrated. No, he told himself, I'm not. But Ramsey was certain to kill Elizabeth Barwick, unless he was stopped.

Soon, he realized that he was driving home. The car seemed to know the way. He parked in the driveway of his West End house and unlocked the door. It was only two in the afternoon; Martin was at school, and his wife was still at work. He moved slowly through the house, and, almost to his surprise, found himself walking down the stairs to the basement.

He had a little workbench there, with a vise and some household tools. He took down a small toolbox from a shelf, found a key hanging on a nail under the workbench, and unlocked the padlock. He took hold of an oily rag and felt the resistance inside it.

He peeled back the cloth to reveal a new-looking, Italian, 9-mm automatic pistol. He had taken it from a cache of weapons found in a drug bust two years before, and it had never been fired. He had run the serial number and learned that it had been stolen in a burglary in 1985. It had never been fired, and his fingerprints weren't on it, because he had never touched it with his fingers. Using a corner of the rag, he removed the clip, which held nine cartridges, the heads of which had been carefully ground flat. These bullets had been intended for cops, probably.

He shelled out the bullets and wiped each of them carefully with the oily rag, then reinserted them into the clip and wiped the clip clean, too. He shoved the clip back into the pistol, then wiped the whole thing once more; then he wrapped the gun in his handkerchief and put it into his coat pocket.

Back in his car, he drove aimlessly. He would have to think very carefully about how he was going to do this. He would have to stop shaking, for a start. He would have to put his oath, his personal guilt out of his mind, and he was not sure he could do that. He wished very badly that he could think of something else to do, but he could not.

CHAPTER

42

*L*iz sat at a light box in her darkroom, an eye pressed to a loupe, viewing a color transparency. She smiled a little, then added the shot to a stack of others and counted. One hundred even, counting the black-and-white shots. That should do for a start.

She took the shots to her desk and packaged them carefully with the prospectus she had written, then addressed them to a New York publisher who had once expressed an interest in her work. It was time to find out whether anyone else thought that what she had done on the island was any good. She got into the Jeep and drove to the inn.

Germaine was issuing the morning's instructions

to the chambermaids, and Liz waited until she had finished.

"Hi, kiddo," Germaine said.

"Good morning, I've got a package for Federal Express; has the *Aldred Drummond* left yet?"

"I'll catch her," Germaine said. She took the package and ran out the back door. She was back in a moment, puffing. "Made it. Whew! I'm getting out of shape since Ron left."

Liz laughed. "I'll loan you my Jane Fonda video-tape."

"Thanks, but that's not what I had in mind." She started to say something else, but there was a roaring outside the back door and the crunch of tires skidding on gravel.

Liz and Germaine walked outside to see James Moses running toward them, looking frightened.

"Miss Germaine," he shouted, "it's Mister Angus! Call the doctor!"

Germaine caught him by the wrists. "Calm down, now, James, and just tell me what happened."

"He came down the front steps, and I had the gelding waiting for him, like always, and I said, 'Good morning, Mister Angus,' and he started to answer me, and he couldn't seem to say anything." James stopped and caught his breath. "Then he put his hands to his head, and he said, 'Oh, Lord,' and he fell down. I picked him up and put him on the couch in his study, and there didn't seem to be anything I could do for him, so I came to get you."

"James," Germaine said, "you go on back to the house and stay with him. I'll get some help."

James ran for the jeep and Germaine headed for her office, Liz in tow.

"Is there anything I can do?" Liz asked.

"You can take me to Dungeness as soon as I've called some help." She consulted a typed list taped to the wall next to the telephone, then dialed a number. When someone answered, she said, "Charley, this is Germaine Drummond on Cumberland. My grandfather is ill, and we need a chopper at Dungeness with a doctor *right now.* It sounds like it might be a stroke. Yes, I'll be there in ten minutes, and don't you take much longer than that, you hear me? Bring everything." She hung up the phone and turned to Liz. "I'll meet you in the Jeep in thirty seconds." She ran out of the office and up the stairs.

Liz could hear her calling Hamish. She went to the Jeep, and, shortly, Germaine and Hamish burst out of the house and ran toward her. The drive to Dungeness was fast and silent; nobody seemed in a mood to talk. Liz screeched to a halt before the big house, and the three of them ran up the front steps, through the front door, and left, into the study.

Angus Drummond was stretched out on a leather lounge, his eyes open, staring at the ceiling. James sat on the floor beside him, holding his hand and talking to him. "You just rest easy, Mister Angus," he was saying, "they're all on the way."

Everybody crowded around the lounge, and Germaine knelt and took Angus's other hand. "Grandpapa, can you hear me?" she asked.

Angus nodded and looked at her, seemingly uncomprehending. Then he nodded his head again.

"Can you talk to me?" Germaine asked.

His jaw worked, but nothing came out.

"Grandpapa," Hamish said, "make a fist with your right hand."

Germaine smiled. "That's a good grip," she said.

"Now make a fist with your left hand," Hamish said.

James looked up at Hamish. "He can't do it," the boy said.

The four of them sat for three-quarters of an hour with Angus, while Germaine and Hamish tried to make conversation with the old man, reassuring him.

"Okay," Angus said suddenly.

"You *can* talk, you old faker!" Germaine said. "You're going to be just fine!"

From outside came the distant chop of a helicopter's rotors. Hamish ran outside. Liz, behind him, ran down the front steps and watched as Hamish stood, both hands raised, guiding the helicopter to a spot clear of the oak trees and the house. As soon as the copter was on the ground, a man and a woman alit, and the man ran with Hamish for the house. Liz went and helped the woman with two large cases.

In a moment they were in the study, and the nurse was unpacking oxygen equipment while the doctor began his examination.

"I'd appreciate it if you'd all wait outside until I'm through," the doctor said.

Reluctantly, Hamish, Germaine, and Liz left the room. James stood aside, but stayed, and nobody quarreled with him. Hamish led them across the hall to the drawing room, one Liz had only glimpsed. It was a huge salon, decorated in the Victorian fashion, and hung with family portraits.

Hamish flopped onto a velvet sofa. "I can't believe this," he said. "I can't remember him being ill with anything worse than the flu."

"It had to happen sometime," Germaine said, sitting beside him. "I felt it coming, I think."

"I didn't," Liz said. "I was with him yesterday, when they were reburying his grandmother's coffin at the new plot, and he seemed just as he always has since I've known him. He took me to a carpentry shop and showed me his coffin."

"He's had a coffin made?" Hamish asked.

"He's had three of them made," Liz replied. "He said one was for Buck Moses, who he wants buried with the family."

"And the other one?" Hamish asked, looking alarmed.

"He said that one was for 'just in case.'"

Hamish looked relieved.

"Who did you think it was for?" Liz asked.

"I don't know, I just wondered," Hamish said.

The doctor entered the room. "He's had a stroke."

"I knew it," Germaine said.

"He's suffered some left side paralysis, and his speech is intermittent, but I think he's fairly stable—as stable, anyway, as anybody can be who's just had a stroke at his age, even a mild one."

"What now?" Hamish asked.

"He doesn't want to go to a hospital, and I can't

disagree with that. There's not all that much we could do for him there."

"That's like him," Hamish said.

"I think the best thing to do is to get him into his own bed now, and my nurse will stay with him overnight. I'll arrange for some regular care by tomorrow. I assume that in a house this size there's somewhere for a nurse or two to sleep?"

"No problem there," Germaine said. "I'll tell the maid to get something ready."

"I sent the colored boy out to the chopper for a stretcher," the doctor said. "If you could give me a hand . . ."

A few minutes later, Angus Drummond was in his bed, and the nurse, an attractive brunette, was pottering about the room, arranging her equipment.

"You staying?" Angus asked her.

"Don't mind me," the woman said.

"I don't mind at all," Angus said, managing a crooked smile.

Hamish, Germaine, and Liz burst out laughing.

"You're incorrigible," Germaine said to him, tucking in the covers. "Watch out for him," she said to the nurse. "He'll have his hand up your skirt, first thing you know."

"I'll watch him," the nurse said.

"I'll be staying down the hall," Germaine said, "in case you need me."

"I don't think that'll be necessary," the doctor said.

"But there's no phone here," Germaine replied.

The nurse produced a small cell phone from a pocket and switched it on. "Works," she said, looking at the instrument. "Just give me your number."

The three walked downstairs with the doctor.

"I'm going now," he said. "Jennifer is very good; she can do just about anything I could do for him in an emergency, so I'll get on back. I'll be checking on his condition with her, and I'll come right out here again, if I'm needed."

Hamish thanked him, and the doctor walked toward the helicopter.

Germaine walked into the study, went straight to Angus's desk, and began going through the papers.

"What are you looking for?" Hamish asked.

"His will," Germaine replied.

"He's made a will?"

"I'm sorry, I was going to tell you today. Liz told me about it; she witnessed it."

Hamish joined her at the desk. "I'll help you," he said.

"Oh, there's something else I didn't tell you," Germaine said. "You've got an uncle."

"An uncle?"

"James Moses. Grandpapa admitted it to Liz awhile back."

"I'm not surprised about James," Hamish said. "I'm surprised that Grandpapa came right out and said it, though."

"You may have a worse surprise coming," Germaine said. "According to Liz, he's come right out and said it in his will, too."

"I don't guess that troubles me much," Hamish said. "Does it trouble you?"

Germaine kept going methodically through the papers. "I'll tell you when I've seen the will," she said.

CHAPTER

43

*L*ee Williams looked at the bedside clock. It was twenty minutes past one, and the house was as quiet as it ever got. He could hear his wife's heavy breathing in the darkness; she was in that sleep that only she could manage—deep, dreamless unconsciousness. Not even the telephone would wake her from this state.

Williams got carefully out of bed, slipped off his pajamas, picked up his clothes, and walked quietly into his living room. There he dressed—same underwear and socks, same shirt and tie that he had recently taken off. He did not want his wife to ask when she did the ironing how he had used up a fresh change of clothing.

Out of habit, he went to his son's room and

checked on the boy. He was sprawled wildly across his bed, sleeping soundly, like his mother. Williams left the house and got into the unmarked police car.

He drove onto 75 North, the interstate that ran through downtown Atlanta, exited north of the central city at Moores Mill Road, then drove to Collier Road, and found a phone booth at a darkened service station. He did not want a record of the call on his car phone bill. It was five minutes before two o'clock in the morning.

He checked his notebook and dialed the number.

"Hello?" the voice said. It was not sleepy.

"Bake, it's Lee Williams. Sorry to disturb you at this time of night."

The voice took on a hostile edge. "What do you want, Lee?"

"First of all, Bake, I want to apologize for the way I conducted myself in our interview. I was almost as upset about Mary Alice's death as you were, and I let it show."

"I guess you were doing your job."

"No, I let myself get personally involved, and that was inexcusable, then I took my feelings out on you. I'm very sorry I did that."

"It's okay, Lee." The voice relaxed a bit.

"But that's not why I called." He took a deep breath; he didn't want to sound nervous at this stage. "I called because I was dead wrong about you. I know now that you didn't hurt Mary Alice."

"Yeah?" The voice was disbelieving.

"I've found out who killed Mary Alice."

"Who?" There was interest in the voice.

"A professional burglar named Ace Smith. He's pulled half a dozen jobs in Mary Alice's apartment complex, and I've got the goods on him."

"Have you arrested him?"

"No, I'm going to do that now. I thought you might like to come along."

"Me?"

"Well, you said you'd like to get your hands on him. I might just find a way to give the two of you a couple of minutes alone."

"I'd like that. Where do I go?"

"Can you meet me at Mary Alice's apartment in, say twenty minutes?"

"Sure, I can!"

"I'll be there, and I'll leave the door unlocked. I've got word that Ace is doubling back tonight to strip the apartment. It's part of his MO, coming back later. Lots of burglars hit the same place twice, when the victims have had a chance to replace the stolen things; Ace doesn't have to wait for that, in this case."

"I'll see you there in twenty minutes," Ramsey said, and hung up.

Williams hung up the phone, then wiped it down with his handkerchief. I'm getting paranoid, he thought. Nobody would ever think to dust this particular phone. He got back into his car, drove to the rear entrance of the apartment complex, and let himself in through the self-service back gate with the card the security lady had given him. He drove slowly to Mary Alice's apartment, opened the front door with his key, and left it ajar.

He reached into his coat pocket and retrieved the

9-mm automatic, wrapped in a handkerchief; then he sat down in a comfortable chair and waited for Ramsey to arrive. He used the time to try to regulate his breathing and heartbeat and to accustom his eyes to the darkness.

Exactly on time, the front door creaked, and Ramsey filled the doorway, backlit by the light from a streetlamp. "Lee?" he whispered.

"Come on in, Bake, and have a seat," Williams said conversationally.

"I can't see much," Ramsey said.

"We can't turn on the lights. There's an armchair to your right about four feet."

"Got it." Ramsey sank into the chair. "What's the drill?"

"We've probably got the better part of an hour before he shows. I'll take him, and then you can have him."

"Sounds good to me. We just sit here until then?"

"Oh, we can talk a little."

"Sure. What's on your mind?"

"I've got most of it, I think. Maybe you'd fill in the gaps for me."

"What gaps?"

"It was Elizabeth the whole time, wasn't it?"

Ramsey said nothing.

"You wanted Elizabeth. That's why you did Al Schaefer, but Al wouldn't tell you, would he?"

Ramsey still did not speak.

"So you had to do the Fergusons, too. Raymond Ferguson told you where she was, didn't he?"

"Are you recording this, Lee?" Ramsey said finally.

"No, it's just you and me."

"Yeah, Ferguson told me. Once I had his wife, he'd have told me anything, anything at all."

"Where is Elizabeth?"

"A place called Cumberland Island, just north of Jacksonville."

"About Mary Alice: you did what you did to her, because you thought she had told me something."

"That's right. Mary Alice always liked it in the ass; I thought I'd give her a treat."

The blood pounded in William's head; he slid his finger through the trigger guard, the handkerchief protecting the trigger from his fingerprint.

"You're going to kill me, aren't you, Lee? You can't prove anything, so you're going to kill me."

"That's right, Bake. You deserve to die, and I'm going to kill you. Or rather, you're going to kill yourself."

"I see. And why do you think I'm telling you all this?"

"Because you think you're going to kill me first."

"That's right, Lee, I do."

"Don't worry, Bake, I know how quick you are. You've always been quick for such a big man. What is it, six-three, two thirty?"

"Two forty, this year. The steroids have been adding some weight. But I'm faster than ever."

"When had you planned to kill Elizabeth?"

"This weekend. We've got an off day on Sunday, and I'm going to slip down there and play with her a little bit. I'm going to do things to Liz that will make what I did to Mary Alice look like a little kid's game."

As Ramsey said this, Williams got up and, the pistol held in front of him, moved quickly across the room to Ramsey's side and held the gun to his temple. The football player did not move.

"Very good, Lee," Ramsey said. "Quick, and very nicely timed."

"It's over, Bake," Williams said. "I'm going to send you to hell now."

"Just one thing, Lee; will you do me a favor?"

"What is it, Bake? I—"

Ramsey's timing was good, too, and, in the darkness, Williams missed the move. Suddenly, Ramsey's hand gripped his wrist and moved the barrel away from his head. To Williams's astonishment, the grip was so tight that his trigger finger would not work. Then the grip tightened further, the detective's fingers involuntarily opened, and the pistol fell from his hand.

"Funny, isn't it," Ramsey said mildly, "when you press the wrist like that the fingers don't work."

"Shit!" Williams said, and it was almost his last word.

Ramsey jerked, spun the detective, and got an arm around his neck; he pulled him to the floor, his forearm pressing on the carotid artery.

The darkness swam before Williams's eyes. "Bake," he managed to say as he came close to blacking out.

Ramsey lessened the pressure ever so slightly. "Yeah, Lee? A last request?"

"Bake, the security guard saw you when you came through the main gate. You can't get away with this one."

"Oh," Ramsey said, "I came through the back gate with the pass Mary Alice gave me. Good night, Lee." He cupped Williams's chin in his hand, released the stranglehold, and grasped the back of his head with the other hand. One quick, powerful jerk, and the detective's body relaxed.

Williams heard a loud snap, and he began a swift descent into a deeper darkness.

"There, that's better," Ramsey said.

Those words were the last sound Williams heard before the darkness overtook him. He saw things, though. He saw his son's face, his wife's profile; he saw himself at four or five, riding in the back of a wagon, lying in hay; he saw his mother's back as she bent over a cast-iron wash pot; he saw a puppy his father gave him, his first. Then he saw nothing.

CHAPTER

44

Dr. Blaylock looked around the Drummond family plot with some satisfaction. He and his crew of students had unearthed the remains of twenty-one Drummonds, and the last two were ready for the trip to the new plot and reburial. In addition to the coffins, he and his students had recovered a hundred and thirty items of some archaeological or anthropological interest, among them, pottery, clay pipes, tools, a pistol, several bone buttons, and a brass box containing three thousand dollars in Confederate one-hundred-dollar bank notes. Their work was finished, now, but for one last item.

"All right, young people," he said to his group, "I want two volunteers to dismantle the erstwhile resting place of General Light-Horse Harry Lee and reassemble it in the new plot, in the space designated by Mr. Drummond. I'm afraid there will be no artifacts to find—just the hard work of removing the covering and base." He waited for his volunteers and got none. "All right," he said, "you and you." He pointed to two hefty young men.

The boys sighed and took hold of tools. The former grave consisted of a single, large slab of badly weathered marble, resting on a base formed by four smaller slabs, which had been embedded deeply in the earth. The top slab lifted away easily enough and was loaded into the truck with the coffins. The base slabs required digging; one boy manned a pick, the other a shovel. They had dug down a couple of feet when they stopped.

"Dr. Blaylock, come take a look at this," the boy wielding the pick said.

"What have you got?" Blaylock asked.

"A bone, I guess," the boy said.

Blaylock took a trowel and began removing small amounts of the sandy earth. The other students gathered around to watch.

Three hours later, Blaylock stood back to survey the results of his work. "Comments?" he asked no one in particular.

There was a long silence, then a girl said, "Male, over six feet."

"Good," Blaylock said. "Age?"

"Not terribly old," the same girl said. "He's still got all his teeth."

Blaylock reached down and gently rotated the skull of the skeleton. "Cause of death?"

"Bullet in the brain," a boy said.

"Do you see a bullet in the skull?"

"No, sir," the boy replied.

"Do you see an exit wound?"

"No, sir."

"Blow to the back of the head," the girl said.

"Good," Blaylock said. "How long would you say these remains have been in the ground?"

The girl frowned, then bent over and plucked at a bit of cloth with a pair of long tweezers. "My guess is twentieth century," she said.

"Why?"

She held up the fragment. "There's a copper rivet in this cloth. Looks like Levi's to me. Levi's go back to the nineteenth century in the West, but I'll bet not here."

"You're very observant," Blaylock said. "Now, what most of all strikes you as unusual about this skeleton?"

There was a lot of weight shifting and head scratching. "Just that it's in awful good shape," the girl said.

"You disappoint me, all of you," Blaylock scolded. "Have you all given up movies and TV?"

"What do you mean, Dr. Blaylock?" a boy asked.

"I mean that it looks very much as though this man was murdered and buried in an empty grave," Blaylock said. "And not too many decades ago."

"Holy shit," the boy said.

"Not a very scientific observation, but an appropriate one," Blaylock said. "You," he said, pointing at a young man, "take the truck to the inn, and ask Germaine Drummond to call the sheriff in St. Marys. And don't mention this to anybody but her."

The sheriff, Dr. Blaylock, and Germaine stood at the graveside and stared down at the skeleton.

"Dr. Blaylock," the sheriff said, "you want to hazard a guess as to how long this fellow has been in the ground?"

"It's only a wild guess—you'll need a pathologist for something closer—but I'd say twenty or thirty years."

"Germaine, do you remember anybody disappearing around here? Anything mysterious like that?"

"No, and if someone had, I'd certainly have remembered it."

"Well, I'll get somebody down here from the state crime lab to look at this," the sheriff said, "but I'm damned if I know how they're going to be able to identify it. There's no jewelry or wallet or anything else we can use to establish an identity."

"My guess is that you'll never know," Blaylock said.

"How about the teeth?" Germaine asked. "Isn't that how they identify bodies?"

"Yes," the sheriff replied, "but that only works when you've got some idea of who it is, and you just want a confirmation. You need some dental records for the comparison."

"Well, we've got a bunch of those," Germaine said.

"Dental records?"

"Yep. About two hundred yards over there, in back of the main house, there's a dentist's office. A man used to come from the mainland regularly to treat the islanders, until about ten or twelve years ago, when Grandpapa decided that the cost of putting in up-to-date equipment couldn't be justified by the reduced number of people working on the place. Everybody has gone to Jacksonville or St. Marys since then."

"Was there an X-ray machine?" Blaylock asked.

"Absolutely. Nothing was too good for the island folk, as far as Grandpapa was concerned."

"Sheriff," Blaylock said, "I'll be happy to go through those records and see if I can get a match."

"Go to it, Doc," the sheriff said. "If you can identify him, then I won't need to call in Atlanta."

"I'll get some close-up Polaroid shots of the teeth," Blaylock said, "and then you can take me to your dentist's office."

"I'd like all of you to keep this quiet, until we find out who this is," the sheriff said to the group. He looked at the skies. "We're going to have some rain, this evening, I think."

"In that case," Blaylock said, "I think we'd better move this skeleton."

Late in the afternoon, Dr. Blaylock sat hunched over a light box in the dusty dental surgery, a small file drawer on the table beside him. He picked up a magnifying glass and made one more comparison of the radiograph films on the light box with the Polaroid photographs of the skeleton's teeth. He switched off the light box and stood up, massaging the back of his neck. Then he picked up the film, placed it in an envelope, and put it into his inside coat pocket. He was confused, and when he was confused about a problem, he liked to sleep on it before making a decision. He certainly was going to sleep on this one.

He turned off the overhead light and left the room. The sheriff and Germaine were waiting for him under a huge live oak.

"Any luck?" the sheriff asked.

Blaylock shook his head. "I haven't got a match yet," he lied, "and it'll take me until at least noon tomorrow to get through the rest of the records. Why don't you go on home, Sheriff, and I'll call you when I've got an answer for you."

"All right," the sheriff said, turning toward his helicopter. "I'll wait to hear from you."

"I'd better check on Grandpapa," Germaine said, and turned toward the main house.

"I wouldn't tell him about this," Blaylock called after her, "until we have some answers." Maybe not even then, he thought. He got into his truck and headed for the inn, a hot bath, and some dinner, which he reckoned he much deserved. He still didn't know who the skeleton was in Light-Horse Harry's grave, but now he knew why Buck Moses hadn't wanted the Drummond family plot disturbed.

"Holy shit," he said aloud to himself.

CHAPTER

45

As Liz drove through the front gates of Dungeness, she could hear the blades of a helicopter beating the air. She looked up as she alit from the Jeep and saw it coming in from the west. James Moses was standing at the foot of the steps, holding the gelding, as if it were an ordinary day.

"Good morning, Miss Elizabeth," he said.

"Good morning, James, I just dropped by to look in on Mr. Drummond." As she started up the front steps the nurse, Jennifer, appeared at the front door and saw the approaching helicopter.

"Thank God," the woman said.

"What's wrong?" Liz asked, alarmed.

"Mr. Drummond is having some sort of spell,"

she said. "I can't do a thing with him; he's thrown me out of his room twice. I called the doctor and Germaine."

Liz rushed past her into the house, then up the stairs. She turned right at the top and found Angus's room. The door was closed. Timidly, she knocked.

"Come!" a strong voice said.

She opened the door and stopped. Angus Drummond stood near his bed, stuffing a steamer trunk with clothes.

"Oh, it's you, my darling," he said, beaming at her. "I thought it was the bloody chambermaid again. She insists on coming in here while I'm running around in my skivvies."

"I see," Liz said weakly. Angus was transformed. From the sick old man she had seen only the day before, he had become authoritative, even youthful again; in fact, he seemed decades younger. "What are you doing, Angus?" she asked.

"I'm packing, that's what I'm doing," he said, walking over and putting his arms around her. "I've decided I'd rather hear you sing Mimi in Paris than hang about here out of season. I'll be with you in just a few minutes." He kissed her firmly on the lips, then returned to his packing.

"Paris?" she said, unable to think of anything else.

"I've ordered a water taxi; we'd never make the morning train in a gondola, and if we miss that one, we'll have to change trains in Milan, and that's a four-hour wait. I hate hanging about railway stations, don't you?"

"Yes." She felt she should do something, but she had no idea what. All she could do was humor him until the doctor arrived.

"I didn't tell you last night," he went on, taking neckties from a closet and hanging them in the trunk, "but Cipriani gave me the recipe for the bellinis. When you come to Cumberland, I'll make them for you with real Georgia peaches!"

"That would be wonderful," Liz said. She could hear hurried footsteps on the stairs.

"Angus," she said, "I don't know where my mind has gone; what year is this?"

He stopped packing and stared at her for a moment, then burst out laughing. "Why, it's nineteen twenty-three, you goose!"

The door opened, and Liz turned to see the doctor and his nurse, followed closely by Germaine, Hamish, and James. She turned back to Angus.

"Goddamnit!" he bellowed, "I'll ring when my luggage is ready! I don't need the whole bloody staff in here!" Then he looked back at Liz and seemed to see her for the first time. "Oh, good morning, Elizabeth," he said. He put a hand to his head and his knees buckled.

Liz caught him in her arms, and the doctor moved forward to help her; they laid him on his bed. Liz saw his pupils dilate, then there was a rattle in his throat, and he stopped moving.

The doctor produced a stethoscope from his bag, bent over, and listened at the old man's chest; then he stood up straight. "He's gone."

Germaine, James, and Hamish moved to the bed-

side, and Germaine took her grandfather's hand.
"What happened?" she said to Liz.

"Oh!" said Liz, beginning to cry, "I wish you
could have seen him! He was wonderful!"

By noon, Angus Drummond's body had been
washed, dressed in a blue suit, placed in his coffin, and
stored in the Dungeness wine cellar, the coolest place
on the island. Hamish, Germaine, James, and Liz sat
in Angus's study. The doctor came in and handed
Germaine a sheet of paper.

"His death certificate," he said. "You can bury
him whenever you wish."

"Thank you, Doctor," Germaine said. "And
thank you, Jennifer," she said to the nurse.

The nurse stepped forward and handed Germaine an envelope. "Mr. Drummond gave me this last
night and asked me to give it to you. It was as if he
knew."

The doctor and nurse shook hands all around,
then left.

Germaine sat slowly down on the big leather
couch and opened the envelope; she held up a single
piece of paper. "It's the combination to his safe," she
said.

"What safe?" Hamish asked.

"I didn't know there was one, either," Germaine
said. "Where do you suppose it is? James, do you
know?"

"No, Miss Germaine," James said.

"James, we'd better get something straight right
now," Germaine said firmly. "Grandpapa let us know

about you before he died. You're his son, which makes me your niece and Hamish your nephew. You don't ever have to call anybody in this family mister or miss again, all right?"

"All right, Germaine," James said, and he managed a small smile.

Germaine smiled, too. "Do I have to call you uncle?"

James laughed aloud. "No, Germaine."

"Now about this safe," Germaine said.

Liz chimed in. "In the movies, safes are always behind pictures."

As one, the group turned and looked at the Turner hanging over the couch. Germaine got up and removed it from its hook, to reveal a large, floridly painted safe in the wall. Consulting the paper in her hand, she worked the combination and turned the handle; the door swung silently open. The safe was stuffed with papers, and on the top shelf Germaine found a large, sealed envelope. "Last will and testament," she read.

They all sat down, except Hamish.

"Excuse me," he said, and started to leave the room.

"Don't you want to hear what's in it?" Germaine said.

"I think I know, more or less," he said. "You read it." He left the room, and, a moment later, the front door of the house opened and closed.

Germaine turned over the envelope, tore open the flap, and removed several sheets of paper. "Here," she said, handing them to Liz. "You're the disinterested party, so you can be the lawyer. Read it to us."

Liz unfolded the pages and looked at them. "The other witness, besides me, is one Ronald Cummings; who is that?"

"You remember my Ron." Germaine sighed. "He never told me about this."

Liz began to read.

"I, Angus Aldred Drummond, being of sound mind, if not body, do hereby make this last will and testament, and I wish all concerned to know that it represents my true wishes without the undue influence of any person.

"I appoint as executor of my will, my eldest grandchild, Germaine Drummond.

"My executor is instructed that all my just debts and all the inheritance taxes due are to be paid from the liquid part of my estate, before any bequest is taken into account.

"I wish to state that the young man known as James Moses is my natural and much-loved son, the issue of a loving union between his mother, Helen Moses, and myself. It is my wish, if he consents, that, after the death of his grandfather, Buck Moses, he change his name by deed poll to Drummond, so that all the world may know that he is my son.

"I have established a trust, known as The Cumberland Island Trust, which shall hold title to all the land on the island, excepting certain bequests, which follow. Attached to this will, and signed by me, is a map which divides the island into tracts of land of approximately three hundred acres each, which are to be used in the disposition of the island among my heirs. No tract of Cumberland land shall ever be sold by any heir to a person who is not a direct descendant by the male or female lines, of Aldred Drummond, who received Cumberland Island in a grant from

King George III of England. Should any of my heirs die without issue, such land as I have bequeathed to him or her shall revert to The Cumberland Island Trust, but may be occupied by the heir's spouse until his or her death.

"I do give and bequeath the house known as Greyfield, and the tract of land on which it rests, to my granddaughter, Germaine, to use as she may see fit, along with the sum of two million dollars.

"Oh, Lord," Germaine said, "he was sweet, but he didn't have two million dollars."

Liz read on. *"I do give and bequeath the house known as Plum Orchard, and the tract of land on which it rests, to my grandson Hamish, along with the sum of two million dollars.*

"I do give and bequeath to my grandson Keir any other tract of land on Cumberland Island he may so desire which has not been bequeathed to another, along with the sum of three million dollars, in the hope that he will construct a house of his own on this land.

"I do give and bequeath to my natural son, James Moses, any tract of land on Cumberland Island which has not been bequeathed to another, along with the sum of three million dollars, to be held in trust until his twenty-fifth birthday. It is my desire that James receive the finest education that he can absorb, and that he use funds from his trust to travel widely, as I did in my youth. I appoint as his trustees Germaine Drummond and my friend Elizabeth Barwick.

Liz turned to James. "We'll have a lot to talk about," she said.

"I do give and bequeath to my great-grandson, Aldred Drummond, the sum of three million dollars, to be held in trust until his twenty-fifth birthday, except that the income of the trust may be used for the purpose of education and travel. I appoint as trustees his mother, Hannah Drummond, and his father, Hamish

Drummond. On reaching his twenty-fifth birthday, Aldred may choose any tract of land on the island which has not been bequeathed to another, and the trust shall pay him the sum of one million dollars, adjusted for inflation, to be used to maintain the land and to build a residence for his use, if he so chooses.

"I specifically exclude my grandson James Weathers from any inheritance from my estate, and I instruct the trustees of The Cumberland Island Trust to bar him from the island at all times. I do give and bequeath to Martha Weathers, the wife of James Weathers, the sum of two hundred and fifty thousand dollars, on the condition that none of this sum be spent directly on her husband.

"I herewith instruct my executor that, in perpetuity, if any United States, State of Georgia or county politician shall advocate the purchase of any part of Cumberland Island for public use, the sum of fifty thousand dollars from the residue of my estate be made available to that politician's principal opponent for use in his campaign."

"I love it." Germaine laughed.

Liz read a list of small bequests to servants at Dungeness and workmen on the island. There were also cash bequests to a number of charities.

"Finally, I do give and bequeath the residue of my estate, including all the unbequeathed lands of Cumberland Island, and all my stocks, bonds and cash, to The Cumberland Island Trust, the liquid part of my estate amounting to approximately seventy million dollars, before taxes, administrated by the Morgan Guaranty Trust Company of New York."

"Good God!" Germaine exploded, "he must have been hallucinating. He didn't have any real money, just the island. I mean, there was some money a few

•
370

generations back, but I thought it had been frittered away."

"Records of these funds and a financial statement are to be found in the safe in my study at Dungeness."

Germaine was on her feet, rummaging in the safe. "He wasn't crazy," she said breathlessly. "Here's a brokerage statement dated last month, with a balance of more than twenty million dollars! Where did it come from?"

"I suppose he must have invested wisely," Liz said. "It would be interesting to know if he got out of the market before the 'twenty-nine crash. Now sit down, Germaine, and let me finish."

"I appoint as trustees Germaine Drummond, Hamish Drummond, Keir Drummond, Elizabeth Barwick and a representative of the Morgan Guaranty Trust Company of New York, to be chosen by the bank. I appoint James Moses a trustee, to be effective on his twenty-fifth birthday. The trustees are directed to meet not less than four times a year to discuss the management of the estate, and those trustees who are not employed by the bank are to be paid salaries of fifty thousand dollars per annum each from the Trust. When a trustee becomes deceased, the trustees will elect a replacement.

"I instruct my named heirs to remove from the house called Dungeness all furniture, silverware, books, works of art, and any other effects which might be useful to them or any other person. I wish them to divide these possessions among themselves and their friends. Should they be unable to agree on the ownership of any object, that object shall become the property of the Trust and shall be sold at auction for the benefit of the Trust.

"It is my view that Dungeness is an anachronism, and that it should die with me. No member of my family wishes to live in

it, and I have no wish for strangers to occupy it. It is for this reason that I have allowed the house to deteriorate for the past twenty years. It is my wish, and I so instruct my heirs, that when all worthwhile furnishings and objects have been removed, the house be set afire on a windless day, and, when the structure has been consumed, the land be cleared and planted in trees, flowers, and other plants indigenous to Cumberland Island. It is my wish that, apart from an appropriate and modest tombstone, this new planting will be my only memorial.

"Finally, I wish to say to my heirs and my friends and to anyone who knew me, that I have lived, for the most part, a joyful and rewarding life, comforted by the generosity of my forefathers and the love of my family and friends, and the respect and affection of the people who toiled in my service and that of Cumberland Island. I leave this life a happy and contented man, and I wish that same happiness and contentment to those I love."

"That's all," Liz said, tears rolling down her face. Then she looked and saw that tears were on the faces of Germaine and James, as well.

She wondered where Hamish was, and why he had left.

CHAPTER

46

*T*he three of them, Liz, Germaine, and James, sat silently in Angus Drummond's study, drained. Nobody seemed to know what to do next.

"I suppose we ought to think about a time for the funeral," Germaine said finally. When no one said anything, she went on. "Today's Thursday. We'll want the announcement in tomorrow's papers, and we'll need to allow some time for people to travel— Hannah and Aldred will come, I'm sure, and there'll be others from Atlanta and Jacksonville. I think Monday morning should be good. We'll have a special run of the *Aldred Drummond* Monday morning, and I'll give everybody lunch at the inn after the service. What do you think?"

"That sounds sensible," Liz said.

"It's fine with me," James said. "I'll just miss school that day."

"Well"—Germaine sighed—"there doesn't seem to be anything else to do here. I'll go back to the inn and phone the papers. I'm fully booked this weekend, too, and I've got some things to do around the place."

They rose to go, and, as they did, the doorbell rang. They went together to answer it and found Dr. Blaylock standing on the front porch. The sheriff's helicopter was just landing on the front lawn.

"I've just heard about your grandfather, from Hamish," Blaylock said, and he looked upset. "Please accept my sympathy, Germaine; he was a wonderful man and my friend for a long time."

"Thank you, Dr. Blaylock," she said. "What's the sheriff doing back, I wonder?"

"I'm afraid I called him, as I said I would yesterday. It was before I ran into Hamish and learned about Angus's death. I'm sorry this is such a bad time, but I really must speak to you and the sheriff now, Germaine."

"All right," she replied.

"And you, too, Miss Barwick," the professor said. "We're going to need your advice, as well as the family's."

"If this is a family matter, then James should be there, too," Germaine said. "He's my grandfather's son, and everybody had better start getting used to the idea."

"All right," Dr. Blaylock said.

The sheriff had alit from his helicopter and was striding toward the house.

They all stood in the disused dentist's office, and Dr. Blaylock had switched on the light box. He took an envelope from his pocket and arranged some radiograph films on the box; then he produced a set of Polaroid photographs.

"I've been through all the dental records and X rays; I began by eliminating the women and children and older men. There weren't that many more records to search." He paused. "I've found films that match the teeth of the skeleton we found in the Light-Horse Harry Lee grave."

"Who was he?" Germaine said. "If he had his teeth worked on here, I must have known him."

"He didn't have his teeth worked on, except on one occasion," Blaylock said. The professor was starting to look uncomfortable.

"So?" the sheriff said.

"I've got a very good match, here," Blaylock said, holding up the Polaroids next to the film on the light box.

"Looks the same to me," the sheriff said. "What's his name?"

"I don't know that, yet," Blaylock said.

"Wasn't his name on the dental records?" the sheriff asked.

"I'm afraid there were two names on these records," said Blaylock. "There was no indication which X rays belonged to which person." He held up a file folder.

"The Drummond twins," the sheriff read aloud.

There was absolute silence in the room while everyone absorbed this news.

"I'm missing your point, Dr. Blaylock," Germaine said finally.

"My point is, the skeleton in the Light-Horse Harry Lee grave is one of the Drummond twins, either Hamish or Keir."

Liz suddenly felt as if she had been struck in the chest with a heavy object. She wanted to run from the room.

"But that's clearly impossible," Germaine said reasonably. "You've met Hamish, and Keir is here on the island, too; I've seen him, and so has Liz. The records have obviously been mixed up in some way."

"No," Dr. Blaylock said, "there's no mix-up. Neither of these boys ever had so much as a filling in his head. The only dental work they ever had, apart from an occasional cleaning, was when they were sixteen; they both had their lower wisdom teeth removed on the same day. That's when these films were taken." When Germaine still did not seem to grasp what he was saying, the professor spoke again. "My point is that one of the twins is lying over there in that shed. Or at least, his remains are."

Germaine stared disbelievingly at Blaylock, but did not seem to be able to speak.

"Are you saying," the sheriff said, "that one of those boys murdered the other one and has been pretending to be his brother?"

"No, I'm not saying that. I have no idea how or

when that boy was killed. But," he said, "it's my guess that Buck Moses can tell us."

"I think you're right," Liz said.

"Why do you think Buck knows?" Germaine managed to ask.

"Buck stole the toolboxes from the professor's camp," Liz said. "I saw them at his house. He must have done it because he didn't want the Light-Horse Harry grave disturbed."

"I think that's exactly right," Blaylock said. "I think Buck buried the boy in that grave on the day he was killed."

Germaine sank heavily into a chair.

Liz held on to a table, trying to gain some control over her emotions. "Germaine," she said at last, "when was the last time you saw the twins together?"

"I remember exactly," Germaine said. "It was the day they left to go off to college, in September of— let's see, the twins are thirty-seven, and they were eighteen then—nineteen seventy. Buck Moses took them to Fernandina in Grandpapa's launch." She rubbed her temples with her fingers. "Hamish arrived at Princeton, I remember, but Keir didn't. We didn't hear from him until Christmas, when we got a letter from New York. Grandpapa and I nearly went crazy waiting to hear from him. Grandpapa had private detectives looking for him."

Dr. Blaylock turned to James Moses, who had been listening in silence. "James, has your grandfather ever said anything to you about this?"

"No, sir," James said. He looked as stunned as Germaine and Liz.

"Well, I think you'd better go and get him and bring him to Dungeness," Blaylock said.

Buck Moses sat in Angus Drummond's study, his hat in his lap, and wiped his face with a bandanna. "Them boys loved each other like nothin' I ever seen," he said, "until that girl come to the island."

"I remember," Germaine said. "Gilly something—I can't remember her last name. Her mother brought her down here from New York for the month of August that year."

"They loved that girl," Buck said, "both of them. They loved her to death. I never saw 'em like that, 'cept that one time."

"What happened, Buck?" Germaine asked, putting a hand on his shoulder.

"I come here to Dungeness to get 'em, to carry 'em to Fernandina, to get a taxi to the airport. They was havin' breakfast."

"I remember," Germaine said. "We said goodbye to them, Grandpapa and I. They didn't want to change into suits."

"Tha's right. They was wearing them jeans, and they said they's gonna change on the boat. Well, I got 'em on the boat, and they started arguing somethin' awful, 'bout that pretty girl, the way boys do, and they had a fight. I stop the boat, but I couldn't do nothin' with 'em, I just couldn't. They was rasslin' around, and they fell down, and one of them boys didn't move no more. They was blood on the back of his head, where he done hit it on a bronze cleat." Buck closed his eyes. "They was brains on that cleat."

"Which one hit his head, Buck?" Germaine asked, leaning close to the old man.

"I swear to God, I don't know. I didn't never know. I put the other boy off at Fernandina and tole him to go to school and keep his mouth shut, and I was gon' take care of his brother."

"And he went off, just like that?"

"He in a daze, like. He just do what I tole him to do. I put him in the taxi and sent him off. Next time I see him, he was home at Christmas. He was Hamish." Buck wiped his face again with the bandanna, and tears rolled down his ebony cheeks. "Next time I see him was the next summer, and he was Keir. He done got to be both those boys."

"And what did you do with the other boy when you left Fernandina?" the sheriff asked.

"I brung the boat up through the marsh to the graveyard, and I put him in ol' Harry's grave, and I said my prayers over him. Then I come back to the dock at Dungeness and didn't say nothin' to nobody, never again, 'bout that day, 'till this minute. I never even said nothin' to Hamish and Keir—whichever he was. He act like it never happen, and so did I. We never said nothin' again 'bout it."

Nobody in the room said anything for a long time; then the sheriff stood up. "Germaine," he said, "this is no business of mine; I've got no interest in what's happened here. There's no crime, as far as I'm concerned, only an accident—involuntary manslaughter at worst, and the statute of limitations ran out on that years ago. I'm not about to arrest somebody as old as Buck for covering up a death, twenty years ago. It's history, and family history, at that, and I'll leave you to do what you will about it." He flicked dust off his Stetson. "I'll bid you all good-bye, and I'm going to forget this day just as fast as I can. Germaine, I'm real sorry about Mr. Drummond." He left the room and the house. Moments later, the helicopter departed from the front lawn.

"Buck," Germaine said to the weeping old man, "I don't know if you did the right thing, but I know you didn't do wrong. You've got nothing to feel bad about. I want to thank you for letting me have my . . . brothers for all these years."

James stood up. "Come on, Granddaddy, I'll take you home."

The two departed, and Dr. Blaylock stood up. "I'm going to tell my students that I didn't find any matching records. I'm going to tell myself that, too." He handed the X-ray film of the twins to Germaine. "Here, you get rid of these."

He left the house, and the two women were alone in the study.

Germaine looked at Liz. "Oh, Jesus, honey," she said, "what are we going to do?"

Liz spoke through her numbness and grief. "We're going to get some help," she said.

Liz sat at Germaine's desk and held the telephone, while Germaine anxiously listened in.

"That's the worst story I ever heard," Dr. Douglas Hamilton said. "What have you done about it?"

"Nothing, so far," Liz said.

"Then you've done the right thing," Hamilton

said. "This man has spent the past twenty years pretending to be . . . no, not pretending—actually *being* two people. It's a sort of self-induced schizophrenia, and it's very deeply ingrained. I'll wager that when he is one of the twins, he has no conscious memory of what happened when he is the other."

"That doesn't seem humanly possible," Germaine said.

"The human mind can exclude whatever it wishes, if it's well enough motivated. Your brother's guilt is such that it is unbearable, so he has excluded the memory of his twin's death, and the only way he can keep his twin alive is by living his brother's life, as well as his own."

"But how can we stop this?" Germaine demanded. "How can we help him?"

"You can't stop it, and you can only help him by continuing as before." Hamilton sighed. "Germaine, if you force him to confront reality, you will destroy him. For an identical twin, the act of killing his brother is tantamount to suicide, and the only way he could avoid that was by refusing to acknowledge it. If he is made to acknowledge it, then it's very likely that he would take his own life."

"If you saw him, could you treat him?" Liz asked.

"I doubt it; not everyone is treatable psychiatrically, you know, just as physical illness is sometimes untreatable. From what you've told me, he is successfully conducting two different, but reasonably stable existences, and only if the tissue separating those two lives is torn is he likely to show symptoms of mental illness. If that happened, and if he survived the experience, then he might be treatable, but I doubt very much if he could survive."

"How long is this likely to last?" Germaine asked.

"Until his own death frees him," Hamilton said.

"Thank you, Ham," Liz said. "We won't take any more of your time."

"Liz," Hamilton said, "I gather that you are in love with this man."

"I am," Liz replied.

"Then I had better warn you of something. I think Drummond has found a way to live with himself, and that he can go on functioning that way. But you know something he doesn't, and knowing it is likely to make life with him difficult, perhaps impossible for you. You're never going to have more than half of him, or, at best, all of him for some of the time. And you're never going to be able to sublimate his secret, as he has; you'll have to live with it every minute. Before you decide to continue with this relationship, you'd better think hard about whether you can live with that."

"Thank you, Ham. Can I call you again sometime?"

"Any time, Liz."

She hung up the phone and turned to Germaine.

"Well, Jesus," Germaine said, "this is going to be tough enough on me, but what the hell are you going to do?"

"I guess I'm going to have to find out if I can live with it," Liz said.

CHAPTER

47

*L*iz got herself ready on the drive back to Stafford Beach Cottage, but when she arrived, Keir was not there.

She curled up on the couch, exhausted, and her eye fell on something familiar on the coffee table: Angus Drummond's handwriting; her name. It was the envelope he had given her at dinner, the gift he had asked her to accept. She had left it in a pigeonhole of her desk. Keir must have put it where she would see it.

Carefully, she opened the envelope and read the single sheet of paper inside. It was dated the same day as his will.

LEASE

As the sole trustee of the Cumberland Island Trust, I do hereby grant a lease on that property known as Stafford Beach Cottage and five surrounding acres marked on a map in my safe, to Miss Elizabeth Barwick, for the term of her life, the lives of her spouse and/or any of her direct descendants. Should she or the last of her descendants die without issue, this lease shall revert to the Cumberland Island Trust. I do hereby direct that the Trust shall pay all of the expense of the upkeep of the exterior of said cottage and the surrounding property, upon request of the leaseholder. Further, I direct that the leaseholder be entitled to keep vehicles on the island, and be entitled to the use of the island's roads, docks, waterways and airstrip, without charge.

It was the second time that day that she had wept.

Liz didn't see Keir until the following day. He arrived at the cottage late in the afternoon and looked for a drink in the kitchen. He filled a glass with ice, then filled it with bourbon.

She was ready for him; she thought he looked different. "You've heard about your grandfather?"

"Yes," he said, "Germaine told me, and I wasn't ready for it. I suddenly realized that I always thought he would outlive me."

"Oddly enough," she said, "I felt the same way; he was such a vital man. Somehow, I thought of him as much younger."

"I don't think he ever got any older than about twenty-two."

"He was that young again for a few minutes before he died," Liz said, and she told him about it.

Keir chuckled. "He was pretty wild in his youth, you know."

"I didn't, but it doesn't surprise me. He did tell me that he had traveled in Europe for some years."

"Traveled isn't a strong enough word. The story in the family is that he cut a swath from London to Stockholm to Cannes to Rome to Madrid to Paris and back, with a diva on one arm and a prima ballerina on the other. Germaine told me she once found a list Grandpapa had kept of his lovers, and there were more than a hundred of them."

"Good God!"

"It makes me think I've led a sheltered life."

"Haven't we all, compared to him!"

"Did you open the envelope?"

"Yes."

"He gave you the cottage, didn't he?"

"A lifetime lease, the dear. I guess you'll have me as a neighbor."

He kissed her lightly. "That's okay with me."

"Did Germaine tell you about the will?"

"Yes," he said, and quickly changed the subject. "By the way, she asked us to the inn for dinner tonight."

Liz looked at him, amazed. "And you want to go?"

"Sure, why not?"

He had shunned the inn since she had known him. "Why not, indeed? I'd better get into something a little less informal." She looked at the cutoffs he was wearing. "How about you? You going like that, or do you think you should wear the loincloth?"

"Oh, I think the loincloth," he said. "The shorts are so dressy, and the inn is such an informal place."

An hour later they arrived at the inn. Liz snuck another look at Keir. He was wearing baggy linen trousers and an old silk shirt. "You look rather elegant," she said. "Do you know, it's the first time I've ever seen you in trousers?"

"Shhh, what will the guests think?" They climbed the front steps. "Actually, these were my father's clothes. I could manage white tie and tails, if I had to."

At the top of the steps, Liz stopped and looked up at the darkening sky. "Looks like rain," she said.

"A lot of rain, I should think," Keir replied.

There were two couples in the bar, and Germaine was pouring drinks. She looked tired, but chipper.

"Evening, you two." She grinned. "What's your pleasure?"

"Bourbon all around, I think," Keir said. "Busy night?"

"You bet. On top of everything else, it's the first time in weeks we've been completely full. I've even got somebody in that horrible little single—a man, no less!"

"Careful, Germaine," Keir said, leaning close. "No screwing the guests."

"That's *my* rule, so *I* don't have to keep it," Germaine said slyly. She handed Keir the drinks. "Both the Atlanta and Jacksonville papers will run an obituary tomorrow. I've made the arrangements for Monday."

"Please let me know if there's anything I can do to help," Liz said.

"Where I'm going to need you is when we clean out Dungeness. I need a good eye to help me decide what to keep and what to throw away."

"I'd be glad to help."

Germaine turned to help other guests who were entering; Liz and Keir found a sofa and flopped onto it.

"So, what's it like being a social animal again?" Liz asked.

"I'd forgotten," Keir said. "I haven't been in a room with this many people for weeks."

"You should try it more often."

Dr. Blaylock entered with a woman about his own age.

"Good evening, Dr. Blaylock," Liz said.

"Ah, Miss Barwick, may I present my wife?"

"How do you do," Liz said. "And this is Keir Drummond."

She held her breath. She wondered what his reaction would be.

"Mister Drummond, I've heard about you," Blaylock said smoothly. "I'm very sorry about your grandfather's death. He was my good friend, and I'll miss him."

"Thank you," Keir said.

"I hear you know this island as well as Buck Moses."

"Nobody knows this island as well as Buck." Keir laughed.

"Old Buck does seem to know things no one else knows," Blaylock said.

"Well," Keir said, "Buck lives in a different world from the rest of us. His father was a slave, brought to this island in the middle of the last century. There's still a lot of Africa in Buck, I think."

"No doubt," Blaylock said.

"How much more work have you to do?" Keir asked.

"We're done. We moved the last two coffins yesterday. We should have all the stones in place in time for the funeral on Monday."

Germaine's voice rang out. "Dinner is served."

The group finished their drinks and began moving toward the downstairs dining room.

There was a rumble of thunder from outside, and rain began to fall.

"That will be Hurricane Iago, I expect," Dr. Blaylock said.

"A hurricane?" Liz asked, alarmed. "Is it going to hit here?"

"Not likely, according to the National Weather Service. They're predicting landfall somewhere on the North Carolina or Virginia coast," Blaylock said. "Charleston is pretty worried, though; they're not back on their feet after Hugo."

"I'm glad Iago is heading north," Keir said. "We haven't had the full force of a hurricane here for a good fifteen years, and we were a long time clearing up after that one."

They reached the dining room, and Germaine steered Keir, Liz, and the Blaylocks to a table. "I'll join you in a moment," she said. "I just want to check the kitchen before I sit down."

Keir held a chair for Liz, and she sat down and unfolded her napkin; she took a sip of water and glanced around the room. Her gaze stopped on a familiar back at another table, and a shudder ran through her.

"Is something wrong?" Keir asked.

Liz tried to speak, but couldn't.

Keir leaned close. "Liz, you're as white as marble, and you're shaking. What's wrong?"

The back rose high and wide, and at the top of it a closely cropped blond head sat on an impossibly thick neck. The head turned, and she saw the familiar chiseled profile; the eyes swept the room, falling on, then passing her.

"Get me out," Liz managed to say. "Quick."

"Please excuse us for a moment," Keir said to the

•

Blaylocks. He got an arm around Liz's waist and helped her to her feet and into the kitchen.

Germaine got a glimpse of her and hurried over. "What on earth is wrong, sugar?"

"She's not feeling well," Keir said. "I'll take care of her; you go on and see to your guests."

He led her into the staff dining room and got her into a chair, then grabbed a pitcher and poured some water.

"No, I don't need that," Liz panted.

"What's wrong? Do you think you need a doctor?"

"No. My ex-husband is in the dining room."

"What? The guy who . . ."

"Yes, the very one."

"But Germaine wouldn't have let him in here."

"Germaine doesn't even know his name. He's probably not using his own name anyway."

"I'd like to meet the guy," Keir said, straightening up.

"No!" she nearly shouted. "Don't you go anywhere near him!"

"All right, if you say so," Keir muttered, but he didn't look happy about it.

"We've got to call the sheriff."

Keir took her by the shoulders. "Now, Liz, be sensible. What would we tell the sheriff? The guy hasn't done anything. Also, nobody's crossing Cumberland Sound tonight, not in this weather."

"Just get me back to the cottage, will you?"

"Of course I will."

He helped her up the stairs and out the front

door. Lightning flashed, and they hurried down the steps in the rain, which was heavier now. The huge live oaks on the inn's lawn swayed and groaned in the night.

"I've got to get off the island right away," she said, as they drove away from the inn.

Keir put an arm around her and pulled her close. "Liz, that's impossible," he said. "Just look at this weather. Anyway, I think you're overreacting. Why should he want to hurt you? The marriage is over."

"That's just the point. It's over. Baker always hated to lose, and after he got on drugs, he became absolutely paranoid about it. I think he looks at the divorce as a kind of public humiliation, and it pushed him right over the edge. It was when I told him I wanted the divorce that he nearly killed me. Now he wants to finish the job. I'm not safe here anymore."

"Did he see you?"

"He looked at me, but I don't think he recognized me. My hair used to be very long, and I'm a lot thinner than when he last . . ."

"Then maybe he doesn't know you're here. Maybe it's just a coincidence that he's at the inn. It's possible; lots of people come to the inn."

"It's no coincidence," Liz said. "He's come here for me." Her hand went to her mouth. "Oh, Jesus, we've got to tell Germaine about him."

"There's no point in alarming her. Even if you're right, and he's here for you, he's no danger to her or anybody else at the inn. Look, why don't you just get some sleep? I'll be with you, and if you still want to go in the morning when the storm has blown over, I'll get Grandpapa's boat and take you myself."

They reached the cottage and ran inside, through heavy rain and rising wind. Liz flung herself on the bed and tried not to cry.

"You stay right here," Keir said. He left the bedroom and came back with a very large bourbon. "Now, get outside this; it'll relax you."

Liz took a swig from the glass. "God knows, I need it." She turned and looked at him. "You won't leave me tonight?"

"Of course not." He smiled. "I can't think of anyplace else I'd rather sleep."

She handed him her glass. "Hold this for a minute." She left and returned with a twelve-inch chef's knife from the kitchen. "I hope you don't mind my sleeping with this, too."

"Not as long as it's on your side of the bed," Keir said, eyeing the wicked-looking blade.

"Keir, tomorrow I want you to do something for me."

"Anything."

"I want you to find me a pistol. I mean it."

"All right. Grandfather has some handguns in his study. I'll find you something menacing."

She took another swig of the bourbon and rested her head on his shoulder. "If I can just get through tonight, I think I'll be okay."

Just after midnight, when she thought all her guests had retired, Germaine was washing glasses in the bar. A man walked into the room.

"Well, Mr. Sutherland, you're still up?" she said, giving him a dazzling smile.

"Call me Bob," he said. "Everybody does."

"Call me Germaine. Can I buy you a nightcap, Bob?"

"You certainly can. Cognac would be nice."

Germaine poured a stiff one for both of them and set his glass on the bar.

He picked it up, sniffed it, tasted it, never taking his eyes from her.

Germaine leaned on the bar, allowing him a glimpse of her handsome breasts through the v of her blouse. She never wore a bra.

"You're an extremely attractive woman, Germaine," he said.

Germaine smiled. "Somehow, Bob, brandy doesn't seem to satisfy you. Is there anything else I can do for you?"

He smiled, revealing large, even teeth. "Where do you lay your head, Germaine?"

"In a cottage just across the lawn."

"Why don't you show it to me?"

"I'd love to," Germaine said. "Bring your drink." She picked up the cognac bottle, grabbed a large umbrella from the stand by the front door, and led him out into the night.

48

The first thing he saw was the darkness; the first thing he heard was the silence. Then there was a beeping—dim, regular—and then another sound.

"Shhh," a female voice said. "Don't try to talk; I'll get the doctor."

There was a rustling of clothes, the squeak of rubber soles on vinyl, and then only the beeping. A long time seemed to pass, and he tried to orient himself. Before he could do so, there was a male voice close by.

"Don't try to talk," the voice said. "Open your eyes."

He opened his eyes. The man was so close he was fuzzy.

He tried to speak, but his mouth and throat were too dry to make a sound. Someone put a glass straw in his mouth, and when he sucked, wonderful, sweet water flowed. He rinsed his mouth, then swallowed. He tried to speak again.

"What?" the man asked. "Say again?"

"Haynes," Williams managed to say.

"Right here, Lee," Haynes's voice came back. "Your wife's here, too."

"Hey, baby," she said.

"Just hold your horses, Captain, Mrs. Williams," the other man said.

There was a sharp pain in his foot.

"Did you feel anything, Lee?" the doctor asked.

"My foot," Williams said.

"See if you can wiggle your toes."

Williams wiggled.

"Now the other foot."

He wiggled again.

"Grip my hand and squeeze."

He squeezed.

"Now the other hand."

He squeezed again.

"Watch my finger. Without trying to turn your head, follow it with your eyes."

He followed the finger.

"Good, very good. Lee, you came out of surgery a little over an hour ago, and you're in a pretty elaborate neck brace. You have some broken vertebrae in your neck, but the surgery was successful, and you have no, repeat, no paralysis. Do you understand?"

"Yes," Williams replied. "Ed?"

"I'm right here, Lee," Haynes said. "Doctor, may I have a moment alone with him, please." It was not a question.

"A moment, no more," the doctor replied, and left.

"Lee, was it Ramsey?"

"Yes."

"I think I know what you were doing there. Don't worry about the gun; it's gone."

"Thanks. Cap, the woman is at a place called . . ." He tried to remember; it wasn't a familiar name. "An island somewhere."

"In Georgia?"

"I think so."

"Lake Lanier?"

"No, the coast."

"Jekyll? Sea Island? Cumberland?"

"That's it, Cumberland."

"Anything else? Do you know where on the island?"

"No. How long have I been out?"

"Three days. It's Friday evening."

"You better move fast; he's there by now."

"Okay. Anything else to tell me?"

"Just get him."

Haynes hit the ground running. "I want a map of the state," he said to a detective. "See if you can find one in the hospital."

"Right over there, Captain," the cop said, pointing to a wall. A framed map of Georgia hung there.

"Okay," Haynes said, tapping the glass with a

finger. "It's right here, just north of Jacksonville. You call headquarters and get hold of a chopper—the big one. I'll get hold of the sheriff down there."

"Right," the detective said, and ran for a pay phone.

Haynes commandeered the night nurse's desk. A couple of calls later, he found the sheriff at home.

"This is Captain Haynes, Sheriff, chief of the Homicide Bureau, Atlanta PD. There's a murderer loose on your turf, and I'm coming down there just as fast as I can."

"Who and where?" the sheriff asked.

"His name is Bake Ramsey."

"Football player?"

"That's the one. He's on Cumberland Island, and he's going to kill a woman named Elizabeth Barwick, unless we can stop him."

"I was on the island yesterday, and I saw Miss Barwick. She's among friends there, and it's just as well, because neither one of us is going to light on that island for a while."

"What do you mean? How far offshore is it?"

"Less than a mile, but that's a mighty long mile tonight. We got ourselves a hurricane that's going to come ashore somewhere around here, maybe tonight, and we've already got fifty knots of wind. That means no chopper can fly, and no man I know is going to try to cross the Inland Waterway in a boat. There's probably a seven- or eight-foot sea running in the waterway, and that's sheltered water."

"Shit," Haynes said. "Excuse my French, Sheriff; are there any phones on the island?"

"One, at Greyfield Inn. Hang on, I'll give you the number." He came back shortly and recited the digits. "It's one of those cellular jobs. There's no phone lines running to the island."

"Thanks for your help, Sheriff." Haynes gave his own phone numbers. "Will you call me the minute the weather lets up?"

"I sure will, and I'll get over there myself just as soon as I can."

Haynes hung up and dialed the number the sheriff had given him. It rang a few times, then a recorded message said, "The BellSouth customer whose number you are calling has left the vehicle. Please try later." He tried half a dozen times more and got the same reply.

The detective approached the night nurse's desk. "The flight department tells me nothing is flying tonight, unless it's going north or west. There's a hurricane off the coast, all of southeast Georgia is bad news, and they expect it to be for at least twenty-four hours."

"I heard already," the captain said. "The sheriff down there says no boat could make it, either. We've got to think of something else."

The two men stood mute at the desk and thought.

"I can't think of anything," the detective said after a while.

"Neither can I, except to keep trying to telephone the inn down there. There's been no answer."

The detective's face brightened. "Maybe we

could . . ." He frowned again. "No, it's got to be a chopper or a boat, hasn't it?"

"That's right."

"I can't think of anything."

The captain picked up the phone and dialed again. "Hello, honey, it's me," he said. "Don't wait up. I may not be back until tomorrow night. Business. You, too." He hung up and turned to the detective. "You got a wife?"

"No, sir."

"Then come on, we've got a long drive ahead of us."

They headed south out of Atlanta, on Interstate 75, the red light on the dashboard clearing the way. An hour south of Macon, heavy rain began to hammer against the windshield, and Ed Haynes had to slow to eighty.

CHAPTER

49

James Moses Drummond was wakened by a huge sighing noise, followed by a groaning crash. It took him a moment to figure out what it could be: a tree, and a big one. The wind and the cabin itself were making so much noise, he was surprised he had heard it at all. There was no clock, but it felt like the dead of night. He glanced at his grandfather's bed; it had not been slept in. A glow from the other room of the former slave house told him that the fire had been built up.

James got out of bed and, shivering, pulled on his jeans. He went into the other room and found Buck Moses sitting in front of a roaring driftwood fire, rocking in his chair, staring at the flames, and making a tuneless humming noise.

"Granddaddy, what you doing up this time of night?" he asked.

Buck Moses noticed his grandson for the first time. "Big wind done come," he said.

"You right about that," James agreed. "I never heard so much wind."

A gigantic gust came, and the house seemed to move. The noise from the rafters was frightening. James moved closer to the fire to warm himself.

"You be a good boy," Buck said, looking fondly up at his grandson. "You keep on bein' good."

"I will, Granddaddy," James replied. It had been a long time since his grandfather had said anything to him about his behavior.

"You got a good life before you," Buck said. "You goin' to see places, see the whole world."

"I am?"

Buck nodded. "But you don' forget about this island, you hear? You got some roots here; don' you forget about 'em."

"I won't, Grandaddy."

"My peoples is calling to me," Buck said, looking into the fire again. "It's 'bout time I be goin'."

A chill ran through James, in spite of the hot fire. He couldn't think of anything to say. A squall of heavy rain pounded on the tin roof; the noise was terrific. "Granddaddy," he shouted, to be heard over the din.

As he spoke, the wind rose to a howl that drowned out even the rain on the roof. The little house groaned, and James looked up at the rafters. He went to a window to look out, and, as he did, the cabin moved with the wind. This time, it kept moving. There was a loud groaning and the splintering of timber, and, more slowly than James could have believed, the house began to come down. Not knowing which way to run, he stood and looked at his grandfather. As the house came down, the brick chimney came with it, falling like a tree onto the spot where Buck Moses sat rocking.

When James woke, it seemed that only moments had passed. He lay under a pile of boards, and broken glass was all around him. The wind was louder than ever now, and the rain came in torrents. The remains of the driftwood fire sputtered out. James found that he could move, could shove the debris aside and free himself. He struggled to his feet and immediately was blown off them by the wind. No man could stand up to that, he realized.

He crawled to where his grandfather lay under a pile of bricks and, keeping low, began tossing them aside. As the last of the fire went, he felt for Buck under the debris. Then, taking a good half hour to do it, he dragged the old man, inch by inch, out of the ruin of the cabin and across the ten yards to the tiny church, which, given some shelter by two old live oaks, still stood up to the hurricane.

Finally, when he had managed to shut the door during a momentary lull in the wind, he got a candle and matches from the altar and brought them to where he had dragged his grandfather. The light showed blood on the old man's head. James felt at his throat for a pulse but could find none. He leaned against the church door and pulled his grandfather's tiny frame into his arms.

Buck Moses was dead, and all James could do was wait for the hurricane to pass. His crying mingled with the roar of the wind and rain.

50

*E*d Haynes sat braced in the passenger seat of the patrol car and tried to see beyond the headlights.

"I'm going to have to pull over until it lets up," the detective said, steering the car onto the shoulder. "How much farther is it?"

Haynes switched on the interior light and looked at the road map. "About twenty-five miles, I reckon. To tell you the truth, I'm amazed we've gotten this far."

"I've never seen anything like this in my life," the detective said. "There must be six inches of water on the road; it's like driving down a river."

Haynes turned on the radio and searched for a Jacksonville station.

"Here's the latest on Hurricane Iago," a voice said. "The storm made a sudden forty-five-degree turn about four hours ago, and made a landfall a hundred miles south and hours earlier than had been expected. The eye is expected to hit the coast north of Jacksonville around dawn, and the Weather Service tells us that the worst should be over by midmorning."

"Well, that's something, I guess," the detective said.

"I'm glad we drove," Haynes said. "At least we'll be able to get onto the island at the earliest possible moment. If this would just let up, we could make the sheriff's office in half an hour."

"It's not letting up, yet," the detective said. "If it's any consolation, Ramsey's got to be pinned down just like everybody else."

"Christ, I hope so," Haynes replied, watching the windshield wipers swim over the glass.

51

*L*iz sat bolt upright in bed, groggy and disoriented. She was dressed in nothing but a T-shirt, and Keir was not in bed with her. The wind howled around the house, bellowing, like some prehistoric animal in heat. What was going on? What had awakened her? It was pitch dark—no moon, not even the light of the stars—and incredibly heavy rain was thundering on the tin roof of the cottage.

The alarm clock at the bedside glowed green, reading just after 6:00 A.M. Above the sound of the wind and rain came another noise, a banging, crashing, shattering noise. The front door, she thought; less wind than this had blown it open before. She stumbled out of bed, hating to give up the warm covers;

she groped her way toward the door to the living room, and she had reached it before she remembered that she had forgotten the chef's knife. Then the memory came flooding over her: Baker was on the island.

She was about to go back for the knife, when a protracted flash of lightning brilliantly illuminated the room. Standing in the middle of the living room, locked together in silent combat, were Baker Ramsey and Keir Drummond. Baker was striking Keir on the back of the head, while Keir had a handful of Baker's short hair in one hand and was clawing at his eyes with the other.

Liz stood, transfixed, as the flash of lightning faded and, a moment later, was replaced by another. The attitudes of the two men had changed; Baker now had both arms around Keir's slender body and was hauling the smaller man to him in a powerful bear hug. Just before the light went away again, Liz saw Keir lean into Baker's head and come away with an ear in his teeth. A scream rent the darkness.

She had seen something else in the flash of light: a wine rack on the counter that separated the kitchen from the living room. Finding her way from memory, she reached it and moved toward where the two struggling men had been. When the lightning came again, she was in position.

She held the neck of the wine bottle in both hands and swung it with all her strength at the back of Baker's head. The bottle exploded, showering red wine everywhere. Baker let go of Keir and fell to one knee, momentarily stunned. The light winked out, and, rushing at where Baker had been, Liz raised the jagged neck of the wine bottle and brought it down. The lightning returned, showing the glass embedded in the top of Baker's shoulder. Bringing all her weight to bear, she drew the broken bottle down his back, shredding his white shirt and leaving a bloody track along his spine.

Baker screamed more loudly than Liz would have believed a human being could, and, in the momentary darkness, she threw herself sideways as he wheeled to strike her. As she did, she caught a glimpse of a crumpled and unconscious Keir on the floor.

She was Baker's goal, and she knew he would come for her, not Keir. She ran to the kitchen and grabbed her car keys from the table before the lightning flashed again, showing Baker her path of retreat. She fled the house, tripping over a light ax on the back porch, knowing he would be after her, and flung herself from the landing. She struck the ground in the darkness and rolled; then the lightning came again and showed her the Jeep.

The wind gusted, throwing her off balance, and she had to correct her course, leaning against the gust as she ran as if it were a wall. She reached the Jeep and got the door open. The lights came on inside the vehicle, blinding her when she closed the door and they went out. Searching for the keyhole, she was vaguely aware of a large tree branch landing on the hood of the Jeep, then blowing away. She yanked on the gear lever and stomped on the accelerator, forgetting the headlights. By the time she remembered and got them on, she was heading directly for Germaine's pickup truck, which lay across the road. She swerved, but still struck a front fender of the truck, moving it sideways as if had been kicked by a giant, then she was on the road and moving fast. How had Baker got hold of Germaine's truck?

Not too fast, she kept telling herself. He couldn't catch the Jeep on foot, and she had hurt the pickup. Anyway, there were no headlights behind her. Still, she drove faster than she had ever driven on the island, along the side of the airstrip, headed for the main, north-south road. Not the inn, she thought; Baker would find her there. Where could she find shelter? A place that Baker didn't know? Plum Orchard. At the T-junction, she swung right and bore down, sending the Jeep hurtling through the wild night.

Suddenly, the Jeep left the ground entirely, then landed, skidding. She whipped it back onto the road and thanked her stars. These roads, which had seemed quite all right at twenty miles an hour, were something else at sixty.

Squinting at the road ahead of her through the driving rain, she forced herself to slow to forty and thought about Keir. Would Baker hurt him? No, he was single-minded; he would come after her, if he could. His back was cut, and he was missing an ear, but that wouldn't slow him; he would come, eventually. She thought about help. The sheriff was only a few miles away and had a helicopter, but she had no means of summoning him, and, even if she could, he could never reach the island in this awful storm.

A fork in the road was approaching, and suddenly she slammed on the brakes with all the force she could muster. A huge pine tree lay across the road at the turning for Plum Orchard. She swung right without stopping and bore down again. Wherever this road went, she was going. She was still in the full flight of panic, and simply putting distance between herself and Baker was all she wanted.

She worked hard at calming herself, to slow her heartbeat and her breathing. Nothing worked. A part of her mind marveled that she could sustain this level of raw fear for such a long time. The Jeep hurtled on through the night, its headlights boring a tunnel through the trees. Then, very suddenly, there were no trees, and the headlamps illuminated nothing but rain and flying debris. She had broken into some sort of clearing. At the moment she moved to stop, something more powerful than brakes dragged the car to a halt. She lurched forward, struck the steering column with her chest, then fell back against the seat.

Blinking, she peered out of the car and saw blue sky above, and the light was improving by the second. There was water all around her, but the car had not sunk. Confused, she tried to orient herself, then she realized how she could be in water and still be on the road. The dike that stretched across the lower end of Lake Whitney was underwater, inundated by the downpour. She glanced out the passenger window, then back out the driver's side. As she did, an obstruction appeared between her and the lake. It was a face, a familiar face, upside down.

Baker Ramsey was on top of the Jeep.

CHAPTER

52

Haynes huddled in the entryway of the sheriff's office and hammered on the door. He and the detective were already soaking wet, just from running a few yards from the car. He peered through the glass. The office was dark, except for an eerie glow coming from a back room.

"I don't think anybody can hear us," the detective shouted over the wind.

Haynes tried the door, and it swung open, banging against the wall. The two men hurried inside and, together, managed to get the door shut.

"Who's that?" a voice called. A man stood silhouetted against the light from the back room.

"It's Captain Ed Haynes, Atlanta PD. You the sheriff?"

·

He stuck out a hand. "I am. How the hell did you get here from Atlanta?"

"We drove."

"You must be out of your fucking mind," the sheriff said, his face incredulous.

"Probably so, but when this storm lifts, I want to be on that island at the earliest possible moment."

"Come on in my office, and I'll give you some coffee," the sheriff said, escorting them into the back room. A television set glowed in a corner. "That's running on my emergency power," he said. "Everything's out around here. Take a look at that, will you?" He pointed to the television. "That's radar off a Jacksonville station."

Haynes and the detective peered at the screen. "Is that a hole in the storm?" he asked, tapping the glass.

"That's the eye of the hurricane," the sheriff replied. "It's right over Cumberland now."

"It's a pretty big hole," Haynes said. "Could we get over there in a chopper?"

"I was right, you *are* out of your mind." The sheriff laughed, pouring coffee. "We aren't in the eye here, yet, although we might see some of it. If we go over there, there's still the backside of the storm to worry about, you know, although it's supposed to break up pretty fast over land."

"How long?" Haynes asked.

"A couple of hours, maybe, if we're lucky. I've tried phoning the inn a dozen times, but I'm getting no answer. They've only got the one cellular phone over there, and it's in Germaine Drummond's office. I doubt if anybody can even hear it over the storm."

Haynes sipped the coffee and stared at the eye of the hurricane. "I've never felt so frustrated in my life," he said. "I'm what—five, six miles from a murderer, and I can't get to him."

"You might as well be a hundred from him, until this hurricane passes," the sheriff said. "I just hope my chopper survives the storm."

CHAPTER

53

Liz hammered on the door lock, forcing it down. The central locking secured all four doors and the tailgate. Baker slid off the roof of the car and into knee-deep water.

Baker's face, streaked with blood from his torn ear cartilage, smirked at her from outside the Jeep. He drew back with his right arm and drove his elbow at the window glass. Liz recoiled as he struck, but it did not give. Oh, wonderful, strong car, she thought, to stand up to Baker Ramsey!

Baker looked as surprised as angry; then he disappeared.

Some cloud scudded away, and more blue sky appeared, sending more light down onto the scene.

Dawn is coming, and the change in the storm is remarkable, she thought. She still couldn't see Baker.

What am I doing here? Why am I waiting for him to come back? she asked herself. She restarted the car and struggled to get it into four-wheel drive. As she was about to drive away, she realized that she was sufficiently disoriented not to know where the dike lay. If she moved ahead, she might drive along it to the other side, or she might simply drive off it into deep water. Then she remembered what was in the water, and she froze.

The windshield exploded into a thousand fragments. Shielding her eyes, she could see that it was still held together by the lamination. Then she caught a glimpse of Baker outside the car. He had what looked like a fence post, and he was drawing back to swing again. He hit the windshield again, and this time the post penetrated, leaving a hole as large as her head. Baker's arm followed it, snaking inside toward her.

She rolled sideways on the seat, and reached the passenger-side door, clawing at the lock. She got the door open and jumped out, looking over her shoulder, determined to keep the car between her and Baker. He was wading around the front of the Jeep.

She moved toward the rear of the car, and, as she did, she suddenly became aware that another vehicle had pulled up behind hers. The door of the pickup opened, and Keir climbed out. He seemed to be struggling, and there was pain in his face. In his hand was a light ax, the tool from the back stoop of the cottage.

Baker did not seem to notice the truck; his eyes

were riveted on Liz as he rounded the front of the Jeep and moved toward her.

Liz stood her ground, waited for him. His path would bring him near the truck. Then, as he came around the rear of the Jeep, he saw Keir, too late.

Keir had leaped to the hood of the pickup, and he was swinging the ax.

The flat side of the implement struck Baker alongside the neck, and his head snapped sideways, followed by his body. He let go of the fence post and fell down.

Liz thought he must be dead, but she had reckoned without the training and the muscle-building drugs that had gone into the development of that neck.

Baker struggled to his feet, and, his face distorted into a mask of insane determination, came after Keir.

There was something in Keir's face Liz had not seen before: a coldness and cunning, a deadly calculation that excluded reason. She knew what he meant to do.

Keir started his swing, and this time the blade of the ax pointed the way. With a sound like a lumberjack striking a tree, the ax drove into Baker Ramsey's neck, and the handle snapped. Blood sprayed both Keir and Liz, who was no more than three feet from where Baker still stood, a look of astonishment on the once handsome face.

Then, slowly, like a great tree in the forest, Baker Ramsey fell forward, gushing blood, into the knee-deep water. Liz, horrified, jumped out of his way, and his momentum carried him, face down, off the dike and into the rushes at lakeside, painting the water red with each faltering beat of his dying heart.

Liz stared at him for a moment, then turned to Keir, who had slumped to a sitting position on the hood of the pickup.

"Are you all right?" she asked, reaching for his hand.

"I don't know," he replied, and there seemed little strength in his grip. Then he was looking past Liz, with an odd expression on his face.

Liz turned and followed his gaze. Baker Ramsey was moving again.

In a blur of motion, Baker turned over on his back, then sat bolt upright, his jaw slack and his eyes blank. He was in that position for a split second, then his head snapped back, the ax blade still embedded in his neck, and he went backward under the water.

"What is he doing?" Liz said, staring in wonder.

"He isn't doing anything," Keir said, a small smile on his face, "Goliath is."

Suddenly, a huge, wet trunk broke the surface; then the twenty-foot alligator's head came out of the water, clutching Baker Ramsey in its enormous jaws. The beast whirled furiously on its own axis, whipped its head sideways, and a snapping sound seemed to come from Baker's body. Then the two vanished under the lake. The water churned for a moment, then slowly became quiet, ripples lapping against Liz's legs.

The wind was rising again, and the blue in the sky disappeared. Liz went to the truck and helped Keir into the cab. She brushed the golden hair away from his eyes, which looked up at her gravely.

"Keir, are you all right?" she asked him a second time.

"When I hit him that last time, something stuck me inside," he said, slowly. "That guy had some bear hug." Then he coughed, and blood rose over his lips.

"Oh, my God!" Liz cried. "What's wrong?" Keir leaned against her, and she put her arms around him.

"I think he broke something," Keir said, seeming surprised. His head fell onto her shoulder, and his breath came in short gasps.

She held him, talking to him, stroking his hair, while the storm rose around them again. After a while, he seemed to sleep, and, her stores of adrenaline depleted, she slept alongside him.

She was awakened by stillness and by the sound of a helicopter. Starting, she looked up and saw the aircraft hovering over the water next to the truck. She watched as it moved a few yards and set down on the lakeshore.

"We've got some help, now," she said to Keir, turning his face up to her.

He didn't wake, and he was cool to her touch.

She looked up to see the sheriff and two strange men splashing toward her across the submerged dike. Then she pulled Keir's face into the hollow of her neck and began to cry.

CHAPTER

54

"I'm sorry about Mr. Drummond," Haynes said. "We got here just as soon as we possibly could. We'd have been here sooner, but for the hurricane."

They were sitting in the bar at Greyfield Inn, and the sheriff had poured them all a drink. Liz clutched the blanket about her, gripped the whiskey glass, and took another swig; it was creating a warmth in her belly that let her know she was still alive. "What I don't understand is why you're here at all," she said.

"We *wouldn't* be here at all, except for a very determined cop named Lee Williams."

"The one I talked to on the phone?"

"That's the one. It was Lee who got Ramsey to tell him where you were." He told her the story.

"I hope he's going to be all right," she said.

"He will be. He'll be very gratified to know what Mr. Drummond did."

"Not as gratified as I." She was talking on automatic pilot, now, just responding. The shock was wearing slowly away, although she could still feel Keir's cold skin against her body. What about grief? she thought. Grief must come with reality. It was still not real.

From outside the room there was the low sound of voices and footsteps on the stairs.

"The guests are stirring," the sheriff said. "It's after eight o'clock."

"Germaine will be getting breakfast for them," Liz said absently. Then she stood up. "Germaine!" she dropped her glass and ran from the room, down the stairs, hanging on to the blanket, followed by the sheriff and the two policemen. She ran across the kitchen to Germaine's office and tried the door. Locked. "Oh, dear God!"

"What's the matter?" Haynes asked.

"Baker was driving Germaine's truck. He would have to have gotten the keys from her." She ran up the stairs and out the front door of the inn. She flew down the front steps and, trying her best to hold on to the blanket, sprinted across the inn's lawn toward Germaine's cottage. The lawn was littered with tree limbs and other debris, and she had to detour more than once to make it across the expanse of grass.

As Liz neared the cottage, she could see shingles missing from the roof, but nothing else seemed damaged. The front door was locked. She ran around the house and entered through the kitchen, then stopped. Everything seemed quite normal there. With trepidation, she walked into the living room; a brandy bottle and two glasses rested on the coffee table.

"Germaine!" she called. No answer. Slowly, Liz went to the bedroom door. As it swung open, she saw a shapeless form on the bed, covered with a sheet. The policemen came into the room behind Liz and stopped. "Germaine?" she said again, her voice quavering.

Liz walked slowly around the bed and stopped. She reached out, took a corner of the sheet, and pulled it down. Germaine's still face was pressed partly into a pillow. Liz tenderly moved a lock of hair from across her eyes.

"What?" Germaine said, startled, and sat up. She was naked, and the men were staring at her breasts. "Oh, Liz," she said. "What's going on?" She saw the men and pulled up the sheet.

"Are you all right, Germaine?" Liz managed to ask.

"Sure." She shook her head. "I had a pretty weird evening with a guy, though. All he wanted to talk about was you."

CHAPTER

55

My dear Ms. Barwick:

I was very pleased to receive your photographs and your prospectus the other day, for two reasons: first, your book of sports photographs came into my hands a few weeks ago, and I think it is brilliant; second, my wife and I spent a weekend on Cumberland Island three years ago, and we were so overwhelmed by its beauty that we have been fighting, unsuccessfully, ever since to find the time to return.

Having seen the real thing, I would like to say that I think your photographs do it justice, and that is high praise indeed. I also found your text to be delightful, in spite of your protestations about not being a writer.

Enough praise; now to business: My firm, as you probably know, has published a series of regional, nature-oriented books, and some of them have turned out to have national appeal. I would very much like to publish your book, and I think I can promise you not only a substantial advance for a book of this sort, but a first-class publication.

If that interests you, let me know who your agent is, if you have one, and then you should come to New York, so we can sit down and see what sort of book we can make together. I look forward to hearing from you at the earliest possible moment.

She looked around the cottage. It looked quite different—more elegant, more permanent—with the old leather couch from Angus's study and a dozen good pictures from the house. Germaine had insisted she share in the furnishings of Dungeness when Liz had been helping with the enormous chore of stripping the house.

She locked the door, now covered with a sheet of plywood, until it could be repaired. A month after the hurricane, glass was still in short supply. Outside, the morning air was chill with autumn. She nearly remarked on it to Keir, before she remembered, for the thousandth time, that Keir was not there. She paused for a moment and pushed away the pain. She had almost stopped doing that, speaking to Keir. She was better, now, and when she could stop speaking to him as though he were there, she'd be fine, she was sure of it. Time was supposed to heal, and she was sure it did, but time simply would not pass quickly enough. She tossed the last of her bags into the Jeep, and drove away from the cottage.

At the inn, she found Germaine in her office.

"Sit for a minute," Germaine said.

Liz sat.

"I haven't said this to you before, but I feel I must. I'm so sorry I told Ramsey where to find you."

"It's all right," Liz said. "You didn't know who he was. He would have found me, anyway, if it was the last thing he did."

"God forgive me for saying it, but I'm glad it was," Germaine said. "Come on, I'll walk you down to the dock."

"I've got another stop to make, before I catch the boat."

Germaine came to the door with her and took Liz's hand. "How long will you be in New York?" she asked.

"I don't know, exactly. As long as it takes to write the rest of the text and put the book together. Several weeks, at least."

They stopped at the Jeep, and Germaine put her hands on Liz's shoulders. "I'll miss you," she said. "You're practically my sister, now."

Liz hugged her. "That's right, I am." She looked around. "I had hoped to say good-bye to James."

"He's down at Dungeness, and I have to join him in a minute. It's a windless day."

Liz looked out over the placid water. "It is, isn't it?"

A few minutes later, she stopped at the new Drummond family plot and got out. Among the old, transplanted headstones were three new ones: Angus's bore simply his name and dates; the second stone read

Buck Moses, ?–1989
Good and faithful servant
Grandfather of an heir to Cumberland
Island

The single stone that marked the double grave of the twins read

Hamish and Keir Drummond, 1952–1989
Two brothers, at the end of one life.

She had contributed that.

She walked along the line of markers, touching each as she passed. Then, she bent and kissed the twins' stone.

Out in Cumberland Sound, halfway to Fernandina, Liz looked back at the island. A puff of smoke rose from the roof of the big house, which could be partly seen through the trees, and after a moment came a lick of flames, then more smoke. Dungeness was dying with Angus Drummond, as he had wished.

Liz turned away from the island and put her face into the breeze the old barge made. She took off her cap and let the wind blow through her hair.

As the *Aldred Drummond* reached the Fernandina dock, Liz turned and looked at the island again. She had traveled only a few miles, and she was surprised to feel something she hadn't experienced since childhood.

Elizabeth Barwick was homesick.

ACKNOWLEDGMENTS

I would like to express my gratitude to Gogo Fuller, for sharing her knowledge of her beloved Cumberland Island, and for her warm hospitality in her home there; Dr. John Griffin, for his advice on traumatic injury, emergency room procedures, and restorative surgery; Dr. A. J. Nicholas for medical advice; Robert Coram for information and advice; and Howard Hunt, of the Atlanta Zoo, for information on the habits and noises of alligators. I particularly want to thank Judy Tabb, in whose company I discovered Cumberland Island, for her photographic advice and for the use in the book of her equipment (sorry about the tripod).

I am grateful, once again, for the advice and support of my literary agent, Morton Janklow; his associ-

ate, Anne Sibbald; and their colleagues at Janklow &
Nesbit.

My thanks go also to Trish Lande and Cheryl
Weinstein, for their efforts.

Finally, I must thank Eddie Bell, Ed Breslin, and
all the people at HarperCollins for their unbounded
enthusiasm for this book and all their hard work.

AUTHOR'S NOTE

Cumberland Island is a real place, as are Greyfield Inn, Plum Orchard, and the old slave quarters. Dungeness was real, but the house burned many years before it did in this book. However, its ruins, the outbuildings, and the old cemetery are still there. Stafford Beach Cottage is a figment of my imagination. Real people live on the island, and none of the characters in this book is meant to resemble any of them in the slightest.

Cumberland has been designated a National Seashore, and most of the island is under the control of the National Parks Service.

The Suspense Isn't Over

Follow Detective Sergeant Stone Barrington
into a masterful tale of intrigue in Stuart Woods'

NEW YORK DEAD

laine's, late. The place had exhausted its second wind, and half the customers had gone; otherwise she would not have given Stone Barrington quite so good a table—number 4, along the wall to your right as you enter. Stone knew Elaine, had known her for years, but he was not what you would call a regular—not what Elaine would call a regular, anyway.

He rested his left leg on a chair and unconsciously massaged the knee. Elaine got down from her stool at the cash register, walked over, and pulled up a chair.

"So?"

"Not bad," he said.

"How about the knee?" Anybody who knew him knew about the knee; it had received a .22-caliber bullet eleven weeks before.

"A lot better. I walked up here from Turtle Bay."

"When's the physical?"

"Next week. I'll tap-dance through it."

"So what if you fall on your ass, tap dancing?" Elaine knew how to get to the point.

"So, then I'm a retiree."

"Best thing could happen to you."

"I can think of better things."

"Come on, Stone, you're too good looking to be a cop. Too smart, too. You went to law school, didn't you?"

"I never took the bar."

"So take the bar. Make a buck."

"It's fifteen years since I graduated."

"So? Take one of those cram courses."

"Maybe. You're coming on kind of motherly, aren't you?"

"Somebody's gotta tell you this stuff."

"I appreciate the thought. Who's the guy at the bar?" To a cop's eye the man didn't fit in somehow. He probably wouldn't fit anywhere. Male Caucasian, five-six, a hundred and seventy, thinning brown hair, thick, black-rimmed glasses adhesive-taped in the middle.

"In the white coat? Doc."

"That his name or his game?"

"Both. He's at Lenox Hill, I think. He's in here a lot, late, trying to pick up girls."

"In a hospital jacket?"

"His technique is to diagnose them. Weird, isn't it?"

Doc reached over to the girl next to him and peeled back her eyelid. The girl recoiled.

Stone laughed out loud and finished the Wild Turkey. "Bet it works. What girl could resist a *doctah?*"

"Just about all of them is my guess. I've never seen him leave with anybody."

Stone signaled a waiter for the check and put some cash on the table.

"Have one on me," Elaine said.

"Rain check. I've had one too many already." He stood up and pecked her on the cheek.

"Don't be such a stranger."

"If I don't pass the physical, I'll be in here all the time. You'll have to throw me out."

"My pleasure. Take care."

Stone glanced at Doc on the way out. He was taking the girl's pulse. She was looking at him as if he were nuts.

Stone was a little drunk—too drunk to drive, he reckoned, if he had owned a car. The night air was pleasant, still warm for September. He looked up Second Avenue to see a dozen cabs bearing down on him from uptown. Elaine's was the best cab spot in town; he could never figure out where they were all coming from. Harlem? Cabdrivers wouldn't take anybody to Harlem, not if they could help it. He turned away from them; he'd walk, give the knee another workout. The bourbon had loosened it up.

He crossed Eighty-eighth and started downtown, sticking to the west side of the street. He lengthened his stride, made a conscious effort not to limp. He remembered walking this beat, right out of the academy; that was when he had started drinking at Elaine's, when he was a rookie in the 19th Precinct, on his way home after walking his tour. He walked it now.

A cop doesn't walk down the street like anybody else, he reflected. Automatically, he checked every doorway as he swung down Second Avenue, ignoring the pain, leaning on the bourbon. He had to prevent himself from trying the locks. Across the street, half a dozen guys spilled out of a yuppie bar, two of them mouthing off at each other, the others watching. Ten years ago, he'd have broken it up. He would have now, but it didn't look like it would last long. The two guys turned away from each other, hurling insults. Neither was willing to throw the first punch.

At Eighty-sixth Street, two hookers were working the traffic. He'd have ignored them on his beat; he ignored them now. He remembered when Eighty-sixth was Germantown, when the smell of sauerbraten wafted from every third doorway. Somewhere along here there had been a place called the Gay Vienna that served kalbshaxe—a veal shank that looked like a gigantic drumstick. The place had had a zither player, the only one he'd ever heard. He'd liked it. He'd lived over on Eighty-third, between York and East End, had had a Hungarian landlady who made him goulash. She'd put weight on him, too much weight, and it had stuck. He'd lost it now, five weeks on hospital food. He was down to a hundred and eighty, and, at six two, he looked slender. He vowed not to gain it back. He couldn't afford the alterations.

Stone rubbed his neck. An hour in one of Elaine's hard, armless chairs, leaning on the table, always made his neck and shoulders tight. About Seventieth Street, he started to limp a little, in spite of himself. In the mid-sixties, he forgot all about the knee.

It was just luck. He was rolling his head around, trying to loosen the neck muscles, and he happened to be looking up when he saw her. She was free-falling, spread-eagled, like a sky diver. Only she didn't have a parachute.

Con Edison was digging a big hole twenty yards ahead, and they had a generator going, so he could barely hear the scream.

Time slowed down; he considered whether it was some sort of stunt and rejected the notion. He thought she would go into the Con Ed hole, but she didn't; instead, she met the earth, literally, on the big pile of dirt the workmen had thrown up. She didn't bounce. She stuck to the ground as if she had fallen into glue. Stone started to run.

A Con Ed man in a yellow hard hat jumped back-ward as if he'd been shotgunned. Stone could see the terrified expression on his face as he approached. The man recovered before Stone got there, reached down, and gingerly turned the woman onto her back. Her eyes were open.

Stone knew her. There was black dirt on her

face, and her red hair was wild, but he knew her. Shit, the whole city knew her. More than half the population—all the men and some of the women—wanted to fuck her. He slowed just long enough to glance at her and shout at the Con Ed man. "Call an ambulance! Do what you can for her!" He glanced up at the building. Flush windows, none open; a terrace up top.

He sprinted past the scene, turned the corner of the white-brick, 1960s apartment building, and ran into the lobby. An elderly, uniformed doorman was sound asleep in a chair, tilted back against the wall.

"Hey!" Stone shouted, and the man was wide awake and on his feet. The move looked practiced. Stone shoved his badge in the old man's face. "Police! What apartment has a terrace on the Second Avenue side?"

"12-A, the penthouse," the doorman said. "Miss Nijinsky."

"You got a key?"

"Yeah."

"Let's go!"

The doorman retrieved a key from a drawer, and Stone hustled him toward the elevators. One stood open and waiting; the doorman pushed twelve.

"What's the matter?" the man asked.

"Miss Nijinsky just took a dive. She's lying in a pile of dirt on Second Avenue."

"Jesus God."

"She's being introduced to him right now."

It was a short building, and the elevator was

slow. Stone watched the floor numbers light up and tried to control his breathing. When they hit eleven, he pulled out his gun. As the elevator slowed to a stop on twelve, he heard something, and he knew what it was. The fire door on twelve had been yanked open so hard it had struck the wall. This noise was followed by the sound of somebody taking the steel steps of the fire stairs in a hurry. The elevator door started to open, and Stone helped it.

"Stay here, and don't open the apartment door!" he said to the doorman.

The fire door was opposite the elevator; he yanked it open. From a floor below, the ring of shoe leather on steel drifted upward. Stone flung himself down the stairs.

The guy only had a floor's start on him; Stone had a chance. He started taking the steps two at a time. "Stop! Police!" he shouted. That was procedure, and, if anybody was listening, he wanted it heard. He shouted it again.

As he descended, Stone got into a rhythm— bump de bump, bump de bump. He concentrated on keeping his footing. He left the eighth floor behind, then the sixth.

From the sound of it, he was gaining. Aiming carefully, he started taking the steps three at a time. Whoever was below him was hitting every one. Now Stone was barely a flight of stairs behind him. At the third-floor level he caught sight of a shadow. The ringing of the steel steps built to a crescendo, echoing off the cinder-block walls of the staircase, sounding much like a modern composition a girl had once dragged him to hear.

The knee was hurting badly now, and Stone tried to think ahead. If the man got out of the stairwell before he could be caught, then he'd have the advantage on level ground, because Stone wouldn't be able to run him down before the knee went. Stone made a decision; he'd go for a flight at a time.

On the next landing, he took a deep breath and leaped. He landed right, pushed off the wall, and prepared to jump again. One more leap down the stairs, and he'd have his quarry in sight. This time, as he jumped, something went wrong. His toe caught the stamped tread of the steel step—not much, just enough to turn him in midair—and he knew he would land wrong. When he did, his weight was on the bad knee, and he screamed. Completely out of control now, he struck the wall hard, bounced, and fell backward down the next flight of stairs.

As he came to rest hard against the wall, he struggled to get a look down the stairs, but he heard the ground-floor door open, and, a moment later, he heard it slam. He hunched up in the fetal position, holding the knee with both hands, waiting for the pain to subside just enough to allow him to get to his feet. Half a minute passed before he could let go of the knee, grab the railing, and hoist himself up. He recovered his pistol, and, barely letting his left foot touch the floor, lurched into the lobby. The guy was gone, and there was no hope of catching him now. Swearing, he hammered the elevator button with his fist.

He pressed his cheek against the cool stainless

steel of the elevator door, whimpering with pain and anger and sucking in deep breaths.

The bust of the century, and he had blown it.

Look for
NEW YORK DEAD
Available wherever you buy books.

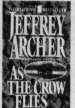
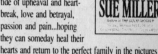